Guardian

Guardian

The Wildlands

Book One

Tyler Tillerson

For the writers struggling to decide.
For the characters who are patient anyway.

Ty lun tol.
Tol kar nim olsa.

Table of Contents

Table of Contents............6

Adult Content Warning............9

Prologue............13

1 – Birthday Surprise............16

2 – Too Close............24

3 – The Wrong Angyr............32

4 – Tense Intentions............38

5 – The Calling............48

6 – Galrend............58

7 – Tal and Kara............66

8 – Evocation............74

9 – Reading and Riding............84

10 – Wrong Angyr, Again............92

11 – Family Dinner............100

12 – A Woman and her Dog............112

13 – Angyrian Future............120

14 – Pretender to the Crown............134

15 – War Comes............140

16 – Fear of the Known............148

17 – Learning to Survive............156

18 – The Sound of Terror............164

19 – Changing Love............170

20 – Perfectionist............178

21 – A Crown Too Heavy............184

22 – No Goodbyes............190

23 – Failed Guardian............198

24 – To Be Different 204

25 – The Angyrian Witch...210

26 – Regret and Rage...218

27 – Sisters in Pain..224

28 – Immortal Combat 232

29 – Blood and Kin 242

30 – Magnificent 250

31 – Planning to Lose..258

32 – Everything Considered 266

33 – Sisters of Choice...272

34 – No More Pretending..280

35 – Mother of Nothing 292

36 – Colliding Crowns..300

37 – Guardians 308

38 – The Dead do not Lie 318

39 – The Cost of Everything..326

40 – Wild and Heartless 334

41 – Burying the Future..338

42 – Returning the Past..346

43 – Hunting the Present...354

Epilogue 360

Acknowledgements...369

Resources: Lore..370

Resources: Reader Wellbeing 374

About the Author 378

Adult Content Warning

The Wildlands is an <u>adult fantasy series</u> featuring explicit content, such as erotic scenes, descriptive gore, and foul language. Discretion is advised for readers below the age of 18. While these traditionally taboo themes are present, they are *not* the focus of the plot!

In layman's terms: *The Wildlands* is <u>not</u> smut but it does contain sex, cursing, and violence.

Additionally, victims of emotional, mental, or sexual trauma may be triggered by certain scenes within the book. **To be perfectly clear: abuse, of any nature, is never ok.** If, dear reader, you find yourself triggered by any portion of the book, I sincerely encourage you to seek professional counseling. At the end of the book are resources to seek help. Trauma does not have to be faced alone, contrary to the faulty thinking of many protagonists (real and imagined).

Finally, *The Wildlands* sometimes features content that involves abuse or non-consensual encounters. I want to be absolutely clear that reading it in *fantasy* does not make it right or permissible in real life! These scenes exist to make characters relatable and authentic, not *correct* nor *ethical.*

No means no.
The gift of choice is sacred and should be treated as such.

. . .

I hope you enjoy Merelith's journey, wild and dangerous as it is. I also hope you see your own path is not so different. The world is harsh, people are like animals, and good often stumbles in the face of evil.

The wild survive it all.
May you as well.
-Tyler

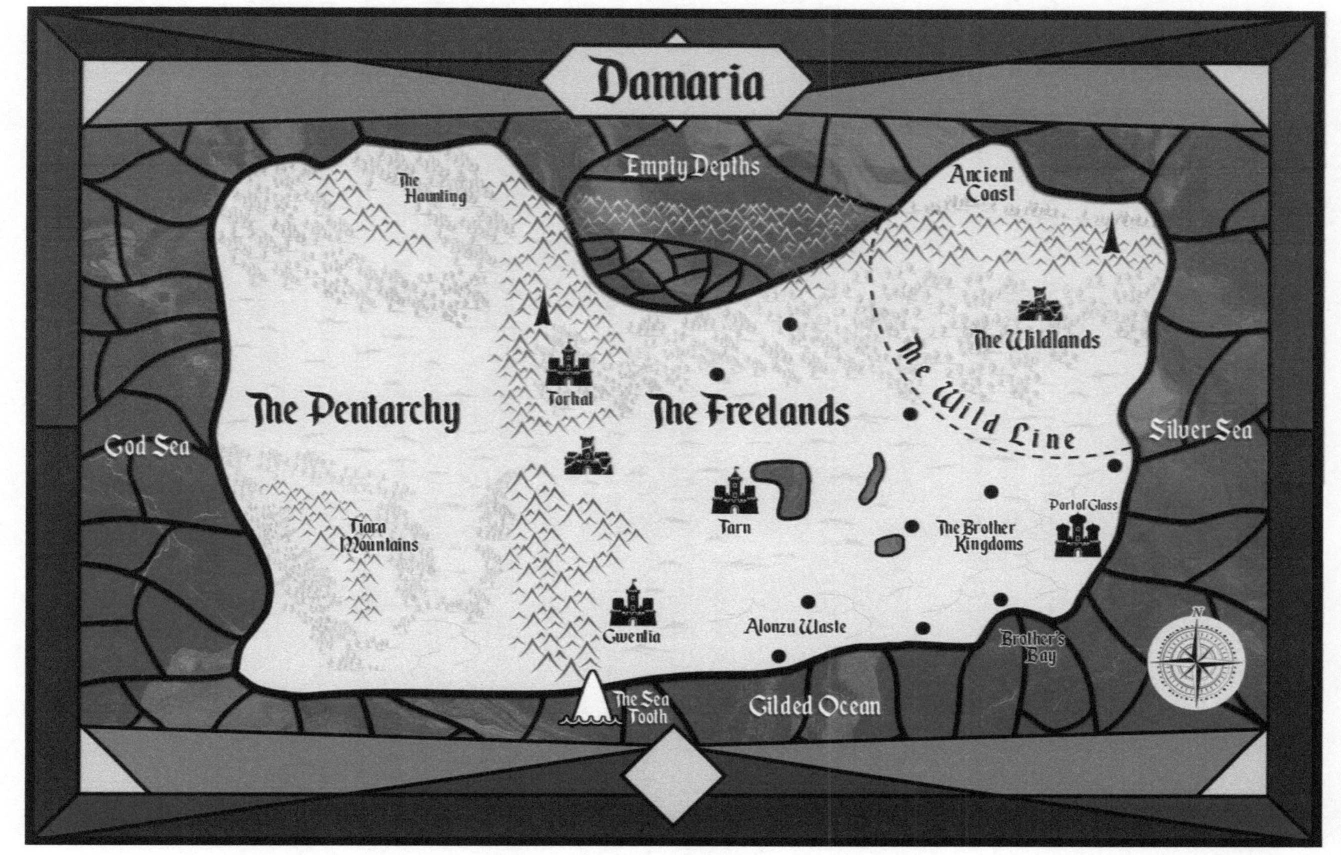
Damaria
Empty Depths
The Haunting
Ancient Coast
The Wildlands
Torhal
The Pentarchy
The Freelands
The Wild Line
God Sea
Silver Sea
Tiara Mountains
Tarn
Port of Glass
The Brother Kingdoms
Gwentha
Alonzu Waste
Brother's Bay
The Sea Tooth
Gilded Ocean

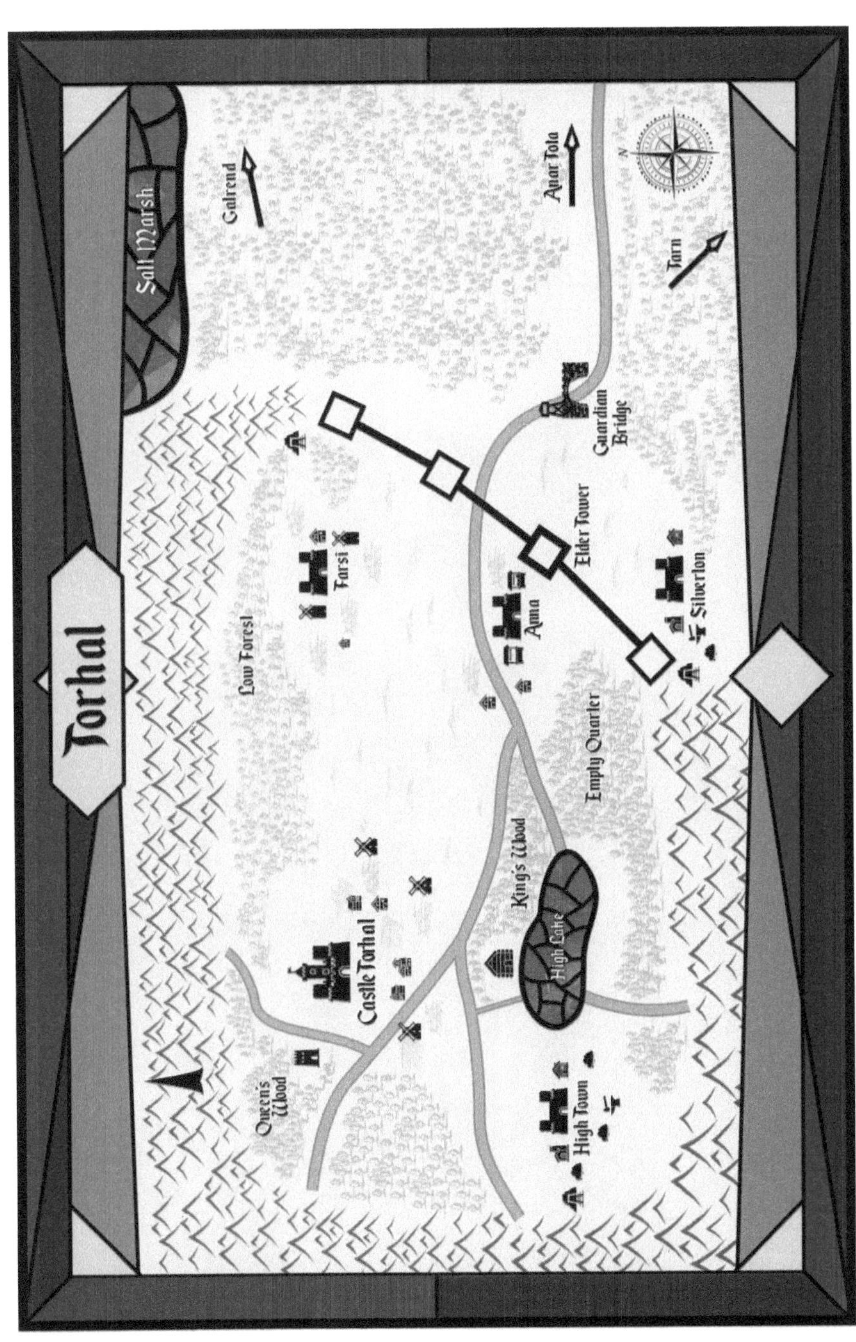
Salt Marsh
Galrend
Anar Tola
N
Turn
Torhal
Guardian Bridge
Elder Tower
Farsi
Low Forest
Ajna
Silverton
Empty Quarter
King's Wood
High Lake
Queen's Wood
Castle Torhal
High Town

Prologue

Wild

In the northeast corner of Damaria there was, for a time, a region called The Wildlands. It was named thus for a simple reason: for almost a millennium it was where angyr traveled to and lived. Of all the animals, man and beast alike, nothing was wilder than an angyr. Or, at least, that was the prevailing perspective on the topic at the time.

How the wildlands even came to be is a story unto itself. Prior to the War for Freedom, angyr lived all over Damaria as slaves and soldiers for the Autarchy, an empire that stretched over the whole of the continent. Ruled by six mighty war-casters, the Autarchy was an uncontested power thanks to its vast armies of angyr.

Yet power often corrupts, as any tale might go, and five of the autarchs turned on the sixth in a bid to attain the impossible: absolute immortality. With imperviousness to death, time, creation itself, these five hoped to expand from Damaria and conquer their world.

And worlds beyond, if they could.

Yet the betrayed autarch, Galrend, had the last laugh: he cursed his former comrades using the very ritual they had sacrificed him to. As he vanished from Damaria, consumed by void magic, he let loose *wildness* into Damaria: an affliction that causes gradual loss of self in those who are touched with void magic.

Galrend had been beloved by his portion of the Autarchy, and the people rose up in defiance. Of course, the newly made 'Pentarchs' were immortal and all-powerful. Yet it was not long before they realized something had gone terribly wrong. Their angyrian soldiers turned on each other, and everything around them, and the might of the Autarchy collapsed instantly into bloody chaos. Worse, the Pentarchs themselves began to lose their minds and realized Galrend's curse nearly too late.

They fled west across the mountain range that divides Damaria and warded it to protect them from the curse of wildness that emanated from the ritual site in the northeast. There they remained, plotting to undo Galrend's curse and resume their quest for dominion of all creation. Through powerful magics and arcane collars dredged up from the distant past, they regained control of their angyrian soldiers but only on their side of the continent.

On the eastern half, Damaria descended into civil strife and over time the War for Freedom resolved into the beginnings of the kingdoms that became The Freelands. As for the angyrian soldiers and slaves? Most lost themselves to wildness. Many were killed, but some survived long enough to migrate toward the source of their wildness: the ritual site. There they mysteriously remained, unwilling or perhaps unable to leave, creating a region impossibly dangerous to inhabit or civilize. Thus, The Wildlands were named and marked.

Nine hundred and some odd years later, The Freelands was a thriving hodgepodge of kingdoms, nations, guilds, and clans. Wars came and went, rulers rose and fell, but the threat of the immortal Pentarchs became distant. With them, too, the notion that the wildlands had not always existed.

A quartet of angyr would soon change that.

The story of how the wildlands ended begins with the first of these four: a rare angyrian child who was raised openly, beloved by her people and parents, and taught how to manage her wildness that she might protect those she cherished rather than harm them. Daughter to an immortal king and sorceress queen, her birthright was not a throne but a purpose: to protect her mother and her younger sister, the crown princess.

This angyrian child would go on to create the quartet and, eventually, gift me this name: Wild. Then she, along with the others, would do the impossible: they would end the wildlands, forever. She would go by many names such as the silver guardian and *Tal Kara Sti*, but let us start with the day before she felt the calling. Back then, she was just a girl becoming something much more than a woman.

Her name is Merelith Torhal and, even now, she is still the wildest of all.

1 – Birthday Surprise

Merelith

A dry, cold breeze billowed in from the northwest, as if exhaled from the cave of the Silver Alpha peak itself, over the canopy of the queen's wood. The majestic mountain was wreathed in what little snow had survived summer and its long dress of trees had begun to fade into the golds and reds of autumn. Huffing her way down that sloping terrain was a girl, perhaps more woman now that she was eighteen, with hazel eyes that matched the earthen tones beneath. Auburn hair gleamed with a shine the trees would envy.

Anyone in their right mind would know that thin and chilly air was a great reason to not venture so far and high, but Merelith couldn't care less about the biting breeze as she scurried and scrabbled down the side of a trickling creek bed. She wore a determined scowl, despite enjoying her outing, though it could have been because of long bangs constantly covering her eyes. With one hand clutching a cloak tightly and the other serving to balance her as she navigated down to the valley floor, Merelith had to resort to blowing her hair out of her face. True to her nature, she couldn't be bothered to stop and tie it back.

It wasn't that she was in a hurry but rather that she probably *should* be. Merelith had learned long ago that the appearance of unintentional tardiness was best achieved with unintentional hurrying: fast enough to work up the stench and look of the harried, slow enough to still be late on purpose. And when it came to her sister and crown princess, Merelith was unambiguously *always* late. On purpose, too.

She could have picked ANY other day than today, the demanding brat. But no! No, no, she MUST have her guardian at her side while she does such and such for this or that reason on MY FUCKING BIRTHDAY! Couldn't even be bothered to ask me herself. I knew I shouldn't have opened that damn letter before I left...

Merelith nearly caught a pine branch betwixt the eyes. She skidded, caught herself with a free hand on the offending branch, only for it to break off and smack her in the face anyway. With a hard thud and no small amount of cursing under her breath, Merelith lay in the soft mud and detritus of the hillside and glared up at the pine tree as if it bore personal responsibility for her lack of decorum.

"On *my* birthday," she grumbled, "During *the* one week I can go anywhere, do anything, and *not* have to watch her back. Stars!"

She sat up, dusted her auburn hair of long-dead leaves and needles, then surveyed her surroundings. All her life, she had explored and played in the queen's wood. She loved to visit the towns, too, yet if given a choice between the bustling market of Anna or the endless wilderness of the northern wardens she wouldn't think twice about disappearing into the places even the hunters left alone. Her mother had long intoned that Merelith's heart was as wild as wild could be, and that she was meant to be so. It was what made her Torhal's guardian, afterall.

She was near to the bottom of the foothills but still high enough to look out over the canopy of the queen's wood toward the castle. Somewhere in that ancient place was a fifteen-year-old crown princess stomping about and probably demanding to know where her guardian was. Merelith rolled her eyes at the thought and resumed her descent.

Nevermind the place is packed with thirty royal guard. Or surrounded by the second company from last week's festival. Oh! AND protected by a sorceress queen and her immortal king. Oh, no! Need to have the guardian who isn't ACTUALLY an angyr yet. If ever…

"Shut up, Merelith," she mumbled, her thoughts annoying even herself.

Truth be told, the lack of *any* sign of her angyrism had been bothering Merelith for over two years now. Her mother regarded the lack of transformation as a positive sign that she was at balance with her wildness, but Merelith saw how it troubled her father. The queen would know better, but the guardian's heart had long been tied to her father's approval and pleasure. The only person who *wasn't* in a hurry for Merelith to become an angyr was her sister. The reason why had Merelith forcing her mind to consider the forest around her instead.

She loved this place, not least because the magic that infused it was so familiar to her. Though Merelith could sense it, she had no means with which to grasp it. Unlike her sister, who was fast proving a natural wild sorceress just like their mother. It didn't bother Merelith, though, that she couldn't make trees grow taller, or stones fly like birds, or water curl into beautiful shapes and then freeze. Angyrism, not magic, was her birthright.

Or, at least, it would be eventually. She sighed with frustration and rested a palm on a towering pine tree.

"Shut *up*, Merelith," she repeated to the tree.

"Have you considered, perhaps, that Anise is hoping to do something *for* you?"

Merelith's back straightened as if struck by lightning. If her hair could have stood on end, it would have. Then she registered the voice was her mother's and instantly relaxed. The girl kept looking up into the canopy and shrugged.

"For ten years I have spent every birthday in these woods, Mama. For the last *five* I spent them climbing to the Silver Alpha's mouth *alone*. If Anise wanted to do something for my birthday *on* my birthday, she should have told me what it was before I left."

"You left six days ago. At *midnight*," her mother drawled.

Merelith snorted and said, "It isn't my fault she loves sleep so much."

Nobody spoke of the crown princess with such irreverence. They certainly didn't do so to her mother, the queen. Merelith knew she was both right *and* wrong, and kept her eyes skyward to see what her mother would do. When she did nothing, curiosity got the best of Merelith's wild heart, and she looked down and over her shoulder towards the queen. Much to her surprise, the blood ruler of Torhal was dressed similarly to her eldest daughter: leather boots, wool pants, a sturdy belt with a large hunting knife, a dyed-yellow cotton shirt under a heavy wool vest, all under the protective warmth of a bear-fur cloak. Not a soul would recognize Annelle Torhal, queen and wild sorceress, if not for the silver circlet adorning her thin-as-silk head of brown hair. Bright, emerald eyes surveyed the guardian with a mixture of mirth and annoyance.

The queen cocked an eyebrow as her eldest child surveyed her back with obvious curiosity. Then Annelle snorted and motioned with her chin towards the castle. Wordlessly, the queen strode off through her wood. Merelith's eyes sparkled as bright as her teeth, now bared in equal parts excitement and savagery, as she trotted after her mother. There were only *two* reasons the queen ventured into her woods: to train the guardian how to hunt, or to hunt herself. With elemental mastery at her fingertips, Queen Annelle's knife had more utility as an oversized nail cleaner than a real weapon, giving Merelith hope that another lesson was *finally* forthcoming.

The last had been over six months ago: a brutal game of hide and seek in a lethal blizzard of her mother's making. Merelith had loved every moment of it, despite only finding her mother once out of five attempts. Deadly cold, whipping winds and shifting snow had been hand-crafted into the perfect coverup of the queen's trail. This in turn had forced Merelith to rely on her most basic instincts to succeed: deep knowledge of the wood, mathematical acuity to gauge how far she might have traveled, and observational alacrity to notice the few clues Annelle had left to be found in the storm. Were she already angyr, the game would have been child's play for Merelith: between a powerful nose and heightened sensitivity to magic, the queen wouldn't have stood a chance.

Yet that was precisely why Annelle, not her husband, trained Merelith. Someday, hopefully soon, magic would be necessary to keep the guardian's skills as sharp as her new claws, fangs, and feathers. Annelle led her daughter until they came upon Antila's stream, which would eventually feed into the mighty Torhal river that stretched the length of the kingdom and deep into the Freelands beyond. The queen unsheathed her hunting knife and held it out for the guardian to take it.

"I *should* be forcing you to run back to the castle" her mother intoned with care, "and I *should* be scolding you for not heeding your sister's request, since I *know* she told you *before* you left."

"Yet here we are" Merelith replied with a hint of amusement, taking the knife from her mother.

"Yet here we are" the queen repeated, a wisp of a sad smile gracing her lips.

Annelle looked her daughter square in the face and Merelith felt as much as saw her mother go rigid. It wouldn't be the first time the sorceress had started combat at such close quarters. Yet the queen only stared for a long moment before sighing and motioning to the knife as she spoke. It was a thing of Torhalian beauty: a sharp steel blade with blood channels, wrapped in a silver hilt with filigree that gave the appearance of feathers adorning it. The pommel was shaped into the head of an angyr: wolf-like, its four ears pinned back as it roared in feral aggression. Merelith had long adored the blade but never known the story behind it. Until now.

"When I was still a little girl, not much younger than Anise is now, my sister – Reeta – gave me that. I could protect myself, she had said. At the time, I didn't know what to do but accept the gift and leave it at that. I thought that, perhaps, she didn't *want* to protect me."

Merelith gulped, well aware her mother was sharing a story few alive would know. She hardly ever spoke of *her* guardian, Reeta Torhal, long ago vanished. Much of Merelith's childhood and upbringing had been shaped by hard lessons learned by her mother in the absence of a guardian and sibling. The queen sighed and forced another sad smile at her daughter. Merelith cringed. All stories had a lesson, and she had a sinking feeling this wouldn't be one she enjoyed.

"Looking back, I realize Reeta was trying to help me feel more secure. She was empowering me, reminding me that I *could* protect myself but did not have to. My mother was too wrapped up in her own throne and my father in protecting *me*…I did not see how isolated Reeta was until it was too late. I did not understand she knew *exactly* how isolated I myself felt."

Annelle tapped the blade in Merelith's hand and winked at her daughter.

"Why am I telling you this story, Merelith?" she asked with a whisper.

Merelith pursed her lips but bowed her head in respect as she considered an appropriate answer. Obviously, the *implied* lesson was she should be supporting her own sister. That is what a good guardian would be doing, anyhow. Anise wasn't handling the troubles her mother had, but the fact remained that being crown princess wasn't exactly an easy life. Certainly not as a wild sorceress only just grasping her power.

As guardian, Merelith's sole responsibility was the protection of the crown heir. So it had been for centuries of angyrian guardians and their second-born siblings. Someday, Anise would marry and raise a husband into immortality – just like Annelle had – and they would conceive an angyrian child as their firstborn, continuing the tradition that had kept Torhal safe for generations. A tradition that had been broken by Merelith's Great Uncle Merel, her namesake, when he left before Reeta was ready to protect Annelle.

"I…I don't know, Mama" she finally answered, the truth of it stirring her heart a little.

Annelle replied, "A threat was made against Anise's life two weeks ago."

"*WHAT!?* Why didn't anyone tell me?!"

Annelle's sad smile remained and Merelith felt that stirring in her heart plummet into a pit of remorse and guilt. Of course. Why *would* they tell her? She was neither angyr nor really a particularly good guardian. Afterall, she was out here enjoying her birthday week while her sister was probably wondering if her guardian even cared to know.

I thought she just wanted me for show or to do some stupid decree on my behalf, so she'd look like a good princess. If mother is telling the truth...

"Why didn't *she* tell me?" Merelith asked, not wanting the answer but needing it all the same.

"You know why, Merelith."

"What would I even *do*, Mama? I'm just...me!"

Merelith motioned at herself with the knife and grimaced. She knew her way around a sword and bow, sure, but one eighteen-year-old soldier wasn't going to save the crown princess' life! Besides, Anise hated her sister. Or, well, it felt like that most of the time. The more Merelith thought on what her mother had shared, the more she doubted the truth of it.

"Anise wouldn't have asked for me" Merelith said in a flat, challenging tone.

Annelle considered her daughter and, once again, Merelith felt and saw her mother become stiff. Either the guardian had crossed an unspoken line, or the queen was calculating her next words to have maximum impact. Probably both.

"No. She did not. Nor did she ask for you today. I did."

Merelith felt a brief wave of satisfaction for being right before it tumbled off a cliff of dull realization. She was *the* guardian and her sole charge, whose life had been threatened, had opted to *not* ask for her. Her *mother* had asked her to be there, today. The queen. Not that it mattered: Anise would one day be queen herself and it was Merelith's literal *life purpose* to ensure that day arrived and continued on.

"Is...is this a test?" Merelith asked sheepishly.

"It was," her mother answered in a grave tone that made it clear Merelith had *failed* that test.

"I...Mama...how am I supposed to protect her if...?"

Merelith paused at the uplifted hand of her mother. Annelle sighed and motioned for the knife back. The guardian hesitated then sighed herself and let go of the blade. Not for the first time, Merelith had missed the mark. The queen sheathed the knife then tilted her head towards the distant castle through the wood.

"I'm not sure what else to say, Merelith. We don't know how the letter containing the threat got to Anise, in her own room. It is a serious breach. Lord Thadeus has his best on the trail, but until we know more…there is little else to be done."

"If I were an angyr…" Merelith began, but her mother cut her off.

"*IF* you were an angyr, your sister would still be unprotected because you'd *still* be out here instead! We only found out about the letter because your father saw Anise shaking at dinner the night before you left. Something angyrian sight *isn't* needed for."

The lecture was as sharp as her knife. Merelith bowed her head lower, taking it all. It wasn't as if her mother had said anything untrue. Annelle took a deep breath then let it out in a huff fit for an angry queen. Her next words gutted the guardian further.

"She is still waiting for you at the gate. Enjoy your birthday however you see fit."

Then the queen strode off into her woods, making it clear she did not expect nor wanted her daughter to follow. Merelith stood alone for a brief moment. Then she took off running toward the castle, not entirely sure what she would say to her sister when she got there.

2 – Too Close

Anise

It had been eight days since Anise had accidentally burnt her dress, frozen a stone off one of her pieces of jewelry, or sprouted flowers in the castle. Most practitioners of magic had such things under control by the age of five or six. Yet, the crown princess of Torhal was *not* a typical elementalist or healer. She was a wild sorceress, born of a womb suffused with wild magic, substantially more powerful and equally more dangerous. To herself as much as others.

Just…breathe. It's fine. It's fine that she's here. At least she's being quiet.

She stole a glance at her older sister and caught the guardian staring at the cobbled path underfoot rather than around. As usual, Merelith was somewhere in her head rather than *here*, where she was wanted. Or needed, Anise supposed. She certainly didn't *want* her sister there. The princess had the sneaking suspicion that her mother had put the guardian up to it.

On her own birthday. Stars, she probably hates me right now! Nothing to be done for it. One more stop then maybe…maybe it can be a better day for everyone?

"Last one," the princess said loudly, pausing on the path.

Merelith looked up toward where her sister pointed. They were on the southern edge of Torhal proper, among the fields situated between the Torhal River and High Stream. Over centuries, Anise's forebears had enriched these particular fields to be perfect for the vineyards that stretched almost out of sight. Officially, the crown princess was visiting several farmers to personally thank them for their freely given casks at the fall festival and reward them with a small stipend. Secretly, the young sorceress was trying to surprise her sister on her birthday.

The guardian approached the last cottage to be visited while the crown princess waited on the cobbled street a short distance away. Torhal was, by and large, a safe kingdom and the royal family rarely traveled anywhere with more than a handful of guards. Considering Anise and Annelle could both incinerate a would-be attacker with a flick of their eyes, even Merelith's presence was a bit unnecessary. Although that had more to do with the guardian still being little more than a woman. Or, well, looking like one anyway.

Merelith rapped her knuckles on the door and said loudly, "Attention! The Crown Princess Anise II requests your presence immediately."

Anise grimaced at her sister's tone, drawling and full of boredom. Merelith *had* arrived red-faced and apologetic, earlier. The princess had even believed her guardian's words. There had been a sadness in the angyrian woman's eyes, though Anise couldn't guess why. But now? It was evident Merelith would much rather be *anywhere* but here. The crown princess shoved aside her annoyance and smiled brightly as an elderly man and his family of six emerged from the cottage. The farmers acknowledged the guardian with a quick bow then prostrated themselves on the street before Anise.

"Peace and prosperity, Your Highness," the older man said, his family echoing him.

"Peace and prosperity. Rise! I come bearing thanks and a gift," Anise said.

The farmer's eyebrows shot up as he stood. Anise motioned to Merelith, who released a tiny bag of coin from her belt – the last of five – and proffered it for the farmer.

"O-oh! Thank you! Thank you, Your Highness!"

Anise replied, "You are most welcome. The crown endeavors to recognize goodwill with goodwill. Your family's gifts to the festival were both generous and appreciated. Lord Regis was adamant that such contributions be recognized and celebrated."

The old farmer bowed his head low and said with deep reverence, "Lord Regis is ever a kind man to us. We only follow in his steps, your Highness."

Anise smiled and nodded. Then, as usual, a tense silence followed. Now was when a commoner might make a request. More often than not, they just squirmed under the gaze of their crowned heir until she bid them farewell. The queen and king were far better at making graceful exits, something Anise was still trying to master herself. She cast a wary glance at Merelith and found her sister staring back with amusement. Then she rolled her eyes.

Merelith quipped, "He's also *very* fond of wine. I'm sure that isn't related."

Anise shot a glare at her sister, yet the farmer chuckled and nodded agreement. Just like that, the tension evaporated, and the family turned its attention toward the guardian.

"That he is, Guardian! That he is!" the old man agreed.

A woman, likely his wife, added, "The good lord is very particular about our process! I daresay he missed his life's purpose, taking up the tabard for your father rather than the plow!"

Merelith snorted and said, "Trust me when I say, you would *not* want Regis ordering you about. He'd have you sweeping the fields of loose dust! The man is *insatiable* when it comes to orderliness."

That is LORD Regis, Mer! Stars and moon…she is so disrespectful sometimes.

The farmer's family hooted with laughter at the guardian as she bent down to touch the grass, rub her fingers, and tut at finding dirt there. Anise managed a grim smile at her sister's antics. Lord Regis Hardy *was* rather rigid. It was a trait that endlessly annoyed and pleased her father, and the principal reason he was Lord over Torhal and High Town, the cultural and economic hearts of the kingdom, respectively. The crown princess cleared her throat, and the guardian noticed. Merelith rolled her eyes, again, but took the hint.

Merelith motioned at the coin purse and said kindly, "Spend it as you see fit, friend. Peace and prosperity to you and your family."

The farmer nodded and then bowed to both the guardian and princess.

"Peace and prosperity, Guardian. Your Highness."

"Peace and prosperity," Anise replied, bowing her head slightly before turning to walk away.

Merelith trotted to catch up and the two were in lockstep back towards Torhal. Until Anise took a right turn and walked straight off the road toward the king's wood. The guardian dutifully followed, though Anise saw in the corner of her eye that her sister had perked up at the change in course. The crown princess was pleased to find herself smiling a little, too. Surprising Merelith was notoriously difficult, not least because they generally avoided each other.

The king's wood was a vast, curated reserve that was enclosed on all sides by water: a manufactured canal to the west, High Lake to its south, the Torhal River along its north, and the lake's eastern tributary that fed back into the Torhal river. It wasn't even half the size of the queen's wood, which dominated the northwestern corner of the kingdom, but what it lacked in size it made up for in accommodation: a beautiful hunting lodge sat off High Lake and three families of dedicated huntsmen and gatherers personally curated the woods. Many a merchant or envoy from beyond Torhal craved a chance to hunt the majestic forest.

Anise loved the king's wood most of all, unlike Merelith, who preferred the untamed wild of their mother's wood. This place, too, had generations of magic layering it but there was a structure and orderliness to the latent energies not found elsewhere in the kingdom. She also preferred it because if the king wasn't gardening in his spare time, he was here, often just enjoying the sights and sounds of his reserve. Today, though, Anise was here for her unwilling escort. Right on cue, her sister got up the nerve to ask *why*. Except she didn't ask why they were there.

"Why didn't you tell me, Anise?"

"Well, it *is* meant to be a surprise…" the princess replied with a smirk.

"No, no…I mean the, um, the threat. To you."

Anise stopped in her tracks, the breath taken from her briefly.

Oh. That. Oh no. I don't want to talk about this! Shit.

Magic surged in her veins, and she took a moment to breathe it out in a thin, chill stream of air that she hoped her sister couldn't see. Which was preposterous, come to think of it, because Merelith would definitely *feel* it. Having an angyrian sister really did have drawbacks at the worst times. To her credit, the guardian didn't make a face nor seem bothered by Anise's long pause.

She's been watching me do this my whole life. Relax. She won't take it personally. Yet.

"U-um…" Anise stammered.

The princess pinched her eyes shut and shook her head. She turned, took a step toward Merelith, and felt as much as heard the grass underfoot crunch like broken glass. Anise glanced down and was horrified to find a neat circle of hoarfrost surrounding her and reaching almost to Merelith's right boot. The princess raised her gaze to the guardian's and found her sister shaking her head with a sorry smile.

"Please tell me about it. All of it."

Anise heard her sister's words but found her mind wandering to a dark bedroom eight days ago. An open letter in neat handwriting lay on her dresser. The paper was too crisp to have been pressed from the local woods. The ink had traces of magic in it, nothing of any power but rather a residual from whoever had penned the words. The message had been short and to the point.

This guardian will fail you, too.

"There was a letter on my dresser. It, um, it said *your days are numbered.* Nobody knows where it came from."

A lie, but not far from the mark. She'd told her parents the same. Considering how sensitive the queen was to any notion of Merelith becoming a failed guardian, Anise had opted to hide the letter and say nothing. Yet prodding from her observant father had seen her lose control later that night and burn the letter, ostensibly on accident. Pressed for answers, she'd simplified the threat to protect Merelith's own peace of mind. Anise had seen Merelith lose herself to wildness before and had no desire to risk such an event again.

"I am so sorry, sister. That…must have been frightening," Merelith said with calculated care.

Anise replied with a false shrug, "It was, but I'm ok now."

"Anise…"

"It's ok, really. Come, we're almost there!"

Anise started to turn and walk off but was stopped by a hard grip on her hand. Magic curled around her instinctive urge to flee, but she kept it from scalding her sister. Merelith wore a warped scowl, her upper lip quivering. The princess paused, began to insist everything was fine, when the guardian stepped closer until she was nearly nose to nose with her sister.

"You are shaking, sister," whispered the guardian, "You are *not* ok."

"Probably because you are too close."

Fuck. Wrong words.

Merelith's eyes dilated, in and out, twice. It was a simple thing most folk did not notice, but Anise couldn't help but *always* notice. The guardian's nose flared, too, but rapidly. Her sense of smell was no better than Anise's, but instincts drove her to try anyway. Such small, simple quirks that reminded Anise every day that her sister was *not* human. Did not think nor feel like a human. Consequently, Merelith also did not hunt or kill like one, neither. As Anise had seen firsthand, almost a decade ago.

Anise took a purposeful step back from her guardian. Merelith's hand went limp and released the princess. The wild rage in those eyes raced away, leaving the hollow look of a spurned sibling. The princess tried to find the right words before she spoke them, but the guardian didn't give her a chance.

"I will *never* hurt you, Anise. I love you. I didn't mean to scare you, just now."

Indeed, but you would hurt anyone else for me, too. Have. Even if I didn't want you to.

"I know that," mumbled the princess.

"I'm sorry."

"No need."

"I'm sorry that…that I haven't earned your trust. That I am not the guardian you want or need."

"Mer…please. Stop. I, it was a mistake on my part, too."

The guardian pursed her lips but didn't agree nor disagree. Sensing an opening, as much to close the conversation as the wound inflicted, Anise pressed on.

"I should have told you *first*. Stars know, you'd have known how to tell Mama and Papa. I certainly didn't. I was afraid it would, y'know, make them get weird. You know how they can be about that sort of thing when it comes to you and me."

Truth. I just wish I'd thought of that in the moment. I could have hidden the letter from you, but you really would have known how to tell them. I'm not the princess you want nor need, too.

Anise felt her heart lighten at Merelith's thin smirk.

"Yeah…given how my lecture went this morning? I suspect Mama didn't take the news well."

Anise rolled her eyes and nodded while replying, "Nope. Poor Regis probably hasn't slept since she found out."

"*Lord* Regis" Merelith quipped, "Come now, Anise. You are *better.*"

Anise was startled by the jab. Then she laughed. It was a real, genuine laugh. Too high pitched – like her voice – but she didn't care in that moment. Her sister had caught her, fair and square. The crown princess was notorious for correcting her elder sister's manners. Weeks, months, *years* of it. Yet Merelith was an ever-patient predator when it came to Anise. The princess raised her hands in supplication and shook her head.

"Fair," the princess said with a smile.

"Hardly," replied the guardian, her own smile faltering.

"Why do you say that?"

"Too much is expected of you, sister…and too little of me. It is not fair. You *are* better."

Anise sighed then shrugged and shook her head.

"At being a princess, maybe. Not so much a sister."

"That makes two of us," Merelith allowed.

The princess felt a flutter in her chest, the same she always felt when a lie was getting too close to being too heavy. Fire darted between her fingers, burning the inside of her dainty gloves. She clasped her hands to extinguish the magic before Merelith saw it as much as felt it. She saw her sister's face fall further and realized Merelith might have misinterpreted the magic.

"No," Anise said quickly, "Not two. Just me. You didn't have to ask."

"I asked too late."

"I never asked at all, Mer. You can't be there for me if…if I don't tell you *where* I am."

"I still should have noticed."

Anise wasn't sure how to argue with that. On the one hand, Merelith was right. On the other, Anise much preferred when her angyrian sister *didn't* notice. The princess shrugged and forced a smile.

"We can both be better, how's that?"

Merelith managed a small smile, nodded, and answered, "Yes."

"Come on, then. No more of this. Today is your birthday!"

Anise hoped her enthusiasm sounded more real than it felt. She *did* want to surprise her sister. She'd just rather not do it right after *that* kind of conversation. Heart to heart was most certainly not her strength. Especially when it was a human heart to an angyrian one. The princess kept up her smile as she led her sister deeper into the king's wood toward the birthday surprise.

3 – The Wrong Angyr

Merelith

It was a poor apology, and Merelith knew it, yet finding the right words when it came to Anise had never been easy. The age difference alone, nearly three years, didn't help. Anise also *hated* when Merelith got too close. The core reason was a memory best left alone, but plenty of other excuses existed. The guardian was both taller and more mature in form, with chest and hips that had long attracted the attention of wandering eyes. Anise was built like a living *doll*. Flat and thin, with the voice of a six-year-old.

As they traveled into their father's reserve, Merelith tried to think through a better way to reach Anise. It didn't have to be today, granted, but she was confident her parents would expect some kind of breakthrough after *this*. Her and Anise's strained relationship was an open secret throughout the castle and probably the kingdom. Which, as the king often pointed out during their sparring lessons, only made the princess *and* guardian bigger targets for outside forces.

Well, let's start simple. Be super excited, right now! It's probably a stupid carriage or, stars forbid, a horse. She would know better than that, right? Bah, focus Merelith! It doesn't matter what it is. What matters is that I like it, and she knows I like it. Or believes it, anyway.

Merelith felt like her face might fracture if she smiled much more. Anise wasn't even looking back. The guardian dropped the smile, and it was as if her whole face sighed in relief. Then her heart cracked instead. She really *was* a terrible sister, which almost certainly made her a terrible guardian, too.

The quicker I feel the calling, the better. If angyr are anything like wolves, they probably look happy most of the time, anyway. Or maybe hungry? Huh. That might be worse. Except everyone would expect that, so…

The guardian was pulled from her thoughts when she bumped into her sister's back. That Anise didn't protest was Merelith's first clue something was wrong. The second clue came when Anise whispered in that child-like voice her sister's nickname.

"M-mer?"

The word was laced with terror. Merelith peered over her sister's shoulder to find the source of that fear. What she beheld set off every alarm in her entire body. Standing not fifty yards in front of the crown princess and guardian was a creature that hadn't stalked Torhal in over two decades: an angyr. A *real* angyr.

"Get behind me, Anise. Now."

Merelith surprised herself with how calm the command came out. Moreso when she stepped around her trembling sister and, in a fluid motion that also drew her sword to a defensive posture, took up position between Anise and the creature. She absolutely *did not* stand a chance against an angyr, but what mattered in that moment was that she was the visible threat instead of Anise. To her credit, the crown princess didn't immediately try to run. The unknown angyr's black eyes rimmed in gold focused on Merelith's blade and it began to stalk towards her.

We're going to die. Stars and moon and void, we're going to die.

"Anise, signal the queen. Now."

From behind her, Merelith felt the surge of magic in her sister. It started as a deep inhalation that seemed to pull an invisible breeze towards the princess. Then she exhaled it as a low, reverberating pulse that only the magically inclined could sense. Including the angyr, who paused at its approach and tilted its head in curiosity before baring its fangs at Merelith in a gut-punching low growl.

"N-now what?"

"Run when it attacks me. Ice the ground behind you, tangle the roots beside you, and don't look back until you find Mama or Papa."

"Wh-what!? What about you?"

Merelith didn't answer the question, instead stepping forward and closing the distance between her and the angyr. In response, the beast growled another warning and spread its legs wide in a show of dominance. The guardian noticed an odd detail: it had no wings to also spread. Rather, terrible scars ran down each side of its back where they should have been.

What happened to you? Please don't kill her. Stars, that must hurt awfully. Please don't kill her.

The larger pair of its ears rose up and danced back and forward. It kept its fangs bared, but Merelith saw the head dip and rise slowly – a sure sign of territorialism. Which, in the guardian's mind, didn't make sense.

You're obviously not Reeta...this isn't your home. You don't seem lost to wildness, unless you're somehow passing through Torhal on your way to the wildlands.

Gold eyes mark you as male. Merel? No, he had brown fur. You're black. Did you come over the mountains?

Merelith's blood chilled at the thought. She looked past the massive head of the angyr to find what she was looking for. Her heart sank: a bronze collar encircled the creature's neck – a sure sign the angyr had once been a slave to the Pentarchs. Possibly even one of their experiments. *Nothing* good came out of that cursed empire.

Oh, shit. Shit, shit, shit. Breathe. Stand tall. Buy her time. I am here. I am here. I am…

As if sensing Merelith's faltering resolve, the angyr suddenly broke into a sprint right at her. The guardian set her feet into a defensive posture and waited for instant death. The best outcome was that the angyr would quicken and kill her before she even knew it. The worst outcome was that the beast either didn't know *how* to quicken, or didn't care to, and would kill her the old-fashioned way: fangs that could crush steel plate and foreclaws that could shred chainmail. At least the feathers that could be sharpened into blades weren't present.

The blow never came. Merelith did as she was taught, waiting until the last three steps of the angyr before stabbing her blade forward – a tactic to hopefully catch the angyr in a lunge. Instead, the predator dodged sideways and *ignored* the guardian. Merelith's heart felt like it might explode as she whirled around, fully expecting to see the angyr shredding into her sister. Anise's eyes were wide with terror as the angyr lunged at her. Then over her.

The crown princess screamed in horror, falling back then throwing ice straight up into the air. Yet the angyr kept barreling into the wood, away from the two sisters. Merelith rushed to Anise's side, blade still at the ready, and demanded to know if she was hurt.

"N-n-no. I…I'm ok…I…stars, Merelith, it c-c-came right at me!"

"Stay put. Signal Mama again. I'm going after it."

"WHAT!? N-no! You need to…"

Merelith was already rushing after the unknown angyr. If the thing had wanted to kill her sister, it already would have. It was heading north, now, towards the Torhal river. She could barely make out its silhouette in the wood as she gave chase. A quiet voice in her mind warned she should go back. Another warned that if she lost the angyr, it might kill without warning. The fact a pentarchy angyr had crossed the warden mountains into Torhal was bad enough.

Yet it didn't take long for her to lose sight of the creature. Angyr were, afterall, as quick as most steeds and she was on foot. Not for the first time, Merelith cursed her own angyrism for being so slow to come on. The guardian resorted to tracking the angyr's large pawprints through the forest. Eventually, she burst from the king's wood onto the southern shore of the Torhal river. Just across was the kingdom's highway. A pair of merchants were off in the distance, heading toward Anna, and seemed unbothered.

Now out in the open, Merelith saw the tracks disappeared into the river and did not seem to emerge elsewhere. Had it gone back into the wood? Surely a large, black-furred beast of legend would stand out in the dying grasses lining the road? It had to have gone back into the wood to…Merelith's heart stopped, and she nearly dropped her sword as the accompanying thought struck her like a gut punch.

Anise.

Merelith whirled around, sheathed her blade, and ran as fast as her worthless human legs could carry her. She tried to suppress the dull realization that she was now, for the second time in her life, running as hard as she could to stop something from hurting her sister. Except this time, the king or queen probably weren't there to help. Merelith vaulted over fallen trees and swung herself around low branches, scratching her hands and knees as she went.

She knew these woods as well as her mother's. She knew *exactly* where Anise had been left, knew exactly how to get there as quick as possible. None of which mattered when she arrived to find the princess *not* there. Merelith choked down a horrified sob, dropping to the ground where Anise had fallen after the angyr had lunged at her.

Footprints. Several sets. Some aren't ours. Ok, ok, ok…I'm coming Anise!

Merelith bolted down the trail of new footprints, one set her sister's. She didn't have to go far before she barreled right into a heavy tree branch swinging at her like a club. She dodged it, only to be grabbed at the ankles and have her legs ripped back out from under her. With a sickening thud, the guardian cracked her chin on the forest floor and saw stars dance in her eyes. She didn't register a man's angry shout, nor a woman's shocked gasp. Nor the murmuring of other men nearby. Only the scream of her sister.

"STOP! IT'S MERELITH! STOP!"

"Stars and moon, Annelle! Could you not tell it was her!?" the man demanded.

"I didn't…Orren, I…" stammered the woman.

"*She's bleeding!* Mama, do something!" screamed Anise.

Sister! Sister in danger!

Merelith felt a hand take hold of her chin and gently lift her face. Then it registered someone had a hold of her head. The guardian's blade came out in the blink of an eye but was disarmed by the skillful intervention of the man.

"Merelith! It is us!" shouted the man, who increasingly sounded familiar.

"Merelith, love, relax!" added the woman.

NO! NO! SISTER! SAVE SISTER!

She tried to bite the hand on her face, but it pulled back before she could. Then a different hand, dainty and cold, took hold of her. It shook violently, as did the high voice that accompanied it, but Merelith heard.

"It's ok, Mer. I'm ok! Please calm down. Please! Not again. Please, don't lose yourself again."

Sister? Sister safe?

"You're ok. I'm ok! Please."

I am ok. Sister…Anise. Anise is ok. Stars, why does everything hurt so much?

"Anise?" Merelith mumbled.

"Y-yes! Yes, I'm right here. So is Mama and Papa. See?"

Sure enough, the man and woman came into focus as her parents: Queen Annelle and King Orren. Her mother's face was ashen with shame. Her father's cheeks were red with fury, but Merelith saw a sigh of relief escape his lips as the guardian managed to smile up at him.

"Is anyone…hurt?" Merelith asked.

"Nobody but you, love" Orren replied, a smirk gracing his lips.

"Oh. That's good."

"Hardly" the king grunted.

Merelith watched her father turn to the other men, royal guards she now saw, and ordered them to spread out into a defensive formation. He then glanced at his wife and shook his head. Annelle bowed her head low and shrugged. The silent exchange seemed odd until Merelith realized what had struck her down was her mother's own magic. She chuckled, though it hurt.

"What? Why are you l-laughing?" Anise asked, still holding Merelith's head.

"Mama thought I was the angyr, didn't she?"

"W-well, yes. We all did. You weren't very quiet on your approach."

"I thought you had been taken."

"She was. Just not by enemies," the queen said stiffly.

The king barked, "Annelle! Not now."

She was? But she's safe…oh.

"I…I am sorry, Anise," the guardian murmured.

"Whatever for!? You…"

"Left."

She saw the understanding in her sister's eyes. Then Anise forced a grim smile and shrugged. The crown princess stroked a few stray hairs from Merelith's face and told her not to worry about it.

"I'm ok," she whispered.

Merelith replied, "I'm glad."

Anise added, "You'll be ok, too."

Merelith's heart caved and, without warning, she began to cry. Anise was startled by the sudden outburst but seemed unable to do or say anything else. She simply stroked Merelith's scalp. Nearby, the queen shook her head before kneeling beside the distraught guardian and lightly touching her forehead. The king, too, came closer and rested a heavy hand on Merelith's shoulder. None of this helped. If anything, it made it all so, so much worse.

Anise should be crying, not me. Mama defending us, not me. Papa chasing after it, not me.

The weight of it all crushed her soul and Merelith realized what had been eating at her for almost a decade. A *real* angyr was needed to deal with dangers like this. A good sister was needed that didn't abandon her own. The Torhal family needed a better guardian.

Not me.

4 – Tense Intentions

Anise

Whenever the crown princess or guardian was scolded, it was a tense affair. In any other kingdom, it would already be a delicate balance of parenting: teaching valuable lessons to a royal child without inflicting wounds or imbuing resentment that might one day punish the people. The castle's scriptorium contained no less than thirty different books on the topic of raising highborn children, some dating to before the War for Freedom. Unfortunately, only one of these books detailed how one might parent a royal *angyr*: the diary of Queen Annabelle, Anise's great grandmother.

Given how much Annelle was yelling, Anise was confident that the queen either did not read the diary or found its contents too lighthearted to be of any use. To be fair, Queen Annabelle was regarded as one of the weakest rulers in Torhal's long line. She had been aloof and silly, beloved by her people and family but soft on foreign policy and economic prosperity. Her daughter, Queen Anise, had been a polar opposite in every way imaginable: cunning and ruthless. Given how history described that queen's guardian, Merel, it wasn't hard for Princess Anise to understand why her great uncle left her grandmother after Annabelle died of old age.

That abandonment had ostensibly triggered a series of events that led to the current crisis unfolding in the throne room of Castle Torhal. The chamber doors were sealed, barred on the outside by Lord Regis himself and ten of his best royal guard. Outside the stained-glass windows that allowed the evening's failing light in, another fifty guards were stationed below the castle's rear. The second company had been staged across the castle grounds and walls, each man within arm's reach or, more likely, clutching a crossbow. Angyrian quickening had no normal counters, but time manipulation could be made complex by a wall of hide-penetrating bolts.

Like most of Castle Torhal, the throne room was austere in its grandeur. Much of the beauty came from carved stone pillars, tapestries of momentous events, and the four, immense stained-glass windows set high over the thrones' dais. Each window depicted an angyr in some sort of regal pose. Who they were and why the castle was adorned with such imagery was a question only its former owner might know: the mad pentarch, Anisterosa. Castle Torhal had been captured by Anise's ancestor, a war-caster named Antila, during the War for Freedom over nine hundred years ago.

That story was among Anise's favorite, most of all for how the name Torhal had come about: a peasant soldier had had the nerve to ask a newly crowned Antila how the tyranny of her magic would be any different from Anisterosa's. His name was Woden Torhal and, before it was all said and done, the man won Antila's heart and became the first immortal king of Torhal, named in his honor. Anise imagined that her father and Woden might have been twins in spirit. Given how the current lecture was unfolding, it certainly seemed like Orren Torhal was endeavoring to curtail the tyranny of his queen's wrath against the current guardian.

"Annelle, love, she is but *eighteen*! Merelith's logic is also sound: the angyr *could* have easily harmed either of them but did not…"

"IT ALSO COULD HAVE BEEN DRAWING HER OFF FOR AN EASY CAPTURE!" the queen bellowed.

Anise interjected, "I was prepared to defend myself when you arriv…"

"SHE IS TO BE AT YOUR SIDE *ALWAYS!*" screamed the queen.

King and princess both winced and huddled into their shoulders at the declaration. Yet the guardian didn't so much as flinch. Merelith stared her mother in the face as the queen rounded on her, again, and shouted the same thing she had been shouting for the last hour.

"*ALWAYS!* Always, Guardian Merelith Torhal! ALWAYS!"

"Yes, My Queen" whispered the guardian in reply.

Flame coursed along Annelle's arms while ice knitted her brow in fury, her evening gown long since incinerated. To an outsider, it would have made a peculiar sight: a naked queen wreathed in elemental fury haranguing her eldest daughter. It had been some time since Anise had seen her mother's magic so out of control. Evidently the same applied to her father, as King Orren shook his head and sighed. Anelle continued her tirade.

"Do you even care!? Do you not understand the day *will* come when your presence may decide if she lives or dies!? Have you learned nothing of your purpose!?"

This isn't fair. I mean, sure, she wasn't supposed to leave me…Mama is right, I could have been captured. Yet she has to see the whole situation was far beyond anything Merelith would have been able to handle anyway? She hasn't felt the calling yet, afterall. And besides, it's my fault we were there in the first place!

"My queen?" the princess ventured, "It was because of me we were…"

The queen snapped, "*You are dismissed,* Princess! I already told you to go."

"Annelle…" began the king.

"You may leave, too, Orren."

Anise's eyebrow cocked in unison with her father's. Then she watched a different side of the immortal emerge. One that was both fearsome and praiseworthy. The king strolled toward his wife, still pulsating with lethal elemental energies, and grabbed her by the wrist. The flesh on his hand instantly burned and melted to the bone. Annelle's eyes narrowed into a glare of warning. The king's own did the same right back.

Orren stated, "That. Is. Enough."

"I am queen, Orren! I decide what is enough when it comes to *our* guardian."

"I am her father, Annelle. I decided she was enough the day she was born!"

A strangled sob escaped Merelith's lips, quickly silenced by her own self will. Yet the noise was enough to snuff out the queen's magic. Just like that, the sorceress went from being the harrowing embodiment of wild magic to the sorry look of a beleaguered mother at her wit's end. Her arm slouched in Orren's bony grip, now gradually rebuilding itself sinew by sinew into his original hand as if no burning had occurred at all. Anise looked away, her father's quickened immortality always troubling to her stomach and heart. Particularly since *his* heart didn't even beat. It never had in her lifetime.

"Take my coat. Go to the balcony with Regis. Remain there until I come for you."

"O-orren, she must understand…" mewled the queen.

"Annelle Torhal, *you* must understand!" the king cut in, "YOU must understand who you are speaking to is *still here.*"

Merelith's brow furrowed at that. Anise felt like her heart might stop. The king spoke of Annelle's own guardian, Reeta. Or perhaps her father, former king Doran, roaming the southern freelands. Both topics fraught with literal danger. Especially with the queen already in such a state. Orren might be immortal, but neither of his children were. An outburst from the queen could see the future of Torhal's line snuffed out! Such a tragedy wasn't unheard of, unfortunately. Yet the queen only stared with the hollow look of defeat back at her husband before nodding like a lost child. The king pulled his heavy cloak from his shoulders and encased his bare wife in it. A short conversation at the doors later, and the throne room was silent.

Anise kept shifting her eyes from her father's backside to her sister's. Merelith gazed up at the four windows with a familiar look of hopeless longing. Orren rested his forehead on the aging doors of his own throne room. Or, well, his when Annelle didn't point out to whom the actual lineage belonged. Both seemed content to stew in silence. The crown princess *hated* silence, a rare quirk she shared with her mother and sister.

"Why would the pentarchs send an angyr into Torhal?" she asked, hoping to change the topic.

"It could be a spy," the king answered, "Or a messenger. It may be a runaway? Escaped experiments aren't all that uncommon further south."

"Why pretend to attack us then…disappear?"

"To draw me off," the guardian whispered, "were you not listening?"

"Yet there was no one there to take advantage of your absence," Anise countered.

"Probably because Mama and Papa were already too close. It was luck."

"It was *not* luck, Merelith," the king groaned, "It was tactics, and you did the best you could in the moment!"

"My best isn't enough," Merelith replied.

The king turned from the door and stared a hole in the back of his eldest daughter. His lips moved, but no words came out. Evidently, he didn't know what to say to the guardian's admission. Anise, too, was speechless. Merelith kept staring up at the four windows, though she seemed fixated on one. Probably her favorite, Anise reckoned. It was a female of red fur with white-tipped wings, her long feathers spread forward as if to protect what sat between her forepaws: a small flame. She was outlined in silver and, unlike the other three angyr, looked ahead as if to watch the viewer.

It must be awful, seeing what you could be and not knowing how to get there. I wish you knew I felt the same, Mer. My best has never been enough, too. Not for her. Not for anyone.

"Sometimes it won't be, love," the king answered.

Anise watched as her father moved to behind the guardian and wrapped his arms about her neck. She was almost as tall as him, now, an oddity in Anise's mind. Merelith had certainly inherited their mother's height. Her beauty, too, Anise remembered with a pang of self-loathing. She shook it off as she went toward the pair and rested a pale hand on her sister's elbow. Merelith finally looked at her sister, the first time since the incident.

"I'm sorry I wasn't there."

"I'm sorry you were," Anise replied.

Merelith's lips danced with sorrow and Anise wondered if her choice of words had been wrong again. Changing tack, she looked at her father and forced a smile.

"Can we leave this until tomorrow evening? I…I don't think there's anything else to say."

"Indeed," the king said with a nod.

"Agreed," the guardian mumbled.

Anise tried to sound hopeful and cheery as she asked, "Papa, did they bring the present back to the castle yet?"

Anise's heart skipped a beat as she saw Merelith's eyes light with curiosity. Perhaps the day could yet be salvaged. The king's own eyes sparkled with joy, and he nodded. Before the princess could ask more, he pointed up at the ceiling.

"It is in your room. Do not tarry too long, I will be asking for dinner as soon as I leave from here. A meal, even in silence, will help quell our queen's fears."

"Yes, Papa. Mer…would you like to see it?"

The guardian nodded quietly then turned and hugged her father. She muttered another apology, but King Orren shushed her and instead heaped praises upon her.

"You are a *fine* guardian, Merelith. You *were* there, today, and you *did* defend your sister exactly as we have practiced. Your mother's fear is simply getting the best of her. We knew it would. We knew it might be like this, the first *real* time?"

"Yes, Papa," whispered the guardian.

"And what did we agree to do?"

Anise was unaware of this conversation and suspected her father was sharing it in front of her for a reason. Merelith stepped back from his embrace, took a deep breath, then stood tall. Shoulders back, head held high, she looked the king right in the eye as she spoke.

"Remember that I'm still here."

"Are you?" asked the king.

"Yes, Papa. I am."

"Were you earlier?"

"I…"

Anise saw the conflict in her sister's face and felt a pang of fear in her chest.

No. She wasn't. She was lost to wildness. Again.

The king nodded and said, "You were."

"Papa, I didn't see you…I…there was only…"

"There was only Anise. Yes," the king agreed sagely, "which is *precisely* who you are. So, I ask again: were you there earlier?"

Huh? Only me? What does he mean?

Merelith gulped then nodded slowly. The king seemed satisfied with this answer. He then tapped her on the nose and smiled.

"I will always be there for you, Mer, if you promise to always be *you*."

"*Me* isn't enough, Papa," grumbled the guardian.

"Were you there earlier?"

"Well, yes, but…"

"Then that is enough."

The guardian furrowed her brow, in confusion or disagreement the princess couldn't tell. The king kissed Merelith on the forehead then rested a hand on Anise's shoulder. He winked at her and suddenly it all felt a little less heavy, a little less scary. How the king did that, the crown princess did not know. She was glad for it most times.

"Go on, you two. I will see you at dinner."

"Yes, Papa," intoned both daughters.

The walk to Anise's room was silent but less tense. Every time Anise looked back at her sister, she found Merelith meeting her eyes and forcing a timid smile. It was a poor way to present her birthday gift, but Anise held onto the brittle hope it might lift her sister's spirits. Or at the very least make the entire day a little less awful. She made her sister wait in the hall as she went into her room. Sure enough, the gift lay on her dresser.

Anise had planned to present it atop a famous stump in the king's wood, unwrapped and bathed in afternoon sunlight so that it shone with royal beauty. Here in the dim candlelight of her bedroom, its splendor was greatly diminished. Still, Anise felt her heart beat a little quicker with excitement. Merelith's tastes had always been hard to pin down and the princess hoped she'd maybe found her mark this time. She tucked the gift behind her back and returned to the hall. Merelith hated being in her sister's room as much as Anise hated being in Merelith's room. The guardian eyed her sister cautiously as Anise cleared her throat.

"So, um…it was supposed to be sitting out in the sun for you to find. Obviously, that didn't happen. Uh, I'd warm it up for you but I'm afraid I might melt it…"

"Rough day, yeah, I wouldn't try," Merelith murmured.

Anise couldn't decide if she should be offended. The assumption she *would* melt it sat poorly with her, yet it was also proof Merelith understood Anise better than most. The guardian had a knack for predicting when the princess could, or couldn't, control her magic. She shook off the feeling of annoyance and continued her presentation.

"Right, so…so try to *imagine* it being warmed by the sun? S-sorry. Erm…well, here. I, I hope you like it. Happy birthday?"

She held it out in her hands, for it took both to balance the oversized cuff. Merelith's eyebrow cocked in curiosity as she leaned forward to examine the jewelry piece. Anise bit back the urge to *tell* her sister to take it. Instead, she explained it while her sister studied rather than accepted the gift.

"It's solid silver. The filigree is spinel…I figured you wouldn't like the sparkle of ruby dust…and the design is…"

"It's her. The Silver Guardian."

She has a name for it? Huh. Ok, well, she SEEMS to like it. I think?

The cuff had a perfect copy of the stain glass angyr etched into its silver surface. Her eyes were two pricks of onyx and between her paws was the flame, formed from specks of garnet. The wings and body were made of spinel, with ivory points marking the feather tips. The interior of the cuff was lined with supple deer hide. A simple message along the cuff's upper rim read, 'May the warmth of this cuff feel like the warmth of your love, sister.' Merelith stared a long time at the cuff before gingerly lifting it from Anise's hands. It was apparent that the cuff was too large, even for her sister's upper arm. The princess waited until Merelith tried to don it before explaining.

"It is…it is for later. When, y'know, when it *will* fit. I know that has been bothering you but, um, but I wanted to give you something that would last. It should fit great when, when it happens."

Stars. Stop making it more awkward.

Anise clamped her mouth and watched Merelith slide the cuff from her upper arm back down to her elbow, where it easily came off. It was so large it could probably be fitted around Anise's tiny neck, the princess realized. Maybe she should have waited on this particular gift? Merelith visibly swallowed then mumbled a question.

"Where…how did you find the size?"

Anise replied, "Mother. She, um, she showed me a cuff her sister used to wear" the princess paused, then added slowly, "She, um, she offered it to me…to give to you, I mean. I thought you might want one of your own instead."

Merelith nodded but didn't say anything else. Her face seemed blank to Anise, and the princess struggled to not ask the question burning on her tongue. Moreso, she struggled to ignore what her magic could feel in her sister: the unnatural calm of a killer. The same calm she had felt earlier that day, and on a day not unlike it ten years ago.

Why now? Is it a bad gift? Why are you losing yourself here, now?

"Mer?" whispered the princess.

"Yes?"

"Do you like it?"

Only then did Merelith's face show emotion: profound regret. She looked up from the cuff and stared at Anise for what felt an eternity. Then she set the cuff back in her sister's hands and shook her head.

"No," she whispered, "I hate it. It's everything I should be…and am not."

Merelith turned from her sister and silently left. Anise felt the cold of the silver in her palm matched the cold in her sister's calm. She had not cast her judgement in hate nor anger. Her eyes had not burned with fury or loathing. As her guardian turned the corner of the hallway and disappeared, Anise felt an emptiness yawn inside of her.

She hates it. She hates what she is. Who she is.

Anise was shocked to find cool tears dribbling down her nose onto the floor. Too big emotions swirled inside too small a heart, yet her magic didn't seem to respond as it might elsewhere. An emptiness permeated her, its hollow echoing with Merelith's unspoken judgement.

I hate that I am your sister instead of your guardian.

Not for the first time, Anise felt the opposite. She returned to her room and set the cuff in the back of a drawer in her dresser. She did not go to dinner nor did her father come looking for her that night. Chances were good both king and queen realized their daughters were best left alone, though Anise hoped they might visit Merelith again. Her father always had the right words and, when she wasn't being driven by her own fears, her mother, too.

Anise never had the right words, for anyone. It often felt as if she only had the right words for herself. Tonight, she couldn't get those words out of her mind as she fell into troubled sleep.

I hate that I am your princess instead of your sister.

5 – The Calling

Merelith

"You should probably apologize."

"It was a dumb gift."

"It was a dumb way to respond."

"You weren't there. You wouldn't know."

"Nope, I'm here now. Telling you it was a dumb way to respond."

"Eric, it was a literal cuff for an angyr...*which I am not*, STILL!"

"Merelith, when has your sister *ever* given you a gift that implies she looks forward to you *being* an angyr? To being her guardian?"

The question stuck, though she wished it wouldn't. That was the trouble with venting to Eric Smith, royal scout, and best tracker in all Torhal. The boy knew how to navigate Merelith's wild heart as easily as her homeland. Her silence saw him huff with a grin then resume his work. The guardian shoved her hands into her pockets and glumly followed.

Eric had, so far, succeeded where the royal guard had failed: the mysterious angyr had indeed passed into the river and then crossed it a short distance to the west – opposite of where Merelith had seen the pair of merchants the previous day. Technically, she was supposed to be in the castle right now. To guard Anise or not expose herself to additional threats depended on who was asked. Yet the guardian had been sneaking out of her own home for years. If the queen of Torhal really wanted to find her, she could. Merelith hoped she did. It would send a clear message at least.

Better that I'm out here than in there with her. Or you. Find someone else to protect her. I can't.

"I *will* send you back if you don't cheer up, Mer. I swear, that scowl of yours could curdle milk."

"Funny," grumbled the guardian.

The scout added, "You didn't answer my question."

Eric followed the tracks north, across the plains of Torhal. To the west, Merelith spied the edge of the capital city. Behind them, an aging gray horse meandered along in their wake. It paid no mind to Merelith, an oddity she ever found endearing. She heard Eric clear his throat, though he kept his eyes on the large paw prints underfoot.

When has she ever looked forward to my calling? Never. Not since then, anyway.

"I dunno, Eric. She hasn't."

"So why give you the cuff?"

"I dunno."

Eric groaned, shook his head, but said nothing else. The sound stole a flash of a smirk from her lips. She liked when he was frustrated. Even if that frustration was because of her. Yet the scout said no more and Merelith understood he expected her to reason through the topic. She sighed up at the sky and felt a pang of longing. Someday, she'd be able to fly up there. Someday. If ever. There was no record of angyrian children *not* feeling the calling. Delays were unusual but none had ever been permanent. More importantly, delays usually tied to a specific cause: the angyrian child's inherent wildness was so balanced that the calling couldn't be triggered.

"She does try…I just, it's always at the *worst* time, y'know? Mama had just ripped me a new one for a *very* good reason. Papa heard me but didn't. Anise just…tried to smooth it all over. Like she always does."

Like spreading a blanket over a sinkhole in the road. Looks pretty, still can't walk on it.

"Common sense isn't exactly her gift, Mer. Cut her some slack, she was trying to cheer up the one person she normally avoids."

There was truth in his words, but her cracked heart didn't care for it. She did care for him trying, though. She sighed again up at a lonely pair of clouds drifting apart then turned her gaze on Eric's back. Tall, lanky, with dirty blonde hair almost as long as hers tied up into three braids, Eric was like a living painting of the workmen of Torhal. Less the muscles and heavy coats, since the boy was unusually hot natured and plied his trade with his eyes rather than his hands.

Those same eyes had found a twelve-year-old Merelith hiding from her father after she'd accidentally lopped his favorite rose bushes in half with a sword as tall as her. Unlike any other dutiful citizen, Eric had led Merelith to a *better* hiding place where they'd spent the afternoon fishing while Torhal's monarchs mustered a thousand men to find their missing guardian. About the time Lords Regis and Thadeus were as far from the castle as one could get inside the kingdom, Merelith and Eric had strolled right up to the main gate. A practiced apology and hug later, Eric Smith found himself gifted both an apprenticeship as a ranger and a spot at Merelith's thirteenth birthday celebration a year later.

"Why do *you* care?" Merelith said.

Eric paused and turned to face her. He wore a smirk that softened into a kind smile the longer he stared. Long enough to make Merelith's breath turn shallow. He then winked at her and the cracks in her heart felt warm.

"It's you. Why wouldn't I care?"

"What should I do?" Merelith asked.

The scout furrowed his brow and looked at the grasses between them before shrugging. He then cast a gaze toward Torhal and its castle looming over it, the northern wing sparkling with the large glass windows of the scriptorium. Merelith looked, too, and wondered if one of her family was atop the balcony above the ancient library. Lunch time had only just come and gone, and the day was gloriously calm. Still cold, but a breezeless autumn day was perfect for eating on the balcony.

"I think you should keep being you."

"Not helpful, Eric."

"I beg to differ. You *were* there. The king is right about that."

"And now I'm *here*. My mother is right about that, too."

"True. Doing exactly what Reeta did, too. I've never heard the queen call *her* a bad guardian."

No. She loved Reeta. Or thought she did. She'll be all weepy tonight after last night. Probably for the next week. She hates losing her temper with me…reminds her too much of Grandmother. Still can't believe Papa pulled that card.

"She never found the killer," Merelith mused.

Eric countered, "Nope, but she *did* come back. She *was* still there until your grandfather lit her up. Hey! Don't give me that look! You know I'm right."

"Mama isn't afraid I'm going to lose my mind, Eric."

"Anise is."

"Yes, I'm well aware…" Merelith groaned.

"And *still* she gave you a gift that *proves* she wants you around."

Damn. I hate when you do that. I love it, too, but right now I just…

"Stars and moon! Can we just talk about something *else*?"

Eric laughed and then shrugged. He motioned to the tracks, then the field of grass surrounding them. A familiar twinkle flashed in his eye.

"Well, we've got your mysterious angyr and a field out in the middle of nowhere."

Merelith smirked and said, "Said field was *somewhere* not too long ago."

"I'd contend it *was* too long ago."

Merelith rolled her eyes then snorted and looked away in a sorry bid to hide the flush sweeping over her cheeks. She hadn't meant to bring up their last tryst. Or had she? She knitted her brows as a slight throb reverberated in the back of her head. It coincided with a tingling sensation in her core. It *had* been too long ago, she realized.

"We're meant to be tracking," she muttered.

Eric drew near and replied, "I am meant to be tracking. You? You can do whatever you like."

"Not true. I probably shouldn't be distracting the royal scout from his mission."

"The tracks aren't going anywhere."

"The angyr that made them is."

"Then we should probably make it quick, huh?"

Ohh stars…you're so wonderfully awful sometimes.

"Eric," she tried to say with an air of authority.

He replied with a chuckle, "Merelith."

"There are more important tasks."

What a stupid thing to say. Anise would say that. I know I want this! Bad.

"Maybe, but you're more important than any task."

A gloved hand swept slowly around her side from behind until it rested firmly on her belly. In a smooth, practiced motion the scout drew her back against him. The small headache seemed to blossom in response, as did the heat between her thighs. Being an angyrian child had certain perks prior to the calling, advantages Eric Smith knew how to rouse with just a touch.

"Let off some steam, Mer. You need this," he reasoned.

"I feel like I *always* need this," she hummed.

"Maybe you do. Best take care of it now, yeah?"

"You're awful."

"Not as awful as you. I can almost see your breath, goof."

Shit. He's not joking.

He gently pulled her cloak from her shoulders and spread it on the ground nearby. Then did the same with his own. And his shirt, which he helpfully folded into a makeshift pillow. Suddenly, it was summer all over again: grasses just high enough to hide a pair of lovers. Eric wasted no time sitting on the layered cloaks and pulling Merelith down to beside him. She danced a hand along his bare chest while he ran a thumb over her ear then across the edge of her lips. She opened her mouth to speak sweet nothings, but only a gasp came out as he rushed his lips to hers.

The surge of need felt like lightning in her veins, tensing her upper body like a steel trap around his. Merelith had kissed plenty of boys, fooled around with a few others, too. Eric wasn't like any of them. Some were timid, some were domineering, and yet others only wanted to kiss as if anything more might summon the wrath of the queen. The royal scout, though, was different. Had always been different. He proved so again when he roughly bit into her lip.

Stars and moon and void…fuck, yes. Yes!

She bit back and he groaned in satisfaction. Then he tugged her down atop him. Their lips separated and there was a flurry of movement. Somewhere in the back of her mind, it seemed comical to Merelith, the way they both raced to undress as if their clothes had caught fire. As if the only salve was each other's cool skin. Despite having a lead on her, Merelith easily outdid him. Not out of skill or experience, but sheer aggression: the guardian *ripped* her shirt off and nearly tore a hole in her pants, too.

"No panties?" Eric teased as she leapt on him again, "That's cheating!"

Maybe I did plan for this. I forgot about that. Ohh fucking empty, dark void…he's so warm.

Merelith didn't respond with words but action: she straddled the scout and forced her mouth onto his once more. Arms danced and legs squirmed, as much to warm one another in the chilly air as to experience every inch of skin. He knew her body, she knew his, but she never grew bored exploring every nook and crevice of his flesh. The small indents on his left hip, a nasty boar attack, the dimple in his shoulder blade, a misfired bolt. There was the stubble on his chin, prickly and dusty, and the luxurious braids she kept twirling around her fist behind his head, as if to hold him on a leash against her.

More.

"I need you, Eric."

"Take what you need."

Gladly, she began stroking her entire body along his. Trembles and tremors heralded a too early climax for her. As if sensing her weakness, Eric released her lips long enough to nip at her ear and hold on. The sensation saw her break over him. She never gave in so easily. The headache throbbed harder, and she had a distinct sense of pressure in her nose, too. Yet the heat of the moment, the throb of him against her thigh, the quivering need...

MORE. I NEED MORE.

She sat up straight and *growled* at him. Eric growled back with a chuckle then gripped her by the hips and pushed her to directly over him. It only took one look for Merelith to make her move. A tight grip with deft aim and she was groaning into the heavens with guttural pleasure. She planted a hand on his belly and ran the other through her hair, as much for show as need. Her scalp felt sensitive and slightly painful. A small fear darted across her mind like a rabbit in a field of wolves.

Why do I hurt?

MORE! MORE NOW!

She swirled her hips on him for only a few moments, a strange impatience overtaking her. It had been too long since she last released. Too long since she'd felt satisfied. Eric grunted in surprise as she slammed her free hand down on his neck and started rocking vigorously atop him. His eyes widened but so, too, did his grin. His hands raced up her sides, graced her breasts then pinched each nipple in rhythm with her thrusts. Merelith growled, long and low, and gradually bent over him.

"More..." she groaned.

Eric growled back, "*Take* more, then."

The command didn't register so much as the sudden upward thrust of his whole body. The sky somersaulted overhead and the guardian found herself below rather than above. Her lover wasted no time pulling her legs wide around him and burying as deep as he could. Merelith shouted in ecstasy and spilled her core once more. Eric did, too, in short order. He began to slow, his breathing heavy and ragged behind a winning smile. Then his eyes bulged as Merelith tumbled him back over and resumed rutting atop him.

"M-Mer?"

"*More.*"

"Shit, give me a moment t-to catch up!"

"*More now!*"

She rammed down atop him, and a peculiar anger rose in her at how soft he suddenly felt. It wasn't enough. None of it was enough. She dug her fingernails into his arms and tried to ride harder, faster, but he only protested.

"Merelith! Hey, take it easy! I…"

MORE. TAKE MORE! GIVE MORE!

He didn't understand. She wanted this, needed this! He would, too, if he could feel it. The blood rushing in her head, the aches along her spine and spidering across her scalp. Nothing kept it at bay like the feeling of him inside, nothing seemed to ward off the pain but more pleasure. More heat. More of everything to stop feeling the nothingness blooming in her mind. He let go of her sides and tried to grab a hold of her shoulders to push her away. Merelith ignored the feeble attempt to stop her hunt. Her prey was so close now, she was so close!

TAKE!

Merelith slammed her hips down as hard as she could and felt her core empty with sweet release. An icy sensation raced down her spine like the pent-up waters of the river Torhal tumbling off the peaks of the wardens. The shiver of relief echoed across her head, down her shoulders and arms, through her abdomen where she shook most violently, down her legs to her very toes. The orgasm lasted far longer than any before and even Eric stopped his protests to marvel at her. In the emptiness of her mind, she felt something new.

Come.

Merelith opened her eyes and beheld a changed world: there was no grass, no castle peaking over it in the distance, no cities or walls or people. Even the wardens were gone, rendered into sloping hills of empty stone and gravel. The entire world was barren. She looked up into a sky impossibly empty of starlight. The void was everywhere. How she saw in the dark, she did not know. She gazed down and found Eric staring at her with cautious curiosity. He spoke her name, but she didn't hear it.

GIVE!

The urge was swift and sudden. Just as an instinct had demanded her hunt for release, now another demanded she return what she took. Merelith bent low over Eric, graced his lips with a soft kiss, then bared her teeth and sunk them as hard as she could into his left shoulder. Instantly, the strange landscape was replaced with the plains of Torhal once more. The void's silence punctuated by the distinct scream of Eric Smith as blood spilled from his savaged shoulder. Just like that, Merelith was herself again. She didn't resist his rough shove, only staring in shock at his bleeding wound.

"WHAT THE FUCK, MER!?"

"E-Eric, I…I…?"

Come.

Words escaped her as her tongue registered the tang in her mouth. Blood. *His* blood. She'd bitten him so hard as to draw blood.

I hurt him. I…what is wrong with me? Why do I keep feeling the urge to…to…

Merelith's mind came to a standstill, even as Eric demanded an explanation. It was happening. She was feeling the calling. Her eyes left the scout's furious face and wandered to the eastern horizon. Toward a place far away and certainly not fit for an eighteen-year-old guardian.

Come.

"Eric, I…I'm so sorry. I, I got carried away a-a-and…"

"NO SHIT!" he exclaimed.

The angyrian child stood and began donning her clothes. Her head spun with questions and fears and a small excitement. An excitement that felt out of place, considering her lover was *bleeding* onto her coat underneath him. She visibly swallowed and pointed to it.

"I…I need to go."

Eric, bewildered, asked, "You're just going to *leave?*"

"Yeah. I…messed up. I'm sorry. It, it wasn't you…I just…I dunno…I'm sorry. May I have my coat, please?"

The scout looked at her hard then threw up his hands and rolled off her coat. Thankfully, there was only a few spots of blood, and they hid easily in the thick bear fur. She bent to pick it up and was surprised to instead see it pulled away. Her stomach turned in worry as Eric stood, naked, and held it open for her. His brow was creased in anger, but he forced a gentle smile. She silently turned to let him clasp it across her neck, a flicker of the uncontrolled desire racing at his touch. Then it was gone, leaving her reeling with uncertainty. Eric pulled her shoulder around so that she faced him.

"I'm ok. Hurts like a bitch, but I'm ok," he said slowly, "Don't, um…don't do anything stupid."

"Stupid?" she asked quietly.

"Y'know what I mean."

She didn't but nodded anyway. The scout's smile felt a little more relaxed and genuine as he sighed and shook his head. Then he motioned toward the castle.

"Go on. We'll talk when…whenever I'm done with this."

"Ok" she whispered.

He nodded at her and began to don his clothing. She left and didn't look back for fear she might see the truth in his eyes again. The fear of prey that was caught. Instincts roiled in her but were silenced, temporarily, by the strange urge that lurked beneath them. That, too, was why she didn't look back at him, back towards the east.

Come.

Somewhere far, far away was the source of that quiet urge: The Wildlands.

6 – Galrend

Lorath

Typical. They have yet to spot my approach. What point is there in conquest if you cannot keep what you take, Tobias? Always such a disappointment, that boy is.

The lone rider shook his head in disgust and carried on, flicking the reins on his mare to incite her to a quicker walk. She blew her lips out in protestation but did as she was bid, though her eyes were ever searching for the next tasty bud cropping up along the road to Galrend. The journey from Gwentia had been long and exhausting, but news of the child's imminent birth had cut short Lorath's plan to enjoy summer in the shining southern kingdom and return to his king's miserable domain.

Of all the kingdoms and nations of The Freelands, Galrend was the oldest. Founded by the autarch and war-caster of the same name, the kingdom was one of only two to have existed prior to the War for Freedom. Situated on the eastern edge of the salt marsh that marked where the northern empty depths penetrated the sunken range, Galrend had been built as a center for research and other scholarly activities nearly three thousand years ago, at the dawning of the Autarch Age. It had never been intended as the seat of an empire but had at several points in history served as a pseudo-capital for the eastern half of Damaria.

Those days of glory were long, long gone. Today, Galrend was a backwater kingdom more famous for its roving bands of thugs and slave trade. Its current king, Tobias Galrend, was a recently made immortal with his consort – he detested notions of crowning his favorite whore – the now wild sorceress Talya Bodisnia. Both aspired to returning Galrend to a place of prominence, ideally at the expense of someone else's coffers. Herein lay Lorath Saltsword's principal purpose as chief advisor to the king and emissary of Galrend.

Lorath tilted his head back to see from under his hood when he heard the call ring out from the nearest sentry tower. *Behind* him. He chuckled, though there was no joy in the sound. Still, once alerted to his presence the local guard wasted no time saddling up and riding out to intercept the solitary hooded stranger.

Oh. They remembered their tabards this time. Not all is lost, I suppose.

A unit of six, four of whom were armed with a sword or mace while the rear pair kept bows unslung and arrows nocked. Lorath bit back the urge to groan at the sight of the longbows. They looked new, which meant Tobias had spent the coin on precisely the *wrong* type of bow Lorath had recommended. One of the lead guards held up a fist and then loudly commanded Lorath to stop and identify himself. The lone rider did as he was told, pulled back his hood, and forced a grim smile. All six men went as white as the clouds gathering overhead.

"S-Sir Saltsword! You have returned!"

Lorath drawled, "That I have, sir…?"

Lorath didn't bother to listen to the man's name nor rank. Instead, his experienced eyes roved over the six men for additional clues to what sort of mockery his king had made of carefully detailed suggestions.

Tabards are bright red on black, which is backwards. Will make for an easier target for archers. Morningstars instead of hammers, waste of coin and flashy. Longswords for riders, good. Healthy horseflesh, all look to be broken, holding formation well enough. Blessed crowns, though, why bows? How many times did I tell that fool boy to get CROSS bows? Idiot.

"…escort you in?"

Lorath shrugged and replied, "This is neither my land nor you, my soldiers. Do as your king would expect."

"O-oh. Uh…"

The lead guard looked back at the others who shared his look of bewilderment. Lorath's mood soured further, though he did his best to hide it from his face. One of the disadvantages of being a teacher was letting your students not only fail but fail spectacularly. He was almost thankful Galrend was too poor a kingdom to be targeted, for an invasion would surely succeed. After some whispering, much of which was easily heard and further proved that better equipment did not make for better soldiers, the lead guard looked back at Lorath.

"We will escort you in, sir. The blooders have been rowdy of late and it'd be our heads if you were made late by them, sir."

"As you wish. Lead the way," Lorath replied, a hint of amusement dancing in his eyes.

"FORM UP! Quick trot."

Blooders. Interesting. I did not think Tobias had the stomach for their work. Perhaps I am being too harsh too soon. Or Talya even more convincing than I gave credit for.

Lorath continued toward the castle, barely discernible in the thick fog that perpetually lay over Galrend's rotting lands. The kingdom had no formal borders, save those made by natural and unnatural formations: the marsh to the west, the mountains to the north, and the wild line to the east. Centuries ago, Anar Tota had been a province of the kingdom but was now a separatist nation led by an elected council. The border between that nation and Galrend was generally agreed to be where the lush pine trees of Anar Tota began to fade into the ugly oaks and cypresses that could survive the salted earth of Galrend. That didn't stop Galrend's hunters poaching in the forests of Anar Tota, nor the gatherers of Anar Tota sneaking into the marsh to harvest rare herbs found only there. Both sides had an unspoken agreement among its citizens: if you got caught, kill or be killed.

Unlike its southwestern neighbor of Torhal, Galrend had no mines from which to generate more coin for the coffers or material for its forges. The sunken range had long ago been plundered of its valuables by the Autarchy, when Galrend had been home to hundreds of thousands of collared angyrian slaves, rather than the meager three thousand humans it commanded now. Trade mostly revolved around trapping, logging, and herbs from the marsh. Thieving and raiding, too, but who was on the king's list of trusted mercenaries changed on a weekly basis. As far as the outside world was concerned, Galrend had become little more than the playground of small-time warlords and slave masters. Precisely as Lorath had planned over three decades ago. External security remained lacking, obviously, but so long as the rest of the freelands didn't look too closely, what really lay at the heart of the old kingdom remained undiscovered.

My, my. You have been busy, Lady Talya. Tobias did not do this on his own.

The noise began before Lorath saw its source: a cacophony of voices, neighing, and hammering of steel. Then the peaks of the tents came into view through the fog. Then the many men and women, all clad in that same incorrectly designed tabard. By the time Lorath's mare wandered up to the gates of the castle, he counted almost six thousand in all.

And that's just the army. Hmm…at least five more of the fanatics.

On the other side of the road lay the second encampment, which was decidedly less outfitted and regimented. Screams of terror and pleasure echoed from the gathered cesspool of Galrend's worst: the blooders, a band of thieves more akin to a cult that controlled any territory Galrend or its neighbors could not. That Tobias tolerated them so close to the castle implied Lady Talya had either eased any fears the king had or somehow threatened him. The latter was unlikely, given Tobias' newfound immortality.

Lorath stepped off his horse in the courtyard of the castle and then bowed deeply to his approaching king. Tobias Galrend cut an impressive figure: tall, broad in chest and shoulder, and fair in both eyes of blue and hair of golden blonde. He was almost a perfect replica of his ancestor, Autarch Galrend himself. Lorath held his bow long enough to suppress the urge to stare at his sovereign.

"Lorath! You have returned just in time! I would trust no other with the coming task."

Always the dramatic flourishes. I do wish you saw how very real the theater of your world is. Bah, play along. It will only make the next steps easier.

"It was a long and difficult journey, My King, but I would not miss the birth of your heir for all the fineries of the world."

"Ha! Spoken like a Saltsword…as if fineries are of any real value to you. Come, friend, let us embrace. It has been too long!"

No, no, no…

Yet the king was upon Lorath and the elder had no choice but to accept the fierce hug of his king. Tears sprung up in his eyes and Tobias laughed when he stepped back.

"I am not so strong, Lorath! Did you miss me so?"

"You have no idea, my king. It is good to be home."

Tobias quirked an eyebrow at his advisor then beckoned him into the castle. As they walked, Lorath was pleased to hear Tobias immediately dive into matters of importance rather than continue to make small talk.

"We stand at nearly six thousand strong in our host, with another five thousand committed from the blooders clan and various companies of less rapport," Tobias paused, then whispered, "Truthfully, I'd call it *three* thousand…a full quarter of the cowards ran during our most recent war exercises. They ran!"

Lorath asked, "And what did Lady Talya make of that?"

Tobias rolled his eyes and said in a sing-song voice, "Oh, Tobias! What did you expect? They are terrorized by the might of your army."

They paused outside an ornate bedroom door and the king sighed loudly. He lowered his voice and looked Lorath in the eye as he vented.

"I appreciate my consort's praise and attention to my needs, but I do wish you'd found someone less *subservient* than her. I swear she has more in her breasts than her head."

Then she is performing perfectly, Tobias.

"Well, Your Majesty, I'm sure the coming weeks will provide ample opportunity for me teach her further. How progresses the pregnancy?"

A grim nod was all that answered the advisor's question. Lorath nodded back and motioned to the door.

"Shall we?"

"You are confident in this, Lorath?"

"Absolutely."

My, my, scared, are we? You had best pray Torhal's angyr doesn't fully emerge before you arrive.

"Good, good," the king replied, though his eyes betrayed otherwise.

Tobias rapped his knuckles on the door, a peculiarity to Lorath, but the king waited for permission to enter. Apparently, Talya was doing far better than the advisor had hoped if she had the king cowed into asking to enter rooms in his own castle. A voice like molten gold called out for them to enter. Tobias opened the door and then, again quite strange to Lorath, waited for the advisor to enter first. He hadn't taken two steps into the room before he understood why.

Lady Talya's quarters were the penultimate definition of refined northern tastes. Every surface imaginable was layered in the finest pelts of predators, each pillow stuffed with the softest of down feathers, and of woven fabric there was not a single stitch. The entire room reeked of leather. A vast, four poster dominated the far wall and was mirrored by an equally grandiose lounger wreathed in the rarest of hides: angyrian fur. The legs were each studded with angyrian claws, angyrian feathers lined the outer edges, and the head of the unfortunate beast dangled off the head of the lounger, its fangs bared at the floor.

When Lorath had first seen the chair, he'd known Talya was precisely who he was looking for. The chair alone could buy another hundred mercenaries, but the woman who lay upon it could buy so, so much more: Talya Bodisnia, Consort to Tobias Galrend, Matron of the Blooders Clan, and very, very pregnant with an angyrian child in her womb. Lorath rarely ogled at women, having found them more trouble than they were worth at a younger age, but Talya was a creature of unparalleled beauty. Slender, ample-bosomed, with perfect symmetry in every line and curve, she was akin to a living statue most men would kill to worship at. She was also a skilled wild sorceress, but the magic of elements had long proven second against the magic of allure and lust.

"Lorath Saltsword. You have returned at last. I was beginning to worry."

I am certain you were. Just like Tobias.

"You need never fear my absence, My Lady. I live for Galrend."

"Indeed, and its future."

Even her jewelry was made only of bone, sinew, and fur. She wore an angyrian claw on her right pointer finger, which she gracefully twirled over the expanse of her exposed belly. Except for the hide of a timber wolf wrapped across her breasts and shoulders, the lady was entirely naked. Lorath cast a glance at Tobias to find his king looking elsewhere. Not out of modesty, the advisor knew, but discomfort. Tobias had almost been drooling at the wedding ten months ago. No, what lay in his consort's womb deeply troubled him and just being in the same room was enough to set a slight wobble to the king's right knee.

"A glorious future," Lorath repeated with a warm smile, "for a glorious kingdom. I will get settled in then return to trouble you after dinner, if you agree, My Lady?"

"Of course."

"Before I go, any concerns I should know of now?"

Tobias shifted weight to his other knee, which now *also* shook. Yet the king said nothing and continued to pay close attention to a spot somewhere beyond the bed across the room. Lorath raised an eyebrow at the lady, and she pursed her lips. No words were spoken, but her eyes darted briefly to the king then back to Lorath. She then breathed deeply and sighed loudly. The sound, like everything else about her, was intoxicating to even Lorath's ears.

"Only those of a future mother, Lorath. The babe grows restless by the day! I fear they may just *leap out* any moment!"

The twitch in Tobias was unmistakable, as was the feral grin on Talya's lips. The advisor chuckled and nodded, hoping the perceptive sorceress saw his underlying disappointment in the king. The child was hardly a threat and would not be for a number of years, if it even lived that long. Lorath bowed his head and motioned toward the door.

"Then I leave you with joyful ponderings, my lady. I am sure many have already said so, but I implore you to rest and eat as often as you desire."

"Of course, Sir Saltsword," the lady said with a devious smile.

Tobias chimed in, "Come, Lorath, I will walk with you to your quarters. There is much to discuss before dinner!"

The king didn't even bid his consort farewell, nor wait for Lorath to follow. The advisor eyed the lady's radiant womb a final time and smiled, genuinely. He then returned his eyes to Talya and made sure to see her smile soften, too. Then he was off, nearly trotting to catch up to his king who was no doubt in a hurry to put as much distance between himself and the child. He said as much when he burst into Lorath's quarters, whirled about, and clapped both hands onto the advisor's shoulders.

"I *sense* it, Lorath," he whispered in fear, "I sense it, and I sense that it can sense *me*. Tell me, man, tell me it can be dealt with!"

"My king…Tobias" Lorath said with fatherly calm.

Channel calm. Channel wisdom. He is a new, idiot immortal. He doesn't know what I know.

"*Please* Lorath, please tell me it can…it can be k-killed safely."

It's a child, Tobias. Of course it can be killed easily. Why must you be so stupid?

"Yes, now sit and I will discuss it all with you right now."

"I know we need the blooders…we need Talya…but that *thing* in her must be gone, a-and…"

"*Tobias*, sit."

A familiar angry quirk of the lip told Lorath he was at the edge of Tobias' trust. The king *hated* being referred to as a familiar. Lorath wasn't sure he'd ever met someone with such a severe superiority complex. Except maybe himself, though he liked to think he'd learned from that time in his life. Still, the king obeyed and sat. Lorath closed the door behind them, suppressing the desire to scold the king about being mindful of who was listening in his castle.

Channel calm. Channel wisdom.

"The delivery will be quick, painless, and she will be none the wiser. Angyrian children are known to be hardy, but they are certainly not immortal as you are, my king. Suffocation by the umbilical cord is not that uncommon. Nor is a broken spine if the midwife grips too hard."

Tobias nodded slowly and he seemed to regain some of his composure.

"I feel it, Lorath. Am I going mad?"

Absolutely. Just not for the reason you think.

"No, My King, you are merely experiencing the harrowing effects of an angyr in close proximity."

"I want it destroyed, Lorath. I want *proof* it was destroyed."

"You will have it, my king. It will not be a fair sight…"

"I don't care!" spat the king, "I want to hear her howl, I want to see its corpse, and I want to hear you declare it has died!"

Crowns, I hope nobody heard him say all of that. The blooders would riot.

Lorath held a finger up to his lips and smiled tacitly. Tobias' eyes widened in recognition and then he sighed and shook his head. The voice of a terrified boy spoke, not that of a king soon to make war.

"I am sorry, Lorath. I…we have come *so far* and there is not much further to go. I am sure you think me unreasonable in this fear, but I cannot shake the feeling of being hunted. By a child not even born! It is foolish and yet…" the king trailed off.

Lorath sagely replied, "…and yet it is a wise king who recognizes what should be feared. It is a strong leader who sees what he fears and seeks to correct it, with courage or combat."

"Would that I could *know* it could be controlled…" Tobias muttered.

Ah, but then YOU would want to keep it. We cannot have that.

"It is my fault, Your Majesty. I should have searched for a better mother."

"No! No, you are wrong, Lorath. Her faults are many, but Talya…Talya serves our purposes."

Serves your cock and your ambitions, you mean. Bah, I did choose her, and she is doing well! I grow weary of managing children wearing crowns of dreams instead of collars of metal.

Lorath kneeled before the king and pressed a fist to his heart.

"On my word, the child will cease to haunt you by the end of the month. Come the end of autumn, your consort will be exclusively serving Galrend's path to empire. Come the end of winter, Anar Tota will be yours. Come the end of spring, Torhal will be yours, one way or another. Then there is only glory ahead."

Tobias smiled at his advisor and nodded.

The king replied, "Glory for Galrend, my friend."

"Glory for Galrend," echoed Lorath.

7 – Tal and Kara

Merelith

One week. Just one week and everything has already changed so much. Merelith perched on the foot of her bed and stared intently into her standing mirror, positioned right in front of her. It'd taken the better part of a half hour to clean the old thing, dusty and disused since it had been gifted to her years ago. Now, the guardian used it every morning and evening to study her face. Or, more precisely, remember what it *had* looked like.

True to the books she had first read six years ago when her mother had *finally* let her study angyrism in depth, the effects of the calling were immediate but subtle. Most of what was happening to Merelith remained hidden from the naked eye, as organs began to swell in preparation for her body's radical transformation into an angyr. That said, minor changes could be seen on the surface if one knew where to look. And, in Merelith's case, where she could *feel* a change.

Walking outside was becoming a minor nuisance, no thanks to her eyes now dilating often and far more than they used to. According to the books, her sense of depth and color would become far greater, but it took the body time to learn this new range. The immediate result was that going inside or outside could feel like staring at the sun or falling into a bottomless pit, the sudden gain or loss of light too much for her eyes to handle for long moments. But in the intervening time between such transitions? Every color popped with vitality she'd not noticed before, cobwebs in the dark rafters of the castle were easy to spy, and *everything* moved. The hardest part of her shifting eyesight was the instinctual urge to look at every single movement of anything. The swaying canopy of the queen's wood outside her window was forever mesmerizing.

What her eyes missed, her nose didn't. Merelith had long dreamed of smelling as the tales and research of the past described. She now realized it was by far the *worst* part of becoming an angyr. Castles didn't smell pleasant to a human nose in the first place. Every day, her personal latrine smelled more toxic. She'd stopped using it three days ago, hoping that would help her sleep better. Dinner with her family was becoming difficult, too, the aroma of food overwhelming and delicious, but the scent of dessert sweets often overpowering to the point of nausea. The guardian feared it wouldn't be long before one of her parents noticed her sudden aversion to pie and sweet rolls. Or her insatiable appetite for all things savory.

Hearing had yet to be augmented, as far as she could tell. Nor sensitivity in her skin, or at least it wasn't sensitive in the ways she had read. What *was* sensitive were her nethers and breasts. Perhaps the only thing preventing her from hunting down Eric for a romp was the fact they'd not spoken since the incident. Each night saw Merelith consumed by a need she struggled to satisfy on her own. That was the conclusive proof that the calling was in full swing: heightened hunger, libido, and emotions were all early symptoms.

It may have even started before I bit Eric. My birthday was a wreck, afterall. Or not. I dunno. I didn't FEEL it until we were in the field, together…stars! I miss him so much. I gotta figure this out, Mer. Figure out how to tell Mama and Papa. And Anise.

A pang of regret washed over Merelith. Eric's words had burned a hole in her all week. The mysterious angyr had disappeared and even Torhal's best tracker had lost the trail. Merelith half-worried that had been her fault, too. He couldn't have been in his right mind after their tryst ended in bloodshed. The angyrian child licked her lips on instinct as a shiver ran down her spine. She had rather liked the taste of him, come to think of it.

Stop! Not at all ok. Angyr are NOT bloodthirsty killers.
No, but the blood of a potential mate tastes so good.
WOAH! Way too far ahead, quit it!
He didn't mind biting me before…maybe I just need to ease him into this?
"You two are *impossible*."

Merelith sighed and shook her head vigorously, as if to shake the new voices from her head. They weren't really *voices* so much as her own inner monologue now speaking in *three* separate ways: herself (or what she took to be her usual self), and the two new instincts inherent to all angyr. Most books called them dominion and docility, two halves to the wildness that afflicted all angyr to some degree. Several millenia ago, a powerful and evil war-caster named Kalligan the Dark had first described the two instincts while studying the only living angyr at the time, Tal'Ar: 'Dominant Void' in the sorcerer's native tongue. Merelith had long preferred the original names given by that ancient war-caster: Tal and Kara, from which dominion and docility had been translated into free speech.

Tal. Dominion. Alpha. Leader. Possessor. You've had lots of names over the centuries since.

The need to take. To consume. To breathe in.

A deep inhale followed and Merelith's heart swirled with worry and excitement. The unmistakable sensation of magic flowed along her airways into her lungs. Angyr, *real* angyr as she was now becoming, breathed more than air. They were literal sources of wild magic itself, living reservoirs of the very stuff that formed all of creation. Each inhale drew the fabric of reality into her. Each exhalation released it back, refreshed and perhaps a little altered.

Kara. Docility. Beta. Follower. Provider. Not so much the opposite of Tal as its perfect partner.

The need to give. To sustain. To breathe out.

"Tal and Kara. Just like the stories of old. You two are going to be ridiculously hard to get a hold of if those old books have any of this right."

And they very likely did, because nine hundred years of Torhalian royalty had relied on them without issue until fairly recently. Taken into the context of what it meant to be angyr, both Merel's departure and Reeta's wildness could be explained. The circumstances weren't at all planned or ideal, but they *were* natural. Or as natural as an angyr could be, considering the creatures weren't even native to this *world.* Merelith turned from the mirror to eye one of the books she had snuck out of the scriptorium: *Legends of the Void Kingdom: A Detailed History of the Impossible Empire.*

How do I ever begin to tell Anise? The cuff really was a good gift, I just…

She is my charge. I don't have to tell her anything! Any who threaten her will die.

"Not helpful, Tal," murmured the guardian.

"Merelith? May I enter?"

Hide! I'm not ready for this!

Shut up, Kara!

Tell her to go away! This is my room and I shouldn't have to answer whenever…

SHUT UP, TAL! BOTH OF YOU! ENOUGH!

"C-come in!" Merelith called, pushing the mirror back into its usual corner.

The guardian hoped her sister's attention to detail only extended to her own studies and not her elder sister. The crown princess opened the door slowly, which Merelith both appreciated and loathed. One instinct had her heart racing in preparation for combat, the other had her legs trembling with the energy to hurl herself out her window to the castle grounds two stories below. Anise entered much the way she did any other time: tentatively and with a slight twinge in her nose.

Anise's various rooms were full of fine linens, lush carpets, and ornate furniture. Merelith's room had a solitary dresser made of pine, a rope and straw bed frame, and a large trunk in the corner that held her collected trinkets. She had a single bear hide for a rug and her bed was perpetually unmade, with only three pillows of plain cotton stuffed with goose down. Yet none of that was why Anise quirked her lips in distaste. Above Merelith's bed hung the fierce, growling mount of a large pine wolf. The same that had tried to kill the crown princess a decade ago.

That Anise was here at all was proof enough something was wrong. Merelith knew her sister despised the mount and, on more than one occasion, the guardian had thought to have it removed to the hunting lodge. Yet beneath the tragedy of that day was a quiet pride she'd never been able to shake. She had, at the age of six, protected her sister long enough for real help to come and deliver them both.

Soon, I won't have to wait for help at all.

None will dare threaten her.

She will be safe. We will be safe, together.

Merelith hoped her sister didn't sense the strange inner monologue, or notice her eyes dilating wide with worry, or somehow detect her heart was beating about five times faster than it should. The extra rush of blood was *not* helping her calm down, that much was certain. Still, the princess stepped into the room, though she left the door ajar. Perhaps for an escape route, Tal suggested. Or to help Merelith not feel trapped, Kara countered. Merelith ignored the instincts and forced a smile.

"Hi," she said, before wincing and adding, "Erm, hello, Your Highness."

"*Stars*, Merelith…stop. Please?"

A surge of fear, a rattle of annoyance, then Merelith found the emotion she wanted: relief. She decided to listen to Kara: Anise wasn't here to do harm. She hadn't been before, afterall. The guardian stood from her bed and clasped her hands behind her back. She started to greet her sister again, but noticed her fingernails felt a tad sharper than moments before.

Really, Tal?

"Hi, Anise."

The princess snorted and said, "Better. I guess. Can we, um, can we visit?"

"We're visiting right now."

Merelith winced again before inwardly scolding herself. Managing Tal was *definitely* going to be hard, she decided. A strange warmth permeated her along with a sense of amusement. Kara. The guardian began to wonder if the instincts were more like two different *people* in her head, rather than just two more facets of herself. She suppressed the curious thought and shook her head physically, too.

"Are…you ok?" Anise asked.

"Sorry. Yeah, I'm…I'm ok as I can be, sister."

"Are you not feeling well? I can come back another time…"

"NO! Please stay!"

Dammit, Kara! That isn't at all how I'd have asked!

"Oh. Uh, ok…? Are you sure you're alright, Merelith? You look a bit feverish to me."

"I'm fine, really. Here, let me open the window."

"What have you been up to? It's not like you to hang around the castle so much…"

Merelith opened the window and was glad to be looking outside instead of in toward her sister. She didn't need a mirror to know she'd just grit her teeth in *fury*. It had been a passing emotion, Tal apparently enraged by what Anise was implying. Now an intense calm settled over her, Kara demanding focus and empathy. One of those mattered to Merelith, but she tacitly hoped the instinct wouldn't make things worse when she turned around.

"Well, I mean…last week *did* happen," the guardian said quietly, "I'm supposed to be here."

Anise moved to Merelith's bed then sat at its foot, right beside where the guardian had been earlier. The princess smirked and shook her head.

"Being here isn't quite the same as being *here* with *me*."

I'm your guardian, not your servant!

Tal, quit! You're right, but seriously, quit. How do I even answer that?

Sit beside her. Be here. Perhaps she is simply lonely.

Tal hated the idea and so did Merelith, but the guardian opted to trust the docile instinct and went to sit beside her sister. Such proximity wasn't *that* unusual, but it certainly felt awkward given the current circumstances. The guardian's eyes searched the princess as she slowly descended back onto her bed. The princess had nothing in her hands, her dress pockets didn't bulge with any unnecessary surprises, and Merelith's nose didn't detect any strange smells upon her. Except that she'd recently pilloried the kitchen for a handful of blackberries.

Anise cocked her head at Merelith and said, "You're really up in there today, aren't you?"

"A little, yes," the guardian admitted with a chuckle.

"Is there anything I can do to, um, to help?"

What. The. Fuck. Is SHE ok? Has she been threatened again!?

WOAH, Tal, relax. Yeah, weird but…uh…

It isn't like her to make such an offer. Her hands are shaking. Breathing is shallow.

Stars and moon, Kara, you, too?

Well, it isn't like I noticed the FIRST time!

"Are *you* ok?" Merelith blurted.

The ensuing silence was excruciating. Anise raised an eyebrow then darted her eyes away from the guardian, which sent both instincts into a tizzy. It was all Merelith could do to *not* grab Anise by the arm and demand an answer. Tal wanted to find whoever was making her sister seem so off, Kara wanted to bolt the door and not let Anise leave until all was well. *Merelith* just wanted her own head back long enough to think clearly. The princess continued to stare across the room at Merelith's plain dresser as she spoke.

"No. I feel awful about what happened. We haven't spoken at all since and…I mean, we hardly speak at all to begin with, but you know what I mean? Anyways, I just, I didn't *intend* to dredge it all up and make you feel *worse*."

Anise paused, shrugged, then whispered words that silenced both instincts.

"Sometimes I hate that you're the guardian and not my sister."

Merelith said cautiously, "Can I not be both?"

Stupid question. Of course not, I'm terrible at both.

Nonsense. I love her and would die for her! That is both.

She hates that I am guardian. Just because I seek her protection does not mean she knows it.

"I dunno, can you?" Anise replied.

Merelith snapped, "Do you think I can't?"

No! No, no, no! Tal, stop! It wasn't a challenge!

Anise leaned back and answered, "No? Er, what I mean is *no*, I don't…"

"You *don't* think I can?" Merelith pushed, "You think I can only protect you or love you, but not both? That I only see threats but not you?"

Now you're BOTH making it worse! STOP!

"Mer, that isn't at all what I meant!"

"Well, what DID you mean?"

"I-I dunno! Why are you so worked up all of a sudden?"

"Why are YOU worked up?! Your hands are shaking, you won't look me in the eye, your breathing is shallow…"

"Perhaps because my *guardian* is scaring me!" shouted Anise.

Anise leapt off the bed and stormed toward the door. Merelith began to give chase but found a hand pressed hard into her chest. Never, *ever*, had her little sister shoved her. Dainty as she was, Merelith only stopped her advance and instead Anise seemed to push off of her toward the door.

"STOP. Just, just stop! I'm sorry, ok?! I'm sorry you were born first and I'm sorry you have to protect me and I'm sorry we're sisters instead of, instead of something *else!*"

"Anise…wait, I…"

The princess raised her voice even louder and said, "Just forget it, Merelith! Hurry up and, and be whatever it is you think you're supposed to be so we can stop *pretending*."

The crown princess stormed out of the room, pausing only to slam the door behind her such that the whole castle probably heard it. If they hadn't already heard her shouted declaration. A dollop of frost lingered on the door frame where she had gripped. Merelith sank to her knees and shook her head in bewilderment.

Pretending?

I should go after her.

I shouldn't leave it like that.

SHUT UP SHUT UP SHUT UP!

It took all of Merelith's inner strength to *not* scream the words aloud. A healthy amount of fear that Anise might *hear* her shout such a thing probably helped. More and more, she understood the instincts were going to be making life extraordinarily challenging. Just because they felt like different people didn't mean they were. Tal and Kara weren't people at all but facets of the guardian's own psyche. Half the books on angyrism were about the pair of instincts alone.

All of them shared the same, unfortunate truth: they were the instinctive nature of the angyr given voice. Merelith was terrified that her instincts were showing a potential truth she'd long ignored: the guardian would protect Anise at any cost, including her sister's love.

8 – Evocation

Anise

Anise curled and bent her fingers in intricate patterns, her hands weaving the invisible threads of emotion around the visible magic of the rune before her. Evocation, the practice of amplifying or dampening magic with emotional threads, was an ancient art few could access without decades of practice. Wild sorcerers, by comparison, came by it naturally at an early age. The rune Anise worked was of delicate glass, formed from the dirt of her mother's forest and fired into glass right there, then gently floated a few feet off the ground. Once completed, it could be ritually 'planted' and would then grow a mature tree of glass in a matter of days.

Such runes didn't serve any real purpose beyond aesthetic applications, but glass runes were notoriously sensitive to emotional swings and thus made excellent tools for teaching evocation. On any given day, Anise practiced some form of elementalism on her own. Once a week, her mother tutored her in whatever she was studying. Anise had started tackling higher forms of evocation the day before Merelith's birthday. She now sorely regretted the decision.

"No, no, no. Love, you are doing it all wrong again! *More* emotion to stabilize it."

"Mama, I'm doing it *exactly* how you showed me!"

"Watch that tone, Anise. Look, you've gone and cracked it again. No, no! DON'T DROP…!"

How's that for cracked? Hmph. YOU said channel more emotion if it gets unwieldy. Well, I just did and look how that went!

The queen sighed in frustration and Anise endeavored to not smirk with vitriolic satisfaction. The rune had fallen to the ground and instantly shattered, the latent magic spreading into the grasses of the meadow they stood in and causing the dying grasses to crystalize. Annelle shook her head then pointed to the patch of glassed ground.

"Look at the damage done, Anise. Look at how far it spread, how quickly?" the queen paused, sighed, and then quietly commanded, "Go ahead and measure it."

"What do you mean by *measure it*, Mama? I can see how far it spread."

"As in *measure* it, Anise Torhal. Give me precise dimensions."

"Why?"

The dangerous glare from her mother warned Anise to not wait for an answer. The princess stepped to the edge of the glassy patch and then carefully stepped off its perimeter for an approximate circumference. She then worked out the diameter, in case the queen asked, and even took a moment to notice some remnant flowers had been tall enough to not be glassed and measured the height of the effect, too. Even magic was affected by gravity, often spreading far wider than high, the acceleration of the latent energies beholden to the truths of the world's workings if not forced beyond those limitations by an elementalist.

"Eight feet wide, about a foot and half tall" the princess said quietly.

"For a rune meant to grow a glass tree no wider nor taller than a foot. Do you see the problem?"

Anise was genuinely surprised by her mother's point. The rune had indeed been shaped and sized for a tiny glass tree, an instrument of practice and little else. Certainly, the queen had no need for a giant glass tree in her wood. Yet if the rune had been correctly sized…

"Why is it so large?"

"You tell me."

The queen's tone was unmistakable: two parts disappointment, one part anger, one part worry. To be fair, Anise was intelligent enough to see that her intentional mistake could have been much, much worse. The glass patch was only a few feet from where she and her mother had stood. Annelle could have shielded them both in time, but still. The point remained that a larger rune could have had devastating consequences.

But why? My emotions couldn't have amplified it THAT much? Could it? I get so frustrated when she's telling me I'm doing it wrong instead of telling me how to do it right. That and…

"Merelith," the princess whispered.

"Merelith?" the queen asked, "What does your sister have to do with this?

"My emotions. They're compromised. We…I shouldn't have been doing this. It didn't even occur to me that I wasn't in a state for practicing evocation. I'm sorry."

"Anise, love, what are you talking about?"

The princess was of a mind to *not* tell her mother. Yet there were so few she *could* tell. Anise had no real friends to speak of. A combination of dangerous magic at a youthful age and the never-ending studies of a crown princess *and* wild sorceress left her with precious little time for even herself. For better or worse, Anise depended exclusively on her parents for guidance and support. Not least because finding it in Merelith was harder each year that passed.

"We…had a fight. Or a tense squabble. I do not know."

"Over what?"

As if you don't already know, Mama. Really? Bah, ease up. That's what Mer would say. Or would have before all this SHIT happened with the stupid letter. I shouldn't have told Papa. Or told Merelith from the start. Hmph. Fat chance. At least now I know how she would have reacted!

"Anise?" the queen pressed.

"More of the same, Mama. Always more of the same."

Anise detailed yesterday's difficult encounter. To her credit, Annelle only listened and nodded understanding. The queen was always sensitive of how the guardian was treated by Anise, an irony considering how she'd handled Merelith a week ago. Yet Anise had learned a long time ago that Annelle Torhal was a woman of *many* conflicting emotions. Given the princess had had her own brush with death, twice now, she could at least sympathize with her mother's sometimes wild emotions. The queen looked at the glassed patch and sighed.

"There is a positive and a negative in all this, Anise. Look? See how mighty your power is when you channel the emotions you have for your sister."

Look, see how devastating that power is. That's what you mean, too.

"I'm sorry," Anise murmured.

"Do not be, you have yet to cause the sort of harm I did at your age. My mother struggled terribly with me. For all my scolding and shouting, Anise, I do hope you someday see how gifted you are. This is a good lesson. Hardly the way I would like to teach it, but…"

The queen shrugged then smirked at her youngest daughter and shrugged again. She then motioned to the glass patch and commanded Anise to correct it. The princess did as she was told. First, the glass needed to be melted down then separated into small enough fragments of slag as to not be dangerous to the environment. A healthy pit of flame and precise cuts of air rendered the glass patch into a barren pile of mineralized ash. Then, the earth was churned with the ash so that it was spread evenly over nearly double the original diameter. This tore up even more of the meadow, but ensured fresh growth would be possible to repair the damage.

The trouble with magic was that damage to the natural environment was often quite difficult to rectify. Despite the name, wild sorcerers couldn't actually *control* wild magic and therefore couldn't change rocks into flowers or birds into trees or any other form of reality alteration. Only wild magic could perform the miracle of raw creation and, as far as anyone knew, only one kind of creature could even *influence* wild magic: an angyr.

Even then, angyr didn't utilize wild magic so much as simply breathe it. No, the creatures from another place possessed an entirely different sort of magic: *void* magic, which could be used to alter time and reality itself, likely *because* they breathed wild magic. Three millennia of sorcerers and war-casters and scholars and witches and every sort of practitioner and researcher imaginable had tried to unlock the secret to angyrian magic for humans. None had ever succeeded and, truth be told, the wiser of that ilk knew success would probably doom Damaria's people rather than elevate them. One sorcerer had already almost destroyed the world with just *one* angyr.

"Good. Now then, let us start over. Previously, we focused on basic, happy thoughts such as enjoying a cool spring day or relaxing in a favorite chair. This time, I want you to focus on *Merelith*."

Anise gulped and said, "That seems like a *terrible* idea, Mama."

"It is, yes? Let's see *how* terrible, hmm?"

Stars. This won't end well. She's in one of those adventurous moods again.

"Humor me, Anise," the queen goaded.

The princess retorted, "This could also be very dangerous."

"Oh, let me disparage you of *any* notion that it could be anything *except* very dangerous."

A wicked grin settled on Annelle Torhal's face and the princess inwardly cringed, not least because it reminded her so much of her elder sister. Merelith didn't *look* like Annelle, but they had many similar quirks. In fact, the guardian didn't look like any of the current Torhal family. The queen had once confided in Anise that Merelith was strikingly similar to her predecessor, Reeta, though her natural swagger was indisputably a direct relation to Merel.

Anise only shared her mother's emerald eyes and her father's black-as-night hair. Beyond that, the princess also looked out of place among her immediate family. Yet in the great hall, where the tapestries depicting the royal families of the past hung, Anise saw her doppelganger in her namesake and grandmother. Stern and sharp even in the aging threads,

Anise had often wondered if she would look as stuffy as she grew older. She certainly felt that way of late.

"Ok, well, here I go."

First was the formation of the rune via air and water vapor. This provided a foundation to attach particles of earth and stone to. This was the easiest part: forming the rune out of the wrong materials. Employed as it was, the rune was more akin to a snare that would rapidly grow a sprawling mess of vines hard as stone. Next came the heating of the rune so that its elements became glass, which was also where evocation came in. The temperature had to be carefully controlled lest the rune warped from overheating and expansion, but too cold and the glass could shatter from cooling too quickly.

Such precise control was easy with enough time. The entire point of evocation was to *reduce* the time needed by achieving the exact amplification needed, then holding it. In effect, channeling the right emotion at the right intensity alongside the magic. Done correctly, complex rituals, powerful elemental manipulations, and far-ranging storms could be created in mere minutes or even seconds instead of hours. Done poorly...

"Are you ready?" she asked her mother, the rune now fully formed and ready for firing.

"Are you?"

"Mama. I am being serious."

"So am I. Think upon Merelith and begin when you are ready." *This is such a very bad idea. Yet...what WILL happen? Ok. Breathe. Merelith. What do I think of when I think of Merelith?*

Anise took a moment to find an appropriate emotion. There was anger and annoyance, of course, but those would warp the rune. Then came sorrow and regret, which typically associated with cold but could be unpredictable if severe enough. The princess sorted through her many emotions and soon found herself astonished at just how *many* feelings she had when it came to her elder sister and guardian.

"I cannot...I, um, I am having difficulty choosing one."

"I imagine so," the queen said unhelpfully.

Anise pursed her lips but didn't bother rephrasing her statement into a question. It was apparent that her mother expected her to figure this out on her own, risks be damned. Not that those risks were really so bad. Annelle Torhal was more than capable of containing any unexpected calamity formed by her daughter. When she was younger, Anise had been afraid of these lessons. Now, she looked forward to them most days. She knew she was safe with her mother.

Yet I'm not safe with Merelith.

Flame erupted from her hands and began firing the earthen rune. The princess carefully wove the heat around the rune as she channeled with her heart as much as her mind the truth she'd dredged up.

She would die for me but no one else. She would kill anyone for me. Even our own father.

A small voice in her mind mused that her control was astonishing. She couldn't quite put a finger on the *emotion* of her thoughts, but there was an unusual calm to it. A calm that made forging glass infused with magic in mid-air easy and intuitive.

There is nothing safe about her. Yesterday was no exception. She is a predator. A hunter. A killer.

Anise furrowed her brow, both at the inner thoughts and how they were making the firing of the rune too easy. This did not feel right, she decided, but still couldn't understand *why* it felt wrong. Easy answers came to mind: she was thinking negatively of her sister, or that calling Merelith a killer wasn't really fair, or that the guardian *had* kept her safe several times. None of those answers seemed satisfactory. The rune neared completion as she continued her line of thinking and wove the odd thread of emotion along her magic.

She's really quite amazing, when I stop and think about it. She is beautiful and confident, like Mama. She has Papa's humor and courage. So many adore Merelith, like those farmers on her birthday! All this work I do, all this practicing and studying, and for what? Most folk don't like me. I'm neither pretty nor respected like she is.

The rune swelled with power, which Anise ignored. The glass didn't fracture as she continued to work, lost in her thoughts, and not seeing the rune had begun to grow. Nearby, the queen worked her own magic, but the princess didn't care. There was only the task before her: build the rune and study the strange emotion allowing her to do so.

Merelith can go wherever she likes, whenever she likes. Mama gets upset that she isn't by me all the time, yet every time I was truly under threat of attack…Mer was there. She doesn't have to dress up nice or spend hours doing her makeup and hair. She doesn't have to listen to boring merchants nor learn histories of kingdoms we'll probably NEVER share commerce with. All things considered, her life is easy! I don't understand why she gets so worked up at me?

"That's enough, Anise. Go ahead and finish it so we can discuss."

"Mhm."

The command registered but her mind remained focused on the emotion.

She has so much freedom. All I have are chains made of gold and silver. A crown I never wanted.

"Anise? Love?"

Is this hate? No, I do not think so. I hate that she is guardian, but I do not hate her.

"Anise!"

I hate that she came first. I hate that she has freedom, and I don't. I hate that she is the guardian and I the princess. She's everything Mama and Papa, even the people, want in a princess.

"ENOUGH! STOP NOW!"

Anise was shaken by her mother's bellowed order. The sensation of being startled out of deep concentration plunged into a well of terror as she saw what loomed overhead. The glass rune was as large as the meadow, spanning over a hundred feet across and shimmering with an extraordinary amount of power. Anise started to open her mouth to ask what she should do when the distinct, heart-rattling sound of a *crack* echoed from overhead.

"BEHIND ME! *NOW!*"

The queen didn't have to ask twice. Anise abandoned all control of her magic and raced behind her mother's forming shield of molten stone, blistering hot and radiating enough heat to instantly incinerate the grasses within an arm's length. As the princess dove behind the barrier, the sky overhead thundered like a fracturing frozen lake as the glass rune caved under the weight of its own power. Anise threw her hands up and focused as much elemental fire into her mother's shield as she could.

"Keep it up until I say otherwise," the queen said with lethal calm, "And hold your breath, too."

"W-why?!"

"It is glass, Anise."

Oh. Oh dear.

The rune tumbled to the ground, its fractures echoing loudly right up until it contacted the meadow beneath. Then the sheer pressure of its weight caused the entire structure to collapse, releasing the imbued magic. Most magics had a distinct sound to them: ice the familiar cracking from rapid contraction due to the cold, fire its well-known roar as it consumed and combusted. Air whooshed and howled, earth often sounded like mush rolling down a graveled hill. What Anise heard now was not like any of these.

Glass *sang*, the billion-billion fragments of the rune acting as miniature chimes while they hurtled outwards with lethal speed, vibrating with energy that could penetrate stone walls thicker than most houses had. It was a short symphony, the ending punctuated by the sickening crackle and crunch of the glass shards pummeling into the surrounding trees and ground or perishing into Annelle's molten shield in a flurry of hisses as they dissolved into mineralized ash. It was over in just a few seconds. Anise held her breath until she heard her mother breathing again. The molten shield collapsed into a rapidly cooling pile of slag and Anise beheld a beautiful and horrific sight: the entire meadow had been glassed. She flinched when a bird crashed down, its corpse shattering not five feet from the queen and princess.

A long silence passed before the queen looked at her daughter with a blank expression. The worst kind, in Anise's opinion, for she didn't know if her mother was impressed or enraged. Or perhaps both.

"What was the emotion?" Annelle asked quietly.

"Huh?"

"What were you feeling, Anise?"

What WAS I feeling?

She recalled her last thoughts before her mother had interrupted and the answer became clear. Anise felt her stomach twist in worry and fear. Sharing such a thing with her mother couldn't end well.

It's not like she can undo the order of our birth. Stars and moon and void...I can't tell her that I'm jealous of Merelith. She'll laugh. Or worse, she'll be furious. I am crown princess! I get to keep my humanity! A whole kingdom!

"I..."

But I won't have freedom. Not like her.

"I'm not sure, Mama. I was thinking on Merelith, like you said, but there wasn't really any emotion. I was just, um, just thinking. Hard, apparently."

The flare of the queen's nostrils warned the lie hadn't been bought, but then Annelle smirked and shook her head with mirth.

"Indeed. *Very* hard. This is incredible, Anise. You really are a natural when you put your mind to it. Now, we just need to sort out how to get your mind *off* it!"

The queen laughed and Anise forced herself to laugh along with her mother. Yet the queasy feeling in her gut didn't subside. It didn't bother her that she was jealous of Merelith so much as the hard fact that there was absolutely *nothing* to be done about it. Angyrism wasn't transferable, nor curable, and besides…her sister probably didn't *want* to be princess. Merelith had always looked forward to becoming angyr. Now, Anise had a much better sense of why. None of which helped her feel better about *any* of it.

9 – Reading and Riding

Merelith

Control of Dominion and Docility are a necessary component of maintaining an angyr that is sound of mind. The greatest risk, as always, is the loss of self to wildness. Once an angyr falls into wildness, there is little chance of return as they lack any sense of self to guide them away from wildness. It is ever imperative to monitor the angyr's emotional and mental state and how the two instincts are driving these measurements.

Merelith sighed and rubbed her temple, unsure if the pain behind her eyes was from reading or continual transformation. She decided to find out, ignoring the book she had been reading – *Angyrian Temperaments and Discipline* – to another titled *Angyrian Biology and General Diagnostics*. Of all the books in the scriptorium, these two were Merelith's favorite. One, they were both easy to read and lacked the typical academic flourishes of a scholar desperate to sound smart. Two, they had exceptionally detailed drawings and diagrams.

Angyrian Biology had been written and illustrated by a pair of researchers almost two thousand years ago, studying enslaved angyr for the mad pentarch in the very castle Merelith and her family now lived. The experiments detailed within were often gruesome, but the diagrams were without equal and detailed in exquisite illustrations *exactly* how a child of the wild binding transformed into an angyr, along with precise explanations for symptoms. Sure enough, headaches were a common occurrence in the earliest stages due to rapid changes in the eyes.

I've got maybe another week or two before they know.

Merelith resisted the urge to rush back to her room to stare into the mirror. There were already small signs of her changes: sharper and longer fingernails that grew back too fast when cut, her canines were sharpening ever so slightly, and her tongue had started to feel a tad too long for her mouth. Her ears were beginning to sharpen at the tips, too. All of which could be easily hidden with gloves, mouth closed, and hair down. What could *not* be kept secret was the coming transformation of her eyes.

Sclera discoloration and eventual darkening will typically begin by the end of the second week, sometimes as late as the third. Formation of the quickened iris follows shortly. Detection of time manipulation via sight is possible as early as end of the first month.

The guardian sighed and looked up at the beams of the ceiling. Very soon, she would wake up and find her hazel eyes were no longer so. More importantly, it would be a *very* obvious sign she had felt the calling. Anyone looking upon her would know the transformation had begun. She looked back down at the book, snorted at her bangs covering her eyes, then felt a strange tingle of excitement alongside the quiet dread.

I won't have bangs. Huh. I suppose that will be kinda nice? Maybe not. Eric loves my hair.

She resisted the urge to look across the scriptorium to another table where the scout in question currently sat, also reading about angyr. He had been granted restricted access to the rare books in the hopes he could discern something new about the mysterious angyr. To date, all that had been confirmed was it wore a pentarchy collar and obviously didn't want to kill the crown princess nor guardian. Another sighting hadn't been confirmed, yet, but several farmers and merchants out in Farsi had claimed to see a large, dark shadow prowling the edge of the Low Forest that made up Torhal's northernmost territory.

I can't decide if I do or don't want him to find it.

And risk him being killed or, worse, taken by another angyr!?

Stars, Tal, really? You think he'd want to waltz off with another angyr? Jealous much?

Eric has long said he looked forward to my change, that it excites him.

I doubt he meant excitement THAT way, Kara.

Since her yelling match with Anise, Merelith had endeavored to relearn everything she could about the instincts, confident she must have missed something for Tal and Kara to so easily take control of her. Yet none of the books really had advice on how an angyr might manage themselves. They had, afterall, been written for the Autarchs and their inferiors with the objective being to control angyr *externally* as tools and slaves. Many of those poor creatures had been killed during the War for Freedom, and many more had escaped captivity. In their wildness, they had answered the never-ending call to journey to the wildlands. Why they did so, these books did not say.

Come.

Scholars agreed it had something to do with the ruins of an ancient capital deep within the wildlands. Who the city had belonged to was a mystery to even the Autarchs that predated the Pentarchs, and getting answers was nigh impossible since the wildlands were called so for a reason: the territory was home to all wild angyr that made it there. One angyr, well-trained and experienced in combat, could devastate twenty men in the blink of an eye. A whole territory four times the size of Torhal worth of angyr? It was a miracle Damaria still existed at all.

Yet the calling, named for the unusual migratory urge, never ended even after arrival. Once a wild angyr *got* to the wildlands, they stayed. The Wild Line, the invisible border of the wildlands, approximated how far angyr were willing to venture away from the epicenter of the calling. Countless expeditions had tried to penetrate the wildlands in search of treasure, ancient artifacts, or a way to influence the calling. Few ever returned, and those that did often did so with severe wounds and harrowing tales of devastation. Wild angyr were known to be aggressive and territorial, with each other as much as any other creature or man.

Merelith returned to her original book and flipped forward to a different section that was specific to Tal and Kara. The Autarchs had developed magical collars that tortured and drove the shackled angyr by manipulating their instincts to react predictably. Essentially, the angyr was 'trained' to recognize painful discharges and associate certain instinctual urges with them. The result was a glorified war hound.

Control of their quickening was never established – only Kalligan the Dark managed that with the first angyr, Tal'Ar – and so most angyrian slaves were just powerful soldiers and little else. The collars suppressed normal magics but reacted violently to void magic. Apparently, securing the collars onto an angyr often involved torturous rituals. That said, the Autarchs never lived in fear of their soldiers: if an angyr quickened, the collar would kill them.

What an awful existence. I wonder if our mystery angyr is the same way? I hope not. That sounds like it would drive me insane, too. Stars, these people really were awful. Let's try this section…

Angyr had long described the two instincts to their captors, but it was up to researchers and scholars to figure out *why* the instincts were there at all. Or, more precisely, why did angyr have a sense of the instincts at a depth no other animal did? Every guardian before Merelith had learned to control their own instincts and live peacefully, and loyally, among the Torhalian people. There were historical records of angyrian problems in Torhal, sure, but they were few and far between and nearly always boiled down to the wrong words or actions were directed at the guardian's charge, resulting in a conflict that often ended in a swift apology lest swift death follow instead.

To be certain, the instinct of dominion is the most easily recognized for external observation. Angyrian aggression is often attributed to this instinct, but such a notion is faulty! Docility can also be a source of aggression. In plain terms: dominion initiates aggression as a means to control, possess, or take. Docility initiates aggression as a means to sustain, provide, or give. A simple example is thus:

Suppose an angyr has a favorite toy and that toy is taken away by a competing angyr who also prefers the toy. Dominion will incite aggression in preparation to take back the toy, likely through combat. Docility will also incite aggression in preparation to sustain the contentment derived from the toy. Both instincts work toward the same goal but for differing reasons. An angyr is most focused, and dangerous, when the instincts align in such a way. Intuitively, they are also at their weakest and most vulnerable when the instincts are not aligned as this confuses them and inhibits instinctual decision making.

Merelith stared long at the last sentence. Perhaps her problem with Tal and Kara was as simple as getting them aligned. Although they had been aligned when talking to Anise and look how THAT turned out! Tal had been worried about protecting Anise, Kara about Anise's emotional well-being, and *both* had spoken through Merelith in a way that wasn't at all helpful.

There must be a way to sort you two without blurting out something stupid…

I am NOT stupid. There is nothing stupid about being an angyr!

Easy! I can do this. I just need to relax and not be so jumpy.

"Hey."

"WOAH, SHIT!"

Merelith leapt up out of her chair, caught her foot on the table leg, and tumbled to the ground. Eric stood over her with a cocked eyebrow and shaking head. Internally, the instincts scrambled to make sense of the sudden and unexpected greeting. Merelith, for once, felt like she had room to just be herself.

"H-hi. Um. You *definitely* scared me that time," she said with a hesitant laugh.

"Never would have guessed, *Beta*" Eric replied.

Alpha. I AM Alpha!

Shut up, Tal. It's a pet name, not a fucking title.

He is a bit like an alpha to me, though? A Tal that is strong and protective and…

STARS AND MOON, are you two ever NOT horny!?

"You ok?"

"Yeah. Um, just jumpy. It's been a rough few days. Week. I dunno…"

"Wanna go for a ride?"

Eric offered a hand to her. She considered it a moment too long and he snorted.

"I'm not gonna *bite* you."

"Way too soon," she grumbled, taking his hand.

He pulled her up and, before she could react, pulled her further into a tight hug. She didn't even tense this time. Instead, she felt like she could melt right into his leather vest. The smell of him was wonderful, the sight of his arms around her shoulders calming, the feel of his breath down her cheek perfection itself. Her heart trembled at the sight of a scar near the base of his neck.

He grinned and said, "I'd debate that."

Take him now! It has been too long!

The scar looks good. I wonder if he likes it, too?

"O-ok," was all she could manage.

The sudden alignment of the instincts was overwhelming but also a bit comical. There was an urge to shove Eric back, rip off his clothes, and have wild sex right there in one of Torhal's most sacred spaces. Then there was the urge to not do *anything* but just stand there and be hugged. Suddenly, the book's descriptions made sense. Tal and Kara both wanted Eric, but they couldn't agree on *how*. Aligned yet not.

"I'd love to go on a ride with you," she whispered into his shoulder, "I miss you."

Eric chuckled and replied, "Aye. I bet you do. C'mon, we'll nab some berries for Sneak. Can't have you slacking paying him off to be nice to you."

They both shelved their respective books – few things incensed the queen faster than a disorderly scriptorium – then made their way downstairs and out of the castle toward the stables just outside the walls. Only the horses of the knights, lords, and royal family were kept within the castle walls. Favored by the king as he was, Eric's own steed was kept in the barracks' stables just beyond Castle Torhal's gate. As usual, Merelith paused outside and waited for Eric to fetch Sneak. Even at this distance, the nearest horses could smell the guardian and were braying their discomfort.

"Anywhere you want to go in particular?" asked the scout, the old gelding following behind him.

Merelith shrugged and held out a hand to Sneak and asked, "What do you think, Sneak?"

Both chuckled when Sneak promptly nibbled at Merelith's fingers then snorted. Eric made a joke about the steed only ever thinking with his stomach. Perhaps that was why the quiet horse wasn't troubled by the guardian. Eric mounted Sneak then hoisted Merelith up behind him. Arms around his waist, head on his back, and the worries of the calling fell away into the familiar and much missed feeling of contentment.

"Well?" Eric asked quietly.

"Anywhere with you."

The scout retorted, "I didn't give you *that* hard of a time, did I?"

"No. You didn't. I really am sorry."

"I know."

He patted a hand atop hers, clicked his tongue at Sneak, and they were off at a slow trot away from the castle. The princess was out and about with the king today, relieving Merelith of her duties. Not that she'd really been performing them in the first place. To what end and where the king and crown princess had gone, the guardian had no idea. She suspected it had to do with the mysterious angyr given all six knights and another twenty mounted royal guard had gone with them. Much as she was curious about it all, she'd opted not to ask. Her family would be finding an angyr soon enough, one way or another.

Eric kept Sneak to the roads, heading south to the kingdom highway then east along the Torhal river toward Anna. Anna could be reached in a day's ride, but Merelith suspected Eric's true destination lay somewhere in the king's wood to her right or the sprawling plains to her left. She considered the dying fields and shuddered. She hadn't meant to hurt him.

"You ok? Need a coat?"

"I'm ok. Thanks," she mumbled into his back.

"You wanna talk about it?"

Merelith winced and shook her head. Then winced again, the motion setting her headache off once more. Internally, the instincts were demanding she *did* talk about it. Mostly to hear his voice reverberate in her ear, its sound soothing and enticing. Yet what she heard next sent her heart racing.

"I mean, I get it. The calling is probably a lot scarier than you thought it would be? Those books certainly make it sound a bit crazy."

He knows!? Or is he just probing? There's no way he could know except…

Except he had been gently rubbing her hand with his free hand the entire ride, the pads of his fingertips regularly tracing the long nails of hers. He'd led her out onto the highway, far from listening ears but not prying eyes, a practiced tactic to make it appear they were simply enjoying a ride together. Not discussing the emergence of Torhal's latest angyr.

"You *bit* me, Merelith. Absolutely lost yourself while fucking me. I mean…I'm not going to lie, it was a bit terrifying but at the same time it completely lined up with what those books said. Not to mention you *never* wait a week to make up with me. Sure as the stars don't act *this* way."

"What…um…what do you mean by *this* way?"

Have I been giving away more than I thought? What if Mama and Papa already know? Stars and moon and void, what if ANISE already knows?! Shit! I thought I was being careful and…why are we stopping? Did I say something wrong again?

Eric had guided Sneak right to the edge of the river and then paused, allowing the horse to greedily gulp from the stream. The scout leaned sideways and looked back at Merelith with a cheap grin. His eyes roved up and down her, which sent Kara scurrying across her heart with need while Tal demanded Merelith not break eye contact with Eric. Some nonsense about being alpha, she figured.

"Merelith Torhal *never* acts like a shy girl that just bled for the first time," Eric retorted.

She wouldn't know, but that was beside the point.

The guardian blushed and shot back, "Be that as it may, I *bit* you! Hard!"

"Aye. Still here. Were you trying to kill me?"

"N-NO! Don't say that!"

"So, it *was* a love bite."

"Well, I-I mean…I guess…I dunno! I just, it was too hard, and you were hurt and…"

Eric cut in, "And now we're riding together and talking about it. I overreacted, Mer. I'm sorry."

Merelith was dumbstruck. Eric shrugged, winked, then leaned back so he could peck her on the cheek. The press of his lips to the corner of hers seemed to temporarily silence the instincts. Then both were pining for him. Or, well, Kara was pleading. Tal was roaring.

NOW. I NEED HIM NOW!

He needs me, too. I can see it in his eyes! He apologized, he missed me, too!

"All good?" Eric asked in a murmur.

"Not yet, but, um…"

"Ask, Mer. You know I'll say yes."

Blessed stars…I love you, Eric Smith.

Alignment. This was what alignment felt like. Sure, Tal wanted to just fall off Sneak and do the deed. Kara was content to just lean into him and be present. Yet Merelith felt far more in control this time around. The instincts wanted the same thing and, honestly, so did she. Which made a lot of sense. They *always* wanted what she wanted. It was just a question of how.

"Can we try again?"

"Are you going to say please?" growled the scout.

Merelith growled back, "Only if you do."

Just like that, Tal and Kara were saying *exactly* what she wanted to say. Not surprisingly, Eric had figured out Merelith before anyone else. Again. The scout had Sneak fjord the river and vanish them into the edge of the king's wood. A blackberry bush near a sufficiently soft patch of ground later, and the lovers were tangling while the old gelding happily gorged himself.

10 – Wrong Angyr, Again

Anise

Though she was practiced in 'sensing' other magics, Anise still had trouble focusing on the act itself because, invariably, the results were nothing short of astonishing to her. The crown princess often practiced under the tutelage of her mother in the king's garden or queen's wood, surrounded by magical signatures she'd known since birth. Where her father and she traveled now was vastly different from those safe places.

The king's wood was *flooded* with magics of every kind, which made magic sensing both challenging and inspiring. Some of the oldest testaments in the scriptorium described the place as the likely original ritual grounds for whoever predated the pentarch that had built Castle Torhal over a millennia ago. The reason why was obvious: wild magic seemed to pool in the area.

When viewed with sensing magic, the trees in the queen's wood flickered like the scales of a fish. The colors were consistent, too: green and gold, her mother's magical signature, with occasional pops of red and gold, her grandmother's magic. Very rarely she saw other colors from even earlier ancestors, but they all undulated and flashed the same way. Like a collage of family lineage, the Torhal family's magic was easily recognized but, with practice, could be individually identified, too. Anise's own magic was a striking crimson with edges of gold.

"What do you sense, daughter?"

Anise startled at Orren's question and mumbled an apology. He chuckled and told her not to worry. He then lightly tapped her forehead with a wink.

"Your mother told me it is always quite the sight for you. Take your time but remember our task. Soak it in, look and listen, but do not forget to *observe*, Anise. The difference between my best and second-best scout is as simple as one remembers what he was looking at and the other remembers *why* he was looking at it."

"Yes, Papa."

The most notable difference was the dizzying array of patterns. She spotted the familiar flashing of Torhalian magic, but there was a litany of other signatures. Two others stood out besides her own family. The first was pervasive and seemed to flow as slow as molasses beneath all the other magical signatures. It was also colorless. It couldn't so much be seen as detected by how other magics collided with it and were rebuffed. This was wild magic in its natural form, drawn to the area for reasons no book in the scriptorium could confirm.

The other was like a scar of deep, angry orange. It had defined edges that stretched across the center of the wood and turned nearly black at its center. This magic pulsated with a heavy throb that was almost sickening to the fledgling sorceress. Other magics seemed to either be absorbed by it or violently rebuffed, a cacophony of reactions that was unseen by the naked eye. This was the magic of the mad pentarch, Anisterosa. None of Anise's lineage had ever figured out why the blemish was there, for it predated the War for Freedom.

Interspersed with all these magics were outlines of life threads. Unlike residual magic, which was left behind from spells or naturally occurring due to elemental forces, life threads were wild magic given direction via time entanglement. Life threads glowed brilliantly against the kaleidoscope of the king's wood, stark white and pulsating with the heartbeats of their respective creatures. Plant-life, though formed of life threads, tended to not pulse at all but instead glow steadily like the wild magic that had formed it. 'Why?' was a question as old as the discovery of wild magic itself.

"I've yet to see an unusual animal. Sickly, dying, or newly born…but nothing out of the ordinary," Anise paused, then smirked and added, "You'll be pleased to know your favorite boar has two sows surrounded by twenty-two piglets."

The king cursed, "*Bastard.* Perhaps we'll take care of…"

"What happened to sporting chance?" Anise quipped.

Orren groaned but then chuckled and nodded.

"Fine. He gets *one* more year of ruining my flowers at the lodge. ONE. Deal?"

"Ha, deal, Papa."

"No angyr?"

"Not that I can see…granted, I'm not entirely sure what to be looking for. I didn't think to try and sense it that day. Sorry."

"No need, you had far more important things on your mind."

"Hmm…hold on, I might have something!"

"Near?"

"Yes, but moving away from us. One moment."

Anise disbanded the magic from her eyes so that she saw normally again. Penetrating sight was the most common form of magic sense, but there were other methods. The young sorceress placed her hands to the earth and expanded her sense through it like a vast, seismic wave of lingering magic. Her mother had told her bats used a similar method – echolocation, with sound – to sense their environment. However, this had the disadvantage of losing the third dimension of sight. Still, Anise's target wasn't hard to find.

It was a trio of living things. One, she was certain, was a man. Humans had innately vibrant life-threads due to their comparatively long lives. Gender was determined by the frequency of the life-thread's glow: men tended to pulsate harder but slower, whereas women pulsed quicker but with less force. It wasn't a guaranteed prediction, children were difficult to type, but Anise was confident this was a young man. The second was right on top of him, or beneath, she couldn't tell. It had the familiar pulse of a beast of burden, like a cow or horse. The third was…something else.

"A man on a horse with…I don't know. It is not like anything I've ever seen or felt before? It might not be a horse; I cannot be certain at this distance. There are three living things in total."

"Could he be riding the angyr?"

Anise considered the question as she continued to feel the presence of the trio. She finally shook her head.

"No, I don't think so. Mother said angyr do not appear like normal life threads. This is a larger life thread akin to a horse. The third, though, I cannot say. It is…"

She didn't know what to say. It was clearly a third living thing, but it also was colorless, like wild magic. The distinct pulse of life came from it, but time seemed to roll over and around it, but not *stick* to it, like a normal grouping of life threads. Anise released her magic, stood, and nodded at her father.

"Time is behaving abnormally around it. It might be our mystery angyr."

"Say no more, mount up. MEN! Prepare arms!"

"Should I head back to the castle, Papa? Signal Mama?"

"I can trust you if you can trust me, Anise. Your mother wouldn't have sent you along if she feared for you."

Anise swallowed down her own worry and nodded. Her heart raced with excitement as she saddled up and pointed the way for her father and king. Orren drew his blade and kicked his steed into a light trot. As they went, Anise occasionally pulsed her magic out to sense the trio. They were easily found now, the peculiarity of the third life sticking out almost as much as the pentarch's scar on the magical landscape. When they were within several hundred feet, Anise told her father so and the king ordered a halt.

"Point where," he commanded.

Anise did so and said, "Straight ahead, behind that oak with the fallen branch on its left. They're outside the wood now, on the river shore heading west."

"Got it," the king swiveled in his saddle to his nearest knight and asked, "Ready?"

"Yes, Your Majesty! Lead on."

"Contain first, then kill if necessary. If the Crown Princess issues a command, obey it!"

"Yes, Your Majesty!" echoed the men.

"Onwards!" commanded the king.

Orren spurred his steed and charged ahead. Anise followed suit, channeling icy magic into her free hand in preparation. The guard surrounded them, all armed with crossbows and swords, while the six knights flanked the king. They burst through the wood out onto the shore. The king shouted for their target to halt, which they promptly did. To Anise's bewilderment, she saw her sister riding behind the king's favorite scout, Eric.

"Eric?! What are you doing here?" asked the king, lowering his blade but not sheathing it.

"My King! Is everything alright?" replied the scout, before apologizing and answering, "I was taking the guardian back to the castle. She had asked me to escort her for a quick visit to Anna."

"Anna?" asked the king, his voice growing exasperated, "What was in *Anna?*"

"It's her, father!" Anise interrupted.

Orren looked back to Anise to find her dismounting, yet still channeling magic in her free hand. It was no longer elemental, though. Anise's eyes glowed with her own magic as she surveyed her elder sister with equal parts amazement and frustration.

"It's you," she said matter of fact.

Merelith glowered at her sister and replied, "What? What are you t-talking about?"

"You've changed. I should have known it was you, but you are different now. What did you do?"

"I didn't do anything!" retorted the guardian.

The king dismounted and stepped between his daughters. Sneak flared his nostrils at the royal and then worked his fat lips in search of a snack. Orren managed a smirk and pushed the horse's head away.

"Yes, yes, wait. I don't have a snack for you this time. Your master *didn't* bring me what we were looking for…" the king eyed the scout and Eric gulped, "…and apparently *did* find something he wasn't supposed to be looking for."

"He wasn't looking for me, Papa!" Merelith hastily answered.

"Enough. Anise, clearly this isn't our prey. I don't know what game you are playing, but…"

"Game? *GAME!?* It's her! I swear it, what I was seeing is her!" the crown princess exclaimed.

Orren replied with a sigh, "Yes, well, Merelith isn't what we are looking fo…"

Merelith interjected, "What do you mean you *saw* me, Anise?"

"Father and I are looking for the angyr that keeps getting reported. Mother tasked me with sensing it, thinking maybe she couldn't. I sensed *you*. I normally can tell it *is* you, though! You are different! You…"

"Well, she *is* the guardian, Crown Princess" Eric offered, "She is meant to be different, right?"

Anise growled, "No, you idiot, she doesn't…"

"Hey, don't call him an idiot!" barked Merelith, hopping off the horse and marching toward her sister, "Apologize right now!"

The king held up a hand to both and loudly commanded, "Enough! Anise, that was uncalled for, apologize. Merelith, back up and stop."

Anise whined, "But she *isn't* meant to look different from a…from…"

Anise's eyes widened with horror, as did Merelith's, which did not go unnoticed by the king and scout. Eric attempted to redirect the conversation.

"My King! I did find tracks matching that of the angyr along High Lake. They were heading east along the northern shore. I suspect it may be dwelling somewhere in the empty quarter. There are several fissures in need of repair by the southern tower, too. It's possible the creature is passing back and forth from beyond the wall. I had intended to tell you when you returned this evening. Perhaps the crown princess might see what I cannot?"

Eric's forced smile did the trick and Orren relaxed. The king considered his scout, then his daughters, then his knights and guard. The men looked at each other with ill-concealed glances of surprise and annoyance. Anise felt her frustration reach a boil. The king looked to her and sternly commanded the princess onto her horse.

"Mount up, we still have daylight. You can pursue this case against your sister another time."

"B-but…"

"*Now*, Anise."

The crown princess sulked back to her horse, opting to not make eye contact with anyone. Once again, her father was taking the side of the guardian.

"Scout Smith, return the guardian to the castle. Report your findings to the queen. Return to the barracks and prepare for a long mission. If this angyr is indeed moving beyond the wall, I'll need you to find out where and why."

"Yes, my king."

"Back up on Sneak, Merelith."

Merelith eyed her father, then her sister. Though Anise kept her eyes down she sensed a shift around her sister. It wasn't magic though, but time itself. Unlike magic, time's signature was measured in movement. All magic, no matter how strong or weak, marched to a constant tempo of the time ascribed to it. Some spells were quick, and this was reflected in how their colors moved, others were slower and seemed to visually ooze rather than dart about.

Near Anise and her horse, time stood stock still in Orren Torhal. Immortality of his kind was not agelessness but a complete stoppage of time. The mystery of the wild binding was how Orren was at once completely frozen in time yet still able to move, to think, and to have emotions. Yet, on the other side of him, time did something quite strange. It bent in on itself. Only when she heard Merelith huff and mount up behind Eric did Anise steal a look directly at the guardian.

Her life threads were colorless yet obviously present. Anise felt the glow and pulse of Merelith's heartbeat even though it couldn't be seen anymore. Beyond the magical sense, Anise felt the time around Merelith and was at once confused and amazed by what she sensed. The queen had once shown her youngest what time felt like as it raced: an anomaly in the mountains that was aging nearby trees hundreds of years in mere seconds. It had been like standing next to a silently roaring river, the sensation of lethal speed overwhelming and exhilarating. That same sensation permeated around Merelith. It boggled Anise's mind that Orren's immortality, so dangerously close to being warped by it, couldn't feel it himself.

"Anise!"

She snapped her eyes to her father and found him watching her with a grim scowl.

"Onwards, child. Stare daggers another time."

"I wasn't..."

"ONWARDS."

She thrust down the urge to set his boots on fire and spurred her steed forward. Chances were good she would have set *him* on fire, and then she'd really be in trouble. The crown princess struggled to not feel slighted. Her father didn't understand and, yes, she had a reputation now for angling to get her sister in trouble. None of which changed that, once again, Merelith was able to do whatever she wanted, and Anise was not.

Except that would soon change, and Anise knew it. Her sister looked and felt different because she *was* different. Soon, the guardian – the real guardian – would be coming. Soon, too, the expectation of a crown that Anise did not want. Frustration at her father fell away into internal grieving as they made their way toward the empty quarter at the south-eastern end of the kingdom. It felt like time was slipping away for Anise. For her entire world, what little of it she really had possession of.

Orren Torhal's immortality rendered his body impervious to everything but natural aging and the quickened strike of another. He would die of old age, but nothing else. Annelle Torhal's magic enabled her to achieve the same fate: she could heal and combat nearly any disease, ensuring a long and healthy rule. Yet both *would* die. Absolute immortality only existed for the pentarchs and, even then, nobody knew how.

Yet Anise couldn't help but dwell on her sister. Merelith had the most time of all: she *was* ageless, and could live for centuries or even eternity, if she were careful. Anise felt she only had time to lose. As the crown princess sensed the time of her own life thread gently flowing away, she wished it could be different, too. Different like her sister.

11 – Family Dinner

Merelith

*S**he knows. She knows and she's going to tell them before I'm ready.*
I should just tell Mama now! Then it wouldn't matter.
After the last week? After today!? No, no, no…that will only worsen things. Mama is already worried I don't care about Anise. Papa, too, I bet.

Will you just stop! Please?

Merelith sighed and slumped against the window overlooking the castle courtyard. She'd been standing watch there for over an hour now. The sun had set, and the king and crown princess had yet to return. Either they'd found tracks for the angyr, or Anise had told the king what she knew, and they were taking their time to come back while they no doubt discussed how best to handle the emerging *real* guardian.

Please. We both said please so many times…

A fire kindled in her core and, briefly, Merelith smiled at nobody. Eric had ravished and ravaged her in the wood. A great many love bites had been shared, though only Merelith's had sometimes drawn trickles of blood. Eric hadn't minded, his lover's aggression only giving him permission to be rougher with her. Tal and Kara both had seamlessly transitioned throughout the romp, Merelith dancing between the two halves of wildness in utter bliss. Then she'd told Eric everything. Her hopes and fears for the transformation, her worries and excitement at sharing it with her family, and her vivid dreams that came some nights of a place empty of stars: the void, where angyr originated.

Eric had listened and marveled and worried right along with her. As he always had. Thinking on Eric quickly turned sour, though: the scout had done as his king had commanded. No sooner had Merelith dismounted, Eric had reported to the queen – thankfully leaving out the part where Anise accused Merelith of 'being different' – then promptly left for the barracks to prepare for a longer mission. How long, Merelith tried not to dwell on. The last time Eric had gone scouting beyond Torhal's borders, he'd been away for over a month.

I hope Papa isn't punishing Eric. It isn't exactly a secret that we're partners, but still…maybe he thinks Eric is a bad influence? I dunno. I hope not. Stars! I just wish today would be done!

Her wish came right then: a loud call went up from the castle courtyard as the king's retinue entered the gate. Judging by King Orren's scowl, the search had proven fruitless. The knights and guards looked weary, as did their steeds. Yet the guardian's keen eyes fixated on her younger sister. The instincts swirled in worry, not at what Anise knew but rather how she looked: broken and disappointed.

Something is wrong. Did Papa lay into her after insulting Eric? Accusing me?

He shouldn't. It isn't her fault if she mistook me for the angyr…I AM an angyr, afterall.

She looks so sad. I hope she doesn't feel like a failure after all that searching.

Merelith felt a strange cold rise under her feet. Below, she heard and saw the queen step out from the castle to greet her husband and heir. The king dismounted, handed off his steed, then quickly went to his wife to kiss her. Yet, when he leaned in, he paused and looked worried. Considering Merelith could feel the temperature drop a whole floor above, she could guess why.

"My love, is everything alright?" he asked, before kissing Annelle on the cheek.

The queen cocked an eyebrow and replied slowly, "Yes? Why do you ask?"

Orren chuckled and retorted, "The tapestries look a bit stiff."

Annelle glanced back into the castle and snorted. Instantly, Merelith felt the floor underfoot warm. The queen shook her head apologetically then shrugged.

"Apologies. I…was worried. You are back far later than I expected. What did you find?"

Orren scowled and shook his head, answering, "Nothing. The trail ended suddenly. As if the damn thing sprouted new wings or climbed into the trees, though I saw no indication of either. Is it possible to summon such a thing and banish it?"

Annelle furrowed her brow in worry but only shook her head in reply. She glanced past Orren to Anise and opened her hand to beckon the girl over. Anise approached, her back stiff and posture erect. Merelith listened intently from above as the sorceress quizzed her protégé.

Annelle asked, "What did *you* find?"

"Nothing of importance," Anise replied stiffly.

"An odd choice of words, Anise. What did you find that was *not* important?"

Annelle asked with a slight hint of amusement, but Anise didn't relax. Orren made to clear his throat and explain his daughter's demeanor, but Annelle silenced him with a finger to his lips. She forced a brighter smile as she spoke.

"Merelith told me, love. I am not asking about that. What did *you* see, Anise, in the empty quarter? Where the trail ended? Anything?"

Anise clenched her jaw before speaking. The king clenched his own, too.

Papa is losing his patience with her. Did she say something else? He would have said something to Mama by now if he knew. Right?

"Just the usual magic. There was nothing different, nothing special."

Annelle pressed, "Why do you think the trail ended?"

"I do not know, Mother."

"Hmm."

Annelle stared at Anise, hard, and the princess lowered her gaze after it became uncomfortable. The queen glanced at her husband with a raised eyebrow once more. Orren looked between them both before sighing.

"Shall we prepare for dinner? It has been a long ride for her and me both."

"I am not hungry," Anise whispered.

Orren replied, "You have not had anything since we left High Lake, Anise."

Annelle interjected, "Humor your father, dear. The day is nearly done."

Uh-oh. Does Mama already know, too? Shit. If they're making Anise have dinner…

"I will fetch Merelith while you two get ready. She should be done with her bath by now."

Indeed, she was, for Merelith had only bathed for a few minutes. Mostly to scrub off the mud that had accumulated under her nails and on her arms and legs. She'd spent the rest of the time staring at her mirror, naked, cataloguing the changes that had occurred in just one day. An angyrian child's transformation into a full angyr took anywhere from a few months to as long as a year and a half. The speed of the transformation depended on the same factor that determined how long it was before the calling was felt in the first place: inherent wildness.

The more wild-like an angyrian child was – or more 'balanced' with their wildness, as Annelle believed – the longer the calling could take. The belief was that the calling was, itself, an instinctual urge brought about as a kind of survival device. Trauma and extreme emotional events, positive or negative, often triggered the calling. Yet if an angyrian child was *already* accustomed to such wildness, the calling was often delayed. Merelith now knew the emotional whiplash of her birthday had likely been the breaking point for her own angyrism.

However, once the calling *began*, inherent wildness didn't slow the transformation but accelerate it. Those who *didn't* want to become angyr often had long, torturous transformations lasting over a year. Those, like Merelith, who had always dreamed of being angyr might fully change in as little as three or four months. Engaging in activities that drove the instincts only hastened the changes. Eric biting her, and inviting her to bite him *more*, had definitely caused an acceleration.

"I *never* wear gloves to dinner," she muttered, "Damn. How am I going to explain this?"

Merelith had raced back to her room and clambered into her tub, freezing water and all. Erect nipples and shivering skin only heightened her instincts. She watched her nails perceptibly lengthen a little more. More astonishing was the distinct presence of a patch of thin hair growing along her elbows. It was still akin to body hair, barely visible and short, but it was thickening. Down fur, she knew. A much larger patch had thickened between her breasts and legs while making love with Eric, something the scout had wasted little time exploring with his face.

Stars…get your head out of the ditch! Mama is coming and I don't need to be horny when she asks why the fuck I'm sitting in freezing water. SHIT! Shit, shit, shit. I just need a little more time to, to figure out how to tell them.

"Merelith? Are you still in here?" called the queen from the bedroom door.

"YES MAMA! I JUST GOT OUT!"

"Gracious, love, you weren't *that* dirty!" called her mother with amusement.

You've no idea. Or you do and are just too kind to say so.

Merelith dried off, again, then took a deep breath and steeled herself. Now was the time her mother would notice if something were amiss. The queen didn't afford either of her daughters any real privacy unless they asked for it. Anise had at the age of eight, but Merelith had never cared. Now, she cared too much and knew better than to say so.

Just…just be like Eric would expect. Confident. Don't ask.

Mmph. I do love when he asks, though.

Stop, Kara. Focus. Help me out, Tal. I need to be the guardian, not some girl freaking out about hair growing between her tits!

I am the guardian. I am angyr. I am Merelith Torhal. This is my secret to share when I'm ready.

She stepped into her bedroom as she had a thousand times before, smiled pleasantly at her mother, and went to her dresser as if nothing were amiss. The queen smiled back and said dinner was being prepared.

"They lost the trail, again. Your father is clearly disappointed. I suggest not asking about it."

"Thanks for the warning, Mama. I won't."

Merelith dropped her towel as she foraged for panties, then paused. Both instincts had her speaking a question she wasn't entirely sure she wanted an answer to.

"How is Anise?"

"Hmm…not well," Annelle replied softly, "I suspect she worries Papa blames her."

"Does he?"

Too sharp! Ease up, Tal. I don't have to be THAT protective.

"Of course not!" the queen replied, "Though he might blame *you* for distracting his scout this afternoon. Anna, was it?"

"Erm…"

"Uh-huh. You are fortunate he is the sort of father he is and prefers your happiness to decorum. Get dressed. We will be in the hall tonight; I think another rain is coming and the balcony is set up for a prolonging ritual to make the most of it. First snow will be any week now."

Merelith gave a meek smile and nodded. Then the queen was gone. The guardian considered her clothing and opted for a simple gown of teal with floral accents in its hem and cuffs. She donned a pair of silver earrings, each sporting a quintet of dangling feathers, then completed the ensemble with a slim chain that had a tiny angyrian head for a charm strung upon it: a gift from her father in the days after she'd learned what she truly was as a child. Then she headed to the ground floor of the castle.

Torhal's great hall served as the nexus of the castle's first floor and much of the crown's business. The hall itself stretched from one end to the other, with the throne room set at the far end. About halfway down the hall were two sets of double doors to either side. On the eastern side lay the royal armory and war room, the latter used as a correspondence room these days. On the western side lay the dining hall, kitchen, and pantry with access to the cellar below the castle.

Merelith's father regularly marveled at how well-built the castle was. It wasn't impressive in size or scale compared to other castles he'd visited throughout the freelands, but it held a certain charm those grander and more famous places lacked. It wasn't ostentatious nor was it primitive, neither complex nor boring. King Orren eventually declared that what made Castle Torhal so special was that it felt like a house despite being a defensive construct. Merelith, who had yet to travel beyond Torhal's wall, suspected he was right. Though she did hope to one day see the grand palace of Gwentia or the Port of Glass in the faraway brother kingdoms of the Heran desert.

She strode into the dining hall to find the servants already laying out the evening's meal: steamed vegetables, pan-seared duck with a honey-almond glaze, and candied apples. An oversized peach cobbler taunted the king to skip dinner altogether. Instantly, both instincts stirred her hunger to near-painful heights. It brought a small smile to her lips as she considered the reason.

I'm a growing angyr. Ha. Maybe I'll finally be able to out-eat my immortal father!

"Your Majesty. How fare you today?" asked a servant with a bottle of brandy ready to be served.

The king replied, "I am well. None tonight, thank you."

"Oh? Did it taste foul yesterday?"

"No, no. I'd rather tea."

"At once, Your Majesty. What may I bring thee, Your Highness?"

Anise mumbled, "Tea."

Merelith watched from the doorway as the king cast a raised eyebrow toward his youngest. Anise stiffened a little before adding her thanks. The servant had already begun walking off, but she paused and curtsied to acknowledge the princess. Orren gave a small nod of approval to both. He'd asked the servants some years ago to make a habit of providing opportunities to improve the manners of his children. The guardian smirked a little then swept in behind her father's chair before he noticed her.

"Good evening, Papa."

The king startled at the peck on his cheek from Merelith. He whirled his head to find her grinning at him and chuckling. Tal huffed with approval at the silent approach. Kara delighted in Orren's wide eyes of surprise and affection.

"Gotcha," teased the guardian.

Orren snorted and replied, "Indeed. I'm starting to think your mother bewitched your feet!"

Annelle glided into the room and retorted, "Perhaps I bewitched your hearing."

Annelle took up her seat around the corner from Orren. Merelith stood awkwardly as she glanced at Anise, who sat several chairs down the other side. The table sat twenty-four in all, but the family had long eschewed royal norms to gather at one end. Of course, this also meant it was painfully obvious when one was in a foul mood. Typically, Anise sat across from her mother and Merelith beside one of the two crowned women. The guardian eyed her mother with what she hoped was a questioning, rather than worried, look.

"Sit, Merelith. Anise is not hungry and likely will not stay long."

"Oh, um, ok. Erm. Yes ma'am."

Merelith tried to ignore her father's questioning stare. She didn't normally care if Anise was in a foul mood, afterall. She heard rather than saw the queen reach below the table and grip her husband's thigh.

"Stop fussing. Shall we begin?" murmured the queen.

Orren snorted and said, "Yes. I'm starving!"

One of the ironies of her immortal father was that, technically, he could not die of starvation. Though his body was perpetually quickened and thus immune to external influences like disease or combat wounds, he could affect change upon himself. King Orren could feel hunger, despite not *needing* food, and could even become fat if he so chose. Yet the king took his gift seriously: he loved to eat, but he loved to be a model of a well-lived life for his children and kingdom more.

"Hmph. So is *that* one! I have been listening to her tummy growl for *hours*," the queen quipped.

Merelith laughed nervously and replied, "S-sorry, I, um, I've not had much of an appetite most of the day. Don't think I ate enough at lunch."

"Why is that? Are you not feeling well?" Orren inquired, slicing into his duck while staring down the table at the peach cobbler with disciplined longing.

"N-no, I'm ok."

Confident! C'mon, Mer. Just make it through tonight. I'll spend tomorrow thinking up how to broach the topic…maybe with Mama first. She'll know how to tell Papa. And how to handle Anise already knowing. I hope. Stars, just one more night to think it through.

Orren furrowed his brow, taking his eyes from the cobbler and resting them on Merelith. She smiled weakly and then seemed to focus on her meal with peculiar intent. She could tell the king was still studying her. The guardian's heart fell into the pit of her stomach when she saw Orren's head swivel towards Anise and study her, too.

No, no, no. Let's not talk about earlier, Papa. Please? Please don't.

Merelith cast a wary glance towards her little sister and froze. The emotion upon the princess's face was as plain as day: anger. Kara began to panic and even Tal seemed to cower a little, as if in preparation for a real fight. Then the king asked a *very* strange question.

"Anise, have you given any thought to what you would seek in a suitor?"

Three pairs of eyes shot to the king. Merelith was shocked, the queen glared with accusatory questioning. Orren ignored his eldest daughter and wife and locked his gaze upon Anise. The crown princess visibly gulped and stuttered out a question in reply.

Anise stammered, "D-do you…h-have some-o-one in m-mind?"

She didn't expect that. What in the world is Papa thinking?! Why does she seem scared?

Maybe they talked about suitors on the ride. Is that why Anise looked so upset? Poor thing.

If Papa tries to force a man on her, he'll have to go through me!

Orren smirked and said, "Of course not, dear. I wouldn't dare choose your husband for you."

I bet not. Good.

Shut up, Tal.

Why is he asking, though? She's only fifteen…surely, they don't expect her to wear the crown so soon? Oh no. Is something else going on? Is Mama ok?

KARA. STARS AND MOON.

"O-oh. Um…do, do I need to d-decide this, uh, soon?" replied the princess.

The king swallowed the bite he had been chewing and laughed, shaking his head. He glanced at Annelle and found her bristling stare to have relaxed. If only a little.

"It is just a question, Anise. What sort of man would you find interesting or acceptable?"

"She has some time to go before worrying about that, Orren…" Annelle murmured.

"You expect her to wait as long as you did?" the king quipped.

"I would have waited longer if not for my mother's death."

Merelith saw Anise's face fall. Beneath the worry and awkwardness, she'd seen what her father had been looking for: excitement. The revelation hit the guardian hard. Eric had come into her life several years ago…which meant Anise had probably wondered when a boy might take interest in her for just as long. The guardian knew her father had tried to have this conversation with the queen before but had been waved off numerous times. Perhaps the king had decided it was time to put it before Anise herself, *without* Annelle's approval.

The king said carefully, "There is no need for Anise to wait so long, love. She has shown tremendous control this year! Today being a fine example of it."

Anise perked up at her father's compliment and he winked at her. A timid smile in return told Merelith that not all was as it seemed. Merelith eyed all three of her family with a bit of confusion, the instincts now uncertain of what, exactly, was going on. She rested her eyes on the safest face: her father. King Orren chuckled.

He said with a broad grin, "Don't fret, *Guardian*. I'm sure you'll have *some* say in what sort of man takes up the crown alongside your sister."

"No, she will not."

The tinkling of Orren's silverware, the soft gulp of her mother drinking, even the breathing of the attending servants, all of it came to a sudden stop. The declaration had been little more than a whisper but may as well have been shouted. The silence was enough to prompt Anise to repeat herself, as if worried they had not heard her the first time.

"No, she will not," said the princess again.

"Anise, your sister will play an important part in…" began Annelle, but Orren rested a hand on her elbow, stopping her with a small shake of his head.

Anise stated, "She won't be my sister by then. She'll just be the guardian."

Annelle furrowed her brow and started, "Anise, she will *always* be your sister! You shouldn't say such things. It is cruel and…"

Merelith interjected, "It's ok! It's ok, Mama, she's um…she…it's alright."

Merelith had tried to wave off the queen, but found herself staring at Anise, an expression of stark terror on the guardian's face. The instincts were frenzied now. A confrontation, again in the same day, could only end in disaster. The guardian defended Anise, as much for her own sake as that of the princess. King and queen both watched her with apparent confusion.

"It's ok," she repeated, "I, I get it. I w-wouldn't want you to pick for me!"

Anise retorted, "There's nobody to pick. You won't be human. It's not the same."

"Anise!" scolded Annelle, "Apologize!"

Merelith cried, "NO! No, it's ok, Mama! Just, um, just leave it. Ok?"

Orren demanded, "What has gotten into you, Anise?! First the wild goose chase this afternoon, now this? Has Merelith done something to you to prompt such, such enmity?"

Merelith pleaded, "P-Papa, please, just drop it, it's ok, it's…"

Anise grit her teeth as she looked at Merelith and said, "Lying won't change it has started. If anything, it will make it quicker. Or is that what you want anyways?"

Another shattering silence. The king didn't understand her words and looked to Merelith. For her part, the guardian could only swallow down whatever answer she had and shake her head. Not at her father but her sister.

No. Don't do this. Not now. Just…just one more day, sister. Please.
Let me get it right. With you, with them.

"Merelith?" he whispered, "What lie is she accusing you of?"

"EVEN NOW YOU ACCUSE ME INSTEAD OF HER!" Anise shouted.

The crown princess thrust back from the table, stood, and stormed to the doors. She paused briefly, hot tears streaming down her face, as she pointed at her father.

"YOU *ALWAYS* ACCUSE ME! YOU *ALWAYS* THINK I AM THE ONE LYING! YOU *ALWAYS* TREAT ME LIKE A *MONSTER* WHEN SHE IS THE ONE *BECOMING A MONSTER!*"

Anise slammed the door to the hall, which promptly shattered into frozen bits of wood. The king watched the great hall darken as the cold of his daughter extinguished the many candles lighting it. He looked to Merelith to find her quietly sobbing into her hands. When the king went to touch her shoulder, she withdrew it and shook her head.

Monster. I not monster! I angyr!

Want be sister. Want sister.

Flee. Heal. Protect anyway.

"Merelith?" asked the king quietly, "What is going on?"

The instincts felt both overwhelming and dull. Her body was flushing with adrenaline, fear, and shame, but her heart was breaking such that she lacked the will to act on the urge to run. Merelith cobbled together what few words she could as she stood from the table.

"I-I g-going tell. Want t-t-time. M-more t-time."

"Time for…wait! Where are you going?" replied the king, "Merelith? Merelith!"

Merelith was already to the door and into the hall, where the servants scattered away from her or pretended to have not heard it all. By sunset tomorrow, the whole of Torhal would know. The guardian hurried away, even as she heard the last words of her parents echo from the dining hall. The guardian listened to the regret and worry in Orren's voice but wondered at the peculiar calm in her mother's reply.

"Her speech…why is she turning wild, here, now? Annelle? Love?"

"She has felt the calling. It has begun."

12 – A Woman and her Dog

Talya

Lady Talya Bodisnia, consort to the king of Galrend, lounged upon her favorite chair in the nude, soaking up the hungry look of her chosen spy as he waited to be questioned. Tobias was a fine man to lay with, chiseled and formed in all the ways that mattered to a woman of her exacting tastes, but he lacked *imagination*. Her hound, on the other hand, was hardly a man but possessed the creativity necessary for truly pleasing her. Pending the news he brought, she planned to reward him with an exceedingly long and tiring night of servicing her desire.

He had returned earlier than expected, but she and Lorath had expected as much after the encounter with the guardian and princess of Torhal. With luck, Torhal's royal family was now focused on a threat from the Pentarchy. Annelle would be channeling her magic to the west and south, rather than the north and east where the real threat lie. More importantly, King Orren *wouldn't* travel beyond his kingdom's famous wall for diplomacy. A roaming angyr was an excellent reason to remain home.

The lady danced a fingernail along a nipple and watched the eyes of her scout intently follow its every movement. Were he an actual dog, he'd no doubt be salivating. Or thrashing her into blissful nothingness. He certainly made better company than Lorath, who sat in a corner and looked on with ill-concealed disinterest. Talya smirked then made a flourish with her other hand toward the spy.

"Tell me everything," she whispered.

He nodded with a grin. Then he did what made her most pleased of all: he lowered his eyes, so that he might focus on the prescribed task instead of her.

Obedience. Submission. So few understand how enticing compliance can be.

His eyes remained down as he spoke. The spy was unhurried, but she sensed his excitement as he relayed all that he had learned while within Torhal.

"No news of Galrend's growing forces is shared. Anar Tota's council still thinks the missing hunters are just a result of territorial sparring and little else. Within Torhal, the hunt for the 'mysterious angyr' continues. Sightings are becoming more common, as instructed. They have found the breaches in the wall within the empty quarter, and they should be repaired by the end of next month. A group of hunters was commissioned to track the angyr within Torhal."

The spy chuckled and Talya felt her core tingle with excitement at his confident conclusion.

"They should be found in the coming days. Mauled and mangled, of course."

"Of course," she murmured, before asking, "Did you follow my instructions?"

"Two of the three I fed to the hound directly. Their bodies are precisely destroyed according to your command. The third has been sundered and defiled at the western edge of the kingdom. The queen has been distracted of late, but I expect her to take notice any day now."

"Excellent. Tell me of this distraction."

He took a deep breath, and she heard the shudder in his lungs. Comfortable as she was upon her bench, Talya tensed as she waited for him to confirm what she had already felt in her own magic.

"Merelith feels the calling. Her transformation has begun."

"Who else knows?"

"Her family, most if not all of the castle servants, and, of course, Eric Smith."

"Ah, Eric. How is dear Eric?"

"He is well and truly in love with his bestial woman."

Talya snorted, hoping it hid the worry uncoiling inside of her. Love was a complication best avoided. Love made boys do stupid things for equally stupid girls. Particularly if that girl was not a girl at all but an apex predator coming into her true self.

"And Merelith? What of her?"

"She trusts none beyond her parents and Eric, I'm sure."

"Excellent. How fares her poor, miserable sister?"

"Anise remains distant to her family. Merelith's changes disturb her."

"The girl isn't remotely ready. What do Annelle and Orren think of all this?"

"The queen is supportive of Merelith but seems overtly aware of her wildness as a threat. The king is unsure of how to handle Anise. Rumor claims the princess is heartless and called her sister a monster. That their love is only pretending."

"Truly?"

"Truly."

"Interesting. Hmm. Lorath may be right about them, afterall."

Lorath. The man with too-old eyes. She was certain his plans might be just as old, too. A pang of regret lanced her heart, but she stifled it. Talya glanced over at the library shelves in her room and grimaced. Galrend had once possessed some of the oldest works in The Freelands but so very few had survived the centuries of inept leadership. Tobias's own father had burned half the library to punish a pair of servant girls that had spurned him. Somewhere in that wasted ash had been one of only two known copies of a book detailing one of the autarchy's greatest discoveries: transference of power from one sorcerer to another.

Idiots. All of them. At least idiots are useful.

I pray Annelle's lot haven't been so careless.

"The ritual?" she asked with a whiff of annoyance, "Did you find anything referencing it?"

"I did. I could not find the ritual itself, but I found proof of it."

The spy produced a stack of vellum tied with a rudimentary knot. He held it out to his mistress and Talya took it, delighting in how his hand trembled with excitement. At having succeeded, or at the rewards that came with success, she didn't care to know. She unfurled the pages and quickly read his chicken-scratch writing. Enclosed were multiple references from the scriptorium, notes on the various tapestries in the great hall, and of particular interest an account detailing the newly made Queen Annelle struggling to combat a fungus in the wood her mother had nearly eradicated before her premature death.

Annelle is weaker than those before her. Mama dearest didn't give her share before the end. How unfortunate, but that should place us on even footing at least.

"What of the cave? Did you go there, too?"

"I…" he hesitated.

Talya dug her nails into the bench but allowed her spy to speak before berating him. When she didn't set into him, he finished his answer, albeit slowly.

"I, I did but…I became lost. I cannot say for certain if I explored the cave fully."

"You became *lost?*" she asked, annoyance replaced with genuine curiosity.

"It is a complex series of tunnels. I left marks, used chalk, even tied string to rocks…" he paused, then gulped before finishing, "…I know little of magic, but it is the only explanation for what happened: my marks were made as if never there, the chalk erased or changed, the rocks vanished from the string, yet the string remained tied. Either a pacifist guardian oversees the cave, or it is magically imbued to prevent exploration."

He paused, took a deep breath, then finished with a hint of excitement.

"I *did* see etchings of many different rituals involving angyr, like Lorath described. There were several that looked to show your ritual of transference. Imagine the power of an *angyr!*"

Talya soaked up his words and smiled at the ceiling. Late autumn rain pummeled the exterior. Even in the dull roar of nature she could hear the breathing of her spy, shaken and lacking confidence. The cave had frightened him.

Poor thing. A shame your wild instinct only serves your hands and cock rather than your head. You dream of muscle, girth, and instinct, like all men. I have no use for angyrism, my dear hound. I am already wild.

"I am pleased with all you have told me."

"What would you command next?"

Talya hummed thoughtfully and watched her spy shudder slightly with excitement. He would be disappointed in her next words, but only briefly. Lorath wasn't one to linger. She considered the old advisor sitting in the corner of her room, his eyes boring holes into the spy. How he could look upon Talya's perfect body and not even twitch forever bewildered the sorceress. It also enticed her: there was control of others, then there was control of self. Yet this man was dangerous and held a precious gift she was sore afraid to lose. Talya looked back at the spy and gave her command.

"Observe for our *illustrious* king. Tobias will be interested in their movements as the declaration draws near. Look for opportunities to exploit the girls. With Orren soon occupied in war, Merelith occupied in body, and Anise in her little mind...Queen Annelle Torhal is stretched thin. We need only find the point of greatest weakness and seize upon it."

"Yes, my mate."

"Burn your boots and cloak. A new set awaits you. Take care, Alpha. Once this war begins in earnest, Annelle's focus will tighten around her daughters. If you suspect she has sensed you...flee. You are more valuable to me alive than reanimated."

"With the speed of the hound."

"Go. Return after dark and we will prowl together. Our kin are restless from waiting on Tobias. We'll put them in order then clean the blood off each other, yes?"

"Gladly, my mate," he growled with satisfaction.

His eyes never met hers as he stood and turned away. His bared teeth, though, spoke to a deep hunger now awakened. The lady marveled at the young man and his voracious appetite. If Tobias could be half as passionate, she'd consider not killing him.

Or not. Everyone should know their place beneath me. Especially you, Tobias Galrend.

Preferably far enough below for the worms to gorge on your worthless carcass.

Once the spy had left, a heavy silence filled the room. As usual, Lorath waited for her to speak first. Experience had taught her the old man had limitless patience for awkward quiet. She waited for the storm outside to grow louder before beginning the next, more sensitive, topic.

"How does she fare?" the lady asked, the rain on her windows nearly drowning out the question.

"Healthy and happy. The nurse maid is forever amazed at her appetite. Seems you inspire hunger in everyone around you."

Talya furrowed her brow and sighed. The babe should have been suckling on *her* breasts. Should have been lying on her in this room, right now. Should have been celebrated for the majestic creature she is, not the monster Tobias feared. Granted, that fear was not without merit.

"Have you named her?" Talya whispered.

"No. Nor will I."

"A child should have a name, Lorath."

She sat upright and turned to face him. Talya hoped she struck the imposing figure of a queen and sorceress. Yet the way Lorath looked at her with disinterest gave the distinct impression she looked exactly as she was: a whore and desperate mother. Not for the first time, she wanted to bury tendrils of earth and stone into those uncaring eyes. She hated the way he looked at her. At everything.

Such emptiness. It isn't natural. Powers unknown, guide me back to her.

"Then I suggest you have one ready for when you two finally meet. Be quick enough about it, and she will never know that she was nameless."

Bastard. Yet he's right. Time is of the essence. Especially now that the idiot Torhal girl has felt the calling. Timing is everything, now.

"You are certain of this ritual?" she asked.

"Absolutely," Lorath replied, "You will need all three of them. *Alive.*"

"Yes, yes. I heard the first time…unlike that idiot you've had me play whore to."

Lorath snorted and said, "I've yet to see you suffer for it."

"My *baby* is in another woman's arms," she hissed.

Lorath replied a little louder, "Your baby is dead, Talya. You really must stop with these delusions or Tobias will think you are going even *more* mad."

She stared daggers at him then sighed and silently nodded. How he kept the lie up so easily was beyond her. Then again, it wasn't *his* child. He hadn't carried her, felt her wild thrashing in the womb, or waited so long to hear those first cries of life only to hear nothing at all. For all she knew, the child really *was* dead. Yet a strange life thread dwelled in a nearby orphanage. The risk was still too great for her to sneak out and meet the nurse maid caring for the orphan babe therein. Lorath only visited the child once a month, ostensibly to check in on boys of age to join the army and be free of the dreadful place.

"I have placed a great deal of faith in you, Lorath Saltsword," she whispered.

"As has your spy and your king. Have I yet failed to deliver on my promises to any of you?"

"No."

No, he had not. She could feel the child with her magic and know it was hers. She could follow her spy into Torhal through the magic of his garments. Magic *Lorath* had taught her. Whatever the Saltsword's true aim, Talya had discerned that he really *did* want Galrend to win its war with Anar Tota and, eventually, Torhal. If all went according to plan, Torhal wouldn't even lift a single sword in its defense. A mother's willingness to bargain everything could always be counted on.

"What else do you need of me?" she asked tersely.

Lorath rose from his chair and went to before her. Then he did something that both excited and worried Talya. The man with ancient eyes kneeled, just like her spy had.

"Capture them, Talya, and I will transfer their power to you," he whispered, "You will be the sorceress Galrend has needed for centuries."

"Why?"

He looked up at her and his smile twisted her insides. It wasn't vicious nor cruel. It held no malice nor hint of deception. It was pleasant, warm even. Lorath smiled like a grandfather might to his favorite granddaughter. He chuckled and the sound almost made her heart lighter.

"Because the Pentarchy *is* coming and only Galrend will be ready for them. Tobias is not fit for such a war. You are. You and your…future…are precisely what is needed to survive that war."

There it was. Talya's opinion of Lorath lessened even more. He looked at her not as an object of desire but a tool of conquest. Of glory or purpose or some other fool notion of legacy. The lady sat back on her chair and sighed up at the ceiling.

Why is it that men turn to women to make their dreams come true? Has a man ever made something without her? How pitiful.

Lorath stood and bowed his head, making it clear he planned to depart now. He made his way to the door but then paused. He spoke over his shoulder, his eyes pinning her to the chair like a hawk might a field mouse. Gone was the warm smile and the tone of his voice felt like cold steel on her ears.

"Be careful with your *dog*, Talya. If you keep feeding his appetite you *will* lose control of his instincts. I warned you to trust me and not send him. Now he knows more than he should. Treading softly around an immortal idiot will be the least of your concerns."

"He is my *hound* and mate. You sound like Tobias. Your worry touches me, Lorath, in all the wrong ways. See to your part and I'll see to mine."

The advisor shook his head then left without another word. His warning rang in her ear, though, and she found her earlier desire suddenly doused. Tobias was as jealous a man as the father he had murdered for the crown. Lorath was right, it would not be long before her puppet king and hound came into conflict. One had an ego the size of the moon, the other had a hunger as constant as the sun. The choice between the two was easy. Surviving that choice was not.

That 'dog' is fucking your queen every chance he gets, Lorath. One day, soon, he'll fuck me over Tobias' grave. Maybe yours, too. And we will laugh at you then howl victory over the blood feast.

Unless his warning was about something else. The spy's excitement about Torhal's guardian had been obvious. Perhaps Lorath saw something she was trying to ignore: her spy had seemed too excited about becoming an angyr. Talya wanted nothing more than to gain the power of the Torhals. Then the power of others.

Until she, too, was a Pentarch…or even more. She had hoped to share in this glory with her spy.

Except now, it seemed, he wanted power of a different sort.

Men always turned to her for their dreams. Her mate wanted nothing more than to be the creature his enchanted clothes made him. She had no doubt he'd want more than that after visiting the cave. Talya sighed with frustration. She forced the worry away and tried to dwell on her nameless child.

My child. My angyrian child. What shall I call you, my dear? How I long to prowl with you. I do not want to BE you; I want to be WITH you. Such is the trouble with men, you will see. They never wish to be with you.

"They only wish to *be* you," she whispered toward the window, "Beautiful. Powerful. *Wild.*"

At that thought, Talya smirked and rose from her chair. She didn't even bother to don a cloak before leaving her room. Let the castle see her naked. Let the people of Galrend see their king's whore waltz to her favorite *dog* and then change them both into the form of wolves. Let the world hear the howl of her bloodletters as they fed and fucked. More than anything, she hoped, let the immortal with a crown and the man with too old eyes see they were *less* than her. Their dreams were impossible without her.

Because in this world, there were only women and their dogs.

13 – Angyrian Future

Merelith

"Merelith? May I enter?" called the queen.

The question felt strange, probably for both of them. It occurred to Merelith her mother had n*ever* asked permission to enter the guardian's room. Tal stirred her nose to scent beyond the room and find only the queen present. Kara urged her eyes to look away from the mirror. It was hard to do so, the silver iris' glowing softly while second, larger rims of the same iridescent quality remained half-formed at the edge of her rounded eye. The whites of her sclera were muddied but not yet gone. Merelith shut her eyes tightly, as if closing them allowed her to choose to look elsewhere.

She opened them to view her room, ever mindful of the sorceress patiently waiting on the other side of her door. Merelith had crossed that threshold a thousand-thousand times in her life and not really noticed it. How special it was. It would be too soon that she'd not be entering this room anymore. Reeta hadn't lived in the castle because *her* mother had abhorred the loose fur and feathers on rugs, tapestries, and gathering up in corners. Annelle demanded a clean castle, too, but she claimed to have no intention of casting out her angyrian daughter over it. Yet the guardian also knew that chances were good she would *want* to live outside the castle.

"Merelith? Love?"

Merelith took a deep breath and released it slowly. Tal and Kara curled tightly into each other, apprehensive yet committed. She rose from her bed and padded toward the door barefoot, pausing briefly to marvel at the lack of sound. Her father's ears weren't bewitched, nor were the guardian's feet. Without realizing it, she was already leaning forward on them more. She continued to the door and heard her mother's soft breathing on the other side. The queen was startled when the door opened rather than her daughter answer. Merelith held it with a trembling hand and a forced smile.

"S-sorry. I, um…I was indisposed."

"Oh, darling, come here..."

Annelle reached a hand toward Merelith's lower lip where dribbles of vomit yet remained. Merelith grimaced but allowed her mother's careful touch. The girl dropped her arm from the door, still quivering, and the queen pulled her into a magically warmed embrace. Merelith sniffled but didn't hug back. Annelle released her and then motioned towards the simple, messy bed her daughter slept on. Merelith trudged over and flopped down, falling onto her back with a heavy sigh. The queen sat on the edge, poised and tense, and surveyed the room in silence.

"I don't understand why everything has to be about *her*," grumbled the guardian.

Annelle struggled to keep a wry smile from showing.

"She would say the same about you."

"She would be *wrong*. I've never done anything to her except be born first."

The queen nodded but didn't say anything else. Enough had already been shouted at dinner. Merelith's stomach turned, the words of her sister stirring her nausea once again.

Merelith mumbled, "Why didn't you say anything?"

"I am thinking, that is all," Annelle replied.
"No, at dinner. You didn't...you didn't even *try*."

The accusation must have stung because the room became markedly colder. Merelith sat up and stared hard at her mother, silently and defiantly daring the queen to make things worse. Tal ached for a fight. Kara braced for impact, not in fear but calm expectation. Instantly the room warmed again. The queen had long loved Merelith's defiance, loved her spirit of challenge. Annelle had once said it had been her favorite part of Reeta. The queen sighed and then spoke.

"I...was not really there, Merelith. I have known this day was coming since before I knew your father. This is not how I thought I would learn of it, but I suppose the answer to your question is this: I was watching you. Seeing you, and the change in you, and trying to make sense of it. I am sorry. I...I should have said something."

"What would you have said?" Merelith prodded.

The queen smiled but then furrowed her brow in concentration. It became apparent she didn't have an answer and after a long silence whispered as much. Merelith sighed before falling back onto the bed with a grunt. Tal huffed in annoyance while Kara sighed in defeat. All of this, the whole ordeal since *before* her birthday, boiled down to Anise. Or, more specifically, Anise's problem with being a princess and her sister being an angyr.

"I wish she were excited for me. I understand she isn't ready to be queen, but it's not like you're throwing the crown at her! We'll all be here. She's not doing it by herself. I'll just be different and…and I just don't understand, Mama. She acts like *she's* the one that is cursed."

"You are *not* cursed, Merelith. You are angyr."

"I know, I know…sorry."

Merelith saw her mother bite back the urge to lecture more. That word, *cursed*, had been hurled around a lot in the previous guardian's life. Annelle had made Orren swear to always validate Merelith's existence, to remind her she was neither cursed nor blessed, but simply what she is: herself. The queen sighed and issued her own apology.

"What for?" Merelith asked, her tone hard.

"It does not matter if I say you are not cursed. If you feel that way…I should honor it."

"Oh. No, not really…I mean, I didn't. Now? I dunno."

"What changed?"

Merelith scowled at the ceiling but didn't answer. The flush of red on her cheeks was answer enough, though, and the queen chuckled. The girl asked why, her defensiveness as plain as her embarrassment. The queen looked at her daughter and winked. It only took one word to see Merelith groan and shut her eyes tightly.

"Eric."

"*Mother…*"

"Come now, there is no shame in it, Merelith. I take it he already knows, too?"

"Yes."

"Couldn't have gone all that bad, then, seeing as you rode with him."

"I bit him."

"Indeed, so he told me."

"WHAT!? *When?*"

Merelith sat straight up, horror and shame written on her face. Annelle smirked and waved her daughter off like it was no matter of importance.

"I had him report to me after dinner. You were still holed up here, so I thought to ask him if anything else had happened before he left. To his credit, he said no, at first. So, I asked him about the wound on his lip. He's a very convincing liar when he wants to be. Fortunately for you, Eric's love is deeper than his loyalty."

"What is *that* supposed to mean?"

"It means he told me everything for *your* benefit."

"E-everything?"

"How did it feel, the shifting of dominion and docility?"

Merelith's cheeks burned as she cast her eyes from her mother. Though there was a tickle of curiosity beneath her embarrassment. Nobody knew more about angyrism in Torhal than Queen Annelle. Until now. Merelith was experiencing it firsthand. It was one thing to tell Eric all about it but entirely another to explain it to someone who had a chance of at least understanding. An old and familiar excitement bubbled up in her chest, almost a decade old.

"It's overwhelming but, um, not in a bad way," she replied in a whisper.

Annelle replied, "Tell me more, if you want to."

Merelith considered the request and then nodded. She sat upright, took a deep breath, and recounted the entire day in her own words. When she was done, Annelle asked of the two instincts and the daughter smiled. In her mother, Merelith sensed the excitement she had hoped for in her sister. More importantly, she could *see* it in Annelle's warm gaze.

"The books are…sort-of right. I get why they described it as predator and prey, but it's not that simple. Or maybe not that complicated? Um…"

"Start with dominion."

"Tal."

"Tal? You call it by Kalligan's name?"

"Yeah…erm, yes ma'am. That's what I call them in my head. Tal and Kara. I liked those names more than dominion and docility. I know, I know, dark language but…"

The queen waved her off, "That does not matter. The black heart is long dead and besides, the first angyr and his mate kept their names. Now then, tell me of Tal."

Merelith felt the calling stir stronger each time her mother said the word. It was like a spell unto itself, as if saying the name gave it strength and power. The instinct flexed within, arrogant and proud to be acknowledged.

"Tal is hungry. Erm, *hunger*. It wants things and makes me take them. It's ravenous, dominant, controlling…" Merelith paused then chuckled and added, "Tal is very, *very* possessive."

"Indeed. That is not surprising. Scholars have called it dominion for that very reason. Tell me of Kara, then, is it submissive?"

"No."

The suddenness of the answer shocked her mother. She watched the queen intently, curious if the queen could sense the instincts with her magic, or even see them in her daughter's new eyes. Kara uncoiled from beneath Tal, stretched luxuriously, then seemed to sit and stare intently through those eyes. Through Merelith, at the queen, long enough to make Annelle twitch with discomfort. That twitch delighted Tal but seemed to have no effect on Kara. Instead, Merelith felt its answer and gave it.

"Kara is not submissive. It is…calm. Content."

Merelith looked away and sighed alongside the instinct, as if feeling longing. Her smile returned as she drew her eyes to a short sword hung from her dresser, a gift from a certain scout. Only then did the docile instinct react, a low growl rumbling in her heart. Not with possessive need, but peaceful want. The guardian considered the calmer instinct and tried to describe it for her mother.

"Kara feels…*everything*. I don't know how to describe it as well as Tal. It's the opposite but, but that's hard to explain. Tal isn't just dominance or control. Tal isn't only possession."

The angyrian girl stared at the sword and hoped the queen could see her daughter was attempting to focus the instincts in question. Externally, Merelith was simply gazing across the room. Internally, Merelith felt her mother's magic gently prodding at the flow of wild magic around her. Tal breathed it in, Kara breathed it out.

"Tal is restless, Kara is peaceful. Tal is…courageous, Kara is careful. Tal wants to take, Kara wants to give? They feel like opposites, but they also feel, um, the same? There's an intensity to them both. Does that make sense? I mean, I don't know how being calm can be intense, but…that's what Kara is like. It's an overwhelming *peace*."

"Fascinating. I had no idea."

"Really?"

"Well, I am not an angyr, love."

"No, but…didn't Aunt Reeta tell you any of this?"

Annelle's face showed her hurt because Merelith immediately launched into an apology. The queen held up a hand for silence and the guardian stopped mid-sentence, clamping her mouth with a cringe of worry. The queen formed her words deliberately. Her voice held no malice, though. Only regret.

"She did not, no. Reeta and I…we were not close, as you know. Rather, I was to Reeta what you are to Anise."

"She…hated you?"

"No, love, and Anise does *not* hate you! She does, I think, envy you."

"Oh, and Aunt Reeta…envied you?"

"Yes."

"Why?"

Annelle's bemused smile had both instincts on alert. Merelith couldn't comprehend why an *angyr* would be jealous of a sorceress. Sure, there was the crown, the authority, and the wealth…but angyr could *fly*! They could manipulate time itself! Ageless, powerful, legendary. Both instincts swelled as the guardian tried to find some way in which she would *want* to be like Anise. It bothered her that no answer came to mind.

"Reeta hated what she was. You…do not."

"No, I love what I am. Why would Aunt Reeta hate herself?"

Oof. Too on the nose. Ease up, Tal!

Or not. Mama is laughing. Although it sounds a bit forced.

The queen replied, "Grandfather Doran was not kind to Reeta. Before I was even born, Reeta was treated like an outsider. What mattered to Grandmother Anise was my upbringing and preparation for the throne. Reeta, as guardian, was a welcome help but little more than an additional tool for ensuring the continuity of our lineage."

"That's awful."

"It was. I had a big sister who guarded me, but I was often unsure if she loved me. When Reeta's transformation began…she had no one. I was much younger than Anise is now, only six when Reeta began to change at eleven. The rest of my life was spent with, well, my mother. Reeta watched over us, but she wasn't really *with* us."

Annelle sighed then shrugged.

"It destroyed her, losing our mother that awful day. All those years, I had thought Reeta was staying for *me*, that despite how she was treated…she loved her little sister, just like you love Anise. It turns out that was not the case. Much like when Merel left my mother."

Merelith ventured, "Is she…you've never said if she's still alive."

"I do not know. I have not felt her presence since the days after my mother was buried. Your grandfather believes she gave into the calling. If she lives, she is in the wildlands now, with all the other angyr that could not keep their minds. Wildness is an affliction if not balanced."

"Will I be this way, too?"

The queen studied her child with a thoughtful smile, shaking her head before speaking.

"No. You are quite different from her, Merelith. You love your family and know your family loves you. You will have all of us, even Anise, in these coming months and the years that follow. Your father and I have an oath: wherever we go, *you* will go, or we will not go at all. You may be angyr, Merelith, but you are also a Torhal. You are *my* daughter, equal in every way to your sister. A crown or a coat of fur will not change that."

The girl leaned into her mother and hugged the queen. Kara basked in the warmth of her love. Tal lapped it up, slowly. Not out of caution, but an abundance of confidence. Merelith stewed in the instincts then felt as if a small bubble in her popped. From within came a billion questions and thoughts from a decade of dreaming of *this* day. She then chuckled and Annelle asked why.

"I hope it's red like my hair."

It took the queen a moment to understand what Merelith meant, then she, too, laughed. They then visited and wondered about what Merelith might soon be. The angyrian child asked a thousand questions that didn't have answers in the books: would her feathers be short and stocky, or long and thick? Would she be bulky and muscular, or lithe and limber? Long into the night the mother and daughter pondered what was to come. Merelith's excitement was palpable, and Annelle tried to share in it.

Yet Kara sensed what the queen hid: Annelle's heart was breaking, too, as old wounds ripped open with shame and grief. Merelith wondered if such conversation was many years too late. Would Reeta have remained if Annelle had asked such things of her? Maybe all that was missing for Reeta was what was missing for Merelith: a sister who was excited and curious. Kara's grief warped to fear as Merelith realized her stability might rest entirely in her mother and father, not her charge, crown princess, and sister. She was of a sounder mind, to be sure, but little else was different.

"What's wrong, Merelith? You look ready to cry. It is going to be ok!"

Merelith realized she had drifted off into her mind and completely ignored whatever the most recent question or comment had been. A tear rolled down her cheek and she forced a laugh to stop the sob beneath it. The queen rubbed her daughter's hand with vigor but kept quiet, so Merelith had time to reply.

I wish she didn't hate me. Or, or think me a monster at least. I can't say that. Mama doesn't think that. I…I just wish…

"I wish Anise were excited. I am so sorry, Mama. I…I don't want to be at odds with her like you and Reeta were. I don't want to lose my mind if…if something happened to you or Papa."

"Oh! Oh, Merelith, love…do not fret so! Come here, child. You need not be afraid of that. You have always come back from wildness and always will."

"I didn't for Papa."

"Oh, but that is not true at all! You did! He was so proud, as was I!"

"Anise wasn't. She was terrified. She was *right* to be terrified…"

"And she may always be, Merelith, but it doesn't change the *truth*: you will *always* protect her. Not because you are the guardian, or an angyr, but because you *love* her and are her sister."

"What if I forget that? What if I am so wild I…I don't remember her? You? Anyone?"

"Ask Tal if it will forget your family. Ask Kara if it will stop caring."

It was as if her heart exploded and imploded simultaneously. Tal roared in furious objection at the suggestion of abandoning her family and seemed to hunker down in possessive aggression, the whole of her being collapsing into a well of primal control. Yet Kara, too, roared with compassionate warning, the idea of not caring causing it to spread its wings wide and shove back the whole of the idea with angyrian might. The guardian wondered if the queen saw this paradox, for Annelle smirked and shook her head with amazement.

"Wildness is the loss of *self*, Merelith. It simply means you live only instinctually. Yet if you instinctually love your family, your people, your kingdom? Terrible and dangerous as you might be, you need *never* fear harming those you love."

"Why did Reeta hurt all those people?"

"Reeta was unloved. Her instinct was not to protect them but instead survive them. The challenge for you, Merelith, is to know the difference between surviving and living. The instincts only want to survive; it is up to you to teach them how to live. To live with us. To live with Anise. Someday you will only have each other and whatever poor man must put up with both of you."

Merelith considered her mother's wisdom then nodded. It seemed to placate both instincts, too, which felt odd. The queen described them as if they were mindless, yet they didn't feel so to the guardian. Thinking on her last words, the guardian snorted at the idea of Anise being married. Not that it was a farfetched fantasy but rather a truth: whatever man got between the two sisters would indeed be in for a world of trouble.

Merelith replied, "I promise not to run off her first pick."

Annelle chuckled and nodded. Merelith grew serious, with a powerful glint of wildness in her eye once more. Wild magic surged into the guardian as she intentionally let Tal take hold. When she spoke, the queen twitched again. Merelith wondered if the authority in her own voice was real or imagined.

"I'll do better, Mama. I'm not just excited for becoming an angyr. I want to be guardian, too. I *want* to protect her. Really. I will always want to protect her. I promise."

"I am glad to hear that, Merelith, truly, but…"

Annelle paused, not to gather her thoughts but sense the sudden rush of wild magic from her daughter. The queen marveled at it, like a breath of pure potentiality, time tumbling about it like bubbles in a waterfall. Merelith knew the queen couldn't feel the peacefulness of the docility instinct, but she *did* sense its intensity. Merelith had switched from intently focusing on preserving her sister to now intently focusing on serving her mother. The queen gulped, smiled, and finished her statement.

"…but who needs to hear it is your sister."

Merelith saw her mother grin and assumed she found her daughter's immediate reaction amusing. It probably wasn't Merelith's outward expression of frustration so much as her internal shift of instinct that Annelle smirked at. Chances were good that even the guardian's eyes reflected the retreat of Kara and the roaring, infuriated return of Tal.

"Ok, look, I meant every word, but…" Merelith began, but Annelle opted to laugh aloud, prompting the girl to demand, "What!? What's so funny? Really, I meant it, I just…she's so…"

You're joking, right!? I've told her a hundred times I'll protect her and, and…

Annelle held up a hand again. This time, Merelith snorted derisively before rolling her eyes and folding her arms. She glared at the floor but managed to put a muzzle on Tal in her heart. It remained a strange challenge, balancing the two instincts. She coaxed

Kara back to the surface once more, willing herself to listen to the wisdom of her mother.

"You have the instinct to protect her, Merelith. We've all seen that with our own eyes, several times. Do you have the instinct to cherish her?"

"She doesn't cherish me," grumbled the angyrian girl.

"Is there something to cherish?"

Merelith glanced up at her mother. Annelle gave away no emotions on her face. It was a trying question for the guardian and the queen knew it. It could easily be asked to her other daughter and have the same answer. Yet Queen Annelle had asked *Merelith*. Tal was unusually still within. Kara, too. As if shackled by the truth of the question's answer.

"No. I, I guess not," Merelith mumbled.

"Love is not the absence of hate, Merelith. It is not transactional nor logical, like hot and cold, or high and low. Many have hated in the name of love, and just as many loved in the name of hate. Anise does *not* hate you anymore than you hate her. That does not mean you love each other, though, does it?"

"I do love her, Mama. It's hard, but…I mean…she's my sister! It's more than being the guardian. I'd feel awful if something happened to her."

"Do you think she feels the same way? About you?"

The urge to answer 'no' must have been obvious to the queen, but Merelith held her tongue. The wild magic flowed in and out of her rapidly, a tug of war between Tal and Kara breaking out. Then it was over, and the guardian released a long sigh. Kara had won out, this time. Merelith nodded and chose her words carefully.

"Yes. For all the ways she tries to…I don't know, get me in trouble? Point out that I'm not a good royal? For all of whatever *that* is…" Merelith paused and said with a wisp of a smile, "I know Anise would feel awful if I was hurt. Really hurt."

"That is love, Merelith. It might seem quiet and timid, too frightened to come forth when it is most needed, but that doesn't change what it is. You have an enormous responsibility, my child: it falls to *you* to protect Anise. Not just her physical body and life, but her heart, too. From men who might take advantage of her and her station, so-called friends that would abuse her generosity, even her own parents."

"Why would I protect her from *you*?" Merelith asked, surprise comingling with confusion.

"Because you are an angyr. Balance is in your nature and the passing of authority, of a crown, from one to another is fraught with unbalance. I am not glad my mother passed the way she did, not happy for how it threw the peace of Torhal into the wind, not content that my father and sister have left me…but I *am* glad that the crown passed. My mother would not have permitted the way I have raised you and your sister."

Merelith considered her mother's words and then nodded somberly. Annelle continued, mirroring her daughter's thoughtful nod.

"I hope to *never* be that sort of burden on neither of you, nor your father. I also know the truth of immortal families: transition is hard, it rarely comes when we want it, and it is rare that everyone agrees *how* it should come. Our ancestors chose to keep the angyrian child for this exact reason: if all else fails, the guardian – you – will be there to protect the future. To be angyr is to seek balance, and there is no balance if your sister, or any future siblings, are not safe."

"Future siblings? Are you and Papa…?"

Annelle laughed aloud and shook her head while raising her hands in defense.

"No! No, no, no, certainly not anytime soon."

"But…you might?" Merelith pushed.

Another sibling! How wild would that be!? I could teach them how to fight and dance and sneak!

I wouldn't be the only one there for Anise, too. We could both support her as our queen.

As our sister.

"We might and I hope we do, someday. For now, our focus is solely on the two of you. I will not make Anise wait too long to find her mate and ascend. Your father and I will cross that bridge when we are confident Torhal is as safe as it can be – a wise, if young, new queen leading with an equally wise, if *wild*, guardian to protect her and her people."

Merelith watched her mother for a time and Annelle became uncomfortable under the intense gaze of the angyrian girl. Finally, the guardian nodded once and then grinned with enthusiasm.

"I'll make it right with Anise," she promised.

Annelle began, "That is good to…"

"I really, *really* want a little brother. Or sister. That works, too!"

"Wha…?"

"Can I teach them to be wild like you taught me?"

Annelle was stunned but managed a snort of amusement. If a sibling was all it took to convince her eldest to try harder…Merelith was confident her father wouldn't be opposed. Of course, if the queen thought about it hard enough, letting Merelith instruct *any* child was a questionable decision. Yet the guardian was pleased to see Annelle not think about it at all.

The queen simply nodded and said with a grin, "Of course, love."

And just like that, Merelith was more excited about the possibility of being an 'aunty angyr' than an actual angyr.

"I could be just like Merel!" Merelith said with a grin.

"Yes, yes you could."

The flicker of worry was unmistakable and Merelith realized what she had said had hit different for her mother. Instantly, Kara surged forward, and the guardian took her mother's hands up into hers.

"I won't leave! I swear it."

"I would not fault you if you did," Annelle said quietly, "It broke his heart, when your great grandmother died. It broke my mother's heart, too. She did not know how to ask him to stay. I think it is why she was so distant with Reeta."

"Yeah. Well, I'm not going! It wouldn't be fair to Anise. That and, honestly? It would have been nice to not be the *only* angyr here. So, I'll be here for the next one, too."

"Then you choose to be the best of Uncle Merel."

"Can we do a silly portrait like theirs, someday?"

The queen laughed and nodded. Tucked away in the darkest corner of the great hall was a family portrait of Queen Annabelle and her royal family. It was also Merelith's favorite painting in all Torhal. It depicted the past queen and her husband standing behind five children. All of them were hanging off a hulking angyr wearing a silly, toothy grin. The current guardian was sure it was also Queen Annelle's favorite, second only to her own portrait.

Merelith had heard the stories of Merel from an early age and had sorely wished to have known him in person. To have seen his strength and courage firsthand, but also his gentleness and compassion. Few were alive today that remembered the beloved guardian. His predecessor had died protecting Queen Annabelle, thrusting a young Merel into the role of guardian for both his sister and mother. He'd risen to the challenge, only to abandon his sister in the days after Annabelle died of age. Why, nobody

knew, but Annelle had suggested it had to do with King Doran –
Merelith's grandfather – and his extreme dislike of angyr.

"What happens now?" Merelith asked of her mother.

The sorceress replied with a wink, "You become what you have always been, love."

The guardian whispered with a grin, "An angyr. A *real* angyr."

14 – Pretender to the Crown

Anise

Of the elements she could wield, Anise favored one most of all: air. It was an odd affinity to have, considering the Torhalian line was renowned for mastery of fire and ice. Annelle had a penchant for flame when she was impassioned and ice when she was threatened. Anise had these same tendencies, too, but her preferred *control* of magic was to manipulate air. Specifically, the air of her own lungs.

It was a dangerous thing to play with, not least because a loss of control could damage or outright explode an organ. Yet Anise had learned control at an immature age and did so now for much the same reason: to calm herself. Sat upon her window seat, legs crossed, and hands folded before her abdomen, she looked to be in a meditative state. Her heart, mind, and spirit were anything but.

What has gotten into you, Anise?! First the wild goose chase this afternoon, now this? Has Merelith done something to you to prompt such, such enmity? Merelith, what lie is she accusing you of?

Always, her father defended the guardian. Always, the queen sided with the eldest. Always, Papa praised Merelith for being a monster instead of a sister. Always, Mama looked on in silent judgement.

Monster. I called her a monster. What have I done?

Anise curled the tendrils of life-giving air into her chest and held them there until she needed more. Then she released it in a whoosh and brought new air in. Through it all, she never inhaled nor exhaled. Her body was statuesque, her diaphragm unmoving, her life sustained by magic instead of will or instinct. She desired to hyperventilate as she considered that word – *monster* – over and over.

Why did I say that? I mean, she IS a monster…angyr are monsters! Kalligan used one to nearly rule the world. The Autarchs enslaved most of Damaria with them. The Pentarchy still experiments with them! An angyr murdered Grandpa Doran's father! Aunt Reeta killed over a hundred innocents after Grandma Anise died! Angyr ARE monsters.

Tears streamed down her face, and she resisted the urge to wipe them, instead using air to curl them up into perfect orbs and march them in a circle around her neck like a string of transparent pearls. She wanted to sniffle, the snot running as free as her emotions, but the air took care of this, too. It gathered it up like any kerchief might then condensed it into a growing block of slime that hovered over her heart. Ugly, disgusting, just like how her thoughts felt.

She isn't a monster. It was wrong to call her that. I was wrong! I am always wrong.

"Anise?" called the king from outside her door.

Her lungs shuddered painfully but she caught the surge of magic before it killed her. She breathed deeply, naturally, and coiled all the collected fluid and phlegm into a single, compact point in her right palm. She considered it, briefly, then opened her window and sent it hurtling out into the dark night over the canopy of her mother's wood.

"Yes?" she called back, forcing a tone of cool confidence.

"I've frozen my fingers to the doorknob. A little help, love."

It was impossible to not smile, despite her heart screaming to remain in its misery. One of the most effective means for containing an immortal was to magically freeze them. It didn't kill, but it also kept them from killing. Many had extreme cases of claustrophobia for that very reason: they *knew* they could be stuck for the rest of their life if not freed. Orren Torhal was a rare exception, neither fearing nor worrying that his wife or daughter would ever punish him so. If anything, the king had a knack for getting stuck on purpose. Like right now.

"Try again," she said with mock indifference.

"Ah! Much better," the door handle swiveled, and the king entered with a smile, "I was there for a bit before I worked up the courage to ask."

"For help or to enter?" Anise replied.

The king smirked and answered, "Both. May I enter?"

"You already have."

The temperature in the room matched her disposition, but it wasn't holding steady. Anise wanted to be annoyed with herself, with her father, with all of it. Yet King Orren had long possessed a knack for bypassing even the worst of his three 'she-wolves' with little more than a smile and a bad joke.

He called me a liar. He also said I did well today, given the circumstances. I DID find an angyr! Just not the right one. That isn't my fault! Besides, why does he always side with her? Does he not remember what she did to him!? Or does he just not care?

Anise fidgeted with her hands and kept her head down, knowing better than to look at her father for long. Because then it would all be fine, and she'd be wrong, and he'd be right, and it would all just go back to how it had *always* been! Which was precisely the problem.

"May I sit with you?" the king asked.

The princess shrugged, for she was afraid to say *yes* and tumble into that deep well of misery only he could rescue her from and determined to not say *no* because she'd much rather be rescued than left alone. Orren made his way to beside her, eyed the thin window seat, then set his back to the wall beside the window and slumped to the floor so that his shoulder bumped her right knee. He, too, looked down at his hands in his lap.

A peculiar silence followed. It wasn't like the immortal father to not immediately launch into an apology, or lecture, or some other wisdom that would smooth it all over. Anise found herself studying the top of her Papa's head and wondering why he was being quiet.

Is he waiting for me to apologize? I won't. He accused me. Wrongly! But I did call my own sister a monster. She IS a monster! Angyr are monsters! But Merelith isn't. Not really. What happened tonight…

"Do you wish you had ever known Aunt Reeta?" Anise suddenly asked.

Orren replied slowly, "That is a…strange question. I suppose so, yes. Why do you ask?"

"Why would you want to meet her?"

The king tilted his head and pondered her non-answer. Then he shrugged, as if deciding he didn't know what to do other than just answer his daughter's peculiar questions.

"Well, she is your mother's sister, for starters. I would have liked to have met Queen Anise, too. Your grandpa Doran says she was quite the warrior in her own right."

"But Aunt Reeta killed all those people."

"She did, yes, but do you know why, Anise?"

A long silence followed then the king looked up at her and she was surprised to find her father scowling. He said nothing and the weight of his glare saw her avert her eyes. It was not like him to be this way, neither. She *did* know why, but she didn't understand why he stared at her so. When he asked again, his tone even harder, she gulped and nodded. Except he didn't accept that answer.

"*Tell me* why, Anise. Tell me why Reeta killed them."

"She was lost to wildness," Anise answered.

"Why was she lost to wildness?"

"Her mother had been killed."

"No."

"No?"

Anise looked at Orren and he shook his head.

"No. That is not why, Anise."

"But…"

"Queen Anise Torhal was murdered on the eighth day of summer. Reeta's rampage didn't begin until the seventeenth. Wildness can come from grief, but it is not so slow. So, Anise, why did Reeta lose herself to wildness on the *seventeenth*? Think upon it."

The truth was she didn't know. The princess knew the story of her grandmother's murder well, and the details surrounding it, yet her father had made a point she'd not ever noticed herself. The princess had asked the queen why, once, and Annelle had merely sighed and shook her head as an answer. Wildness *could* take long – years even – to set in, but Reeta's escalation was unusual in both its suddenness and breadth. She could have killed *thousands* but didn't.

We celebrate her passing on the seventeenth. That was the funeral.

"The funeral?" Anise ventured, "Only then did it hit?"

"Reeta wasn't at the funeral."

"She wasn't?" Anise replied, surprised, "Why not?"

"Doran forbid her to attend."

Anise's eyes widened in horror and understanding. Grandpa Doran had claimed Reeta attacked him, her own father, on that sorrowful day. Yet the angyr had obviously not intended to *kill* or he'd not survived the encounter. Suddenly, an entire tragic history swiveled on its head. To lose a mother, who was Reeta's responsibility to protect, and not even be able to say goodbye?

"Grandpa caused the wildness to set in," Anise whispered.

"It was her fault that Anise died. She had failed to protect the queen. Do you know *why* Reeta wasn't able to stop the murderer?"

"It was a silent attack, she didn't know…"

Orren interjected, "She is an *angyr*, Anise. She could have easily stepped back in time and stopped the poisoned knife long before it struck."

"But…then why didn't she?"

"Because she wasn't there," the king said quietly.

"What? Why not!?" Anise demanded, realizing her grandfather had been right to be angry.

"The same reason Merelith was with you in the wood. It was Reeta's birthday and Annelle had frozen part of High Lake for her to play on."

Anise gulped and the weight of the last days came crashing down. Merelith almost certainly knew this story. She had been ravenous for anything and everything angyr-related as a child. Even the tragedies. The queen spoke rarely of her own mother and sister, but Anise knew the king had answered whatever Annelle wouldn't for the guardian. The princess had thought the king was preparing her to be a *better* guardian. Teaching her the mistakes of the past so she wouldn't repeat them.

"Not once has your mother ever blamed Reeta for what happened. Nor has Lord Regis, whose own wife was killed by Reeta on that terrible day! There is a reason your grandfather has not returned since your mother gave birth to Merelith. All Doran saw was the loss of his wife, rather than his two daughters who needed him. All he saw was that his daughter was a *monster*, Anise, when that same sort of monster had kept generations safe in the darkest days of Torhal since the War for Freedom."

Monster.

The king sighed and laid his head back against the wall. Another long silence followed before he spoke again.

"Help me understand *why*, Anise. Why did you call her a monster? Why did you reveal her calling this way? Why did you choose the most hurtful, most cruel way to tell us?"

Why did I choose the monstrous way. That is what he means. I AM the monster.

"I don't know," Anise replied.

She didn't. Or, rather, she wasn't at all interested in diving in deep enough to find out why. The princess was tired of pretending that it was all fine. That it would work out somehow. On the surface, it boiled down to knowing her sister wasn't human. That she could and someday probably *would* lose herself to wildness. Angyr were ageless and they really only died two ways: going wild and disappearing into the wildlands to be killed by *another* wild angyr or going wild and killing themselves in combat with people. Often the people they had once loved. Reeta's disappearance after her rampage was the exception, not the rule.

"I'm tired of pretending."

"Pretending…what, Anise?" the king asked.

"That this is all going to be ok. That *she* is going to be ok."

The king nodded then stood. His tone was of cold indifference.

"Pretending is a choice, Anise, just like hate and love. Merelith doesn't *pretend* to be something other than what she is. Nor do I or your mother think she is something other than angyr. We do not *pretend* that this will all be ok. We *choose* to make it better. You could choose to make it better, too. You could choose to see why Torhal's guardians are different."

He then went to the door and paused at the threshold.

"Or you can keep pretending you *can't* choose that. I am also tired of you pretending."

Then he closed the door and left. Unlike when he entered, the door was no longer coated in ice to keep someone out. Now it was simply wooden and ordinary. Yet Anise felt like a new wall of impenetrable frost had settled in at her father's words. Not to keep him out, but her in. In the end, it was exactly as it always had been.

They will keep pretending they are right and I am wrong. I won't let her choose my suitor. I found an angyr for Papa. I did channel my emotions correctly. I have worn my crown and learned my histories. I have done exactly what Mama asked. I warned Merelith there was a wolf. I told her we should go back.

On and on, through the night and her fitful sleep, Anise remembered every time she had warned her family or done as they asked and *still* been found wanting. Over and over, it all came back to Merelith. It all came back to her family pretending an angyr was something other than a monster. Merelith wasn't a monster, she kept telling herself, but it didn't change that she could and probably would become one. They all did.

It didn't matter how kind Merel had been or Reeta diligent. They had both left, one of them after inflicting bloodshed. Merelith had *already* inflicted bloodshed and she hadn't even felt the calling at that time! It made so little sense to Anise. The blind trust, the forced love, the baseless tradition of a guardian. It was pretending and she didn't know how to show them.

15 – War Comes

Merelith

The last two weeks had been the longest of Merelith's life. It was hard to believe the night her parents had discovered she was becoming fully angyr was only thirteen days ago. It had felt much longer than that. Anise had yet to leave the castle, choosing isolation over asking forgiveness or just smoothing it all over. On the one hand, this meant Merelith didn't have to worry too much about the crown princess' safety. On the other, it left her *very* bored. Leaving the castle just didn't feel right. Or it was more that leaving the castle felt too right for the wrong reason.

Come.

Every morning had started the same since Anise had called her a monster. Merelith woke then rolled over to stare into her mirror to see if her face had changed more in her sleep. Then she rose and stood at her window that faced east. Sometimes her mother or father found her still staring an hour or more later. The king thought it an interesting quirk but nothing to fret over. The queen always looked worried. That worry somehow stirred Merelith's heart to ignore the calling for another day. She had promised to stay, afterall. Yet the calling was endless.

It was a gentle nudge, always. Persistent but not annoyingly so. Interestingly, neither Tal nor Kara seemed all that lured by it. Rather, it was distinctively *Merelith* that wanted to go towards the wildlands. Tal was more excited about becoming a 'real' guardian, fur, feathers, fangs, and all. Kara dwelled on Anise's isolation and the queen's ill-concealed worry for both her daughters. That was the most difficult part of the last several days: the guardian felt pulled in three different directions. There was an exception where all three facets managed to align. Merelith had decided *that* was why the weeks had felt so long.

Eric. Stars, be safe and come home already. If only so I have someone else to talk to about all this. Someone who will listen and not worry. Or call me a monster.

I am not a monster! I am angyr. Eric would say so. Then he'd roll me over and…

Oof, I miss him so. A quick morning romp would clear my mind I bet. Or a long one.

You two are insufferable. And right. Hmph.

Since leaving the castle felt like a bad idea, Merelith had taken to spending her time in one of two places: the great hall, where she kept watch as her mother or father held court, or in the scriptorium where she continued to refresh all she had learned over the years. It had become something of a routine to spend the morning in the scriptorium then go to the great hall in the afternoon when court was least busy. The books were a small comfort, regularly reminding her that all she felt was normal. Court was a gentle reminder that what was normal for her wasn't remotely so for anyone else.

"How fare thee this morning, Guardian?"

Merelith looked up from fingering her nails to see Lord Thadeus Starling standing over her with a pleasant smile. Commander of the crown guard, Lord Thadeus wasn't but ten years older than the guardian. It occurred to Merelith he was rather handsome, something Kara focused a little too intently on. Tal came to the rescue, angrily scolding his other half for preferring anyone over Eric.

"I am well, Lord Thadeus. And you?"

"A guardian will soon sit in the great hall again. I could not be better!"

I wasn't much of a guardian before this, huh? Oh, stop. He didn't mean it like that.

"Why is that?" Merelith asked, hoping for clarity between insult and optimism.

"Lord Regis has long owed me a hunt! Old bastard keeps bowing out. With you in charge, he'll finally have to let me try my hand at the elk in the mountains!"

With me in charge. I'll lead the royal guard, soon. Or, at least, that's what Papa keeps saying.

Merelith scoffed, "I suspect it will be a while yet. I can't see Lord Regis giving the reigns over *that* quickly! Even if he does, the men may *like* me, but I sincerely doubt they'll *obey* me."

"Only because you've not seen an angry angyr up close!" the lord teased, "Take it from me, Guardian, they'll be obedient on the *first day*."

Merelith cocked an eyebrow but nodded politely. She didn't want to be in charge because the men *feared* her. That wouldn't go well at all. It occurred to her that Thadeus would have known Reeta, if only as a young boy. Yet, if *she* had overseen the royal guard but also never been allowed in the castle…

"How did Reeta lead the royal guard?" Merelith asked.

The lord furrowed his brow then shrugged. He motioned to a spot on the bench beside Merelith and she scooted over that he might sit with her. Across from the bench was one of the many tapestries depicting a past Torhalian family. In this case, it was Queen Anileth and King Alwyn along with their two children, the guardian Arten and the princess Antisa. The monarchs had ruled well and died of old age while Arten had gone on to train not one but *two* more guardians before choosing to go to the wildlands, long after Antisa had died of age, too. The lord motioned to Arten's stern visage, sat beside the thrones of his family, as he spoke.

"She didn't, as far as I could tell. Most of the time, your mother's guardian was skulking about in the shadows. I recall a time when Queen Anise publicly scolded Reeta for being too visible during a visit from an emissary out of Tarn, out in Anna where I was raised. Best I could tell, the guardian didn't coordinate with the royal guard at all. The men watched the royal family. Reeta…was more akin to a *presence* to stave off any foolish attempt on their safety."

"Did she frighten you?" Merelith asked, curious to hear the lord speak more.

"Oh, yes! Terribly. My father and mother? Not one bit. Most of the children I played with found her disturbing, but the adults regarded her as a source of pride and comfort."
"Really?"

"Well, *they* all grew up knowing Merel or about him. And the elders? The few still alive back then? Some of them had even played with Merel themselves!"

The lord suddenly grew dour and returned his gaze to Arten in the tapestry. Merelith could tell the young leader was troubled and, after failing to suppress Kara's need to know why, the guardian tacitly asked what was bothering him.

"Your mother and father, as well as Lord Regis and I, have gone to great lengths to ensure the people know you, Merelith. Yet it cannot be understated that their love for you is because of *you*. I know the rumor mill of the castle has been *busy* of late, but I want to personally commend you for being here. In this spot. Where others might see the guardian is neither a shadow nor a beast to be feared."

Hold it together, Mer. Help me, Tal. And stars above, STOP crying Kara!

The domineering instinct held out, but Merelith's eyes still stung a little. The lord grinned and winked, then motioned up and down the great hall as he stood.

"Owed hunts aside, I also look forward to seeing Torhal's legend walk this hall with my own eyes. You've been a fine guardian, Merelith. I've no doubt Torhal has years of peace and pros…"

"MAKE WAY! URGENCY FOR THE CROWN! MAKE WAY! URGENCY FOR THE CROWN!" hollered a courier from down the great hall.

Merelith went stock still as she heard the song of steel being released from Lord Thadeus' scabbard. Tal bristled with potential rage while Kara growled in warning at the familiar sound that had threatened before. Then the guardian was up and beside Thadeus, her own short sword loosed and at the ready. The lord shot her a glance of surprise but then turned his attention to the courier who had gone pale at the sight of the pair standing in his way. Already, royal guards had begun to filter in behind them from the throne room at the sound of the commotion.

"I am Lord Thadeus Starling of Torhal! Identify yourself, courier, and your business!" barked the young lord.

The courier blanched then hastily bowed his head and replied, "David Swift, Lord! I come from Anar Tota! I have a message from the council to be seen by the king's eyes only!"

In his trembling hand he held out a crumpled envelope that had obviously been stuffed into his pocket in a hurry. The man looked haggard and wretched, with mud caking much of the outside of his legs, indicating he had ridden through at least one storm to get here. The lord looked to Merelith and nodded, then stepped aside.

"This is Merelith Torhal, daughter of the queen and guardian. She will escort you to the throne" he then turned back toward the royal guard and ordered, "You! Summon the king. His Majesty should be somewhere in the stables still. You! Head to the garden in case I'm wrong. You! Find Lord Regis and bring him to the foyer. I will be waiting there for him. The rest, take up your positions and bar any entry to the castle until this is sorted."

As one, the men clapped knuckles to their hearts then raced off to fulfill the lord's orders. Merelith eyed Thadeus as he turned back to her and forced a cheap grin.

"I hope I didn't speak too soon," the lord mumbled.

Merelith nodded and replied, "Indeed. This way, Sir Swift. My mother will take your message."

The courier began to protest that it was for the king's eyes only, but then stopped as Merelith snarled at him. The lord looked on with surprise but then laughed.

"Best do as she says, Sir Swift. The guardian has a nasty bite, I hear!"

Merelith hoped her cheeks didn't burn at the joke as she turned on her heel and led the courier down the great hall into the throne room. Surely Eric hadn't told *others* before he left? Perhaps the lord was simply being a tease. It wouldn't be the first time, Merelith mused. At the doors to the throne room, a pair of merchants with disappointment stretched on their face hurried out. Evidently their business proposition had been interrupted. Aside from a quartet of guards, the room was empty save for Queen Annelle who now stood before her throne. It must have looked odd to the courier, to see a queen standing before *four* thrones, for he didn't immediately announce himself when Merelith brought him before the monarch.

"Er, I am David Swift, courier to the council of Anar Tota. I bring a message of great urgency for the king's eyes only!"

Annelle smiled pleasantly and replied, "The king is not yet here. I will take your message."

"The council was *very* clear that…"

The poor man didn't finish his sentence as his eyes opened with bewildered fear at the long spear of ice floating inches above his bobbing throat. Merelith suppressed a grin as Tal licked its lips in satisfaction and Kara huffed annoyance at the man's ignorance of Torhal's *true* monarch. The queen slowly stepped down from the dais and to beside her spear as she spoke.

"If the council's message is indeed as urgent as you claim, then I suspect they forgot to mention that Torhal's royal line is of *queens*, not kings. King Orren visits your nation for this precise reason: as my envoy and equal. Yet when you address Torhal's throne, Sir Swift, you address *me*, Annelle Torhal, queen and *wild* sorceress, sixteenth of Antila's line."

Merelith leaned in towards the courier and whispered, "Don't bother apologizing. Just give her the envelope."

The man unsteadily lifted his hand with the envelope toward the queen then let out a peep of fear when a breeze from nowhere whisked it from his fingers toward the queen. Instantly, the ice spear vaporized into steam and dissipated. The queen caught the envelope, opened it with a sliver of summoned ice, then withdrew the letter. Any humor in her eyes disappeared and Merelith felt the magic in the room stir around her.

"Are you aware of the contents of this letter?" the queen asked in a whisper.

The courier replied, "I am not, Y-your Majesty. I was given six day's rations and a horse and told to ride until the horse died or I made it."

Until the horse died? That's a bit extreme. Is Anar Tota under attack?

"Guards?" Annelle said a little louder, "Escort Sir Swift to the barracks and see that he is well-fed and his wounds, if any, attended to. The same for his steed, if you please."

The guard did as they were told and all four departed with the courier, leaving Merelith alone with her mother. The queen went back to her throne and, oddly, slumped into it before letting the letter tumble off her hand onto the floor. Only then did Merelith work up the courage to ask what the letter said.

"War comes," replied the queen in a whisper, "Galrend plans to invade Anar Tota."

Merelith felt her heart tumble into her stomach. *War.* The message could only mean one thing: Anar Tota had called for aid. Torhal had but one true ally and it was now under attack from its one and only true enemy. Tarn had given up on controlling Torhal centuries ago and the other nearby kingdoms weren't wealthy enough to wage a real war in the first place. Galrend wasn't supposed to be able to, neither.

"What will we do?" asked the guardian.

The queen did not answer. At first, Merelith thought her mother had not heard her, perhaps lost in her thoughts. Torhal had not contended with war in nearly five centuries. Large gangs of bandits, disrupted trade from other wars and the like, yes. A direct invasion of an ally that would surely lead to an invasion of Torhal if successful? No.

Father will lead the charge to defend Anar Tota. We are allies, afterall. Anise isn't fit to fight in open combat, and I've begun changing…they won't take me, even if I begged. Mother won't leave us undefended.

"Papa will go alone, won't he?"

Annelle looked up from the letter to her eldest daughter and Merelith beheld an old, terrible fear in her mother's eyes. The queen only nodded. The doors behind the guardian opened for the king and Merelith saw the queen's eyes dart to her husband. Then Annelle began to cry as a bewildered Orren rushed to his beloved and asked what was wrong.

Merelith was bewildered, too, with Kara as confused as Tal. The king lifted the letter and studied it, even as his queen clutched at him and began to wail. Then Orren sighed and began trying to placate his mate.

"All will be well, Annelle. We'll endure this, too. Do not be afraid," he intoned.

"Not again! Please, Orren, not again," she sobbed, "I don't want to be alone again!"

Then Merelith understood and the weight of her title, *guardian*, doubled like a stone in her chest.

16 – Fear of the Known

Anise

I *hate this room so much. Must we meet in this dreadful place?*

It wasn't much consolation that both her sister and mother also seemed ill at ease in the war room of the castle. Granted, they likely seemed off on account of the topic at hand rather than the magic that permeated the former dungeon. Prior to Queen Antila's capture, Castle Torhal – then known simply as 'The Northern Keep' on autarchy maps – had been the experimental playground for Autarch Anisterosa, called the *mad* pentarch for obvious reasons.

The war room, situated across from the dining room along the great hall that formed the ground floor's spine, was a large gathering space set at the end of a long hall with small rooms to either side of it. To the untrained eye, this side of the castle might appear like a cramped guest wing with a large master suite at its end. To Anise and those with magical sense and sight, it was a place forever marred with the lingering magic of forbidden experiments in an ancient dungeon.

Historical accounts in the scriptorium said that Queen Antila had filled this part of the castle with unending fire for over a month, the wretched abominations within not capable of being safely released or healed. As time went on, Woden Torhal had set up his commanders and himself in the wing to make use of the space Antila avoided. It had been that way since, with the royal armory, castle barracks, and war room now occupying the accursed rooms. Anise avoided the wing, just like her ancestors, but today demanded her presence, along with the entire royal family, both lords of Torhal, and several knights from the crown guard.

I shouldn't even BE here. I'm neither queen nor a warrior of any substance. Nor should Merelith for the same reasons! Father will send off the soldiers under the capable leadership of Lord Thadeus and then we'll focus on preparing Torhal for a siege should Anar Tota fall anyway. If anything, mother and I should be reviewing the trade reports against our inventories with winter upon us.

"King Tobias Galrend, of the same kingdom, has declared war upon Anar Tota."

King Orren's raised voice calmed all conversations. Everyone present already knew the news, but both lords shook their heads in concern all the same. Anise's father nodded gravely then motioned to a map of the northern freelands upon the war table that dominated the room. Upon it sat a number of wooden pieces representing towns, castles, abandoned forts, and known military units moving about. Orren pointed to a castle figurine – marking Anar Tota – and the princess grimaced.

Anar Tota doesn't even HAVE a castle. Idiots. Five Torhalian kings have tried to convince those fools to build better defenses. Now here we are, saving them. Again.

"Anar Tota is already suffering the start of a hard winter, according to our courier friend. Sir Swift says that many hunters and gatherers were killed in their wilds in these last months. I say Tobias has been softening them up for a winter offensive. He'll be on the move but fall rains and early snow may make for a long ride in those wetlands. I estimate a five-week march for his men. Lords, what are your estimates?"

Lord Regis stroked his graying beard then glanced at his much younger equal. Lord Thadeus smirked then shook his head before tracing a finger through the land that separated Anar Tota from its northern aggressor.

"It's been a wet autumn, to be sure my king. Merchants that have traveled from Galrend through Anar Tota say the roads were all but mud and puddles that could founder a horse. Neither nation nor kingdom has invested in them in many years. If Tobias wishes to arrive with a well-fed army, he'll be slow going. Slower still if he plans to bring engines."

Orren scoffed, "Engines will hardly be needed for Anar Tota. They can build rams from the very woods surrounding the city, too."

Lord Regis nodded and said, "Indeed, but Thadeus speaks true: a caravan of supplies will be needed either way, and those roads will make transport slow. That said, Galrend no doubt expects an easy journey. Unless bandits decide to risk conflict with an army, Tobias can send his army ahead if he is so inclined and feed them on looting and pillaging."

"Why is he attacking now?" asked the guardian.

Anise eyed her sister with a mixture of surprise and annoyance. She was neither a leader at this table nor a voice worthy of interruption. Yet both lords and the king looked at her and smiled as if the question was a good one.

"We do not know, Guardian," replied the king, "which is perhaps Tobias' best tactical advantage."

Anise answered, "Galrend has a long history of savaging its neighbors for profit or amusement. Ren has seen an influx of mercenaries hunting angyr for years now, making it a difficult and risky target. Anar Tota has farmers and loggers for a standing army, ample hunting lands they cannot control, and a city whose best defense has always been a sack of coin rather than walls even a child thief could climb."

The princess scowled at her sister, even as Lord Thadeus cleared his throat with obvious discomfort at the description. Anise's scowl deepened as her mother shrugged.

"All true, Princess. Yet Tobias need not *declare* war to acquire these things. We should be receiving a courier telling us Anar Tota has *fallen*, not that it calls for aid. He could have had an army there long before we'd know. Instead, he is very publicly telling us his intentions."

Fair, I guess. Also stupid. I'd expect no less from Galrend's extensive line of fool rulers.

"So why attack now?" Merelith repeated, eyeing Anise with a small smirk.

Oh, shut up, Mer. You're not THAT smart.

The queen said, "Tobias is coming for Torhal and seems to think he will succeed."

"I sincerely doubt he's *that* stupid, love," the king replied with a chuckle.

Annelle answered, "Tobias is arrogant and high-minded, he is *not* stupid, Orren. By all rights, he should be wearing that crown on your head if I didn't have a heart, too."

You did not just suggest…Tobias could have been our father!? Why have I not heard this before? Mother has never said he was a contender for her hand! Wait, does that make this a war of revenge? What ELSE is going on, then?

Orren replied, "Ah, but you *do* have a heart, my queen. Thank my lucky stars."

A chuckle went up from all the men, but both daughters eyed the queen with questioning stares. Annelle waved them off and motioned to the map as she continued.

"Anise is half-right: Anar Tota is the easier target *if* Tobias didn't tell us he was coming. I suspect our invading king is hoping to draw out Torhal's forces to a fairer battleground – Anar Tota – before attempting the walls of our kingdom later this year."

"He can't possibly stand a chance?" Lord Thadeus replied, "The wall has stood for nearly a millennium! We have a mighty sorceress queen and immortal king. Soon we will have an angyrian guardian once more, too! To assault Torhal would be folly."

Orren countered, "To assault Torhal *alone* would be folly. Yet there are others who would see the Torhalian line ended, and its riches plundered. Control of Anar Tota invites others to choose the side they think most advantageous. Our defenses are legendary, but we have no escape. If the wall falls, Torhal falls with it."

If Galrend takes Anar Tota…we're trapped. It's always been so, but only Tarn has ever posed a real risk. Tarn AND Galrend? That could get ugly, especially since King Aaron is an immortal himself and his heir a supposedly powerful sorcerer like myself. At least their angyr died in stillbirth. Hmm, I wonder…

Anise asked slowly, "My queen, you mentioned Tobias might have once become ruler of Torhal…"

"That isn't really relevant right now, Anise," the queen said with a sigh.

Anise ignored her and pushed on, "…and thus would have been immortal. Is there anyone else that could have performed the wild binding with him?"

Several men visibly gulped when the queen paled at the question. King Orren glanced between his queen and daughters then sighed. Merelith considered Anise then carefully asked how one might determine if Tobias was an immortal and, if so, for how long. Lord Regis groaned and clapped a hand to his eyes.

"Stars and moon," he muttered, "I didn't even consider that he knew about the ritual *before* he met Annelle. He may well have an angyr of his own!"

Thadeus broke decorum with a whispered curse that saw Merelith snort. Anise shook her head at her sister and grimaced. This was most certainly *not* funny. That the queen's face remained drained spoke to her considering the reality to be more likely than not. Anise cleared her throat and answered the guardian's question.

"Detection of immortality requires direct line of sight. We can sense King Orren because we know his life thread intimately. Tobias…we'd have to see him on the field of battle to know. As for an enemy angyr, it is even more challenging to sense them unless they *want* to be found. Angyr inherently 'blend in' with the residual wild magic of the world, even when quickening. Only another angyr can sense them at great distance with any success."

All eyes swiveled towards Merelith, and she visibly gulped before tapping a finger below her right eye then tapping her right ear.

"I could see it…Tobias' angyr, if he used one, but it'll be a while before I can hear it. Obviously, I can't fight it. Yet."

"I appreciate your courage, Merelith, but you'll be going nowhere near Tobias or his army anytime soon," the king intoned, before turning to Annelle, "You know Tobias best, Annelle. What do you think?"

She doesn't know what to think. An enemy immortal is challenge enough. An enemy angyr? Such a conflict is unheard of. Torhal's guardian has always been a unique advantage. What few know how to perform the wild binding nearly always kill the angyrian child or end up killed by it.

"I doubt he has an angyr" Annelle ventured, "The man was deathly afraid Reeta might return and insisted that, should we marry, she be tracked down to ensure she had left for the wildlands. That extraordinary fear played an influential role in why I spurned him: he would have killed Merelith without a second thought, upending centuries of tradition for sounder sleep."

Merelith quipped, "He sounds like a *wonderful* suitor, mother," before seriously adding, "That also means he would either need to lie to a potential sorceress wife about angyrism or she be just as ruthless. Isn't Galrend home to a cult of blood-drinkers known for earth-casters?"

The queen nodded slowly then looked to Anise with a strange quirk to her lips.

"What do you think the likelihood of such a sorceress is, princess? Assuming Tobias found a *correct* source of the wild binding, how likely is it such a woman gave up her firstborn to wear Galrend's crown?"

Anise easily answered, "The north is rife with elementalists and witches that wouldn't hesitate at a chance for more power, magical or otherwise. Outside of Torhal, no love is lost for angyr and if Tobias were so blunt with you – a princess from a kingdom that openly keeps an angyr as a guardian – I suspect he wouldn't even give his potential mate a choice in the matter. All that to say, Tobias could very well be an immortal but the chance of him having an angyr is nonexistent."

Lord Regis nodded and said, "Agreed, Princess. Yet that brings us back to the original question: why now? Why declare open war that we might aid Anar Tota?"

King Orren answered, "To force me out into the open and potentially weaken Torhal further."

What? Wait. No!

"You can't be seriously considering going out yourself?" Anise asked.

The king eyed her and replied evenly, "If an immortal leads Galrend's army, I *must* go. If Tobias is even half the swordsman he was twenty years ago…he could single-handedly devastate Anar Tota *without* an army."

"But…but he could *kill* you!" Anise exclaimed.

"Or Papa could kill him and stop the entire war," Merelith replied.

"YOU think this is a good idea!?" Anise shot back angrily.

The queen interjected, "Anise, calm yourself. There is nothing *good* about it. Our guardian merely points out the tactical viability of sending our king."

Anise whirled on her mother and pointed an accusatory finger.

"King Tobias has *decades* of combat experience as the monarch of a kingdom *built* on raiding and looting! Papa has decades of experience *gardening* because he's been here the entire time! Sending him out isn't just foolish, it is suicide!"

"If Tobias is an immortal," Merelith remarked.

"AND IF HE IS WE WILL HAVE LOST *TWO* KINGS IN LESS THAN HALF A CENTURY!" Anise hollered, then pointed at the map, "You don't think *that* will convince Tarn to try its luck again!? Torhal has *never* been as weak as it is now. If we lose Papa, there is only Mama and I to provide any real defense! *You* aren't done transforming and even when you ARE, you'll still be unfit for combat for at least another year. Nevermind you might go wild when he dies and kill us all *before* then!"

By the time her tirade was over, Anise was breathing hard, and her chair was coated in a thin sheen of ice. The knights had pressed backwards to the walls, the lords had turned their gaze to the floor, and the king sat in his chair, blankly staring at the map. An empty silence filled the room when, like a boomerang, Anise's words came back, and her eyes widened in horror. She glanced at her sister to find Merelith staring right back at her, eyes filled with hurt. The queen began to speak then stopped as wild magic surged into the room towards her angyrian daughter. It felt like a riptide that threatened to pull Anise over onto the table itself.

Then it stopped. The queen started to speak a second time, but paused as the guardian raised a hand for quiet. Then wild magic barreled out from Merelith, surprising Anise into sitting in her chair suddenly. To the men, it must have looked peculiar. To the pair of sorceresses, it was apparent that Merelith had the floor. Or, rather, her instincts did. Merelith opened her mouth, clamped it, furrowed her brow, then stood and made for the door. She stopped at it, turned around, and looked not at her sister or parents, but Lord Regis.

What have I done? Am I just making it worse? Is…is she lost again?

"Lord Regis. I invoke my right as the final authority on preservation of the Torhalian line, as demanded by Queen Antila and her heirs. Should I ever threaten the royal family, or any innocent of Torhal or beyond, it is my order as your guardian and princess that I be immediately executed without trial or imprisonment."

Lord Regis glanced at his monarchs, both of whom had paled at the declaration.

Surely, he doesn't have to obey such a thing! Besides, that's an overreaction and, and…

"On my soul, Guardian, it will be done" answered the elderly lord.

The guardian gave a terse nod and said, "Good. Lord Thadeus?"

"Yes, Guardian?" answered the young lord cautiously.

"Bring my father home or don't come home yourself. If I am to be a constant *threat*, let me be a threat for the benefit of Her Majesty and Highness."

Thadeus forced a smile and replied, "It will be done, Guardian."

Merelith cast a final glance at Anise, her nostrils flaring, but said nothing to the princess. In the black eyes with silver rims and irises, Anise saw no trace of her sister. What stared back was the monster she'd always known was there. Except that monster was still trying to protect her. The wild magic swirled about Merelith then focused into a pinpoint needle that speared right through Anise's heart at the guardian's parting words.

"I live, only, for Torhal's heart. No matter its condition towards me. As all guardians have lived."

Then she left the room and a dreary quiet settled over them all. Not a soul would look at the princess, who herself found it hard to look at anyone else. When the quiet had become unbearable, she stood and excused herself without another word. That neither the king nor queen acknowledged her departure – not even the men or lords – told her she had crossed a line. An old adage rose up in her mind, spoken in an ancient myth about flying cats.

Always speak the truth, but the truth need not always be spoken.

Anise stepped into the great hall and glanced toward the throne room. To her surprise, she found the guardian sitting on her throne, head in hand and eyes closed as if in deep thought or shallow slumber. Then she saw Merelith's hand itself: fingernails that were too long, and unusually thick, clasped at her thinning red hair. Upon the dais were yet more hairs scattered.

It's me. She's changing faster because of me. I'm the one making her wilder. How is she supposed to protect me if, if THIS is what I do to her? This whole situation is impossible! Torhal would be better off with only her instead of me. Yet an angyr can't wear a crown and I certainly can't change places with her. Hmph, if only.

It was a strange thought, trading places, one that only made sense in moments like these. When she had really messed up. Or really told the truth nobody wanted to hear. Not for the first time, Anise wanted to *be* the monster if only because then she'd be how she felt. The crown princess turned from her sister and silently made her way back to her quarters. She tried to ignore the gentle stream of wild magic pursuing her and willed herself to not look back where she knew Merelith would be watching her with the eyes of a sister instead of a killer.

Only when she turned the corner to go up the stairs in the distant foyer did the wild magic suddenly pull back, the docility instinct's longing for connection falling away to dominance's furious, lonely cry. Anise ignored it, too, for it felt too strong to be real.

17 – Learning to Survive

Merelith

Torhal's training yard was a tiny thing, fit only for a few dozen men at a time. These days, the army did most of its practice and honing of skills on the outskirts of Anna or at the base of one of the four towers along the kingdom's border wall. Within the confines of the castle walls, the 'royal' training yard had been customized over the years to suit the tastes of whatever immortal king ruled.

In Orren Torhal's case, much of the training yard featured just three armaments: swords, shields, and heavy crossbows. An avid hunter that preferred the stopping power of the ungainly contraptions over its lighter forebears, Orren had made it a point to learn all his royal guard in its use. Publicly, he wanted his guard to be able to hunt alongside him. Privately…well, Merelith was still coming to grips with his explanation.

"It is the most effective tool for warding off or significantly wounding an angyr," he had said, the humility and reluctance heavy in his voice.

From the moment she had been born, Orren Torhal had been preparing for the possibility that his own daughter might turn on him. Or, more likely, that another angyr might come and hunt him. Possibly *also* family.

"As such, you'll be learning a great deal about them, love. The greatest lesson I can teach you is one innate to your very being: survival. The trouble with being an angyr, Merelith, isn't that you'll lack the capacity to disarm, maim, or kill your foe. The trouble is you might forget they can do the same to you. In this, you are no different from any soldier caught up in the throes of combat. I aim to change that."

She visibly gulped as he leveled the unloaded crossbow directly at her. Behind the king's recalcitrant grimace, she saw determination in his eyes. She had absolute trust in her father and nearly the same respect for his crown guard. The two dozen men that formed the retinue encircled the training yard, each standing at attention and waiting for their king to commence their sessions. All wore a thick chainmail covered by a fine tabard of verdant green with a silver-embossed tree upon its chest. Most carried a sword and shield, though a few had maces.

One pair, who were twin brothers, sported unusually large hunting knives on their left hips. Slung across their backs were crossbows that were half a man long. Quivers of bolts hung off their right hips. The king motioned to the brothers to come forward and they did so, clapping their chest with their right fist in salute.

"These are Knights Paol and Polo. They were recently promoted to crown guard in light of the coming war. They're excellent hunters and scouts, second only to Eric. And, yes, they are twins. Paol has the big nose" Orren said with a cheap grin.

"Not as big as yours, My King," quipped Paol.

The crown guard burst into laughter and Merelith immediately relaxed a little more. Orren, too, laughed and nodded agreement.

"Helps me aim!" he cried.

"In the woods or in bed?" teased one of the others.

"Hey, hey!" cried Polo, "Not before Princess Merelith!"

The others immediately ceased their laughter and looked to Merelith, who blushed furiously at being called a 'lady' by the guard. Orren chuckled, nodded, and continued his instruction.

"Paol and Polo have one other distinction: they have both had first-hand experience with an angyr. Before coming to Torhal, they were engaged in a mercenary band out of Ren. Suffice to say, they survived several encounters but made it a point to get as far away from the wildlands as they could."

"A wise policy that continues to serve us well, eh, brother?" Paol said, nudging his brother.

Polo nodded and said to Merelith, "We had heard legends of Torhal's past guardians and thought to see for ourselves. As the old saying goes: if you can't beat 'em, join 'em!"

Merelith quietly remarked, "I doubt I'll be quite like those legends, good sirs."

"Aye, the way His Majesty talks, you'll be putting them all to shame!"

Merelith's blush only deepened as the crown guard nodded or hurrahed agreement. For his part, the king simply winked at his daughter, clapped her on the shoulder, and strode off to engage the others in practice. Left between the two armored hunters, Merelith felt vulnerable. Her Kara instinct rose, begging her to flee and preserve herself. Paol raised an eyebrow, smiled, then pointed out she was shaking. Polo elbowed his brother and shot him with a glare.

"Ignore him, Your Highness, he…"

"Please, just Merelith," she interrupted, "I'm no princess."

Paol joked, "So we've heard from Sir Smith."

"*Paol*, shut up!" Polo seethed.

Yet Merelith laughed and Paol along with her. Polo's eyebrows shot up in surprise and she cleared her throat before speaking.

"S-sorry. Um, yeah, you'll find I'm not as proper as my sister. Or family in general."

"That'll serve you well, Merelith," Paol said with sincerity, "Combat is not for the fancy or fine."

Polo then asked, "How fare your instincts? The king learned us a little on what you are experiencing but we'd rather hear from you."

"They are difficult to control. Erm, they tend to quickly shift from one to the other. It's a bit overwhelming."

"Aye, sounds like an animal to me," Paol replied.

Polo hissed, "*Paol.*"

"What?!" answered the brother with an exasperated huff.

Merelith chuckled and said, "He's fine, Polo. Really. It…I *am* like an animal. It makes sense."

A tense pause was had before Polo relaxed and said that Merelith's instincts would be both a boon and a curse. Paol nodded along as his brother explained.

"They'll save your life, to be sure, and allow you to react when thinking will get you killed. However, just like we know from hunting, instincts can make you *predictable* and lead you into a trap without even knowing it. Standard combat is no different. What divides the knights from the squires is as simple as controlling instinct: knowing when to rely on it, and when not to."

Paol rolled his eyes and said, "Alright, alright, mighty hunter! That's enough lecturing. I'll get her started if you'll get the dummy bolts strung."

Polo grimaced and retorted, "Figured *you* would get the dummy bolts strung."

"And leave you to harass the fair lady?" Paol said with mock offense, "I think not, dear brother!"

Polo's cheeks turned crimson, and he stomped off, leaving Paol sniggering. He motioned with his head for Merelith to follow. The hunter-guard led her to a corner of the training yard where a rudimentary obstacle course had been laid out. She'd played on this much of her childhood while watching her father spar. To stand over it now felt odd and a bit childish.

"The king says you know this course well. Show me," commanded Paol.

Merelith smirked and did exactly that: she showed Paol how nimble she could be. The course began with a series of log stumps that grew wider apart with each step. Next came a patchwork of ropes crisscrossed, making for a tripping hazard. After was a short wooden wall with a rope to assist climbing, followed by a leap to a suspended rope that swung to a platform. From there, Merelith skidded down a gravelly hill before sprinting through the obstacle course's final and most unusual portion: a moving carousel of wooden dummies.

The carousel had but two entrances with a wood fence forcing entrants to stay upon it and move counter to its rotation. Within, six wooden dummies erratically spun. The entire contraption was powered by two servants working a crank. Though it didn't move with great speed, the 'carousel of carnage' was an exercise in environmental awareness and agility. Merelith had memorized the thing as a child and easily navigated it now, despite being much taller and thus an easier target for the dummies.

She emerged from the other side with a victorious huff and a winning smile. Paol didn't seem the least bit impressed, though he did acknowledge her successful completion. Tal plucked at her annoyance, but she pushed it down when Polo returned with a pair of small crossbows and quivers filled with 'dummy' bolts: the heads had been replaced with thick cloth bundles. Kara worried away as the pair of hunter-guards nocked their first bolts and then, together, grinned at her with vicious enthusiasm.

"You can probably guess what happens next, aye?" Paol said with a chuckle.

"That…does not seem fair," Merelith replied.

Polo answered, "Said every rabbit ever. Didn't stop them from running, though, did it?"

The instincts warred over Polo's remark – fury at being called a rabbit and terror that she was about to be shot at like one – but Merelith managed a grim nod and returned to the start of the course. As she went, Polo gave new instructions.

"It starts out easy: we'll tell you we're about to loose. It will always be a pair of bolts, and they will always follow one after the other by about a second or two. The goal, Merelith, is *not* to reach the end quickly but rather to not get hit before you do. Take your time, stop and stare at us if you are so inclined, but *do not* get hit."

Paol added with a gleam in his eye, "If you do, you start over. We've got a bit of dye on the ends, too, so don't bother lying about it."

Merelith retorted, "I wouldn't dream of it."

Both men guffawed and Merelith tried to laugh with them. Yet her instincts were on edge, anticipating a challenge she'd not endured before. The men raised their crossbows, Paol made a remark that the bolts shouldn't hurt *too* much, and then Polo shouted for her to begin. Merelith dashed across the stumps, already certain the best approach was to finish quickly.

"Loose!" shouted Paol.

She heard the first bolt whiz past her face and nearly stumbled off the second-last stump. The second bolt narrowly grazed her knee as she tried to catch her balance. The men didn't tell her to stop, so she continued. At the crisscrossed ropes, Paol shouted again. She instinctively ducked down, and the first bolt sailed well above her. She then dove forward as the second bolt blasted right behind her bottom. Merelith heard Paol curse under his breath and grinned.

I might actually get this done on the first try. Ha!

Just gotta hit the wall fast and…

"Loose!"

"OW-OW-OW!" she howled.

Merelith tumbled off the rope from the wall and thudded the short distance down to the pressed dirt floor of the training yard. Her arm stung and, upon lifting it to inspect the damage, found it coated in bright red dye.

"Are you well, Merelith?" asked Polo, the nervousness in his voice apparent.

"She's fine, Polo. Shake it off, Merelith. Back to the front. Good first few dodges!" Paol said with cheer.

Merelith clambered to her feet, dusted herself, then shot a scowl at the pair of men. Polo meekly smiled back while Paol beamed with pride.

"Who hit me?" she demanded.

"Does it matter?" Paol shot back, "Dead is dead. Go on."

The sudden harshness of his tone was like a slap to the face. Polo seemed a bit unsure, but Merelith opted to only nod and return. Her father had promised difficult training. When it was time for lunch, Merelith realized he had been telling the truth. Forty-six times she tried to scale the wall. She was shot down on forty-two of them. The four successes, though, did not end in completion, neither. Twice she was shot swinging on the rope and twice she was struck right at the start of the carousel.

"A good, strong start, Merelith," Paol said with stern praise, "This afternoon, we'll work something else. Every morning, though, will be this right here."

Merelith grumbled, "All this teaches me is to dodge."

Polo replied, "Aye, that's the point. What makes an angyr dangerous is distance. They get inside ten feet and you're dead. Every man with half a brain looking to stay alive knows so, too. Been the tactic for centuries to shoot at them and keep them back."

Polo rested a hand on her shoulder and winked.

"You'll be no different, Merelith. Once close, no man will have the speed to deny you. There's no point teaching you swordplay and the like. Your greatest strength is your weakness, too: those instincts. We hone them, now, as you are able. Once fully angyr, we can hone them even more. They are fearsome things to behold, angyr. They are as lightning, darting, pouncing, and striking. They are so fast that they can cleave through ten men before the eleventh realizes he's about to die."

Paol gripped her other shoulder and nodded sagely.

"It's a fool's errand to hunt them. We would know. That said, we saw the pelts, bought and sold the feathers in the market outside Ren. They're not invincible. Might take fifty men to bring one down but the pay was enough for two hundred. Your father spoke true: survival is your aim."

Merelith whispered, "Why hunt them? For what purpose?"

Both men released her and looked to each other. Paol grimaced while Polo visibly gulped. Finally, Paol answered.

"The same reason we hunt other things that don't need to be hunted. Pride, money, hate. Lotta folk have died to angyr, there in Ren. They don't bother the people too much but sometimes one wanders out too far, kills cattle or some poor farmer's son or daughter fooling around in the fields too far from home. Hunters from across the freelands come looking for the most dangerous prey. Smugglers supposedly sell the parts to witches and the like. Some whisper of the Pentarchy having a whole illegal market for such things."

"Trade with the Pentarchy can't be wise," Merelith retorted.

"No more than going toe to paw with an angyr!" Polo quipped, "Folk do anyways, though. We did. Lucky we survived our idiocy."

"Why did you stop?" Merelith asked.

Polo chuckled and then shrugged. Paol, though, shook his head and rolled his eyes. The brothers eyed each other then laughed together. It was Polo who answered this time.

"Family."

"Family?" asked the angyrian girl.

"Aye, family. Polo wants to be a father and…well, I dunno if I've got that in me but I'll be damned if I'm not around to see him convince some poor, stupid woman to think he's worthy of her. Someone has to warn her, right?"

"Oh, shut up!" Polo said with mock indignation.

"Really? That's it?" Merelith replied, not entirely convinced.

"THAT'S IT!" Polo retorted, "What? Man can't be a bit lonely? Ya think I want to sleep beside *this* noisy bastard the rest of my days?!"

Paol wheezed as Polo struggled to keep a straight face. Despite Merelith's amusement, she held her ground. It didn't seem like the truth. Or the whole truth, anyhow. Seeing they had failed to placate the young guardian, Polo sighed and said more.

"We were the only two that survived, Merelith. By sheer luck, a horse spooked and fell on us both. Darn near killed us, too. We were knocked clean out. By the time we came to, the angyr was gone and…and so was everyone else. Gathered up what we could, wrapped ourselves in splints, and hobbled back to Ren."

Paol added, "Not a soul said a thing to us. Didn't wonder what had happened, didn't ask if we needed help, didn't even acknowledge we were the only ones to return. They'd seen it so many times before that we were just the latest idiots in a long line of idiots."

Polo nodded agreement and shrugged.

"So, we stopped being idiots. Now, instead of hunting an angyr…we're teaching one. Hmph."

Merelith quipped, "I'll try to make you not regret it."

Paol joked, "Too late. I saw you staring daggers at me that last time."

"Fair" Merelith said with a hint of gleeful malice.

Polo retorted, "Hardly. Eyes like yours hunt eternity itself. Unsettles even the bravest man."

Merelith cocked an eyebrow, but the men said no more, urging her to eat well and come back ready for more training. By the time Merelith collapsed into her bed that night, she was exhausted and excited all at once. Paol and Polo worked her hard and she had no doubt they would continue to do so. Yet, Polo's retort had bothered her all day.

Looking in her mirror, seeing yet more changes that even a hood could no longer hide, she tried to understand. Her slipping humanity, or the appearance of it, was understandably unsettling. Yet in her eyes she did not see the hunter Polo saw. Nor the monster her sister claimed was there. Instead, she beheld a pair of eyes staring back: one full of pride and the other intently curious. In those eyes she didn't see a predator but a protector. A guardian, she hoped, too.

18 – The Sound of Terror

Anise

"Your Highness, the harvest ain' so good this year. With the army takin' what they wan…erm, *need*, Your Maj-erm, uh, Highness, uh, there jus' ain' enough for the res' of us!"

"I am sure the castle stores have something to spare," Anise answered, a bright smile on her lips as the peasant beamed at her words.

The queen, though, shook her head and plainly said no. Instantly, the temperature of the throne room fell along with the peasant's smile. Though it was not from Annelle. The queen cast a warning glance at her daughter as she spoke.

"War comes and with it sacrifices many may not be prepared for. We cannot offer the castle stores, should that war progress further than we hope. We *can* offer our promise that no man, woman, or child will starve so long as this family rules. Make do with what you have and return when you have *nothing*, for there are others already without to see to."

"Yes, Your Majesty. Th-thank you, Your Majesty."

Annelle motioned to a nearby guard and commanded, "The court is resting for the remainder of the afternoon. See that those who still wait are directed to return in the morning."

The guards, as one, saluted and began ushering the crowd out. Anise bit on her lip as the last peasant to speak cast a worried glance at her before leaving. She managed to contain her myriad questions until the throne room was empty, save for her and her mother.

"*Why?*" Anise replied with deliberate slowness, "Why do you undercut everything I say? Do I never say any of it right?"

Annelle perched on her husband's throne, back straight and posture still poised with grace and authority. She cast a long look at her daughter, who sat below and slightly ahead of her, before sighing and shaking her head.

"No. You did not say any of it right."

"B-but…"

"Be silent, Anise, and listen."

Anise was of a mind to fill the throne room with the roar of flame or the crackle of fracturing ice. Yet, she obeyed and held her tongue. When her mother didn't speak further, instead casting her eyes toward the far end of the great hall, she realized what her mother had commanded. Even beyond the thick wooden doors that barred entry to the castle, she could hear them. Wailing, crying, shouting, demanding…a throng so large she couldn't recall seeing so many at the castle except during festivals.

They are so loud. Never have so many come, asking so many questions.

"Now listen with your magic."

Anise furrowed her brow but did as she was told, reaching out with her magical sight. All she saw was the life threads of nearly five hundred peasants, merchants, and other folk of the kingdom. Yet when she *listened*, as her mother had commanded, what she heard was unlike anything she'd experienced before. She stopped as quickly as she began, snapping her eyes shut. It had been like a thousand iron nails scraping slate alongside the roar of a waterfall, deafening and *defeating* in its noise.

"What is it?" she asked, her eyes still shut, the noise reverberating in her mind.

"Fear," answered the queen in a somber whisper, "Fear that our people have not known in generations."

"Why? Why does it sound so…so…"

"You know why. Tell me, that I know you have been listening to *me*."

Anise bristled at the jab but didn't bite back. Her mother had been on edge for a week now. Some of it undoubtedly related to Anise being a poor monarch-in-training but the crown princess suspected it had more to do with Merelith and her father. Merelith's training had been brutal and seen the guardian bruised and cut numerous times. She didn't seem to mind but the queen was still coming to grips with her daughter being forged into a weapon. That Orren didn't share the queen's concerns only deepened that worry.

"Life threads are drawn by time. As they move, they hum with action and twist with emotion. Both make sound in their own way. Actions we can hear alongside time passing. Emotions can only be heard when listening to creation rather than its creatures."

Annelle replied, "Yes. So, why does fear sound as this?"

Anise gulped, knowing the answer but not wishing to speak it aloud. Every emotion had a unique sound, a direct product of the 'twisting' of a life thread combined with the action (or inaction) that caused the emotion. While there were hundreds, if not thousands, of emotions, they could all be condensed to just two halves: dominion and docility, the foundational pair of all things wild. However, in terms of emotions, these two halves took on different names: courage and hope. Yet, what Anise heard was the *opposite* of one of these.

"It isn't fear. It is *terror*. Is it…is it so bad, Mama? The war hasn't even come?"

"War often comes long before blood is spilled, Anise. The weapons are not made of steel but of minds, the cost not in blood but trust, and the spoils are named so for a reason: war only spoils. No victory is worth more than what has been rotted in its wake."

"Then why wage war at all?" Anise asked.

"Because war is natural, Anise. All things that live wage war. It is the essence of creation, to destroy and consume so that there is space for things that are new. Time is infinite but creation is not. There are only so many lives with which to build."

"How do we change this?"

Annelle's eyes were bemused as she considered her daughter. The princess knew immediately her question was itself faulty. Still, she didn't try to reword it. The queen's smirk matched her eyes as she answered.

"You do not, Anise. Emotions are the natural derivatives of life. You don't *change* the terror of our people. There are few sacrileges so terrible as to warp a heart to feel something it should not. It is the duty of the crown to change what *causes* these emotions. In affecting change this way, we give space for terror to rot into hope."

"*Rot* into hope? I do not understand, Mama."

"What is terror, Anise, but the aged and withering carcass of courage? They grow from the same root but their fruit changes with time. Plucked too early, it tastes of uncertainty. Plucked too late and it reeks of terror. Harvested when it is ripe…it is courage: to still be afraid yet not too young or old to do nothing about the source of that fear."

Annelle rose from her throne and beckoned her daughter to follow. They wandered the great hall, pausing occasionally before the various family portraits as the queen continued to speak. The ritual of lecture, known to Anise since she could barely speak, played out once more: a queen instructing her princess, a sorceress her apprentice, a mother her daughter. All under the watchful gaze of the mothers, sorceresses and queens that had come before.

"Terror must be rotted into the soil of your people, Anise. It must be allowed to exist so that it can enrichen their lives. It must be answered with sharp words and strong hands, just as the till must be sharp and the horse pulling it strong. The rocks of doubt, the roots of terror, the stems of fear, these must be ripped and torn but *not* discarded. They must be honored and acknowledged for they are the ingredients of a fertile heart ready for seeds."

Annelle paused before her mother's family portrait and Anise watched where the queen's eyes were drawn. King Doran, Anise's grandfather, stood behind and to the right of Queen Anise, sat in a solitary throne. To her right stood a spindly Annelle. Anise realized that the queen was staring at the blank space to the queen's left. The great hall was arrayed with every queen, every king, and every guardian that had ever lived. Except Reeta.

"What you choose, Anise, is what seeds to plant in that soil. Today, you tried to plant the seeds of trust, gratitude, loyalty. These are good seeds and bear many fruits for your kingdom, but they are easily drowned out by weeds of terror in times of war. You must plant something hardier. What, then, would you plant?"

Annelle looked to her daughter and Anise fidgeted under the stern gaze of her living mother and dead grandmother. The crown princess considered the question and framed it against all her lessons. She thrust down the urge to be frustrated.

Merelith doesn't have to think about these things. Why must I be the one to answer such challenging questions? Bah, think. She says terror and courage are the same seed…

"I would plant courage."

"That is the same as terror, Anise. You gamble your people's wits with such a seed."

"It is the only answer to terror? To still be afraid but *do* something. You told him to make do so that he would have courage to press on…" Anise paused then added quietly, "…and hope that if he failed, we would still be there to help."

"Well done, daughter. Yes."

Annelle returned her gaze to where Reeta should have been. Anise opted to look across the great hall at the portrait of her great grandmother: Annabelle. The difference between the two was stark: everyone, even the angyrian Merel, smiled. Queen Anise's family had the regal look of indifference that Princess Anise had found in countless books containing portraits of distant kings and queens. It was strange, seeing a queen so happy and vibrant, across from a queen that was not. Moreso in that, as far as history was concerned, Queen Anise had been a much more adept and skilled ruler.

Is this what I will be like, too? Stuffy and harsh but also wise and powerful? Do I even get a say? Merelith is already gone from me…and father, too, after what I said. Again.

"I am sorry you feel undercut, Anise. I had not planned on teaching you these things for some time still. My mother did not even allow me *in* the court until I was sixteen. You are but fifteen! Even then, I was to only be seen, to listen attentively, and recite *everything* I had seen and learned that day at dinner."

"That sounds miserable," Anise mumbled, before widening her eyes and quickly apologizing.

Annelle let out a cold laugh and replied, "It was. I'm not sure I'm doing much better with you."

Annelle looked to her daughter and forced a sad smile.

"The crown is heavy, Anise, I know. There is so much joy and privilege in it, but that does not change it weighs on you now and then. My mother kept the crown from me for as long as she could. I *thought* she simply did not trust me. It is only now I realize she may have been avoiding placing the sort of burden on me I have placed on *you*."

"You say that like I'll be queen soon," Anise murmured.

"I certainly hope not," Annelle replied, her smile a little lighter, "I rather like being queen and having a crown princess to boss around."

Anise managed a meek grin. Her mother had her moments. Annelle pulled Anise by the elbow to her side and then leaned in such that her lips nearly grazed her daughter's ear.

"Sharing that crown with an immortal husband greatly reduces its weight, too. War has a habit of turning up men of valor and loyalty. Your sister has already found one such man among our own. You have an advantage she does not: you can *see* and *hear* the intent of men."

Anise's cheeks flushed at the implications of her mother's words. Annelle leaned back just enough that their noses nearly touched. She winked then cast a wicked grin at her daughter.

"War brings terror, and it is *hard* to hear through it. Yet if you will sift through it, you'll find those men who bear the fruit you seek. You must *seek* them, though."

"N-now?" Anise replied in a whisper.

"No, not now if you do not want to, but…"

Annelle straightened and pointed to her father, then her grandfather.

"…there are times when hunting is more productive."

The meaning of her mother wasn't lost on Anise. Queen Anise had found Doran in Torhal's time of peace. Queen Annabelle, though, had found her husband during a war between Tarn and Gwentia. King Harold Torhal – then Knight Harold Cotton of Gwentia – had been sent to request aid from Torhal. He had been refused but the fact the man had survived crossing Tarn's lands, alone to protect his own men, had impressed then-princess Annabelle.

What had ultimately sealed their love, though, had been Harold's ensuing quest. He had taken Torhal's dismissal in stride, declared Annabelle's eyes more beautiful than any pair of stars in the sky, and that he would personally enter Tarn's fabled library and find the oldest book on astrology to prove him right. The war ended in a truce, but Knight Harold kept his promise: he asked for his service to be rewarded with the honor of delivering the truce papers to Tarn. Upon arrival, Harold did the unthinkable and snuck into the library under cover of night to steal the book. He was discovered and he fled with the book. Harold's actions nearly started another war.

Tarn's calvary chased the lone knight all the way to Torhal's walls, where a young Annabelle had sensed his passion for a full day. She raised a hedge of thorned vines to protect his entry, and he delivered into her hands the book. As the story went, Annabelle chided him and pointed out numerous stars in the book were more beautiful than her eyes. Harold's retort had been swift and true: their beauty belonged to everyone and that made it less than hers, which belonged to no one. Despite the many romances Anise had read or studied, her great grandfather Harold was by far her favorite.

"I understand," she replied, a small smile on her lips.

"I know," Annelle replied, "Come, it has been some time since we worked the woods together. A bit of fresh, frigid air always lightens the crown. Last night's snow is still crisp."

Anise understood this, too, though she didn't necessarily agree. All the excitement and giddiness of a future as a married queen couldn't drown out the noise of terror she had heard. Such was its nature and, against her mother's many lessons, Anise could not help but hate that it was natural.

19 – Changing Love

Merelith

verything hurt. Even Eric's gentle caress down her spine hurt. It wasn't that Paol and Polo had been so hard on her, neither. As she rested in his embrace, Merelith realized the pain was coming from within. It was neither sharp nor overwhelming. It was more akin to a dull, permeating ache that left every inch of her skin tender, her bones feeling weary, and her senses…

There is so much of everything. Too much.

"I must admit, you're rather boring today."

"You'd be, too, if you felt this way," she growled.

Her ears thrummed with his chuckle, her chest tensed at the vibrations in his, and the lighting of the room seemed to pulsate until he stopped. The headache became that much worse, and she struggled to not scold him. He didn't know. He didn't understand.

"You're worrying me, Beta."

"Hmph."

Get over it, Eric. If you felt half as bad as I do…

Stop, Merelith. He's trying to help. He CAN help, if you'd let him.

I don't need help. I need…fuck, what DO I need?

At first, the changes had come slowly. The only outward differences had been her teeth, eyes, and nails. Even then, a good filing every morning kept the nails looking human. Most of the servants had taken notice of her eyes and teeth, though, so she endeavored to smile less and keep her bangs long. Come to think of it, maybe her hair had changed, too? She hadn't trimmed her bangs since a month before the calling…

I'm losing my hair. Or, well, getting different hair, I guess. Fur. More of it every day. I wonder if it will grow long on my head? I'll have to check the diagrams. Certainly getting long in some weird places. I hope Eric doesn't mind. Shit, why do I feel so tense? So, so worked up? It's like Tal and Kara are going insane in a crate named Merelith!

The closer the time came for the Crown Guard to leave, though, her changes had started to accelerate in small ways. It was only afternoon, and she'd already filed her nails twice. Seeing Eric's grin had set her whole body on fire with need, fear, and anger and…

What is happening to me?

Eric said, "You are becoming an angyr, goof. I thought you read about all of this?"

"H-huh?" Merelith stammered.

"You asked what is happening to you," Eric said with a hint of amusement.

"Oh. I…I didn't realize I said it aloud."

"Yeah, I figured. You gotta get out of that head, Mer. Talk to me. I'm here."

"Today," she mumbled.

"Don't be like that!" Eric chided, "I'll be fine. It's a big deal, too! I can't believe your father raised me up into the Crown Guard. I thought Polo was going to throw a crossbow at me when I told him. Even Lord Thadeus was surprised."

Merelith kept her eyes trained towards the door of her room, even as Eric pulled her into a tighter embrace. Her skull thrummed with his warm breath on her neck. Her instincts seemed ever more at war with one another. Anise's complaining or dark looks stirred up Tal's anger, Eric's teasing and flirting stirred up Kara's longing, Paol and Polo stirred up both depending on the day, and her parents endlessly asked how she was feeling when the obvious answer was that she wasn't feeling better *or* worse, just different.

"Please say something," Eric whispered, "I hate your silence."

"I don't know what to say, Eric."

"Tell me how it feels."

"I already have."

"Tell me again."

For your sake or mine?

Why do you smell different? Is it another woman? Should I care?

Of course, I care, but…I've never smelled him this way.

"Nothing seems the same. None of it is the same. Not anymore."

"What do you mean?"

Merelith sighed and winced at the volume of it, full of annoyance and grief. She mumbled an apology, but he didn't reply. Instead, the scout did what he did best: he waited. The angyrian guardian gathered her thoughts then tried to explain it. Again.

"Everything *looks* different, *smells* different, *tastes* different…it even sounds and feels different. My senses are sharpening but…but I thought it would make things more like they are, not less."

"How is it less?"

"You don't smell like my Eric."

The tension in his body was unmistakable. Perhaps he had found someone else? No, he wouldn't do that. She was certain of his love. For now. When he didn't deign to ask another question, she kept talking, if only to keep that awful silence at bay. She, too, hated the silence.

"There are things on you that are familiar. I smell Sneak. I smell the jerky on your breath. I smell the river water in your hair from yesterday's patrol. You've been in the empty quarter recently because I can smell the rot of those woods on you. Mama hasn't had time to cure the fungus because I can smell *that* on your boots."

Merelith paused, sighed again, then continued.

"There are things that *don't* smell familiar. I smell other women on you. Some of them I know – Mama probably led you by the elbow like she always does – and some of them I don't. You've been on other horses I don't recognize. You've worn clothing that smells new rather than worn. You're taking a tonic of some kind, but I don't know what it is for."

His laughter surprised her. It also sent a sort of ringing through her ears, pleasant and raw at the same time. He hugged her tightly and, through a snigger, explained himself.

"There's a pair of sisters in Anna who have been *throwing* themselves at me every time I pass through. They're so desperate that Sneak gets spooky anytime he sees them. I've been getting fitted for my new Crown Guard mail and jerkin. And the tonic…" Eric snorted, "…is something your mother made for me."

"My mother made you a tonic?" Merelith asked, rolling around to see into his eyes.

Eric grinned back and nodded.

"She said I might need help *keeping up* with you."

"*WHAT!?*" she nearly shouted, "You let my mother give you a tonic for your *DICK!?*"

Eric's cheeks flushed as he hastily replied, "Well, I didn't want to disappoint! You were already tough to follow before!"

"Eric Smith! Why in the world would my *mother* give you *sex potions?* You seriously can't come up with a better lie than *that!?*"

"Shh! Keep it down, you want the whole castle hearing!?" he shot back, "I'll never hear the end of it on the road if anyone else knows!"

The road. Tomorrow.

No. No, no, no, I'm not ready to be alone!

"Merelith? Hey! Hey, it's ok! I, I won't take it if you don't want me to…?"

Tears streamed down her cheeks, and she buried her face into his chest, if only to stop gazing up into those happy, gleaming eyes of his. A fucking tonic. Literally! She didn't know what was worse: that her mother had offered or that he had accepted. Sometimes, the queen was *too* aware of her daughter's needs.

"Is it…is it so you're in the *mood?* Like an aphrodisiac or…or…"

Eric retorted, "As if I need help being in the mood for you."

"You might," she choked out, "I won't be like this when you get back. Probably a lot worse."

"Or a lot better! Did a bit of reading on my own…haven't decided if getting my pelvis crushed is worth it, but why not? Always liked you best before you cut and shaved."

Merelith groaned, "That isn't funny, Eric."

"I didn't mean it to be funny, Mer. It's true."

She looked up at him to find him staring back, a serious look on his face.

"Everything might *feel* different, Merelith. Doesn't mean it *is*. I love you just as much right now, acting like a girl on her first bleeding, as I did that first time we lay down together. *Your* change doesn't change *me*."

Merelith let the words soak in. Her mind scattered in a hundred directions, most of which were questions. She didn't know what a first bleeding was like because, as an angyrian child, she didn't *have* any bleeding. Not until she fully transformed would she be fertile and, even then, only fertile for another angyr. Many of Torhal's guardians had left for the wildlands for that reason alone: the urge to find a mate, to have pups, to *not* be alone in their angyrism.

Anise had bled many times by now. Merelith had never asked her about it. Should she have? It occurred to the guardian that her sister knew *more* about being a woman than Merelith did. Sure, Merelith had enjoyed the fruits of passion, but Anise likely understood courting far better. Moreover, the princess had undoubtedly considered the future of any such relationship. Merelith had not because it didn't *have* a future. She would be an angyr. The *only* angyr in all Torhal, if not most of the freelands.

I'm changing. He isn't. Can this even work?
Should it? Just because he can stay with me doesn't mean…
"We can't have children," she blurted.
"Huh?"
"We…we can't settle down and have children. Have a little house near the castle? Or, or, um…we can't *really* be together, Eric. I mean, I'll be an angyr and you'll be human a-and…"
"How the *fuck* did we get on children?" Eric asked, his bewilderment obvious.

Merelith stammered, "W-w-well you said my change doesn't change you! I, I'm just saying th-that m-m-maybe…I dunno…I…"

Kara was in control, now, charging ahead full of terror and worry. In her mind, Merelith could almost *see* the instinct as a separate person. Or, well, an angyr. Beside her sat Tal, shaking its head and huffing with frustration. Behind them, or all around them, was Eric. A *real* alpha, a man unafraid to lead or pursue her. No matter where or how far Kara ran, it still ran toward Eric. No matter how much Tal ignored Eric, it still respected him. He was everything she wanted and needed. Both instincts knew it.

So why am I fighting this?

"Merelith, I can't imagine life without you at my side. I don't care what you look like or feel like or sound like or smell like or whatever other senses there are. I only care that it's you. You're *my* Beta and I want you."

"B-b-but…"

"But nothing!" he interrupted, his face a shade of anger, "No children? Fine. They're demanding and hungry and shit all over you for years…if we want children, we'll just be there for Anise's children or someone else's, who cares!? No cabin or nice house or whatever by the castle? Fine! We'll sleep in a hole in the woods. I'll have a flying dog to keep me warm!"

Merelith snorted, the idea of *him* curling into *her* both plausible and absurd. She managed a smile, but Eric kept on, determination on his brow as he professed his love.

"If people look at me like I'm weird or insane or what-have-you, so what? They *already* look at me that way. I didn't fall in love with you for their sake. I fell in love with you for *my* sake! I love you, Merelith Torhal, and if I must forge the ring myself so it fits your paw, I have every intention of making you my wife."

Then her smile was gone. So, too, her instincts. It was as if the entire world within and without had fallen away save for Eric holding her. His face relaxed at her bewilderment, and he chuckled. *Wife*. He had said the word she'd never really expected. Knew *not* to expect it.

"No, I haven't taken the tonic yet. My words. I know we're not there yet, Merelith but…I leave tomorrow, and I'd sooner die now than leave you not knowing how much I love you."

"I love you, too, Eric," she whispered, a smile creeping into her lips.

"I know."

They stared at each other for some time before she sat up from him and began to undress. He did the same, no words passing between them. The silence was full of tension and anticipation as they dropped the last of their garments on the floor and stared at each other. Eric looked as he always did: handsome in his nakedness, eyes full of hunger and muscles tensed with need. Merelith had never really cared for his looks so much as what lie beneath: a man whose wildness could keep up with hers.

Merelith, though, did look different and she made it a point to let him see before going to him. Her nails had lengthened in the matter of moments it took to undress. Her eyes glimmered silver in the failing light of sunset out the window. She grinned back at him, well aware her canines now stretched over her lips. His sharp eyes could see the thin hairs that had thickened across her body, too fine to be easily seen except between her breasts and thighs, but not for long. There were yet more changes he couldn't see underneath her sensitive skin.

Merelith cleared her throat and said quietly, "Be gentle, please. I…I'm not sure…"

"Do whatever you need to do, Merelith. I only ask you do it with me."

Tal roared with lust and Kara slowed itself to be comforted. Merelith was unsure what to expect as she stepped towards him. Eric encircled her waist. Tal demanded she bite and claw and *fuck*. Kara whimpered to push into his arms deeper, howled for his kisses to cover her, and dreamed of the future as wife and mate. The two felt so at odds with each other in their intensity.

Yet they are the same person. That's what Mama would say. Mama. Hmm…

"Need your tonic?" she whispered, smiling as he chuckled.

"Let's see how it goes, yeah?" he replied.

"I'm sorry it's been so long."

"I'm sorry it will soon be longer."

He gasped as she dug her fingernails into his back but didn't scold her. Both instincts worked as one, intentions different but their actions the same. She pressed into him but also pressed him backwards to her bed. The angyrian girl crawled atop and wasted no time taking Eric into her but she also did so with deliberate calm. When he tried to pull her into a kiss, she dodged it and bit into his shoulder but made sure to lap at the wound left behind until it no longer bled.

All through the evening, past dinner and into the night, Merelith embraced her instincts. There were distinct moments of each. Tal was indefatigable, joyfully testing and taxing Eric's endurance and pain tolerance. Kara was lachrymose, grieving his too-near departure and determined to know and minister every inch of his body. Eric responded to both in perfect harmony, as if possessed of his own parallel instincts. Perhaps he was, the guardian wondered more than once.

For the briefest of moments, she wished Eric could be angyr. Most of the night, though, Merelith tried to forget she *was* angyr. She loved her instincts, loved how they guided her with him, loved that he so easily matched them with her. Yet it didn't change the underlying fear and anger of earlier. It didn't change that they weren't the same.

She didn't want people to look at him like he was weird. She didn't want him to sleep in a hole in the woods. She didn't want him to find joy in other's children instead of his own. Increasingly, as their lovemaking ended and he slumbered beside her, Merelith realized she loved being angyr but loved Eric *more*. The desperation of her sister, the fears her mother told her of, the few stories she had of her angyrian aunt…they all fell into place.

It wasn't supposed to feel like a curse, but it did. She knew she couldn't change it. And, as she finally fell into sleep beside Eric, she resolved to accept that it *didn't matter*. Eric loved her more, too, and that was more than she could have really hoped for. He was leaving to war, but she had faith he would return. More than that, no matter how different she looked, she had faith he meant every word he'd said: he would return and *still* love her. It was this thought that saw both Tal and Kara curl into each other, deep in her wild heart, and allow sleep to come.

20 – Perfectionist

Lorath

The timing could not be more perfect. Am I finally feeling hope? The advisor with too-old eyes stood upon the battlements of his king's castle and watched the teeming host below. Almost twelve thousand strong, the army commanded by Tobias Galrend and his consort was impressive. Yet Lorath bit down the urge to revel in the moment. Twelve thousand was a fine army, but it paled in comparison to the forces the kingdom had controlled in centuries past.

At the end of the War for Freedom, Tamar Galrend – son of Autarch Galrend – had led a host of *forty* thousand, of which almost five thousand had been mounted. Each man had worn family armor and been steeped in the traditions of war from childhood. Tamar had secured most of the freelands with that army in the aftermath of his father's sacrifice. His army had butchered the crazed and wild angyrian army of the autarchy and sent its surviving rulers fleeing across the wardens to form the Pentarchy. Lorath cast an eye to the east and scowled.

If only that had been enough.

"Lorath! Why so glum, my friend? Do you still find our army lacking?"

Our army. Hmph.

Lorath turned about to find Tobias approaching him with arms wide and a cruel grin on his lips. The Saltsword forced a smile and bowed his head in submission.

"I dwell on what remains to be done, my king. Your forces are more than adequate for the task ahead. Anar Tota will fall to you."

Tobias clapped his hands on Lorath's shoulders and replied, "But one step more unto a glorious future!"

But one step more…by the crowns, why did it have to be you?

"Indeed, My King."

"Are you well, Lorath?" Tobias suddenly asked.

Lorath shoved down his inner turmoil, a strong survival instinct reminding him who Tobias was – and was not – and that a great many more steps remained on his own path. He forced his smile ever wider, shrugged and winked at the young immortal.

"Many years I have waited to see such glory. I worry my bones will not see me to the end of your rise across the freelands. My mind turns towards ensuring you are not alone in that endeavor."

Tobias laughed and retorted, "You are a schemer and a planner to the end of time! Galrend already owes you a debt it cannot repay, Lorath. Allow me to share some of your wisdom with *you*: leave tomorrow to tomorrow's advisor."

The king then swept an arm out over the host below and chuckled. He squeezed Lorath's shoulder with an iron grip that the advisor pretended was too rough. It had the intended effect, for Tobias' smile turned malevolent and his voice impossibly *more* arrogant.

"Leave today to today's *emperor.*"

Insufferable buffoon. Perhaps I should teach you to LOSE to that nobody in Torhal? Bah. Smile and survive, Lorath. That is what father would say.

"I will endeavor to do just that" Lorath paused, then added, "My Emperor."

Tobias' eyes glowed with victorious amusement, and it was all Lorath could do to not shove the immortal off the battlements then and there. How the Galrend line had descended into such poor stock, the advisor struggled to stomach. Lorath knew the answer. Much as he knew the answer for why much of the world was the way it was. Yet a former mentor had spoken true: those who failed to study history were doomed to repeat it; those who *did* study history were doomed to watch. Galrend's steady tumble into obscurity could be traced all the way back to Tamar and his father's absence.

The current king of Galrend nodded with self-assurance then tapped Lorath on the chest as he spoke, his tone shifting to one of authority. Once more, Lorath had to suppress inner emotions at the sound of his king's voice. He endeavored to pay attention while savoring that soon, very soon, he'd hopefully be rid of Galrend's last descendant and his insatiable pride.

"I want you to accompany me to Anar Tota. I am confident I can defeat Orren, but I am not so foolish as to turn away wise counsel and training. I have hand-picked twenty men, as you suggested, and trained them according to your instruction, Saltsword."

Lorath tried to hide a grimace. He was neither needed at Anar Tota nor did he wish to *be* there. More important matters demanded his attention.

"My King, I appreciate your desire for greater instruction, truly, but I am due to go to Tarn and begin expanding our relations there. More coin may be needed should Torhal opt for a siege. The additional aid will serve as yet another aforementioned step."

"King Aaron is an ass and would rather wait until Annelle and I bloody each other before choosing a side, if any!" Tobias countered, "Still, march with us. It will delay you only two months, if that. Once Anar Tota is taken, I will release you to continue south."

Those two months could mean the difference between gaining or losing Aaron, you fool. Would that everyone else could understand the timing so intricately placed…Oh, stop it! Adapt. Again.

"If it pleases Your Majesty, may I send couriers ahead? It will not make as much of an impact, but every advantage counts."

"Do what you must, Lorath" Tobias replied, his tone terse, "You travel with us."

Warning enough, Tobias.

Lorath bowed deeply and the king sniffed in arrogant dismissal. The advisor hastened from the battlements into the castle, all the while fuming at being stymied. In all his years of guiding and directing, no ruler had been *more* problematic than Tobias Galrend. The young king's egotism both infuriated and grieved Lorath.

It is no small wonder you lost Annelle to that nobody. You are fortunate Talya craves your crown enough to endure bedding you! The year cannot pass quickly enough.

Lorath stopped dead in his tracks then shook his head.

"What am I *thinking?*" he murmured in disdain.

Then he continued towards his quarters, introspection overtaking his former rage.

Time is NOT on our side! Idiot. I've been around him too much and now am becoming LIKE him. I desperately needed that trip to Tarn…get over it! Adapt. Smile and survive. Win the long game. I have endured far worse, have maneuvered from more inferior positions, and have grasped victory from the jaws of defeat countless times. This is no different. I am but surrounded by impatient children! I need only frame their whims within mine.

Lorath arrived at his room, took a deep breath, and entered only for his long exhale to catch at what he saw: Lady Talya leaning over his desk, apparently rifling through his many papers and letters. Years of practice kept him from yelling at her. Many more years than that convinced him to say nothing at all and instead glare.

"Such a dour face, Lorath."

"How may I assist you, *Consort?*"

Talya's sweet smile instantly melted into a venomous glare. Lorath didn't resist his own smirk. Some children were too headstrong to control directly, but a well-placed title and insult could work wonders. Tobias *had* wanted to call her nothing at all. A certain advisor had known giving Talya just a taste of power in title would be far more effective in leashing the cult leader.

"You write to many places. Too many places. Why?"

Oh, you wish to snoop about, little bitch? Has your dog been rutting around and now you see my warnings were valid? Or are you just impatient like your would-be husband?

"Kingdoms are built upon the trust of men. Empires are built upon the trust of kings."

"Not queens?" she replied in a whisper.

"There will not be a need for a queen if she is empress."

Oh, such hunger! You will make a fine autarch, Talya. Just keep those beautiful legs closed and your ears open. There is so much I can give you. If you survive long enough to grasp it.

Lorath's smirk faded into a kind smile, and he continued into his room. He paid no mind to her leaning over him as he sat at his desk and began to reorder the letters as if nothing had occurred beyond the small chaos of a curious child. Children like Tobias would be furious to see their 'work' undone. Yet Talya only watched. And waited for him to say more. Lorath carefully fed the bitch the table scraps she so desired.

"I had planned to go to Tarn to resume securing King Aaron's support, but Tobias insists I come along to Anar Tota. It would seem yet more letters will be needed, now."

"I told him to not worry," Talya replied, "He seems like an idiot to me most days, but he easily defeated ten of mine yesterday. Tobias is an excellent warrior."

"I am glad to hear that. I share your opinion. He should have no difficulty with Orren."

"Are you certain Annelle's pet will be there?"

She means Orren. I think. Perhaps I should make sure? No. I am the adult. Guide. Direct.

"Orren will come because they know Tobias will be there."

"And Torhal's angyr? What of her?"

"By my math, Merelith Torhal will very soon reach a point of being utterly useless for at least several weeks if not months. She will not be present."

"Why is she so late? You said…"

"What I said should not be spoken so loudly."

Lorath glanced at Talya and found her glaring at him once more. Then she averted her eyes towards the door to his room and sighed. He suppressed his grin when she nodded in careful submission. The lady *always* wanted to talk about the child and Lorath *always* had to suppress that desire. The result was a leash forged of blood rather than coin, the best sort in his experienced opinion.

Lorath continued, "Torhal's guardians are different. They normally take longer to transform, hence our own waiting. She is of little use to you, Talya, until she has her feathers. Even then, I wouldn't risk a ritual until we *know* Merelith has quickened. I haven't found a single record regarding transference with an incomplete angyr."

"My hound cannot remain in Torhal to observe…Tobias has called him here."

Lorath shrugged and replied, "It is just as well. We need Annelle's entire focus on Anar Tota. Do your work, Talya, and the word *queen* won't have any meaning to you by end of winter."

The consort flared her nostrils then bared her teeth in a feral grin. Lorath ignored all of this, his eyes kept on his desk. She huffed in amusement and then graced his neck and shoulders with her arms.

"How?" she whispered, "How do you not care for me, Lorath? I've not seen you cast eyes towards my most handsome men. Do you simply not care for what is beautiful?"

The man with too-old eyes furrowed his brow, as if in thought. Then Lorath stared right into Talya's eyes as he answered.

"Beauty is the absence of blemish. What then is more beautiful than the void?"

"The void is *nothing*, Lorath," she said cautiously, "Emptiness is not beautiful."

Lorath chuckled and Talya recoiled from him. Whatever magic she sensed about him, she obviously wanted to be clear of it. The Saltsword shrugged.

"Indeed. It is perfection. I have long loved that which is perfect."

Talya quivered in fury as she turned her nose up at him and stormed out of his room. She paused at his door, cast him a final glare, and snorted.

"The void is empty for a reason, Lorath. It destroys and consumes everything."

Then she was gone and Lorath found himself able to chuckle even louder.

Indeed. You only make my point.

21 – A Crown Too Heavy

Anise

Even covered in muddy snow with the stench of horse and mule dung mixed in along every street, Anna was still a beautiful town. The departure of the first and second companies of Torhal had left an indelible mark, though, one Anise couldn't help but notice as she strolled the streets, a half-dozen royal guards always within thirty feet of her. For being Torhal's largest city – really its *only* city – the emptiness surrounding Anise was striking.

She meandered along the southern edge of the city, where the wooden and stone buildings gave way to vendor stalls and tents: the high market, named for its claim as the highest elevation of any in the freelands. It was nearly empty now, not all that unusual given winter had begun, but only a few weeks before it had been packed like the weeks right after the first snowmelt. Merchants had swarmed from Anar Tota to offload their goods before making south towards Tarn, where they would wait for the war to end. Now they were all gone, save a lone painted wagon with a young mule gnawing away at moldy hay beside it.

Anise's eyes drew up from the high market to what loom beyond: the Elder Tower. The first, and largest, of the four strongholds connected by Torhal's famous wall. It was almost the width of Castle Torhal, but the similarities ended there. The Elder Tower was *seven* stories tall, each floor identically built: garrison, armory, and stairs in the center, siege engines, crenulated battlements, and murder holes on the exterior. Only the top floor and roof were different: a large bedroom and bathing room, a dining room, three fireplaces, and a simple kitchen. The roof was bare save for ancient markings predating the War for Freedom: Anisterosa's personal summoning circle while experimenting on Torhal of old.

No queen had yet dared to use the ancient ritual site, for fear of magical traps unseen. Anise didn't blame them, having seen it a few summers ago. Despite the glorious wind blowing between the

Wardens on either side of the pass into Torhal, the summoning circle always stank of otherworldly death.

"Is everything alright, young lady?"

Anise startled at the greeting and looked down to see an elderly woman hobbling towards her from the painted wagon. A witch, judging by the array of trinkets on her neck and wrists. The royal guards wasted little time placing themselves between the woman and Anise.

"Stand down, she's fine," Anise said in a clipped tone, forcing a smile.

"Oh, oh my…such handsome, strapping men!" the witch teased, "what would my poor daughters think, knowing such fine men were in Torhal!"

Anise eyed the old lady as she approached, ogling the royal guards before finally glancing at her with apparent concern.

"They don't seem like brutes…are you alright?"

Anise chuckled and replied, "Yes, matron. I am well."

"*Matron*, oh…*oh*…you have gifts! What a lovely surprise! I had heard a tale that Torhal was *filled* with magic, but I've yet to see any at all. In fact, all I've seen are men and all I've heard is the sound of fear."

"Galrend seeks to invade Anar Tota, soon. Did you not know?"

The matron paled and Anise felt sorry for the old lady. The crown princess studied the wagon, soaking in every detail: iron wheels, rather than wood. Bright blues and reds, not the typical greens and yellows of the north. She studied the witch, too, clad in a shawl too thin for such weather and shoes too dainty for snow.

"From where in the south do you hail?" Anise asked, her tone pleasant.

"G-gwentia, sweety…oh, war…oh, oh…oh my."

"Do not fret, matron, if you leave today or tomorrow, you should have plenty of time to get out of harm's way."

"No, n-no no no! I have kin in Anar Tota, they will need my skills. Oh, how dreadful…how awful!" the witch turned on her heel and began hobbling back to her wagon, "St-stupid. So stupid. I knew better than to come here looking for that angyrian witch…oh! Stupid, stupid."

Anise cocked an eyebrow.

"Angyrian witch?" she asked, "In Torhal?"

Yet the old woman was already out of earshot, it seemed. So, Anise followed, curiosity making the day more interesting than it had been. Besides, her mother had told her many times that kindly witches were always worthwhile company. The guard watched the elder intently, but the crown princess ignored them as she hurried to the wagon's stair and helped the matron to the door.

"Oh, thank you, sweety! I…say, you look familiar? Do you by chance know a woman named Anise? Anise Torhal?"

Anise smirked and replied, "That would be *me*, matron. Crown Princess Anise II, daughter of King Orren and Queen Annelle."

The matron studied her for a moment and Anise was surprised to see the woman frown.

"No. Anise's mother was named Annabelle. And besides, she'd be much older than *you*."

She said it with such matter-of-fact surety that it took a moment for Anise to register what the woman was implying: the witch had *known* Anise's grandmother.

"Y-yes, that is correct. Annelle is *that* Anise's daughter. I am her granddaughter," Anise explained as calmly as she could.

The matron's eyes went wide as she whispered, "Then…oh. Oh my. Perhaps *you* can help me! Um, um, um…one moment! I'll be right back! D-don't you go anywhere *little* Anise!"

The matron fumbled her wagon door open and scurried inside. All manner of clatter and noise issued forth. Anise asked if the witch was alright, but she only heard the old woman mutter under her breath something about stacking pots somewhere other than by the brooms. Anise peered in, but the wagon was eerily dark despite a bright afternoon sun shining overhead. The only window was set into the door, yet even with the door standing open, it was as if Anise could only see a few feet into the interior. She nearly yelped when the witch hobbled forth, right into her.

"This!" the witch said triumphantly, holding out a rather large feather to Anise, "Is for you! Come, come…I'll show you which mountain to go to."

"W-what? I, I don't…"

"Come, come! Right here."

The witch motioned to inside the wagon and Anise clambered in. The guard watched warily but seemed to relax when she winked at one of them and forced a smile. The gloom of the wagon made it hard to see, until the witch pulled back a curtain and sunlight splashed over the equally colorful interior. Anise went to the window as the old witch pointed outside. She whispered excitedly while jabbing a finger towards the mountains in the distance.

"There's an old, old mountain up there, see it? Called the Silver Alpha, they say. Very, very special magic there, by the by, if you ever want to feel the *good* stuff. Anyways, straight down its right side, see that little bump next to it? There. That's where she's at."

"Uh…who, matron?"

"The angyrian witch! If you take that feather to her, she'll enchant it so I can cure my poor grandson of his angyrism. I'd go myself but, well, war has a habit of making a mess of *everything!*"

Anise eyed the feather and felt a tingling in her fingers as she realized what sort of feather it was: angyrian. Large and brilliant white, it could have been mistaken for the flight feather of a great bird of prey except for its unusual texture: silky soft, yet unusually sharp along its edges. Anise lightly flexed the rachis and was amazed to see and feel the vane harden like stone, its edges sharp as any sword her royal guard carried.

"This is his?" she asked.

"Yup! Rumor has it she just needs one of his feathers. Of course, I can compensate you, little Anise. May have to wait until this all blows over, but…."

"She can *cure* angyrism?"

That's impossible. Every single book in the scriptorium makes that clear.

"So the claim goes!" replied the witch with a hearty laugh, "Tell her it's from Maybury."

"Is that, um, is that your name?"

The witch blinked at her with mild shock, then looked down at the muddy snow that had been tracked inside and itched her nose. Then she looked at Anise and gulped.

"I suppose it is. Hmm. I really am forgetting things these days. So, will you go?"

"Oh! Uh, well…that's a long way and war is here…"

Maybury eyed Anise then sighed and held out a hand for the large feather. Anise hesitated then gave it back. The old witch sniffed then sighed again.

"Look," she said under her breath, casting an eye toward the guards outside, "I know a thing or two about being *stuck*, Anise Torhal. Been my profession getting folks untangled for a long, long time. You, my girl, look more tied up than a pig on a spit."

Anise bit back the urge to sick the royal guard on the witch at once. Yet Maybury didn't speak with malice or annoyance. She spoke with kindness.

"I came up here to help my idiot daughter who somehow thought giving birth to a *monster* was a clever idea. He's a sweet boy, but that doesn't change there are moments when he doesn't even know his own kin from the rabbits he likes to chase. It isn't your problem to solve. Yet, I get the sense that you might have a problem of your own."

It was Anise's turn to study the muddy snow and itch her nose. She nodded agreement but said nothing as the witch held out the feather a second time.

"Dunno what you're chasing, girl. Or running from. What I *do* know is that if a war is coming, the crown princess ought to be by her father, not milling around an empty market and talking to nobody witches handing out unusually large feathers."

Anise managed a thin smile. Maybury matched it as the crown princess took the feather again. The witch nodded and winked, then pointed out the window a final time.

"She's up there, somewhere. If she's anything like the rumors, she'll find you, not the other way 'round. Best think carefully. Talk it over with your mother before you go. I've got more of his feathers if you decide not to. I'll get my family seen to in Anar Tota and…well, you'll either be here or you won't. Powers unknown, I hope you are."

The powers unknown. Now *that* was a saying she'd never heard anyone say. More importantly, Anise had only read it a handful of times in books as old as the castle. Books that had survived the War for Freedom. She looked Maybury over then nodded, pocketing the feather. *How* she was going to trek up into the mountains was anyone's guess, but just feeling the feather sparked something she'd not felt in years.

"Is there anything I can do to make your travels safer, Maybury?" Anise asked.

"Get yourself untangled, little Anise. Crowns and magic and war are dangerous things when they're all tangled up. Do that, and the entire *world* will be safer."

Anise nodded then made to leave the wagon. She eyed her six guards and wondered how in that same world she was going to explain such an encounter to her mother. Any idea of *curing* Merelith could not possibly end well. The witch was right: Anise *was* tangled up. No thanks to her mother and father.

"Ok, Vernon! Hitch up!"

The young mule cocked a long ear then obediently moped over to the wagon's harness and pushed itself under. Maybury wasted little time strapping him in before clambering atop her wagon. Above Anise and her various guards, Maybury squinted against the sun and gave a toothy smile.

"Good luck, Crown Princess. Whatever you do."

Then she snapped the reins and a mule too tiny pulled a wagon too large as if it were made of air and little else. Anise felt the edges of the feather in her pocket as she turned toward Anna, her guards in tow. They asked her what the witch had said, no doubt hoping for a vision of the war, but the crown princess only told them the matron was just being polite, visiting with a fellow magic-user. Each time she stroked the feather in her pocket, the same strange feeling permeated her chest.

Angyrism couldn't be cured, said every book in the castle she called home. Angyr were not monsters, said every queen before Anise. Maybury had said there were *rumors* of an angyrian witch. The more Anise considered the entire encounter, the more unreal it felt. Except the feather in her pocket was *very* real. The way Maybury had known that the crown princess did indeed feel like a pig on a spit, slowly roasting over a destiny she couldn't avoid had been real, too.

Above all, the feeling in her chest was real: hope. For Merelith as much as herself.

22 – No Goodbyes

Merelith

It was a bright, beautiful winter morning as King Orren mounted his steed at the center of his crown guard. The elder tower loomed to the east, Anna to the west, with the last of Torhal's forces hemmed between the two. Much of the kingdom's people had journeyed to see the king ride off to war. The royal guard maintained a loose perimeter around the royal family, the trio of women lined up to bid the king farewell and good fortune.

Merelith stood betwixt her mother and sister, an unusual placement given the circumstances. By rights, the crown princess always stood at the side of the queen. Yet today, Anise had chosen to stand beside Merelith rather than her own mother. By all appearances, Anise was validating the guardian's role as her chief protector. Those that knew better would suspect Anise had yet to forgive her mother for sending Orren to war. Or that Annelle had not forgiven her daughter for the words spoken two weeks ago.

Mama is desperate to cry. Poor thing. Tonight will be very, very long.

We could dance and sing? She seemed to enjoy it last night. Even Anise smiled a little!

Not with Anise scowling as she is. Why does she keep ogling me? I can't exactly HIDE these ears anymore. Maybe it's the dress? Mama said to wear something pretty!

The guardian stood out like a sore thumb compared to the queen and crown princess. Annelle wore a veridian dress with a sweeping cape of burnt orange, the crest of Torhal stitched in silver upon it. Anise was dressed head to toe in forest greens and browns, the traditional Torhalian outfit muted compared to what her sister wore: a violent red dress cut more like a summer gown. Merelith wore no gloves nor cloak, her down fur thick enough to provide warmth her human counterparts lacked. Despite her choice of clothes, most folk were more interested in her long, tufted ears and unusually thick, black fingernails.

Merelith glanced over at her sister to catch Anise quickly looking away, burying her scowl too slow. Angyrian smell and sight couldn't discern if the princess was directing her displeasure at her sister or her mother. Merelith assumed it was their mother, although Anise had yet to apologize for what she'd said. The guardian whispered a sigh and already hoped her father's victory was swift.

You two can't smell emotion yet, can you? No…not yet. Hmm. Perhaps it would be best to just focus on Mama and Papa. I just wish I knew what was going on in that head of yours, sister. I know this can't be easy for you.

"Your Highness? Is something wrong?" whispered the queen.

Merelith's left ear cocked backward at the sound of her mother's voice, a strange sensation she was still growing accustomed to. Anise deliberately guided her eyes around Merelith's face to the queen, then forced a smile only for it to falter.

"N-no, Your Majesty" she mumbled.

Then a single tear rolled down her cheek. Annelle visibly gulped and nodded silent understanding. The guardian thought to share encouraging words, but then heard the king kick his horse into a slow trot towards them. All three turned to watch Orren approach, his crowned helm cradled in an arm. The king paused before and over them wearing a grim smile.

"It is time, My Queen" he said, his words a deliberate echo of the last king to leave.

Annelle heaved a heavy breath and replied between tight lips, "Yes, My King."

Orren didn't let his gaze linger on her, no doubt all too aware she would burst into tears at any moment. He darted his eyes to Anise, who bowed her head at his greeting.

"Crown Princess."

"King" she replied, her chin lifting to meet his stare.

"Above all else, your mother serves the people. Above all else, I command you to serve *her*. When her light falters, to you falls the task of kindling that flame in my absence. When her voice is quiet, to you belongs the burden of shouting for her. When her spirit is lonely, upon your shoulders will she find the promise of family. Your crown is a circle, Princess Anise II, to be used to surround the one I charge you with."

Anise gulped again and bowed her head. She stepped forward so that her father could lean down and kiss her hand, then her cheek, then her forehead. He whispered into her ear, loud enough for the royal family and no one else.

"Do not be afraid, Anise. Torhal will never fail you."

"Y-yes, Your Majesty" she whispered back.

Orren nodded with a warm smile, then sat back up. The king turned his gaze upon Merelith and returned her wild grin. Kara grieved alongside her mother and sister, but Tal did not. No, the dominant instinct had held the reigns much of the morning, no doubt buoyed by Eric's declaration the day before. The king winked at her then hailed her by title.

"Guardian" he said, a little louder so that others might hear.

Merelith's throat bobbed in pride before she replied, "Papa."

Kara pined in sorrow, demanding Merelith's heart break a little. Orren's surely did as his lip quivered, whatever speech he had planned lost to her reply. The king cleared his throat, glanced up at the sky as if to let the sunshine return his senses to him, then gazed at Merelith again. Through it all, the guardian watched him with animalistic intensity and stillness. Orren huffed then chuckled before issuing his command.

"Upon your mother's brow rests the past of Torhal. Upon the brow of your sister rests its future. Upon you rests this age, with all its woes and danger. A queen can lead a nation into war. A princess can lead a people out of it. But a guardian…to you, Guardian Merelith Torhal, falls the burden of protecting that queen and princess. To you falls the preservation of both past and future, today. I charge you with the lives of your mother and sister. *Our* family, Guardian."

Merelith bowed her head, deeper than anytime she had before. She stepped forward to her father and reached a hand into his. He kissed it, then her cheek, then paused before moving to her forehead. Over the din of the waiting crown guard, her mother heard his whisper and smiled.

"Do not be afraid, Merelith. Your instincts will never fail you."

Merelith nodded and then mumbled, "They don't know what to make of this."

"No, Merelith. They know *exactly* what to make of this. Trust them and you will, too."

"Yes Pa…Y-your Majesty."

Orren smirked, kissed her forehead, then winked.

"I will *always* be Papa first, my little Alpha" he then sat up, glanced at Anise, and added, "To both of you."

The king looked upon Annelle and the queen released an unsteady breath as she walked towards him. All eyes were on the queen as she reached up to clasp Orren's gauntlet, both rulers the picture of royals bound by duty. Tal kept Merelith's brow steady even as Kara flooded her heart with grief: for the love of her parents as much as her love for Eric.

"Annelle."

"Orren."

The king beamed at her and then shook his head with mirth.

"I have not given you orders before. I am not going to start now."

Annelle choked out a chuckle but seemed unable to form a retort. Orren gripped her hand tightly and cleared his own throat before finishing.

"I love our people. I love our kingdom. I swore that I would, for I knew you would choose no man who saw them as anything less than worthy of love."

He bent down to her, even as he raised his voice a little.

"But I did *not* swear I would love you."

Annelle smiled, even as those surrounding them – including her own daughters – gaped at the unusual declaration. Annelle raised her other hand to rest on his cheek and her smile widened to a silly grin.

"No. No you did not, Orren," she whispered.

"Should I? Lest you lock the gate and not let me back in?"

The crown guard roared with laughter and the surrounding citizenry relaxed. Annelle chuckled and shook her head. Merelith grinned with pride, the banter of her parents always a salve during grim times. When the din had quieted, for all wanted to hear her retort, she spoke.

"No, lest you lock the gate and never let me leave, for I know you would keep me to yourself."

Orren nodded and said, "Indeed. Shall I instead swear to never love another?"

"No, my people need your love, Orren."

"Shall I swear to love only that which *you* love, Annelle?"

"No, for I cannot love myself."

Her daughters each cocked eyebrows at the exchange, as did others, but the older crown guards – those who had heard this vow before – bowed their heads in solemn respect. The instincts seemed to quiet within the guardian, as if to bear witness to a magic unfamiliar to them.

"Then what shall I swear, my queen, my love, my mate?"

"Swear nothing, my king, my love, my mate, for I am already those things and need nothing more."

"Then I will swear nothing and have everything instead."

"Then I will be everything and have need of nothing instead."

"I love you, Annelle."

"I l-love you, Orren."

Her voice broke as he leaned down for a kiss.

She murmured, "R-return to me, Orren. P-p-please return."

"Ask me to swear it and I will," he whispered.

Annelle's brows knitted together tightly, rage and grief and joy and sass openly fighting across her heart. She hated his calm, loved his humor, grieved his courage, and laughed at his offer. The queen shook her head, and the king kissed her again. Oaths were made to be broken, as the saying went, and Torhalians were ever keen to not make them between each other. Instead, she gazed into his eyes and willed her voice under control.

"For Torhal," she stated.

"For Torhal," he replied.

A final kiss, then he was up and riding away without another word. In all their years of marriage, they had never said goodbye. This was the first time Merelith wondered if it was arrogant not to do so. The crown guard began to fall in behind their king, though in no particular order. Some lingered, still wishing their spouses or families goodbye. One made his way toward the royal family and Merelith was surprised to see Eric step off his horse and kneel before them.

"May I have a final word with the guardian?" he asked to the ground.

Annelle smirked and said with regal authority, "That is for her to decide."

Merelith snorted and said with snark, "Stand up, you goof. Now your legs are all muddy!"

Eric did as he was told, glanced at his once-clean leggings, and shrugged. He then visibly gulped, began to open his mouth and say something, when Merelith decidedly shut him up with a passionate kiss. One that set the crown guard hollering with surprise and whooping with zeal. Anise blanched and turned away, but Annelle watched, her smirk never faltering. When Merelith released his lips, the guardian was certain her ears had lengthened another finger-width.

Wife. Mate. You must return, Eric Smith, or I will hunt all the freelands for you.

"Whatever it is, tell me when you get back," she said with a hoarse whisper.

"O-o-ok," he said, eyes wide with surprise and a hint of fear, "Yeah. S-sure. Um…can I have another?"

The queen *did* guffaw at that, along with the others who heard, even as her eldest easily leaned in for a longer, if more delicate kiss. When Merelith lightly nicked Eric's ear with a sharp tooth, she was surprised the man didn't flinch. Anise, though, did. The guardian ignored the princess, even as both instincts were troubled by her sister's response.

"Until next time," he murmured, forehead to hers.

"Until next time," she replied, nodding before standing back from him.

Eric turned to the crown princess, bowed, then did so again to the queen. Annelle kept her smile tight as he gulped again under her gaze, then hastily mounted his new warhorse and set off towards the others. A great deal of back-clapping and teasing ensued, which only saw Merelith grin as broadly as her lover. The guardian was glad her hearing wasn't *too* sharp yet, for she was confident most of those present wondered how such a love could survive the coming months.

Tal snorted in arrogant dismissal while Kara curled beneath its partner in content apathy. A mate had been found, as far as they were concerned, and the taste of Eric's blood washed away any fears for the moment. The royal family watched King Torhal ride out with his crown guard, toward Anar Tota and the approaching army of Galrend. Not until the ancient gate of the Elder Tower ground shut did they begin returning to the castle.

. . .

"So, where will you be tomorrow?"

The guardian tried to sound pleasant as she asked. Her sister's raised eyebrow and grimace told Merelith that this conversation wasn't going to be as hard as she expected. It was going to be so, so much worse. They'd not made it five steps into the castle and Anise was retreating from her guardian's presence.

"Why do you care?"

Because I'm your fucking guardian!

Ease up, Tal! Good grief.

Well, I was. Eric's gone now and…

Shit, focus Kara. Both of you, relax!

Papa needs me to do this. So does Mama. Besides, I want to. I really do.

Merelith sighed, took a deep breath, and before she could answer, Anise was already walking away. The guardian stole a glance towards her mother, now standing by the family portrait in the great hall. The queen glanced back and tilted her head ever so slightly. *Don't give up so easily.* The angyrian woman rolled her eyes, nodded tersely, then followed after the crown princess. She tried to keep her ears from instinctively pinning as she called after Anise.

"Anise! Hey, wait up."

"You are to address me by my title" Anise replied, not even looking at her sister.

Merelith clenched her fists then winced, the motion gouging her long nails into her palms. She could hardly wait to have paws, if only to not have to file the damn things anymore. She continued to follow Anise, who seemed to be making her way to her bedroom, no doubt to shut Merelith out before she made any progress.

Oh…oh stars, that's how you want to play this?

Easy, Tal. She's just being…off. It's just been a tough day, that's all.

She's always off, Kara! Might be time I put her ON. Preferably on a floor with no rug.

That won't help anything, Tal! She's scared. You heard what Papa said.

She's always scared! We could be fully transformed and eating bolts for breakfast, and she'd still be scared. It's time to take the claws out and…

Anise stopped, whirled around, and flatly said, "You really need to learn to control that."

Merelith replied, "Control…what?"

Anise motioned around her sister and simply said, "That."

"What the fuck is *that* supposed to mean?"

"Cursing in my presence won't be tolerated. If you can't act like a civilized person, I have no need of you."

"*Civilized?*"

"What you did earlier today was appalling, *Guardian*. Our people need to have faith in your ability to protect and serve, not flirt and entertain."

Merelith was stunned. So much so that even the instincts were eerily quiet, perhaps too wounded to do anything but retreat to where she couldn't feel them. Anise flared her nostrils and continued, as if her sister's silence were permission to keep haranguing her.

"You deliberately didn't refer to our king by his title and then ruined the sanctity of his parting with our queen by publicly declaring your own passions with a soldier not even a month into his promotion. A soldier you won't even be able to have relations with when he returns, *if* he returns, at the rate your transformation is progressing. Speaking of which, what possessed you to dress in such a way as to *flaunt* your oversized ears, nails, and breasts?"

Ruined their parting.

Can't even have relations with when he returns.

If he returns.

Flaunt? Oversized?

Merelith was speechless. She half-prayed her mother somehow could hear the vitriol spilling forth from her sister's mouth. Why? What had she done to deserve such treatment? The instincts curled tightly into one another, as if forming a ball of nothingness in her heart.

"Well?" Anise demanded, her chin tilting up as if challenging her sister to speak.

Then Tal and Kara rushed forward in unison. Like dogs on a leash just shy of Anise's throat. Or that's how it felt to Merelith, who was holding the other end of that leash. Tal yearned to dig oversized nails into Anise's powdered cheeks and listen to her scream with oversized ears. Kara demanded to clamp a hand around Anise's throat and simply prevent her making a noise ever again. *Never* had the instincts wanted to harm Anise. Merelith…didn't know what she wanted. Not this. She just wanted what was between her and her sister to not be *this*.

"I don't want this," she whispered.

"Yes, well, neither do I" Anise replied flippantly, turning on her heel to continue marching off.

"I don't want you to be my queen."

Anise stopped dead in her tracks. Merelith knew she felt the words more than heard them. They had been spoken by instinct, laced with lethal and unforgiving rage. The crown princess turned slowly, as if half-expecting Merelith to be descending on her in feral violence, but found the hallway empty, the guardian nowhere in sight.

Merelith prayed her absence either haunted Anise into insanity or brought the peace the crown princess so desperately needed. She did not care which. In a matter of hours, Merelith's ears were twice as large, her fingers stiff and heavy, and her back and hips unusually sore. For better or worse, her changes were coming faster than she had hoped. So, she resolved to bring them on as quickly as she could. For her father's sake, if not her sister's.

23 – Failed Guardian

Anise

I don't want you to be my queen. She finally said it. I hope you're right about this angyrian witch, Maybury. I do not know what else to do.

Anise set out in the dark of morning, the sun's glow not even hinting in the east yet. The royal guard had questioned her departure, but she'd easily lied that her destination was her father's garden. In part because it wasn't a lie. She did go there, first. She always went there first. A quartet of guards followed at a safe distance, the guardian and queen both asleep. Probably.

This is really going to scare them. Good! No, not good. It shouldn't even BE this way. Yet it is.

Situated just across Antila's stream, which fed into the Torhal river at the castle's south-western corner, lay the king's garden: a miniature fort complete with ornate gate, sentry tower, and gardener's cottage. Within lay a solitary cherry tree surrounded by thirty-some-odd beds of herbs, flowers, and all manner of vegetables. Not one of which was magically altered, a point of pride for King Orren whose wisdom as a king was second only to his knowledge as a gardener.

Prior to Orren's improvements, the king's garden had been an ancient barracks used by past monarchs for training guardians. Annelle and Orren had both decided Merelith would be trained in the queen's wood or the castle, not some aging enclosure that would make her feel like a trapped dog. Orren had then converted it to his personal garden, something Annelle had gladly supported.

Would that a man care for me as Papa does…I wonder if any of them even see me. Or if they only see Merelith. Stars! I cannot believe she wore such a thing yesterday, dressed like a furry whore and slobbering all over that idiot scout.

Anise paused at the gate to the garden and beckoned her attendant guard closer. They stood to attention as she addressed them.

"I wish to be alone. Please, return to the castle and warm yourselves."

"Are you certain, Crown Princess? We *are* at war and…"

"I am certain. Go on. I am well within the safety of my mother's magic."

"And the guardian's scent, too" chimed a different guard, "Come on, then."

The guards nodded at one another then bid her goodnight. They didn't walk far before breaking into a trot, the cold urging them on. Anise hoped they didn't notice the chill deepening unnaturally quick. Satisfied she was well and truly alone, Anise cast a long gaze at the gate to the garden.

I shouldn't go. It could be a trap of some kind. No, I do not think so. Besides…Papa is tired of me pretending, too. He didn't mean it the way I do, but still. I have to find a way forward. Perhaps this angyrian witch knows a way to ensure Merelith remains herself? Or a method for quietening the monster within. I have to try.

Anise turned from the gate, began to set off into the queen's wood, then stopped.

And the guardian's scent, too, the guard said. He's right. Merelith will easily find me once they know I've gone. Hmm…I suppose I have some things I can leave as false trails. It will take longer, but maybe I can be there by the end of today.

She rummaged in her pack for a hairbrush and then tossed it into the snow by the gate. Then she walked around the garden a full two times before setting off into the queen's wood once more. The guardian had described the trials her mother had put her through over the years. Perhaps, with a little luck and intuition, Anise could recreate such a trial and buy herself time. Hope pricked at her heart as she warmed her boots and cloak against the bitter cold of a coming snowstorm, natural yet begging to be amplified.

Anise knew the perfect emotion with which to do so.

. . .

Merelith

"Where is she?!"

Merelith kept her eyes to the floor and bit back the urge to tell her mother the cold stone was hurting her knees and hands. If not for the fluff of her ears, Merelith was certain frostbite might already have set in. Towering over her, eyes full of fury, was the queen of Torhal wreathed in a lethal chill.

"*Why?*" she hissed, "Why is she missing?!"

Kara begged for Merelith to flee her mother's wrath. She'd seen what Annelle could do, had felt the heat countless nights across the castle, listened to the crackling branches of the woods as they shattered, smelled the earth rip open across Farsi for planting, shut her eyes against the gale winds forcing rainstorms hither and thither. Nature, wild and *furious*, stood above her.

Merelith stammered, "I s-said to her, 'I d-d-don't want you to b-be my q-queen.' I'm sorry, Mama. I'm s-sorry."

"Not yet you aren't."

Merelith braced for a punishment she'd long awaited. Annelle had *never* struck her eldest with magic in discipline, not once. Played with, chased, teased, yes. Harmed intentionally, no. The angyr could feel both instincts preparing in their own way. Kara crying to curl into herself tighter, Tal preparing for fury it believed was righteous. No blow came, though. Not as magic, anyhow. Annelle's next words were harm enough.

"Anise is missing. If harm befalls her…it will be because of *you*. You, who are her guardian. *You*, who your father and I trusted to protect her."

A shot to the heart, sharper and truer than any bolt loosed by the crown guards that had trained her. Barbed with her mother's regret and coated in her father's disappointment. Annelle turned from Merelith, the hallway outside the scriptorium slowly rising in temperature from freezing to only bitter cold.

"I will try to search for her, but she shares my blood. If she deigns to hide from me, I won't find her. I don't care how you do it, *Guardian*. Find my daughter."

"Y-yes, Your M-m-majesty."

Annelle strode into the scriptorium, no doubt to take the stair to the balcony where she would have the clearest view of her kingdom. Merelith rose from the floor, glad to be unharmed and yet feeling guilty for having no wounds. She made haste to her room, grabbing a sword and donning a heavy winter coat. She paused before her mirror and saw the twin instincts looking back with fear and heartbreak. *My* daughter, the queen had said.

Down in the great hall, royal guards waited for the queen to issue orders for the day. Nobody knew Anise was missing, yet. Did it fall to Merelith to tell them? In past courts, the guardian had been the highest commander, second only to the king and queen. All that had changed with Reeta. Merelith nodded at the guards as they opened the doors for her to pass. None asked where she went, none inquired after her mother or sister, none surveyed her sword and cloak with questioning eyes. She was the guardian, wild and free to do as she pleased. Free to say things that might ruin the kingdom, too, it seemed.

Anise would not have been so stupid as to say what I said.

She might be a bitch, but she wouldn't have said that.

What have I done? What will I do, if…

Merelith shook the thought, pausing just beyond Torhal's drawbridge. The castle grounds were eerily quiet, the crown guard no longer there to train or spar. The angyrian woman breathed the crisp winter air deep into her lungs, fighting the urge to wince. Not at the cold, but the pain of stretching organs larger than her ribcage. The next few changes would be among the most painful, and the stresses of the moment were doing nothing but hurrying them forward.

Her heart was already twice its size, its beat nearly *half* of what it had been to compensate while her body caught up. Her lungs, too, were oversized, as were most of her intestines. The sensation of being bloated was constant, as was the distinct impression of her ribs against her too-small skin. Legs, hips, arms, and neck ached as bones warped and lengthened. About the only thing that felt *good* was her spine, the only part of her body that seemed to stretch with ease and ripple the ever-thickening mane of fur growing along it.

Ok, breathe. Just breathe. Smell. Taste. Anise. Where are you, Anise?

Her sister's favorite oil lingered: apple and cinnamon. So, too, did the tang of her leather overcoat, always smelling fresh because it saw so little use. Merelith tilted her head as she sniffed, noticing other smells that didn't belong in the dead of winter: blueberry muffins, salted jerky, cherry wine, metal canteens perhaps filled with water. No one in their right mind would be journeying in such cold, but a broken crown princess might.

"Guardian? Are you well?"

Merelith opened her eyes, her teeth bared as she glanced at the royal guard that had interrupted her sensing. He raised a cautious hand and backed away. She immediately sealed her lips and winced.

"S-sorry. I, I was smelling…I didn't mean to…"

The guard nodded slowly but waited for her to answer his question.

"Inform my mother I have a scent and am following it."

"Uh, of course, Guardian. A scent of…?"

"She'll know."

"Right. Er, yes, Guardian. Good hunting."

He gulped at her flashed smile. Briefly, ever so briefly, Merelith's instincts surged in joy before falling back into worry and grief. In that moment, she decided it was only a curse *most* of the time. She set off across the drawbridge, following the faint scent of her sister. Merelith had no idea what she would say, or how she would get Anise to return with her. Only that she had to.

I am the guardian. She is their daughter.
I will make this right. I want to make this right.

24 – To Be Different

Anise

I don't want you to be my queen.

Anise trudged through the snow of her mother's woods, one gloved hand tightly grasping her pack and the other fidgeting the angyrian feather in her coat pocket. The edges of the coat shimmered yellow and orange, fire magic keeping her toasty even as the wind roared against her. She half-wondered if her mother was adding to the growing storm, too, perhaps to dissuade her from wandering too far.

She didn't dare let her queen know she was alright. Annelle Torhal could summon tendrils of roots in the dead of winter as far as High Lake. A terrible lecture no doubt awaited her return. If she returned at all. At least the princess and guardian agreed on something: Anise didn't want to be queen, neither. The young sorceress felt the vane of the angyrian feather with her finger and prayed that Maybury's quest wasn't some trick but a genuine offer of aid.

The crown princess paused near the northern edge of the queen's wood. The slope of the ground markedly increased here, indicating she'd reached the border of Torhal. Through the snow-clad treetops she saw the Silver Alpha loom high above the other mountain peaks. She huffed with determination and a hint of annoyance. A horse would have been nice but then she'd have to explain to the stable hands where she was going. That, and, she wasn't sure she could have kept the animal from freezing to death. Shared magic was still a weak spot in her studies. No doubt because the best person to practice with hated her guts.

"At least we agree on that, too," she mumbled.

All morning and afternoon, Anise had carefully wound her magic around her to conceal her progress from the queen. She'd gone to great lengths to create numerous false trails of scent for Merelith, too, though she wasn't entirely sure her sister would actually come looking for her. She wondered what Merelith would say to their mother.

Did she tell her the truth? That she doesn't want me to be her queen?

Or did she lie? I wouldn't put it past her. If mother even suspected it was her fault that I left…

Was it? No. I don't think so. I want this, too, just for different reasons.

Would she hurt Merelith?

Anise paused, bracing herself against a pine struggling to stay upright on the steep slope. The question struck deep, and the crown princess felt worry bloom in her chest. Whatever had happened, whatever had been said, Anise's departure would fall squarely on Merelith's head *first*. She was the guardian, afterall, and protecting Anise wasn't just her priority but her sole duty. The *only* thing she had to get right.

I must take care of hundreds, sometimes THOUSANDS, of things. But I can make mistakes, too. Mother isn't all that hard on me, really. What happens if Merelith screws up? Would that make her leave, like Aunt Reeta? Would she lose her mind, too?

The crown princess gulped down freezing air to cool the burning in her gut. She'd not really considered the consequences of her unannounced journey. What the punishment might be for *Merelith*. What she went to do would hopefully benefit both of them, but what if it didn't? Anise pushed the thought away, the feather in her pocket like an anchor in a storm of questions and worries.

Tangled up like a pig on a spit.

Anise snorted at the jab but felt the truth of it settle her gut. Weird and wacky as she was, Maybury had spoken rightly. Anise *did* feel tangled up and held over an open flame, slowly cooking for someone else's pleasure. Onwards and upwards, she pressed toward the short mountain beside the Silver Alpha.

· · ·

Merelith

It was all Merelith could do to not scream in fury and wail in sorrow. Another dead end.

NO! No, no, no! Damnit, Anise, where did you go?!

This is payback. She knows. She knows what mother will do to me if I return empty-handed.

Empty-pawed, more like it.

Merelith glanced at her trembling hand-paws, the stress of the search curling them even more. At this rate, she'd have to return to the castle by dusk, leaving her sister alone. An unacceptable but ever more real possibility. Her hips groaned and she clamped her mouth against a moan of pain. Another week and she'd be bedridden for sure, her hips and shoulders too out-of-whack to walk on two legs *or* four. She had to find Anise.

How? This is the fourth dead-end!

Merelith glowered at the doll, angry and fearful all at once. Miss Molly sat against a tree, smelling just like her mistress and owner. That Anise would be willing to abandon her only doll to throw off Merelith spoke volumes. The young sorceress would not have carelessly left the precious toy unless she well and truly planned to disappear, possibly for good.

No, I cannot allow that to happen.

Oh, I'm going to absolutely RIP her to shreds when I find…

NO! No. She might be scared, lonely, or even hurt! What if she's been abducted!?

THEN I'LL RIP THEM INTO BLOODY SHR…

"SHUT UP!" she screamed into the woods.

So loud was her shout, nearly a roar, that a bit of snow tumbled from a nearby tree. The wind stirred then settled, twirling her sister's scent around but providing no other clues. She'd have to backtrack, again, and hope to pick up a new trail. Her tears burned in the cold as she tried to wipe them away. At least the instincts were being quiet, if only for a moment.

Your instincts will not fail you.

What a lie. My instincts are why this happened, Papa.

I didn't mean it. Not like that. I…I don't want this. I don't want her to be my queen.

I don't know what I want. Just, just not this.

Ah, what would Eric say? Probably that she deserved it…he'd be wrong.

He's wrong about a lot of things. Maybe he's wrong about me, too.

Merelith sighed, willing her mind empty as she trudged back along the trail of her sister's scent. It didn't matter if she was right or wrong, if Eric was right or wrong, or even if her sister were right or wrong. She was the guardian. Anise was her charge. More importantly, she was her sister. For all the cruel words, the ugly stares, the intentional ignoring…Merelith knew she'd never forgive herself if something happened to Anise.

Her mother was right. She wasn't sorry. Not yet. Fear of that sorrow kept her searching.

. . .

Anise

In fifteen going on sixteen years come spring, Anise had *never* been in the mountains past dark. She hardly ever went into the queen's wood past dusk, not since that awful day her sister had saved her from the wolf. Annelle had explained that incident a hundred times; Anise had studied the books on angyrism just as many days. It didn't change the truth: Merelith had been so wild as to forget her own family.

Now, Anise almost wished Merelith were by her side. She had crested the peak of the little mountain to find nothing. No sign of an angyrian witch, no indication any living thing had ever been there in the last century. Worse, Anise was certain something had been following her for the past half-hour. Just before scaling the last ledge, she'd spotted it in the corner of her eye: large, black, and on four legs. Stalking her. Suddenly, Maybury's quest felt very, very foolish.

Her magic had been kept at a near-constant alert since then. She pushed away thoughts that, perhaps, the mysterious angyr that had avoided her parent's scouts – and brutally murdered two hunters – was now hunting her. She had tried using her magic to briefly sense it out, only to realize her mother's sense was mere moments from finding *her*. In that split-second of sight, she had sensed not one but *three* lives. The first was close and laced with unusual magic. The other two had been distant. One high up on the Silver Alpha, bright and brilliant but too far to make out what it was. The other down below her, in the Queen's Wood, dim and perhaps dying.

"Hello?" she called into the dark, not sure anyone could even hear her voice over the blustering wind, "Is anyone there? Maybury sent me!"

Anise looked about and she raised a hand of flame high to light her surroundings. Nothing but rocky outcroppings, powdery snow, and the freezing wind. She turned around to consider heading back down when she screamed in surprise and spewed forth flames in self-defense. They billowed over and around the mysterious angyr, but no harm came to it. Wide-eyed with terror, the crown princess prepared to launch another attack when the angyr *cackled*.

"My, my, my!" it said in a voice smooth as silk, "A bit jumpy, are we? Is that what the rumors say? Find me and then set me on fire?"

Anise's terror deepened into horror as she quickly stammered out, "N-n-no! I'm s-so sorry! No, I didn't come to k-kill you! Maybury sent me with a f-feather! See?! She needs your help!"

Anise practically ripped the feather from her pocket and held it out toward the hulking creature. The angyrian witch sniffed the air then smiled, great fangs and teeth dripping with fresh blood, perhaps from a recent kill. The crown princess mustered as much calm as she could as the angyr plopped its furry behind into the snow.

"And *why* are you here?" drawled the angyr, motioning a great paw at the princess, "Who is this *Maybury* to you? Why do you have a feather of my kin?"

"I…I just wanted to help. She, um, she told me to bring it to you to, uh, to make a cure."

The sound of a woman laughing and cackling out of the throat of a monster was chilling. The witch shook its furry head with mirth then stood and stalked away.

"Well, come on, then. No sense standing in the cold and wasting your magic. You've a long walk back, girl, and you'll need every ounce of it to survive your mother."

Anise tacitly followed, asking, "Do you know my mother?"

"Personally? Pfft, no. *Queen* Annelle Torhal is above our ilk, just like her stuffy mother. Annabelle was such a treat, though. No idea how such a lovely woman made such a loony angyr and heartless daughter. Seems it keeps passing on, though."

Anise bit back the urge to say her mother was *not* heartless. Controlling and high-minded, maybe, but not uncaring. The angyr led her down the southern slope from whence she came then turned east onto a ledge Anise had not seen before. To her surprise and relief, a little cave with a flickering fire within greeted them after a short walk.

Inside, the angyrian witch's abode was sparsely supplied and decorated. A lone cauldron rested over the fire, a handful of trinkets rested on shelves hewn from the cave walls, and a simple bed formed of dried grasses and various pelts sat in a corner. What drew Anise's eyes, though, were the hundreds of *thousands* of runes marked all over the cave. Most she recognized but there were some she did not. She paused at the cave entrance, unsure if she should enter.

The angyr looked back, barked out a laugh, then seemed to glow. The glow grew into a brilliant flash of red light, then the monster was gone. In its place stood a woman of unparalleled beauty. Anise was speechless as the witch gently tugged the other sleeve of her coat off and tossed it to her bed: it was a great black cloak lined with the pelt of a massive angyr, its eyes seemingly still alive and watching her and the crown princess. Yet the collar was not on the pelt. Rather, it remained around the witch's neck.

"Ah, much better. Come in, dear, don't mind all that," she said, motioning to the many runes, "they're not for keeping *you* out."

25 – The Angyrian Witch

Anise

Anise wasn't sure if she wanted to know what the runes were meant to keep out. She had felt the ebb and flow of her mother's magic since before birth, known the tickle and scraping of wild magic as long as her own name, but what flowed in the small cave was unlike anything she'd felt before. The angyrian witch's magic was subtle but seemed to steadily beat like a heart. *Thump-thud-thump*, over and over, its intensity so soft as to feel like the pitter-patter of a mouse's heart-rhythm, yet slow like that of a great bear.

Or an angyr, Anise realized, recalling what she knew of the creature her sister was becoming. Yet, angyr could *never* appear as human. Could they?

"Well then, let's see it. She wouldn't have sent you unless she was afraid to show me herself."

Anise had the distinct impression a lethal threat lay under the witch's observation. The woman didn't look a day over twenty-five, full of life and beauty and glamor. Except for her neck, where the skin looked raw and unhealthy beneath the heavy collar. Yet the witch had spoken of Anise's *great*-grandmother as if they had been best friends. The crown princess held out the angyrian feather to the witch.

"Och," she sniffed, "I told you it had to be a *quickened* feather, Alice."

She lifted the feather from Anise's hands with tender care, as if picking up a newborn or priceless heirloom. She sighed and shook her head, then rather unceremoniously flung the feather into her fire. It instantly curled in on itself, bursting into flame and disintegrating into ash. Anise didn't have time to protest before the witch snorted then spoke.

"Someday, we'll stop pretending to be something else and stop breaking things because of it."

Anise's eyes shot back to the witch, who stared at her with deep curiosity. She then smirked and went to sit by her meager campfire.

The witch pat a spot beside her but Anise hesitated in joining her. The witch chuckled, her laughter sweet and singsong.

"I'm not going bite you, child. These teeth aren't made for such violence."

The witch made to snap her teeth at her, then giggled again as if the joke were merely that. The crown princess visibly gulped, though.

"Who is Alice?" asked Anise.

"Maybury's fool daughter. She found me years ago, asking for advice on how to raise her son. Hmph. He's an *animal*, I said, you feed him and train him and hope he doesn't eat your corpse when you die of old age. Needless to say, she didn't *accept* that answer."

"Can angyrism be cured?"

"Not in the way Alice imagines. It matters not, a quickened feather is needed."

"For what?"

"For whatever reason Maybury sent *you*."

Anise gulped again. The witch saw and grew serious.

"Sit, Anise," she said with quiet authority, "and let me see why Maybury sent *you*."

Tangled up like a pig on a spit.

The crown princess nodded and went to beside the angyrian witch, though Anise sat further around the fire than where she had pat. The witch sighed then scooted her lovely bottom around to beside her. Her brown eyes twinkled with mirth as she pulled her knees to her ample bosom and lay her head upon them, watching Anise like a child might a frog or butterfly.

Or a meal. Maybe this wasn't such a good idea.

"So much in that little head, it's a wonder it doesn't just explode! I suppose that's why they put a crown on children like you. It's a bit like a jar lid. Keeps it all in, hmm?"

"I, um, I don't know what you mean," Anise replied in a murmur.

"Oh, but you do. A girl like you doesn't summon flame into a perfect cone that hones the highest intensity of the heat at just the right distance and *not* know what I mean. Do not play the fool, daughter of Annelle. Heartlessness may be your curse, but idiocy most certainly is not."

Heartlessness. My mother isn't heartless. Is she?

Am I? I said such awful things last night. Heartless things.

A curse. Merelith has called it a curse before. This certainly feels that way.

"Maybury said you could, um, could help me."

"Did she now? And what, crown princess, would you need my help for?"

"I…I don't know. Erm, I don't know how to change it."

"It?"

Anise's throat felt dry, but the witch didn't prod. She instead lifted her head, pulling her luscious hair back over her shoulder and staring into the fire. Then the woman closed her eyes and breathed in the smoke, her sharp canines flashing with a look of pleasure and freedom. The princess found her answer.

"Freedom. I…I want freedom."

"You don't look a slave to me" the witch said, looking up at the ceiling as if to study its runes.

"I want freedom like what my sister has. Like…like what *you* have."

"Me?"

The witch glanced at Anise and those teeth flashed with a smirk.

"What makes you think I am *free*, girl? For that matter, what makes you think *Merelith* is free?"

"You are out here, doing what you want," Anise said plainly, "You are free. You can choose to do whatever you want."

"Such as eat you."

Anise gulped but forced a nod and calm reply, "Yes."

The witch eyed her with what felt hunger. Anise, though, felt her fear slip away under that gaze. She had meant what she'd said. The crown princess lifted her chin a little, forced a small smile, and snorted. The witch cocked an eyebrow and asked what she found so comical.

"Well, you *could*, but those aren't the teeth for it. Said so yourself."

Anise could listen to that laughter all night. It had a quality to it that was pleasant and refined. Or it did when it came from a woman instead of a monster. It reminded her of simpler days with her family, when she was just a girl, not a princess. When her sister was just a sister, not a guardian. Anise realized that laugh reminded her a lot of Merelith's own. Perhaps, perhaps it was the sound of freedom, natural and easy for those who had it.

"Your sister is no freer than you, Anise Torhal."

The crown princess wasn't sure how the witch knew her thoughts. Was not sure she wanted to know, for such thoughts were wrong and selfish. Or so she had long believed. Now she sat with a stranger – a witch no less – because those thoughts had become unbearable.

"You'll find nobody is truly free in this life. I may look it, but I have my own responsibilities. My own oaths and promises and debts. I didn't become what I am for freedom, child. I became what I am because pretending to be something else hurt too much."

"What did you pretend to be?" Anise whispered, her eyes drawn back to the fire.

"A queen."

"Of what land?"

"You would not know it. I was born to a loving family, a loving people, in a loving land. Yet my crown was too heavy. I never had the right words; I didn't have the grace of my mother or the voice of my father. My sister, though, did. She possessed a grace and beauty unparalleled. Ferocity was her birthright and instinct was her brother."

"An angyr."

The witch barely nodded.

"They hated her, my parents," the witch whispered, "Hated a monster lived among them but they were too cowardly to kill her. But to me? She was my sister."

"May I know her name?"

The witch gulped then shook her head.

"I cannot speak it. Some of the price I paid. I loved her, Anise, loved her as surely as I love the summer breeze and winter stillness. I would sneak out from the court and ride her, a child upon a beast that can end eternity, and we would journey together long into the night."

She sighed and Anise saw the tears in her eyes.

"I was happy and she was miserable. I loved the wilds, the woods, and the streams. She hated them. I hated the dresses, the parades, and the never-ending dances with suitors. She loved them. I could go anywhere, though. She couldn't. You think your sister free, Anise, but she is not. The world beyond the court isn't bigger. It is so, so much smaller than the love and adoration of your people, the pride and confidence of your parents."

"What became of her?"

"I loved her but hated myself. She loved me but hated herself. What else could we do? We stopped pretending."

Anise furrowed her brow in confusion, aware the witch was now smirking at the flame as if sharing an unspoken joke with it. The silence was long, and the young sorceress knew the witch was waiting for her to say something.

"How?"

"You cannot tell?"

The witch glanced toward her cloak upon the bed. The wolf's eyes watched Anise, still. For a moment, she wondered if the witch had butchered her own sister. Then, slowly, realization crept over her face.

"You…became angyr. She became a princess."

"Our hearts were already those things. Sometimes, sometimes fate twists and turns just so, and the body and the heart aren't where they ought to be at the same time. It might be easy to say I had my sister's heart, and she mine, but hearts cannot be changed. The truth was that I was pretending my body wasn't hers, and that hers wasn't mine."

"Where is she now?"

"Oh, she died of old age a long, long time ago. Happily married and with beautiful children."

"And you…are ageless, now."

"Yes."

The way she said it was heavy with responsibility but also tinged with joy.

"All of the world for me. Huge and wonderful compared to that stuffy castle. At a cost."

"What was the cost?" Anise whispered, enraptured as she leaned toward the witch.

"What else? Everything."

The spell was broken as Anise let the answer sink in. *Everything.*

"I cannot speak her name, the name of my sister I loved so much. I cannot return to the court, for I robbed them of my presence. I am a monster, free in the world and forever caged beyond the realm of men and women."

"You appear as a woman now, though? I did not think angyr could…"

"The cave is not to keep you out."

Anise eyed the runes, understanding comingling with confusion. *None* of her readings indicated an angyr could become human again. Come to think of it, the witch's angyrian form had no wings, neither. The crown princess opted to not ask why.

"It is ancient. I did not make these but found it by accident. Torhal's angyrian legends are known across the freelands. I had come seeking to learn more of my new life, many years ago. I suspect it was made to offset the powers of this *thing*."

The witch tapped her collar with a grimace.

"It cannot suppress my angyrism, but it *can* suppress my magic. This is the only place I can appear as I do now. The cave keeps out the pentarch's horrible magic."

"Is there no way to remove it?"

"You are welcome to try, princess, but no. I think not."

Anise tenderly reached for the collar and touched it. She felt a jolt of magic sting her fingertip and she ripped her hand back. The witch chuckled, shook her head, then shrugged.

"Worth a try," the witch mumbled, "Far worse has been done to me than this."

What a lonely existence. To have gained her freedom, the life she had dreamed of, and lose everything else. To have been *collared*. And yet…

"Do you regret it?" Anise whispered, "Becoming what she was, allowing her to become what you were?"

"No."

The answer was swift and firm. The witch smiled and shrugged.

"The cost was high, but not higher than the toll of pretending. Not even close. I lost my parents, but I gained myself, and my sister *herself*. We visited as often as I could sneak into the cities she visited. Sometimes she would ride me into the dark, like I had as a child…" the witch paused, her voice wavering as she finished, "…she would cry, not at what she'd lost but what I had gained. She had never seen me so happy and I, I had never seen her so happy."

"I wish to know how to do this."

The words came easily. Anise didn't know if the cost was lower than the toll she felt. Wasn't even sure if Merelith would *want* such a thing. Yet the way the witch spoke, how her story pierced Anise's longing heart, the princess knew without a doubt how the witch had felt before. Maybury had sent her here for this reason exactly.

"Last I looked, your sister seemed pleased with what she is."

Anise did her best to not growl as she replied, "She was. She is in love now. With a man. He loves her, too."

"Are you so sure?"

"His kiss was as pure as any I've seen between my mother and father. Eric loves her, will love her even as she changes. Neither were afraid to let the whole kingdom know it. I'm sure he means to marry her when the war ends."

It was the briefest flicker, of pain and remorse, but Anise saw it. Anger, too.

"Your sister had fallen in love, too, hadn't she?"

The witch cocked an eyebrow in surprise then composed herself and nodded. She sighed, looked to her pelt, and shrugged.

"He was a strange man. He would have loved her as a beast, but he was thrilled when she was a woman. I do not know if this Eric would be the same. Besides, you assume she wishes to trade with you. You do not *know* it, as I did."

"What if I brought her to you? Let her hear your story as I have?"

"Why not tell the story yourself?"

The question rammed Anise in the core of her being. *Why not tell her yourself?* She couldn't. She knew she could not. Merelith couldn't possibly trust her after all she had said. As if sensing Anise's apprehension, the witch sighed and stood from the fire. Each step she took from Anise felt like the opportunity of a lifetime slipping away.

"I do not think she would trust me," Anise croaked.

The witch paused and asked, "Why not?"

"B-because I…I don't know. I am cruel. I am heartless."

Anise's eyes watered as she looked at the cave floor in shame, the truth of her words echoing in the hole forming in her chest. The witch nodded then continued toward her bed to gather the pelt. She slipped one arm in, paused, and glanced at Anise.

"I will consider your request if you consider what you have told me."

Anise nodded dumbly, too raw to say anything else. That the witch would even consider telling her was more than the crown princess deserved. She knew it. A brilliant flash of red and the hulking angyr was back. Anise stole a glance to see that it had two great scars where the wings should have been. The witch-wolf cocked her head, looked at her own side, then nodded slowly.

"The pentarchs think themselves gods when really, they are just monsters. It is as I said. We hurt others less when we stop pretending to be what we are not."

The collared angyr padded to the edge of the cave, stopped, and looked at Anise with silver eyes.

"Do you pretend to be heartless, Anise Torhal, or are you?"

Anise stammered, "I-I don't know."

"You'd best find out, girl. A heartless angyr is far more deadly than a heartless queen. Your mother would know."

The witch left the cave and disappeared into the winter night, vanishing into the shadows of the few pines clinging to the side of the low mountain. Anise reached into her pack for her last possession not left to draw off Merelith: Augie the Angyr, an old doll made the day after she had learned what Merelith *really* was.

Anise sat in the cave by the fire, gently stroking the stuffed angyr long into the night. She pondered the witch, who wandered alone. She considered the queen who shared her name, wise but seemingly heartless. Above all, though, she thought upon her sister, whose eyes were silver instead of gold like Augie's. Her sister, who she knew to be searching in that frigid wood below the mountain. Whatever Merelith's feelings, Anise knew her sister wasn't heartless.

A heartless sister wouldn't have come looking. Anise prayed that her search for a way to change was proof she wasn't heartless, too.

26 – Regret and Rage

Merelith

Merelith stirred beneath the snow, shivering and chilled to the bone. Then her eyes shot open at realizing why. The motion of sitting up was too swift and she barked in pain. Literally. She raised a crumpled hand-paw to her mouth to find its lips pushing out a little. She wondered what she looked like, not-quite human and not-quite angyr. Dawn's light crept at the edges of the mountains to the east.

"Anise," she murmured, before forcing herself up and shaking off the snow that had covered her.

My daughter.

Merelith fought back the urge to cry in devastation. She had fallen from exhaustion in the freezing storm and her mother had not come for her. The message was clear. *My daughter or don't come home.* The guardian forced her nose to work, to find some lingering scent of the crown princess. The trail, like her surroundings, was cold. Too cold. Everything was too cold, suddenly.

She shook off that lethal shiver and took stock of her surroundings, eyeing the mountain peaks through the snow-topped pines. She spied the Silver Alpha and groaned. Of course. Where else would a sorceress-child go to hide from her mother and sister? Merelith hoisted her leg forward to free it of the deep snow and promptly fell face-first. Shock and fear laced her veins.

I can't walk.

She stumbled to a sitting position, working her hips and legs as she grappled with the truth echoing across her aching body. It wasn't frostbite. No, this was something else. She stood again and felt the distinct *offness* of her balance. She had been too cold to feel it the first time but now, now it was as obvious as the towering mountain ahead of her. She had changed more in her sleep. She gingerly made for another step and, while successful, stumbled and fell when she tried to move her other leg ahead.

Changed too much.

Oh no. Oh no oh no oh no!

Anise. Sister! I must find Anise.

Merelith forced back tears, not of pain but terror, as she rose again. At least she could still stand, though it was stilted, her back unwilling to straighten upwards. Rather, she felt top-heavy, her spine forcing her to lean like a crone. The image stuck as she stumbled and scrabbled her way to the nearest tree. Her hands were covered in thick fuzz, now. The nails had begun to square, too, not just elongate. She still had rudimentary control of her fingers, at least. Enough to wield her sword and hack away at a low but sturdy branch.

Eric would probably laugh at this part of the story: his beloved, bent over like an old woman, hobbling with a pine-branch cane, traversing snow almost up to her knees. Then she wondered what the man would do, or say, to her mother. How loyal was Eric Smith when the beast-woman he'd proclaimed his future wife was found to have been left in a snowstorm, searching for a sister that hated her, for a mother that had disowned her?

She didn't disown me. She's upset, and rightly so. I…I shouldn't have said it.
She left me! In the storm, she left me! My daughter, she'd said.
This is Anise's fault. I was just, I didn't mean to…

Merelith paused, wincing and sighing as she tried to straighten and stretch her back, finding it no more willing now than when she'd first stood. It'd taken half a day and into the night to get this deep into her mother's wood. That was *before* she was crawling along like an invalid. The guardian forced down the self-pity, feeding it to Tal's determination to not give up. She called up on Kara's intense serenity, bidding the instinct to lead her on.

"She is my sister," she said aloud to nobody, "She is my sister."

Anise probably wished otherwise and, truth be told, Merelith had wished it more than once herself. Not right now, though. The twin instincts seemed to prowl around the words.

"She is my sister."

They did not look inwards, at Merelith's conviction, but outwards.

"She is *my* sister."

Tal growled with possessive rage. Poor words or not, Anise belonged to her. Belonged to her protection. Belonged to her love. Woe betides anyone that would harm her.

"She is my *sister.*"

Kara stared with compassionate fury. Poor words or not, she belonged to Anise. Belonged to her crown. Belonged to her family. Woe betide Merelith if she failed this task.

"I don't want you to be my queen, but I do want *you.*"

On and on, Merelith whispered these words. Around and around, Tal and Kara circled the guardian's heart, hemorrhaging with terror and grief but pumping with pure, unadulterated *anger*. At herself, at her mother, even at her sister, but mostly at herself. King Orren had said she could trust her instincts, trust them to make sense of whatever she was feeling, so she let go of her thoughts and dwelled instead on the tempest within her heart.

In turn, each step gained the unfailing willpower of Tal. Each breath the steady patience of Kara. She was angyr, an apex predator and among the most feared creatures in all of Damaria. Merelith recalled the stories and legends she had studied since learning what she was. Stories of her forebears, like Merel, but also tales of angyr in the distant past. To her instincts she fed every word that had been used to describe these creatures of the void.

Silent. Fierce. Noble. Ruthless. Compassionate. Devastating. Intelligent. Feral.

On and on, the guardian whispered to herself. Farther and further, she trudged towards the great mountain. Deeper and deeper, she followed the instincts, no longer circling her heart but now leading it. Guiding her where magic sight could not see, where false trails and scents could not hide. The pair hunted what only they could: the wildness of a sister.

. . .

Anise

Anise paused at the edge of her mother's wood, took a deep breath, and prepared to release the magic hiding her. It was still morning, the sun glinting off the frozen trees and casting the queen's wood in a cacophony of rainbow sparkles tinted in the soft gold of sunshine. The crown princess curled and uncurled her fingers, as if trying to remember *how* to not hide. The thought struck a chord, and she sniffled.

I am so tired of pretending. Perhaps, perhaps that is all I should say? No, no she would never understand. She probably wouldn't want to…I don't know. I don't know.

"Sister?"

The young sorceress stilled at the whispering of her name. Her heart pounded at what she beheld emerging from behind a pine tree some fifty yards off. At first glance, it was a woman bent over, hobbling along with a broken branch for a cane. Yet a recognizable sword hung from her shaking hip, a well-worn cloak cast about her hunched back, and those eyes…

"Merelith?" she whispered back.

There was such beauty in those eyes, wild silver rimmed with the sheen of tears. Her sister tried to hurry forward, but her legs would not obey, and she stumbled, clinging to the pine branch to keep from going face-first into the snow. The crown princess wasted no time rushing to Merelith.

"What happened? A-are you hurt? W-w-why are you limping?"

Merelith rose again as Anise reached her, only to stop at what she beheld up close. Under the hood of the coat was someone, *something*, that did not look like her sister yet spoke with her voice.

"Sister," she said quietly, "Is me. Merelith. I…"

"What happened to you?" she replied, wincing at her words before hastily adding, "Nevermind. Are, a-are you hurt?"

"No."

A bald lie if ever there was one. Anise grimaced and placed a firm hand onto Merelith's, forcing her magic into her sister to see where the damage was. She was startled when her sister growled.

"Not hurt! You? Pain?"

Those beautiful eyes dilated with what looked feral hunger. The growl had stopped her seeing much, but Anise had seen enough. Merelith wasn't wounded but she *was* in terrible pain.

"No. I…I am not hurt."

What gazed out from under that hood was not human. She wasn't even sure it was her sister. Merelith nodded slowly, then seemed to relax again. A great sigh escaped her lips and, without warning, she dropped her makeshift cane and fell to her misshapen knees. Anise yelped her sister's name, but Merelith seemed to *bury* her head deeper into the snow. The crown princess tried to lift her sister up, yet Merelith kept forcing her way down.

"Merelith! Merelith, what is it? Tell me where it hurts and I, I, I can help! I…"

"I *sorry*, sister. Much, much sorry."

Never, in her whole life, had she heard such a broken voice. Not even her own.

"Love you! Never want hurt! I sorry! I so, so sorry. Not want hurt. Not want this. N-never!"

"Merelith…"

"I do it. I do you want. Please. Home. No leave again. So sorry! Your Mama needs you! P-please. I so sorry, sister. I so sorry!"

YOUR Mama? What did she do to you, sister?

Anise knelt into the snow before her sister, even as Merelith quaked and shivered with grief. And fear, the sorceress felt fear as she let her magic gently tease and tug at her sister's own threads. Fear so strong, so *old*, it predated any recent conversation with the queen. It was not hard to guess how far back that fear went.

Loony angyr and heartless daughters.

"Merelith, I…"

She had no words. What could she say? The longer she gazed upon her prostrate sister the more she understood the witch's words. Annelle Torhal might not have been able to find her sorceress daughter, but she damn well could see her angyrian daughter. Merelith hadn't just traveled across the snow-bound wood this morning, judging by her body's advancing transformation, a familiar dolly poking out from her coat pocket, and the thick ice crusting her hood.

Mother let Merelith brave that snowfall. In the dark. Alone. Not out of faith, but punishment. Heartless. This…this was heartless.

Something snapped in Anise and, without a word, she stood up and released her magic covering. Let her mother know where she was: beside her sister, crippled and freezing. Let the wise and loving ruler see she was anything but. The crown princess resolved then and there what she would do. Or rather, what she *wouldn't* do: be a heartless queen.

"No more pretending," the crown princess whispered under her breath, before looking down at Merelith and stating flatly, "I don't accept your apology."

The angyr-woman tensed, and Anise cringed a little.

"You have nothing to be sorry for, Merelith. I don't want to be your queen, neither. I'd rather just be your sister. You didn't come out here because of a *fucking* crown."

She plopped into the snow before her sister, grabbed her hood, and pulled it back to reveal tall, fur-lined ears poking from a scalp of red hair and down-fur beneath it. A second pair of ears had begun to form just below and behind the first. Anise forced a hand under Merelith's elongated chin and pushed her sister's eyes up to where they gazed into hers. A beast stared at her, not a woman, but Anise did not care.

"You came for the same reason I did. You're my sister."

"Yes," whispered the guardian between an array of crooked teeth, some still flat and others still sharpening.

"I…I d-don't know how to change this, Merelith," she said, motioning between her and her sister's head, "But I swear I never want to change this."

She thrust her other hand down to her sister's chest, heaving and shaking, right above her too-large heart throbbing with too-large emotions. Merelith's eyes widened as Anise pushed her face close, so close she could see the irises dilating as only a wolf's might. Focusing and draining every mote of light from around them, taking in every detail of Anise's face and their surroundings.

"I will *never* change that I love you, sister. You must *never* be sorry that you love me. No matter what *our* mother does to us."

The sob that left her distorted face chilled Anise to the bone. The wild eyes shut with pain unimaginable. Merelith fell into Anise's embrace, her mouth widening to let loose what started as a wail and ended in a howl of agony. Anise dove deep into her magic, pouring every ounce of it into her senses, allowing Merelith's emotions to resonate with her own.

The sorrow was unearthly. The shame as violent and bitter as Anisterosa's scar upon the king's wood. The fear deafening, so loud as to leave the terror of Torhal's people behind like a whisper. How could such things exist in one person? Who could have the power to break a spirit so completely, so *quickly*? Anise knew the answer and swore again and again she would never be the same. The curse the witch spoke of would end with her.

The royal guards arrived with horses a few hours later. It took several minutes to get Merelith into a saddle, in no small part because her legs and hips simply wouldn't swing wide like a human's might. The guards asked a hundred questions of both princess and guardian but neither answered anything more than that they were unharmed. That the queen herself was not there only deepened Anise's fury. She wondered at that fury on the ride back. Was it kin to her mother's and grandmother's? Or was it kin to the instinctual rage that had guided her sister to her?

Whatever the case, Anise settled on a simple truth: only a heart could feel such rage. Hers.

27 – Sisters in Pain

Merelith

"The fighting started this morning."

Merelith's eyes slid open at the whispered words and, for a moment, the world was too bright and fuzzy to make sense of. Then the colors settled, and she beheld the ceiling of her room. As she had for the last six days. Merelith kept waiting for the novelty of her sharpening vision to wear off, the amazement at depth and detail she'd never noticed before. She could count the splinters in the wooden beams, see where moisture had migrated during a humid summer, even mark the faint stain of oiled or sweaty handprints that had set the stone countless generations ago.

"I can still feel Papa."

Merelith labored to raise her head from the pillow towards the voice. Lying on her back was nigh impossible, her spine too curved to allow any comfort despite the overstuffed mattress that had been brought in for her. The urge to prop herself up on an arm was frustrating. She couldn't hardly do that, neither. Her arms could not swing out that wide at the shoulder anymore. Perhaps the most irritating aspect of her changing was that the only way to *really* look around was to lie on her belly. So, she flopped around, got her arm-legs under her, and looked back to where Anise sat at the foot of her bed.

"Is he ok?" the guardian whispered back.

"I think so."

Anise stared out the window of Merelith's bedroom, but the angyrian sister knew she wasn't really looking. Magic, a crimson with streaks of gold, gently arced around open hands upon her lap. Every morning, since returning from the queen's wood, Anise had come to sit and tell Merelith their papa was alive.

Merelith asked, "How can you tell that they are fighting?"

"The horizon is dimmer than yesterday."

Less life threads. Oh, Papa. Please come home.

Merelith nodded somberly and sat in silence except for the slow stretching of each leg and arm. Her back had a furious itch on it, too, but she waited for Anise to ask. In part because the quicker Anise began ministering to her, the quicker she would leave. It was strange, this new dynamic, as the instincts seemed to sigh with satisfaction at her presence. What now existed between her and Anise was both brittle and ironclad, a bit like a bridge of glass built around a single truss of pure love.

Anise released her magic, visibly swallowed, then shut her eyes tight. Merelith felt Kara stir. She rolled onto her side again and gently stretched out a leg to press against Anise's hip. She was too sore to rise, too broken to hug her sister, but not so much so that she couldn't at least prove to Anise she was not alone in her fear. A small hand, cold as ice, rested upon Merelith's foot-paw before stroking it. It was strange, to be stroked by someone she was certain had wanted to throttle her not even a month ago.

"He'll be alright, Anise."

The crown princess only nodded, opening her eyes to gaze at Merelith. She forced a small smile and said the angyr looked more comfortable. An attempted shrug ended in a wince, shared by Anise.

"How bad?" asked the younger sister.

"Not as bad as yesterday."

Merelith spoke true. She made to exit the bed and Anise wordlessly rose to fetch a cane, carved from the very pine branch Merelith had used in the Queen's Wood. The guardian wriggled her hips so that her legs 'fell' off the bed onto the floor below, allowing her to stand and support herself off the bed frame. She then took hold of the cane from Anise and stretched as best as she could. Stretching, her sister had advised, was the only consistent method of relief during these hardest weeks of the change.

"Does it feel as awful as it looks?" Anise asked.

"Depends."

"On?"

"Does it hurt? Only a little. Is it a shitty way to get around? Absolutely."

Merelith grinned as Anise tittered. It was such a wonderful sound, a giggle that was high and pure. The guardian had made it a point to find some way to make Anise laugh every day, usually at the expense of her warping body, if only to hear a sound she'd not realized was so precious to her. Kara rested in that noise like a cat in sunshine. Tal snorted in mirth, pleased to have caused it.

Anise shuffled a foot then asked, "Would you like help to the privy?"

"It's that or you pick it up off the floor like I'm a poorly trained pup."

That *did* get a guffaw, and Merelith's heart sang as she laughed along with her sister. She had always marveled at Anise's manners, but she'd also always grumbled at her sister's penchant for being too proper. Anise ensured the door to the privy stayed open while Merelith hobbled in. The crown princess stabilized her sister as she flopped onto the seat and relieved herself, ensuring she didn't tilt too far and fall off.

The crown princess. Helping me take a shit.

Eric is going to die from laughter. Or amazement.

I'm supposed to be taking care of her!

This is nice, though.

"*Mothers before*, Merelith! What crawled inside of you and *died!?*"

Anise gagged but held firm, letting Merelith finish and rise off the seat, laughing with perhaps a tad of Tal's pride. Another calling card of the changes ravaging her body was a *very* unhappy digestive tract. At least she could still wipe herself, albeit with some difficulty as her wrists realigned. She tried not to think about how mortifying *that* might be, asking Anise to do such a thing. They were quick to exit the privy, Anise mocking another gag with an ill-concealed grin.

"Oh, shut up," Merelith retorted, rolling her eyes, "You'd be no better if it were you."

The tension rippling across Anise was unmistakable, sending both instincts into heightened awareness.

"What? What is it?" Merelith asked, "What is wrong, Anise?"

The crown princess shook her head and replied, "N-nothing! Why?"

She was lying and Merelith knew it. Yet, she didn't press. Hadn't, every time she'd felt that strange tug across her sister. In part out of fear that she'd somehow lose Anise again.

"I…it seemed like something was bothering you."

"Oh, no. I'm ok. S-sorry."

"No need."

"Ready for stretches?" Anise offered, changing the topic.

Merelith nodded, dropped her cane, and promptly fell forward onto the floor. Anise groaned but Merelith sighed. Lying on her belly was the *best*. Nothing hurt in this position, at least not at first. Anise wasted little time in repositioning Merelith's legs and arms to begin. The crown princess had spent the first two nights back studying every book she could find on easing angyrian children through their transformation. Even now, Anise opened a familiar book beside Merelith's head to ensure she was performing the stretches correctly.

The pages were dappled and worn, a testament to how old this particular tome was. It smelled of thousands of people to the angyrian sister, but only one smell stood out: that of her mother. Merelith sighed and Anise asked if something hurt. The angyr said no, then sighed again, and asked the question she knew her sister didn't want to answer.

"What happened with Mama?"

. . .

Anise

Anise paused at the question, the answer forming in her mind along with a swell of magic that would surely kill her sister if unleashed. She forced both down, unsure of how to separate the two. Merelith tensed, her angyrian instincts no doubt detecting that swell. The crown princess was still marveling at how perceptive those instincts could be.

"S-sorry. I...I don't know how to talk about it, Merelith."

"I understand."

She heard the resignation in her sister's voice and cringed.

"It's ok, Anise. Really."

Anise mumbled, "I sometimes wish you couldn't sense how I feel."

"But only sometimes?" her sister asked, mirth lacing the words.

Anise smirked and nodded. Though her sister could not see, she knew Merelith could feel it. Sense it. Somehow, a relationship now existed in place of the void that had been there just over a week ago. The wild magic that her angyrian sister inhaled and exhaled was no longer chafing but welcoming. If she focused enough, Anise could almost make out the twin instincts twirling about in her sister's life thread.

"I know you're angry at Mama, but..."

Anise tensed again, her sister's words halting at it. The crown princess willed herself to relax and listen. It was enough, that they only agreed to love each other but not much else. How Merelith could forgive their mother for her actions, Anise didn't know. How the guardian could forgive the princess, Anise didn't know. Yet she had, and it only made Anise angrier.

"...she really is sorry, Anise. I *know* she is. It was a lot, Papa leaving. Grandpa hasn't come back a-and, well, *you know*...it's a lot. When she said those things to me, it really hurt, but…what I said to you was just as bad, right?"

You're not going to call out what I said to you, are you?

No. You're too broken, still. Too much a tool and not my sister.

She did this to you and I don't know how to show you that.

"Mhm," was all Anise could manage, changing from one leg to the other.

Merelith remained silent, no doubt trying to think of another way to broach the topic. Anise kept her focus squarely on her sister's stretching and massaging. The work wasn't necessary, but it relieved a great deal of pain during the transformation. Bones guided into their new rotations, muscles relaxed and tensed to prevent atrophy from disuse, and nerves activated to help the mind adjust to its changing range of motion.

Overwhelmingly, the most common cause of pain in the transformation was cited as being the mind grappling with its new body. During their transition, angyr had three distinct periods of heightened discomfort or outright pain: the reshaping of the spine and sockets, the emergence of the wings, and the first quickening. The latter two were known to be quite painful, but swift, whereas Merelith's current condition could take as few as two weeks to several *months*.

Anise paused to massage her own wrists and relax her fingers before starting up the spine. Merelith stretched herself forward and the crown princess smirked. This was by far her sister's favorite part. It was odd to think of Merelith like an oversized *dog*, but the similarities were too great to ignore. Though her sister still wore a chemise or gown when sleeping, the distinctive mound of *fur* protruding from her spine and steadily thickening away from it would eventually render clothing unnecessary. Mostly, if the female diagrams were to be believed.

"I can't make you forgive her, Anise, and I won't."

The younger sister paused her hands and sighed. Perhaps sensing an opening, Merelith continued in a low voice.

"I just want our family back. She loves you, Anise."

"Not enough to come looking herself."

The words were out before she could stop them. It was a miracle she didn't singe the lovely fur between her fingers. Merelith had tensed, though, at the sudden flash of warmth.

"S-sorry" Anise muttered.

"You were hiding from her, Anise. She can't find what she can't see."

"She could have found you."

She prayed Merelith thought the heat in her hands was intentional and suspected her sister's instincts knew it wasn't. Still, Merelith's tension relaxed as she countered.

"Finding me and facing me aren't the same thing. She couldn't face her own sister, Anise. For better or worse…Mama is afraid of me as much as she is afraid *for* me."

"You love her. She has nothing to fear."

"She loves you. You have nothing to fear."

"*Enough.*"

Anise lifted her hands, eyes wide with worry as she looked at Merelith's back. Thankfully, the fabric of the shirt was undamaged. The gout of flame had left an acrid smell in the air, though. Her sister sighed, then chuckled. Her next words were like a slap to the face.

"You really should learn how to control that."

Merelith continued to chuckle, though it sounded forced to Anise. Still, the crown princess willed her anger and shame into check. Perhaps she, too, had instincts that needed heeling. She'd never thought of her emotions that way. Her mother *had* said Merelith was akin to a vast focus for her magic. Maybe, maybe her sister was right.

"I'm sorry. I…it was a stupid thing to say."

"It wasn't stupid, Anise. You were right. I *do* need to learn to control Tal and Kara. It's the way you said it. That is what hurt my heart. I'm saying it now because it *isn't* stupid."

That is what hurt my heart. Because she HAS a heart.

Merelith cocked her elongated neck sideways and glanced back at Anise. Her oblong face tried to smirk, but it looked more like a half-snarl. Still, Anise saw the twinkle in her sister's eye as she spoke.

"The more I've thought about it, the more I've realized…you'd probably make a great angyr, Anise. You have so much more control than you give yourself credit for."

Anise gulped and asked, "Do you think you'd make a good princess?"

Merelith snorted then shrugged, "I don't know. Maybe."

She then lay her head back down on the floor. A tense silence followed. Just before Anise resumed massaging Merelith's spine, the guardian spoke.

"I feel like it would have been easier, for you and me, if it had been that way."

"That way?" Anise asked, though she knew what her sister meant.

"If you had been born first. I think you would have liked it. This."

"Do…do you think you would have liked being princess?"

Anise was practically holding her breath as Merelith sighed before answering.

"Eric would have."

That was answer enough for the crown princess.

28 – Immortal Combat

Tobias

"Tell me, Consort, how did you come to be the matron of such an…*unusual* host?"

Said host was spending as much time tearing at an incomplete palisade as it was the people of Anar Tota. Galrend's legitimate army had already penetrated the city proper and begun engaging Torhal's more formidable warriors. Tobias had opted to hold back and observe the bloodletters clan, as much out of curiosity as tactical necessity: he needed to know what to expect when they besieged Torhal.

They are animals. Ferocious, implacable, mildly effective, and overwhelmingly terrifying.

All of Lady Talya's people wore a single pelt of varying animals, typically as a cloak or a crude jerkin, and nothing else. Needless to say, an army of naked blood-drinkers had quite the impact on Anar Tota's initial defenders. The cultists were seized by a peculiar lust for gory violence and unholy desecration. Anar Tota's defenders were decapitated with simple axes and knives, their arms severed and shared among the host for bloodmeal or a spare club, and the hearts gouged out and employed like sponges of perfume across their bodies.

Talya's smirk was beautiful and insane as she replied, "The same way all leaders are made, my king: I lied until the lie became truth."

"And what lie did you tell them?"

That they could live in houses and eat normal meals, I'm sure…

"That I had consumed the heart of an immortal. It is rather convenient yours no longer beats."

Tobias glanced at her and found the smirk of his consort had widened to a feral grin. His loins bid him to grin with equal ferocity back. A small voice in his stomach warned he would need a new queen sooner rather than later. The bloodletters were dismantling Anar Tota's wall out of practicality, not strategy: Talya had said they would use the wood later that night for pain and pleasure, both for themselves and any doomed survivors they kept.

"You forever surprise me, Consort," was all Tobias could think to say.

You and Lorath both. Hmph. Where is that ancient windbag anyway?

"Have you seen Lorath?" Tobias asked as he surveyed the carnage.

Talya shrugged and replied, "I was under the impression that he would leave for Tarn today?"

"Not until the battle is completed."

"Oh. Hmm."

Don't toy with me, bitch.

"Where is he, Talya?"

Ah, good. At least you remember who your king is.

Tobias smiled with satisfaction as Talya considered him with a wary eye before casting a hand toward Anar Tota itself. He furrowed his brow as she chuckled.

"You asked him to show you how to fight Orren Torhal, *love*. I have yet known Lorath to be tardy. I imagine he is waiting for you among your men. Orren is here, afterall."

"You are certain?"

Talya only nodded and then tapped her left eye, which glowed blood red with magic. A thrill went down Tobias' spine. He didn't bother to say goodbye as he spurred his horse into the flaming streets of Anar Tota. More than once, he had to kick or slay one of Talya's own, the savages too deep in their bloodlust to recognize the king that had brought them this feast. A massacre played out in the outer districts of Anar Tota, just as expected.

The council district, however, still held. The only complete wall in Anar Tota surrounded just seven buildings, all of them administrative. Within lay what remained of Anar Tota's leadership and Torhal's defenders. Tobias smirked as he hauled on the reins to stop his steed beside Lorath Saltsword, bedecked in his familiar if tattered traveling cloak. His mare was burdened with supplies and a trunk that contained a portable writing desk, papers, and ink pots. Tobias ignored the experienced stare of his advisor as the king surveyed the final gate to be breached.

"Torhal prepared them better than expected, Your Majesty, but the gate should fall soon. They are all but routed. Anar Tota will be yours before sunset."

"Talya claims he is here."

"I can confirm that he is," Lorath replied, "He made a valiant stand at the gate as the last of the council leadership fled into the district."

"Valiant my ass, Lorath. He is *immortal*. Valor belongs to those who fear death."

"Indeed, My King. Well said."

One of these days I'll grow weary of your ass-kissing, Lorath. Yet your resourcefulness never ceases to improve your standing in my court. A shame you are not younger. Replacing you may be impossible when death finally calls.

The last wall was defended by a paltry handful of crossbowmen, with one falling to the hail of arrows launched by Galrend every half minute. A crude battering ram formed from roped together logs stripped from the outer palisade wall hammered at the final gate, its fractures already bristling with spears from the defenders behind it. Standing at attention not fifty feet behind the ram was Tobias' crown guard, each mounted and equipped with unusually long glaives.

"You are certain in this plan, Lorath?" Tobias asked, hoping to sound confident.

"Absolutely. They have demonstrated unity precisely as prescribed. You need only enter their center and do your part."

Tobias was of a mind to rip into Lorath for his choice of words, in front of subordinates no less. Yet the king was too preoccupied with the meaning of those words. He'd never killed an immortal before. A king, yes, his own father, but the poor man had been blind drunk and as good with a blade as a dog with a quill. A small shiver ran down his spine again: excitement, dread, and a strange feeling he'd not known before.

"You feel him, do you not?" Lorath asked.

"I am unsure," Tobias answered.

"You are yet new to your immortality, but have grown accustomed to the…constancy…of your life thread. The lack of time affecting it as it does the rest of us. It is when you feel that time being tickled, that is how you know another is near. It is why you sensed the babe in the womb."

"How do you know of this?" Tobias asked.

Lorath smiled pleasantly, but Tobias saw the cold in his advisor's eyes.

"The study of immortality and agelessness has been the purview of the Saltsword family for generations, My King. I have read a great many first-hand accounts of past immortals. Few things are more regularly mentioned than the distinct sense of time *slipping* from them."

Time slipping. Hmm, yes, that is this feeling, I suppose.

The advisor nodded sagely along with his king, then turned his head back to the gate at the sound of a resounding *crack*. A hinge had been broken from the stone on the left door. Four more pounds, and Anar Tota's heart was laid bare to Galrend's army. Tobias cast a glance at Lorath and nodded. The advisor smiled.

"You are ready for this, Tobias," Lorath said, "Go and begin Galrend's glorious future."

"Glory for Galrend, my friend."

"Glory for Galrend, My King."

I told you, Annelle. I told you Orren would be a poor choice. Now I will show you why.

The king of Galrend spurred his horse right into the fray of the gate, his twenty-guard falling in around him, with the host of his army pouring around them like a river might a solitary stone. The interior of the district lay before them, with Torhal's remaining lines forming up for a final stand. Before them was a mounted company of thirty. At their head was King Orren Torhal.

Annelle's immortal husband was clad in practical chainmail beneath a sturdy leather jerkin and, aside from his crowned helm, looked no different from his crown guard. Tobias couldn't help but laugh as he charged directly at Torhal's line, knowing full well his painted plate armor made him a nightmare Torhal's men would never wake from. Even Orren's voice sounded weak as he courageously called for a final charge.

Perhaps a thousand of yours remain, Orren. I have well over eight still! What folly is this? Maybe Annelle is not so keen as Talya. Surely you sense my own immortality by now? If not, this will be too easy.

Horse, man, steel, and flesh crunched and clattered as Galrend's army struck Torhal's last line before the council hall of Anar Tota. Then it swarmed around it and past to pillage the hall and its remaining survivors. Tobias' orders had been clear: had Anar Tota wanted to survive this war, they should have surrendered and sworn fealty over a month ago. A surge of satisfaction filled the king's heart as he heard King Orren call for his people to force a retreat and escape. Tobias called his own orders to his crown guard. He needed Orren Torhal to bleed. He needed Annelle Torhal to know she chose wrong.

Farms could be replanted, mills rebuilt, merchants replaced. His ancestors had obliterated Anar Tota before. He had no qualms repeating history and reminding the world that Galrend would never yield its empire back. Lorath's time had been divided between training an army to effectively annihilate opposition and training the immortal king for this moment.

"ORREN TORHAL! FACE ME, COWARD!" Tobias bellowed over the din of battle.

A sword caught Tobias in the leg, and he looked down to behold a soldier of Torhal. Tobias kicked the man back with a plated boot, reached down to remove the sword from the crevice the soldier had managed to pierce, then tossed the blade aside. Two kicks of his spurs, and the fellow was a heap of gore beneath the king's warhorse.

"CROWN GUARD! HOLD FOR ME!"

Tobias looked up to see Orren charging toward him on his own horse, driving down Galrend's front line without care for his steed. Tobias smirked as his own guard fanned out to do battle with Torhal's best. As expected, Torhal's crown guard drove deep into his surrounding troops and made to surround him. They aimed to make a ring in which only Orren and Tobias could do battle – the only two who could actually harm one another. Lorath had advised most immortals tried too hard to keep their distance and made it that much easier to be pinned down.

Orren will want this fight, my king. Give it to him and you will win.

Are you trying to stoke my ego, Lorath?

No, My King. I am trying to open the way to Annelle and her throne. Orren Torhal is a skilled warrior, but I am confident you are superior. He will seek to protect his crown guard, both to ensure their safety and to give space to deal with you. It is a common and effective tactic IF he is the superior warrior. He is not.

What is to stop his crown guard from hindering me?

Orren will be above that. You need only inflict a mortal wound, Tobias. Slaying Orren at once is the best course of action, but if the battle turns do not hesitate to send Annelle's choice home as a reminder. Your own guard will ensure you have space to do so.

Oh, I rather like that thought. What would I do without you, Lorath?

Find someone else, My King. You are resourceful.

"TOBIAS! We end this now!"

Orren Torhal forced his horse forward and went straight for Tobias's neck. The King of Galrend grinned beneath his visor and easily dodged the blow, opting to ram the pommel of his own sword into Orren's passing head. The king of Torhal fell from his horse in a clatter of steel but was swift to rise to his feet.

As if it were just another day of riding, Tobias Galrend dismounted his own horse. Both crown guard fought around them in a circle, one eye to their kings and one eye to the host swarming them. Tobias tried to not be annoyed his own soldiers didn't grant this moment to progress unhindered. It was so rare, two immortals willingly doing battle. As far as the King of Galrend was concerned, everyone there should have been on their knees and watching in silent, rapturous awe.

"I look forward to showing Annelle what a *real* immortal can do to her," Tobias taunted.

Orren didn't even bother to reply, opting to instead charge his opponent. Steel clashed on steel and Tobias' hairs stood on end as he felt the time slipping reverberate with the blow. Felt his muscles ache, his fingers numb a little, and his heart attempt to beat. It was thrilling and horrifying. Unlike his father, Tobias was certain Orren would put up a real fight, too.

The first five or six blows were parries, with the occasional leg sweep and other maneuvers. Orren held his ground well and Tobias grit his teeth as he realized that Lorath's assessment might have been a tad overzealous. Yet the weaknesses were there, the openings small but present, and he could see the weariness starting to form in Orren's hardened gaze. Tobias went to the defensive, allowing Orren to assail him, knowing the young king likely felt he was gaining ground.

When a crown guard got too close to Tobias, he broke from Orren long enough to slice the back of the horse's legs, sending the rider tumbling. Before Torhal's king or his men could intervene, Tobias deftly drove his blade through the visor, instantly slaying the man. It had the intended effect. Orren's blood-rage blossomed, and he charged with wild abandon.

"A friend of yours?" Tobias taunted between pants.

"DIE, FILTH!" Orren roared.

"You first, Orren," Tobias replied with a cool smile, before slipping a dagger right into Orren's exposed armpit.

Immortal blood spewed across Tobias, and he reveled in it. Orren Torhal's sword arm went limp, and he narrowly avoided Tobias' follow-up with his own blade. The King of Torhal stumbled backwards and the King of Galrend pursued. A hint of surprise crossed Tobias' face as Orren picked up the fallen blade of a slain soldier in his left hand.

Ambidextrous. Impressive, Orren! I had hoped for a battle worthy of this occasion.

Orren made to charge again, but it was a poor attempt. The bleeding was taking its toll, his immortality unable to repair the equally immortal wound. Tobias easily blocked Orren's attack, spun his borrowed blade away, and drove the sword's tip into a crevasse in the Torhalian king's left leg. Orren howled with pain as the blade penetrated. Tobias hoped it had also severed a major artery or at least a fair few nerves.

Orren Torhal collapsed to the cobbled streets of Anar Tota. Tobias Galrend moved to execute the king, his blade raised high, when he heard the wild charge of another clad in Torhal's colors. He yelled with the voice of a man just barely out of boyhood.

"GET AWAY FROM HIM!"

The King of Galrend grinned viciously and saw fear bloom in Orren's eyes. Oh, yes. The king of Torhal understood now that he was beaten. That his final view would be of yet another crown guard throwing his life away. A child-knight no less!

"E-eric! No!" cried the king of Torhal.

Tobias howled laughter as he engaged the young guard. To his credit, Eric put up a half-decent fight, though his swordsmanship lacked in elegance. Tobias disarmed Eric and prepared to run him through when two heavy bolts slammed into the king's chest. Tobias stared at them in shock then up at the pair of crown guard that had fired them, both already nocking a new bolt.

No pain. There should be none, but these are inside me. Inside my own heart!

Tobias gripped one of the bolts, ripped it from his plated chest with a grunt, then smiled apologetically at the boy soldier before slamming it into his shoulder. Eric screamed in agony and fell before the king of Galrend. He then made to charge at the pair of crown guard preparing second shots when he heard the yelp and groaning of his original opponent. Tobias whirled around just in time to see a pair of crown guard hoist Orren Torhal up, deftly defending the king from Tobias' own.

"NO! *NO! GET BACK HERE!*"

Yet before Tobias could even hurl his sword at the injured king, another pair of bolts slammed into his back, staggering him. He whirled around in fury to find the pair charging away, the limp form of a boy thrown across one of their saddles. Just like that, Torhal's crown guard and king slipped from Tobias' grasp.

"Orders, My King?! Shall we purs…*gluk!*"

Tobias slung his sword, burying it into the knight's neck.

"No! You have failed me already and will not do so again."

Tobias ripped the dead man from his horse, retrieved his hurled sword, then leveled it at the remaining crown guard. What few remained of Torhal's forces had fled with their king out a back gate, trampling bloodletters too stupid to be of any help stalling them. Galrend's forces cheered, save the remaining crown guard who warily regarded their king. Tobias himself stared at the gate and tried to remember this *had* been the plan.

Annelle would know her husband had been beaten. Orren was injured, though Torhal's queen could fix that with time. What mattered was that Torhal's king would return home, defeated and shamed, paving the way for a siege that would, hopefully, never occur.

Annelle will bend the knee to preserve her family, my king.

I say we do as Lorath says, sweety, but let us hedge our bet, hmm?

Tobias breathed in fury for his quarry slipping him, but breathed out ruthless satisfaction that all was going according to plan. Talya would become a mightier consort. Queen, even, if she kept her clan in line. Annelle would become his latest plaything in the aftermath, a living reminder to future conquests of what resistance would bring. Yet even as Anar Tota burned around him, Tobias could still feel the time slipping in his bones. He tried to tell himself it was battle weariness, as it had felt before he had become immortal.

Deep inside, he knew it was fear that he was just another pawn, too. That fear had existed long before Lorath had arrived or Talya's body gifted him immortality. Whatever plans had been laid beyond his knowledge, Tobias could feel their strings tightening with every yard that grew between he and Orren.

Moreso when he could no longer see the Torhalian king.

. . .

Merelith

Merelith had not known what to think of it, that glass-shattering scream, as she hurtled down the halls of the castle towards her sister. Tal and Kara forced her body past the excruciating pain of moving too swiftly. She came upon Anise's room to find the princess wild with grief, sobbing and shouting incoherently as she hugged herself upon the floor. The guardian sensed no immediate threat, saw no wounds, and immediately set to trying to calm her sister, to no avail.

Then the queen burst into the room, left arm wreathed in white-hot flame and right hand armed with King Orren's ceremonial sword, ready to disintegrate or dispatch any who threatened her daughter. The surprise on her face at seeing Merelith there was both worrying and insulting. Then Annelle lowered her arms and asked what was going on. The guardian considered the shivering form of her sister in her arms then whispered her answer.

"It's Papa," she said, then asked louder, "It's Papa, isn't it?"

The queen didn't dare answer, dropping the sword and magic and swooping in to hug her children instead. Anise violently shook, unable to even speak as she curled into herself. Merelith, too, shivered but she kept her silver eyes trained on her mother. Searching. Pleading. Raging. Yet the queen did not answer her, instead stroking Anise's head and whispering that all would be well. The instincts did not agree and Merelith endeavored to ignore them.

The royal guard came shortly after, but the queen shouted for them to go away. To wait in the great hall until she came for them. Though Annelle didn't answer their questions, Merelith saw in their eyes that they all wondered. Perhaps it had been a nightmare, one mused, as they walked away. Lord Regis, the eldest of them, nodded but said nothing more.

Merelith saw that he knew. She felt Tal's confidence melting into fear, Kara's calm warping into panic. This was indeed a nightmare, the guardian was sure, but not one of the void. Anise's nightmares were few and far between, but they all had the same ending.

Had always had the same ending for ten years.

29 – Blood and Kin

Merelith

Merelith's eyes shot open at the sound of Anise barreling down the hall. The guardian was already moving herself to the edge of the bed when the crown princess burst into the room.

"Papa is here!" she said between huffs, then she was gone, racing toward the stair.

The guardian tried to ignore the twang of anger with a subtle pinch of shame beneath it. Anger that her sister had forgotten Merelith might need help getting down the stairs. Shame that her father would soon know what she had done the very day he had left. Merelith forced herself up on all fours and stretched as best she could, then gingerly lowered a leg to the floor. A soft tap echoed from her clawed toes. She dropped the other leg down, another tap, then backed up as far as she could.

At least it doesn't hurt anymore. Just horribly awkward.

Is Eric ok? Shouldn't I be more worried about Papa?

What will either of them think of…of this?

At least a shirt still fits. For now.

Merelith glanced down her underside, forcing a grim smile. Her breasts now sported thick fur between them that was, every day, inching up and around them. The mane proceeded all the way down her stomach, thankfully hiding her new array of nipples, where it thickened yet more in her crotch. Her back was nearly identical, making for a *very* strange appearance when she was naked: thickly furred down her back and front, but bare skin still visible under down fur along her sides and hips.

Ugly. Absolutely ugly. It isn't forever! It isn't forever like this. Just gotta keep going. My back looks nice at least. Onto the floor now. One, two, three…

The impact sent a small shiver down her arms. Her back still lacked the necessary curve to walk on all fours with any comfort. On the bright side, her hips were nearly finished, and she could sit back on her haunches with ease. This left her decidedly shorter than anyone standing around, but it made her have a sense of still being a person rather than an animal. Granted, that's precisely what she looked like: a human pretending to be a dog, sitting up as if waiting for a treat. Merelith's large ears pinned back at the thought. Then they flicked up at the sounds echoing off the stone hall beyond her door.

A great commotion could be heard from below, but she detected three distinct sounds. First, the hurried explanation of a crown guard. Second, the gasping and crying of her sister. Third, the trembling but confident command of the queen.

Injured or dead. Stars! I need to get down there. For both of them.

Merelith leaned to the side and reached for her cane. Though her hand was larger and more lupine, she still retained some dexterity. Her thumb had begun receding up her arm, a change that sometimes made her stomach turn if she stared at it too long, but her four remaining fingers could still grasp at things. If the books were true, angyr never lost the dexterity of their hands in their forepaws. Using tools was simply a matter of learning to do so without a thumb.

Cane acquired, Merelith looked to her mirror to decide how much she cared about her appearance. A plain, white dress covered most of her body, its skirt cut to allow her canine legs more room to stretch forward and back. A thick silken binding held her breasts, but panties had been forgone in light of her emerging tail – little more than an ugly stub with a tuft of red hair at its tip – and her hips being too constrained. She wore no jewelry, the holes in her ears healing too quickly to bother keeping and necklaces tangling too easily in her fine fur.

She managed a toothy smile. Her face was so strange now, so *long*, but she saw a beauty there she'd dreamed of. At least her upper lip had begun settling over most of her teeth. She gave her head a rolling shake and marveled, as she did every morning, at the radiant red of her mane and withers. Her human hair had been shedding for weeks and the last of it had fallen out just three days ago. She'd cried at that. Now, though, she beheld – and felt with her own paw – luxurious fur that put away any doubt about losing her hair. Her smile widened, briefly, at wondering what Eric would think of it.

The stairs proved treacherous, and the going was agonizingly slow. She half thought to call for a servant to help her. The easiest way down was crawling backwards, humiliating as it felt, one step at a time with a pause to bring her cane with her. She had nearly reached the bottom when a servant came hurrying over.

"Guardian! Oh, my dear, you should have called! Here, let me aid you."

"Thank you," murmured Merelith, her instincts on high alert at the offer.

Is it that bad? Does she know something about Papa? About Eric? No, no, no…relax. Deep breath. DAMN! Easy, woman! Don't snap, don't snap, don't snap…

"S-s-sorry, Guardian! Are you, uh, are you alright?"

Merelith winced as the servant rotated the guardian too quickly from the stair, prompting her left hip to burn with the overexertion. Merelith sat back on her haunches and held up a hand-paw. The woman stood stock still as the angyr caught her breath and forced a polite smile. With as few teeth as she could manage. The unmistakable shudder that ran down the servant's spine had Tal growling with vicious pleasure and Kara wondering about the servant's unusual willingness to touch her at all.

"I am fine. Thank you. Truly. Where is he?"

"S-sir Eric is being kept at the royal garrison, Guardian."

Kept?

"Alive?" was all Merelith could whisper, her throat clenching at the word.

The servant nodded vigorously and added, "Gravely wounded, Guardian, but he will live. Would you like assistance there? I understand he is awake a-and…"

Merelith was already turning toward the entry doors of the great hall when the woman's choice of words struck her. Deep shame penetrated the guardian as she stopped.

"No. Where is my father?" she asked in a whisper.

"He…he has been moved to the dining room. The queen asked me to fetch you so that you might visit Sir Eric? We can…"

The dining room? For more space. Oh no.

"How fares the king?"

"Oh, well, u-uh…"

The queen expected me to visit Eric, first? No. Mama sent you to keep me away.

Merelith turned her gaze fully upon the servant. The portly woman seemed to shrink, despite looking down on the guardian. Silver-rimmed eyes bore into hers as Merelith whispered her command, a soft growl beneath it warning against anything but the bare truth.

"Tell me."

"H-he lives. J-just. The k-k-king."

Merelith only nodded and began hobbling towards the hall that led to the dining room. The servant, to her credit, neither protested nor offered any additional assistance. Before Merelith had turned the corner into the hall, a familiar smell struck her nose, and she felt her heart tumble into her gut.

Blood. Papa's blood.

She hurried along as best she could, keeping to the side as a pair of nurses rushed out, their hands filled with bloodied sheets and cloth. One nearly stumbled at the sight of Merelith. The guardian ignored the stare of horror. All she saw were the doors to the dining room. All she scented was the blood of her father. All she heard was the slow, rasping breath of a man she thought invincible. A snarl curled across her lip at the thought of Tobias Galrend. She turned into the doorway and stopped, the snarl dropping at the sight before her.

All but two chairs had been shoved to the far corners, allowing as much room as possible around the spacious table. Two Torhalian doctors, the castle healer, and the queen stood around it. Anise sat on a child's stool – once reserved for Miss Molly in years past – before the roaring fireplace, her eyes empty as she watched. Six baskets, filled with bloody cloth, sat in the corner. Merelith managed to tear her attention from Orren's breathing to hear the doctor's words.

"…is keeping up, but it will take time to shut."

"Tobias knew what he was doing," Annelle whispered.

"Indeed, Your Majesty. How do you wish to proceed?"

"No sense closing it up, it'll just pool and clot inside of him. Call for a smithy. Anise?"

Annelle turned to her youngest. Anise swallowed then nodded that she was listening, though she still stared at her father on the bed.

"Scriptorium. Fifth row. Second or third shelf. *Immortal Bloodletting.* Fetch it, please."

"Yes, Ma…Y-your Majesty."

"Mama is fine, love. Hurry. If you see anything else on blood siphoning, bring it, too."

"Yes, Mama."

Anise rose, turned to the door, and spied Merelith sitting just inside it. Annelle noticed the crown princess pause and looked, her face going white with fear.

"M-merelith?" the queen asked quietly.

The guardian tried to not feel hurt. She was well aware of the profound impact blood could have on her instincts, especially blood of kin. Add in emotional trauma *with* an active crisis, and the situation could quickly become dangerous. Still, Merelith managed to tear her eyes from her father's limp hand and meet her mother's stare.

She whispered, "May I see him? Papa?"

Annelle tried to wipe the blood coating her hands onto her dress as she hesitated in her answer. Then she took a tentative step, then another, toward her eldest daughter.

"It…it is not good, Merelith. He will live, but…"

"Please," she growled.

Every human in the room stilled at that noise, subtle yet loud enough to make the threat clear. If ever there was a time Annelle or Anise Torhal were going to draw a line, this was it. Anise glanced between her sister and mother, then took a step back. No, the crown princess would not be aiding in this decision. Tal was pleased. Kara was not. Merelith did not care either way. The queen stood to her full height, as if trying to summon courage before she spoke her answer. Then her eyes widened at the slight flare of Merelith's nose, the widening of her irises, the hackles rising just slightly.

"Everyone out," the queen said with too-quiet authority, "Anise, that book, please."

Every single person, even Anise, kept to the far side of the doorway from where Merelith sat. As they left, the angyr turned her eyes onto the table and the man bleeding upon it. It trickled like an endless, gentle stream from beneath his left arm. It was pooling under his side, too. Orren's eyes were closed, his breathing erratic, as he looked up at the ceiling. Death was not far from this man, but it was far enough. Merelith's eyes shot back to the queen as she also backed away from her husband on the table.

"Do not touch the wounds. You are not quickened, but your inherent magic may have unintended consequences."

Merelith only nodded, as if one professional acknowledging another.

I should be crying. Or at least respectful.

He is MY Papa! He spoke for me before anyone else.

Please, please make it through.

Merelith hobbled to beside the table, propped her cane on a chair, then laid a hand-paw upon Orren's brow. The instincts surged as her senses took it all in. How cold and clammy his forehead was. The immortal blood replenishing itself inside the wound, the putrid tang of old blood in the sheets beneath him, separated from him and dying. The shallow, uneven inhalations and the whoosh of the exhalations as if it took all his strength to even hold a breath. Beyond the five senses, though, Merelith felt something different. The instincts both balked, unsure of what to feel but certain of what it was.

"He is afraid," Merelith whispered, before turning to Annelle and asking, "Why?"

The queen's eyes guttered, and she let loose a long sigh before replying. When she did, Merelith's own fear swelled for a moment.

"For Torhal, Merelith. He is afraid for our people. For our family. He…we did not expect this defeat. The army was far larger than we thought and Tobias, King Galrend, far stronger."

Tobias. I will end you for this!

Merelith growled, "Tell me how to to kill him."

"NO!" screamed Anise.

The timing of the question could not have been worse. Anise flung out a spear of ice to stop her sister, Annelle narrowly intercepted it. The crown princess was already preparing another spell when Annelle thundered for her daughter to stop.

"TO KILL TOBIAS, ANISE! STOP!"

Anise's eyes widened with horror at what she'd nearly done. Widened further when she realized Merelith had done little but stretch her arms wide to shield the fallen king.

"M-merelith?" Annelle asked, the shield still in place.

The angyr didn't immediately answer. Her arms were shaking, her hackles as tall as either woman had ever seen them in the last weeks. Neither knew the battle happening inside of Merelith's heart, the two instincts warring over how to respond. Tal demanded the blood of the crown princess, stupid and untrusting. Kara demanded the answer not given, to have a path to prevent her Papa ever being harmed again. Merelith felt like a distant spectator, unsure of who to support or if she even cared, her eyes still trained on her father's quivering chest.

"Merelith, love? A-are, are you alright?" asked the queen.

The crown princess stammered, "M-merelith, I, I…I am s-so sorry! I didn't, I thought…"

Merelith did not answer. Instead, she gently wiped her father's brow of sweat and pressed her almost-muzzle to his cheek. Then she took up her cane and hobbled toward the door, where Anise stepped aside, a pair of books clutched to her chest. Not until Merelith reached the doorway did she speak.

"Your fear is as wild as mine, but I do not think your love is. I will kill Tobias Galrend, not out of fear, but love. I will always protect you, all of you, not out of fear, but love."

She forced her eyes to meet Anise's and raised her head slightly. Stared at Anise long enough to force her sister to blink in fear.

"Wild fear is why you keep hurting others. Wild love is why I refuse to hurt you. Any of you," she glanced at the queen, her mother, huffed, and added, "Even if you deserve it."

She looked back toward her father and allowed her face to soften.

"Do not be afraid, Papa," she whispered, "I go wherever you go."

Then she left, not for the garrison to find Eric, or her own room for solitude, but for the scriptorium. Before the day was done, Merelith had every book on angyrian combat and quickening spread across a desk. She had read them all before, most before she was even ten. Now, she made to commit their words to memory. None dared interrupt her study in the following days, not even the crown princess nor queen. All saw the look of Tal's demand for blood in her eyes. All felt the calm wrath of Kara in her presence. Before, the guardian had felt like a wild woman, unpredictable but still human. Now, whatever little instinct the castle staff possessed begged them to keep their distance. A predator dwelled in their midst.

. . .

Lorath

Merelith's vow of vengeance spread through the kingdom like wildfire and soon reached the ears of Galrend through spies at a dinner held on the road outside Anar Tota. Tobias laughed it off, though Lorath heard the tremor in his voice and knew the men did, too.

"A half-finished whelp, no doubt even weaker than Orren!" the king declared.

Talya had looked worried, too, but Lorath knew she didn't fear the angyr so much as her spy's ever-deepening fascination with Merelith. The lady knew she was dancing on a dangerous precipice between the competing hungers of her husband and hound. She had been quiet for the rest of the dinner. A pleasant silence, as far as

Lorath was concerned. It was good, this unreasonable fear of an angyr not even quickened. Merelith's threat was an unexpected gift, one the Saltsword would make effective use of in Tarn.

It had sent a chill down his spine, but Lorath's smile was genuine. He couldn't help but grin at the news. An angyr would soon be hunting within Torhal. *Again.* He laughed along with the king, but for quite different reasons. All was progressing as planned. The journey south would be bitter cold, but the warmth of his success here would keep him comfortable.

30 – Magnificent

Merelith

"Never, in my wildest dreams, did I imagine a person could…could do *this*."

Eric marveled at the book, a hand absentmindedly roving through Merelith's withers. The guardian nudged her head into his stroke, content within his lap as he continued to read. It was a blissfully wintry morning, filled with fresh-fallen snow that glittered like a sea of diamonds out her window. His shoulder remained bandaged but time would heal all but the ugly scar made by the bolt. Time, Merelith realized, that couldn't pass quick enough.

"Because they can't," she murmured, "You'd have to be cursed with angyrism."

"It isn't a *curse*," Eric mumbled, tensing at her words.

"It is when your mother and sister are afraid of you. The whole damn kingdom."

"I'm not. Neither is your father."

"For now."

Eric snorted but didn't bother to continue arguing. Merelith felt her instincts stir with annoyance. Both wanted a fight, if for different reasons. Her father was at least awake and moving about now, nearly two weeks later since returning. Upon learning of what had happened the day he left, Orren Torhal had let loose a great sigh, shook his head, and simply said *I am glad you found her*. No lecture, no disciplining, nothing. Merelith still didn't know what to make of it. Eric had mused that the king likely had bigger things on his mind than a spoiled princess and half-formed, hot-headed angyrian daughter.

More than half-formed. Far more.

"So? What do you think will be best?" she asked, returning to the original topic.

What will be the best way to kill Tobias Galrend?

Eric shook his head and answered carefully, "I…I'm not sure, Mer. Obviously, you need to be able to quicken to actually *kill* him."

"Obviously. I meant the getting-to-him-before-I-rip-his-throat-out part."

"I love when you talk like that."

"Mhm. So, keep talking and you'll hear more."

Eric chuckled and her heart sang with the sound. She loved that he loved her aggression. Not once had he questioned if she was overreacting. Not once had he wondered if planning to kill the King of Galrend was something best left to her father. Eric understood her, understood her *need* as the guardian, as an *angyr*, to do this.

"Well, let's eliminate what *won't* work. Your wings will be too new and, honestly, if they're as beautiful as the rest of you…you'll be an easy target for archers. So, no swooping down, incredible as it may look or feel."

"Fair," she replied, nodding into his lap with agreement.

"That leaves the ground. You'll be fast but…I dunno, Merelith. Tobias is different. It's like he knew *exactly* how to handle your father."

"I am not my father."

"No, you're not," Eric countered, "You're *you*! Younger and lacking that experience. Your father fought well, just not well enough. You might be fast, but I dunno that you'll be fast enough."

"I'll have quickening."

"Briefly. And if any of this is true…"

"Ok, ok…so? Spit it out!"

"Ask nicely, *Beta.*"

Merelith tensed at the taunt. The instincts bitterly disagreed on how to reply. Tal was of a mind to just bite down on his leg. Perhaps a little too close to a certain erect member. Kara wanted to ignore the conversation entirely and roll over for him. Eric's sarcasm had a knack for driving her need. Considering they'd yet to do more than share a few kisses, Merelith was inclined to let Kara win. Ever since he'd left the garrison's sick beds, she'd been dreaming of letting him explore her changes. She was confident the former scout would be thorough.

"Please."

She tilted her head so that she could watch his expression of surprise. And feel him pulsing against the back of her neck. Eric's nostrils flared and then he smirked. He gave a flat reply.

"You're horny."

"No shit," she replied, "Hurry up and answer me."

"Ah, there's my Beta."

"Wait long enough and find out."

She had intended the growled words to sound threatening, but Eric only laughed. He cleared his throat, then ran a hand along hers. She couldn't help but hum and purr as his nails pierced her coat down to skin.

"I think you should sneak up on him…"

Oh, I like that idea. I don't need him to see it coming. I just want him dead.

"…I also think you should ask for your father's help in laying the trap."

She went rigid at the suggestion. Then promptly sat up off him, leaned back on her haunches, and crossed her furry arms with as much frustration as she could muster.

"*What?*" she replied, her teeth bared, "Why? That would put Papa in danger *again*, Eric."

Eric raised a hand in supplication as he replied, "Your father was himself tricked, Merelith. I don't think you'll be able to sneak up on Tobias without help. Without bait."

"My father, *your king*, is not *bait*, Eric Smith!"

The snarl, though quiet, was unmistakable. Any need she felt a minute ago had been washed away in a torrent of wild rage. The mere thought of her father being near the King of Galrend set her blood boiling. So much so she could feel her bones thickening with change brought on by the unbridled emotion.

"You would be there to protect him, Merelith. You asked how to kill Tobias Galrend. I think this is the way. Feel free to ask someone else if you don't like *my* answer!"

Then he was up off her bed, the book cast aside, and walking toward the door. Just two leaps saw her between him and the exit, his eyes wide at her agility. She sat up as straight as she could, arms and paws raised in surrender, silver-rimmed eyes pleading, ears pinned in humility.

"Stop. I…I'm sorry."

He gulped, not in fear but amazement, then folded his arms and waited for her to say more. She *hated* when he waited for her to say more because it meant she *had* to say more. He knew she hated the silence. Yet Kara was in full control, desperate to keep him from leaving, to keep her from facing this challenge alone. The door dug into her back, her wings painfully just below the surface of her skin dragging against it.

"It's just…I can't risk him, Eric. Not again. I…I should have been there."

"You'd have been a cripple."

She gently growled at him, but then nodded acceptance. He was right.

"I *was* there, Merelith. I understand, really, I do! But you're underestimating your father…or overestimating your chances. Or both. I get the feeling you're letting that alpha instinct lie about one and the beta instinct lie about the other. Besides, your father would probably support such a plan *if* you could prove you're ready. Acting like this will prove you're *not*."

Tal and Kara. Why do you insist on calling them Alpha and Beta? Bah, leave it. It makes sense to him and…that matters more. Papa has called me little Alpha for years. I'd rather be misunderstood sometimes than alone all the time.

Both instincts flinched at his words. She lowered her arms and sat fully on the ground, head hung in shame and defeat. He kneeled between her paws and thumbed her furry cheek. She refused to meet his eyes, even when he asked her to. He spoke anyway.

"If all else fails, and he says no, you'll still be prepared to try if the opportunity presents itself. Like it or not, Merelith Torhal, your father is *king*. A good one, too. He isn't going to sit back and let the crown guard lead the defense."

"I know," she whispered, "I'm scared of that."

"He loves you, Merelith. Loves all three of you. He'll use you, but only if he's sure the other two are safe. Or right there in the battle with him. I hope it doesn't come to that."

"Yeah."

"I want a piece of Tobias, too, but not at the cost of my queen and crown princess. I know things have been rough the last weeks, but…you don't want that, neither. So, instead of focusing on how we're going to bag that bastard, focus on how we're going to convince your father to let us."

Us. You and me.

"I love you," she murmured, finally meeting his eyes.

He smirked and replied, "I love you. Love your puppy-dog eyes, too."

"Oh, shut up."

If she could blush, she would. Did, under her fur, as he pressed the bridge of his nose to hers so that his eyes were just beyond her own.

"They are astonishingly beautiful, *Beta*. I could look at them all day and night."

"Only them?" she asked, aware her irises had dilated at the suggestion.

His eyes were smug as he replied, "I have hands for the rest."

One of those hands pressed fingers deep along her spine, gliding through her fur towards her rump. The sensation was exquisite, and she couldn't help but whimper as he moved. The other hand was light and gentle, first exploring her breast before searching out each of her other nipples, a quick pinch prompting her to lean into his face with her own.

"Eric," she huffed.

"Merelith," he whispered.

He brought both hands to her head, larger than his now, and began to stroke at the base of her ears. The massage was both exhilarating and relaxing, though her chest felt heavy at the absence of his hand, her spine still tingling from his rough stroke. She kept waiting for him to tease her about being as easy to please as a normal dog. Yet he said no such thing, even as she tilted her skull to the side as he began to vigorously rub the inside of her left ear.

Fuck. Amazing. Why does it feel so amazing when HE does it?

"Harder," she pined.

"Oh, it'll be harder soon enough."

She snorted even as he moved to the other ear and did the same. Her tongue, longer and wider now, lolled out of her mouth as she sighed in pleasure. She felt ashamed of his ministrations, wondering if all dogs felt this pent-up at such touching, uncertain if her feelings were unnatural or just *too* natural. The shame warred with amusement at it all. She really was a giant dog. A giant, horny dog. A quick whiff from her nose reminded her the man 'petting' her was *also* feeling the heat of desire.

Through it all, Eric kept his eyes on hers, even as she repeatedly closed her own with each tingle and tremble of lust. When he ran a hand over her breast again to cup it, she broke. The first time since the changes had begun. The heat, the intensity of it was unlike anything she'd known before. Her eyes shot open and then rolled up as that initial release roared through her. She collapsed into his neck, gasping as he threw his arms about her and hugged her through the cascading orgasm.

"That was quick," he mused with a chuckle.

Her instincts demanded a swift reply. Or rebuke. To just throw him back and savagely *breed* with him until he begged her to stop. Yet Merelith was stunned, unable to answer her own body's call for more. Beneath the orgasm had been a tremendous *pain* in her back. A pain she knew heralded her greatest change yet. She could feel a trickle running down her left side and knew skin had already broken.

"E-eric," she stammered, "M-m-my wings."

He went tense, then carefully lowered his hands until he found where the wings waited under her fur. First, he traced the right, his touch electrifying her in ways both pleasing and painful. Then he surveyed the left, pausing when he found where she was bleeding.

"Oh. Oh, uh…I…I'm sorry, I didn't…"

"It's ok," she said, pressing into him, "Don't stop."

"You want me to…um, to get it out?"

"No."

"Oh. What do you mean, don't…"

"Don't stop. Please. I want this. I…I want *you*."

His silence and stillness were agony to her. Then he stood back from her, and she was certain his abandonment had begun. Right up until he pulled his shirt off. Then his pants. Then his undershorts He smiled at her, with equal parts hunger and excitement, and held out a hand towards the bed behind him.

"I want you, too."

Nothing else was said. He lay on his back, and she clambered atop him. She almost joked an apology about a crushed pelvis, but then his hands were at her breasts and nipples, and she was collapsing into him again. He kissed, licked, and bit at her lips and neck. Then he thrusted against her abdomen, as if losing control of his own instinct while working her into another release. It came soon enough, and she fell atop him as blood trickled down both her sides, the wings loosening more.

"Now," she groaned in his ear, "Take me *now*."

She shuddered on his first plunge then had to choke back a roar of frustration when his second thrust missed. He ground out a guttural apology, wriggled beneath her, then gasped in surprise when she thrust down onto his tip, too impatient to wait any longer. He didn't seem to mind as she robbed him of his role, forcing herself down onto him rather than allowing him to push up into her. Eric just lay there beneath her, his hands roaming the guardian's chest and face, groaning with pleasure as she fucked him.

And fuck she did. Merelith didn't even see the man below. Tal focused exclusively on working her hips, demanding increased friction, heavier thrusting, and quicker movement. Kara steadied her breathing, felt every nipple flare with his pinches, followed the stroke of his hands around her soft breasts, reveled in his gentle twisting and pulling of her ears, mane, and lips. Even before his breathing turned ragged, heralding his own release, she sensed the change in him. The way he felt less controlling, less dominating, and more pliable and needful.

She bent low and bit him on his shoulder, sinking her teeth deeply and savoring his yelp and whimper. The sound of him yielding to her, then the feeling of him spilling into her, proved enough for her own undoing. The orgasm was cataclysmic, ripping right up her spine and down every bone in her arms and legs. She went stock still as if struck by lightning then shuddered uncontrollably as she collapsed upon him. So great was her yielding to him that she barely registered the ripping of skin as her wings spilled forth across her sides, bloodied, raw, and aching.

They lay still, or as still as they could, for a long time. Each time one trembled, the other did so, too. She buried her head into his neck and lapped at the blood oozing from her bite. He nuzzled into the top of her head, occasionally chewing on her ear, which always sent her trembling again. He softened within her, but she endeavored to hold still so that he remained. Eventually, his hands sought out her wings and explored them. They had little more than crusted down feathers, covered in dry blood and viscera, ugly as a newborn chick. Yet Eric's first word in what felt hours set her soul on fire.

"Magnificent," he whispered.

Then he was hard again, and the pain and ache were gone in her, and they made love once more. Long into the morning, pausing only for Eric to fetch lunch for them both, then again into the afternoon. How the man kept up with her, she didn't care. Perhaps the potion from her mother? Perhaps from deep love, she hoped. How he could stand her strange body, she didn't wonder. On and on they went, trying every position conceivable, learning every inch and hair and bloody feather of her body.

He called her magnificent at the end of each bout. When the moon rose high and he finally joked that his pelvis might indeed be fractured, she relented. He marveled at the fact she could still go on, satisfied as she already was. His only lament was that he wished he, too, were angyr. Merelith hid her discomfort at his words. Hid that she'd rather be human and unable to keep up with *him*, because he was magnificent to her.

Man and angyr curled together in bed, her head pressed under his chin, his legs pinched between hers, her wings thrown back and limp with too-weak muscle. When sleep had nearly come, he reached for her paw and curled his five fingers into her four.

Eric looked down at her and said with a hoarse voice, "I will make you, all of you, mine."

Merelith shivered and she smiled up at him.

"You already have," she whispered.

31 – Planning to Lose

Anise

"You can't possibly be serious!" cried Anise, "What if we are playing right into his hands *again*, Mama?! This plan reeks like the messenger from this morning!"

The queen regarded her heir with an appraising eye that warned Anise to correct her tone or risk the conversation transforming into a series of orders. To her surprise, Merelith's sudden intake of wild magic made it clear the guardian agreed. Annelle eyed her eldest daughter, perhaps in a taunting manner, and the angyr voiced her own opinion. Albeit with far more grace and calm than Anise had.

"The risks seem too great, Your Majesties. I can't see Lord Regis approving of such a plan and, just as importantly, Lord Thadeus being prepared for the fallout if it succeeds."

The queen whispered in reply, "It was Regis' idea."

That surprised both princess and guardian. Anise glanced at Merelith and found the angyr shaking her furry head, though her hackles bristled. The sight of the monster beside her was both comforting and disturbing: that monster was on *her* side. For now, Anise tried to remember.

Mama would listen to Merelith if she wore the crown. Mer has always had better words for this sort of thing. Would probably have better magic, too. Huh. I wonder if she would gain my magic?

The queen continued, "I didn't ask you two to review this with me to punch *more* holes in it. I need you to see the holes already there and determine how best to act."

In case you die pursuing this idiot idea, you mean.

Anise huffed but nodded. Merelith's growl was submissive in its frustration. While Anise studied the map, the guardian looked toward their father standing at the window. The royal family lounged within the reading room attached to the monarch's suite on the third floor. The sight of them would have made a classic painting of Torhalian flare. The queen presided over her heir as she studied a map, the guardian was relaxed yet alert by the entry door, the king stood in thoughtful repose as he gazed out upon the wintry beauty of the northern wardens.

The plan, if it could be called that, had come about as a result of the arrival of a messenger from Galrend's invading army, approximately three days out from reaching Torhal's kingdom wall. He had been delivered to the castle in a prisoner's collar with four long, iron rods attached to keep him a safe distance. Not because the man was rabid or violent. Oh no, Tobias had opted to have his consort *reanimate* some poor sod's corpse.

Parley in three days, at the stream beyond your walls. Capitulate and I will spare your children and Torhal.

Annelle had laughed bitterly and attempted to throw Lady Talya, who controlled the corpse, by asking if she would prefer to be killed by her king or Orren. When no answer had come, Annelle had asked if Tobias had killed their child or been foolish enough to keep it. Talya's answer through the dead man's lips had left Annelle as rattled as her foe.

Three days. Or he will kill yours, too.

Anise used a compass to draw a large circle on the map as she said, "I think I can make it this wide in a day's time, large enough to secure Torhal, High Lake, and most of the plains. After that, it will have to grow naturally…but Galrend will see the thunderhead long before they reach our walls. They'll know."

"That is all I ask, Anise," the queen said with a hint of approval.

Merelith chimed in, "If Tobias storms the wall without delay, you'll have to choose between saving yourself or saving Papa. You won't have time or magic to do both. Not with Talya in the mix."

Orren hummed agreement from across the room and Anise was buoyed by her sister and father. She nodded and implored the queen to reconsider.

"Torhal is *lost* without you. Possibly without just *one* of you! I am not fit to lead if this goes wrong and I'm deathly afraid that it *will* go wrong, Mama."

"If all else fails, Tobias will be bound in ice so thick Talya will have to choose as well: herself or her husband. I am confident she will flee the field and, with her, Galrend's strategic heart. I appreciate your concerns, daughters, but we face a war we cannot win without a major shift."

"Trading monarchs is hardly a major shift, Mama. It's just risky tactics. Too risky," Merelith huffed with a brief flare of her wings.

Agreed! This is suicide! Besides, what if it DOESN'T work!?

"I will not cower behind my people!" Annelle suddenly shouted.

Anise lowered her head, though a small glimmer of hope kindled when she heard Merelith growl back in response. The temperature of the room plummeted, ice began to coat the windowsill Orren had just released with experienced timing, and the rug under Anise's feet noticeably stiffened.

Orren tilted his head as he said, "It is rare, to see you so furious."

Merelith's growl stopped as the guardian cocked an inquisitive ear towards her father. Annelle, too, looked to Orren with a raised eyebrow. The temperature remained dangerously low, but it seemed like only Anise noticed. The king cast a wry smile at his queen, indicating who he was talking to.

"They hurt my mate, threaten my children, and frighten my people," Annelle replied stiffly.

"I had long thought her wildness came from me. But now I see it comes from you."

Anelle relaxed a little at that, if only because his words were probably true. Merelith, too, seemed to ease up, though Anise sensed that the 'Tal' instinct was very much at the fore. Wild magic continued to drift towards and into her angyrian sister. A bottomless well of limitless potential begging to be unleashed. The queen sighed then motioned to the eastern edge of the kingdom on the map.

"If Galrend breaches the wall, Torhal will suffer tremendously. I live for Torhal."

Anise clenched her jaw and replied, "I'd rather trade my life than yours."

Merelith growled, "Give me to him and I'll have his throat out before next sunrise."

"Neither of you are pawns to be negotiated," Orren said firmly, his voice raised.

Both daughters looked to their father and king. Anise sighed and nodded. He was right, much as she did not want to admit it. She looked to Merelith and worried as the angyr regarded her father with an intense, apathetic glare. Evidently, the guardian was in a combative mood in general. The king regarded his eldest for a moment then motioned to the map.

"Tobias' request, while dubious, does present a tactical opportunity."

"How so?" Anise asked.

"He has made it clear what he, or his queen, are after: *you*. Both of you."

Merelith growled, "Why?"

Annelle answered, "You are both weapons of extraordinary power, especially together. Kalligan the Dark was rumored to have controlled his angyr with a sorceress paired to it. The two loved each other and so could be leveraged against one another to do Kalligan's evil bidding."

Anise whispered, "The child of damnation and the dark hound."

"That is little more than a legend, Anise," Merelith said with a huff, before looking to the queen and conceding, "But it makes sense. If he controls one of us, he'd control both of us."

"But not you?" Anise asked, looking to her mother and father.

Orren pursed his lips and waited for Annelle to answer. When the queen did not, Anise's heart fractured a little. The king spoke for both of them.

"No. We love you, would journey to the ends of Damaria and beyond for you…but not over the needs of Torhal. We are, first, the king and queen of these people. To them, not you, do we owe our lives."

Anise's visible gulp saw Orren sigh. Merelith, though, only nodded agreement.

"You are the past," she mumbled, then looked to Anise and added, "You are the future." She glanced back at Orren and asked, "So, what do we do with this knowledge, Papa?"

Orren steepled his fingers as he focused his eyes upon the map, tracing the stream where Galrend had demanded parley take place.

"Our best course of action is to keep both of you from sight. As loyal as Torhal's people are, I have no doubt spies have ascertained that you are not yet quickened. However, they will *also* know you are drawing near to it."

Annelle shook her head and said, "Even then, Tobias probably knows Merelith poses no real threat for some time yet. Even under the best of circumstances, quickening takes weeks to master. He will want her to either ensure her demise or use her as leverage against us."

Orren countered, "His army does not know that, and I doubt he's stooped low enough to encourage them if he's sending cadavers to deliver his messages."

Merelith bared her teeth in a grin as she said, "Eric says they were poorly trained, many in number but not men and women of any great skill. Fear could be a strong tactic?"

The shudder in Anise's spine did not go unnoticed by either parent. Orren kept his focus on the map, only nodding in acknowledgement of the guardian's words. Annelle was thoughtful, as if seriously considering Merelith's suggestion, before shaking her head.

"Spreading fear among Galrend's army is a wise tactic, but such rumors must begin among our own. There are many who have not forgotten my sister's final deed. Loathe as I am to say it aloud, Merelith, fear of you will harm Torhal as much as Galrend. The guardian should be a source of pride and calm, their presence beside the heir a reminder of what and for whom they march: the future of the throne, of their families, of their kingdom."

Silver-rimmed eyes penetrated Annelle but she held her daughter's withering gaze. The angyr sucked the wild magic from the room, the sensation like an endless void ripping against Anise's life thread. The queen had *wanted* Merelith to be this way, the princess recalled. Annelle had wanted a guardian that was brash and independent, rather than cowering before her parents as Reeta had. The king cleared his throat as Anise looked on with worry.

"You will stand down to your mother and queen, Guardian. That's enough," Orren said.

To his credit, Orren maintained a firm glare as Merelith's head swiveled to him, her eyes just as focused and daring as they had been on Annelle. Yet the guardian did not bare her teeth, her hackles did not rise, and the pit into which wild magic was spooling suddenly filled and became a still, placid pool. As if Merelith were holding her breath. Then it began to rhythmically ripple. The angyr bowed her head.

"I...I understand."

Anise was shocked to see those silver eyes look to her again, no longer fierce. The princess' surprise deepened at the guardian's next words.

"Forgive me. I do not care what others think, but I should. If not for my sake, then those of my family. I care only that Tobias dies, but I shouldn't. I should care who lives."

"Well said, daughter," replied Annelle, a firm nod of approval following her praise.

How? How do they do it? Was this what I was meant to have with Merelith?

Perhaps we can. I dearly hope so. But how? How do I even tell her?!

"To the topic at hand," Orren then said, gaining the focus of all three women, "the tactical opportunity is not knowing what Tobias wants. It's realizing what he *doesn't* want."

"How do you mean, Papa?" Merelith asked, her ears standing tall in curiosity.

Anise understood and answered, "A siege that will leave him too vulnerable to keep any of his winnings. Galrend needs a swift victory."

Orren beamed at the crown princess. Annelle failed to hide a titter as she saw Merelith's eyes widen with understanding, though her ears pinned with frustration. The guardian disliked her younger sibling having more knowledge of war. Yet, that was to be expected. Anise had considered countless wars as part of her historical studies. Merelith knew the tactics of combat between men and units, but not kingdoms and empires. The princess continued with her opinion.

"Tobias chooses his battles purposefully. He needs the prestige of a defeated Torhal to draw a greater army, just as he needed a ransacked Anar Tota to draw the horde he has now. The towers have stood since before the War for Freedom. They are mighty but porous, too long for us to truly control after our loss at Anar Tota. Tobias need only infiltrate the kingdom and chaos will ensue. The suffering will be unimaginable, but a siege on this castle will almost certainly fail."

"Why?" asked Merelith, her ears rising again at Anise's explanation.

Annelle replied, "The queen and her heir are both present. Both skilled in magical warfare. Lady Talya's chances of mitigating damage to an assaulting force are poor at best. The siege will almost surely fail, leaving Tobias with a defeated army, a powerful family hunting him, and no recourse but to retreat to Galrend and hope nobody else decides to settle the many debts Galrend owes to other kingdoms."

"Then why take the risk at all?" Merelith asked, "It seems a fool's gamble from the start."

Orren answered, "We would lose most of Torhal, too, Merelith. Tobias gambles our honor against his hubris. We, too, do not want a siege. Anar Tota was a play to force us into the position we are now in: parley or open conflict beyond the wall, if only to spare Torhal."

"We do not have the strength for a pitched fight" Anise murmured.

"No, no we do not," Orren replied with equal quiet, "Our best bet is to hope for winter to crush them before it comes to that."

Annelle nodded and said, "Indeed, hence the plan: a sufficient storm could ensnare Galrend and drive the horde to abandon the campaign, immortal king and sorceress consort be damned."

The queen looked to the guardian, who watched her with a renewed intensity. It was not aggression that flowed from her daughter, but exacting scrutiny. Merelith, Anise realized, was agreeing to the plan. She had been convinced. The princess felt her heart sink.

"No," Anise said.

"No?" the queen asked, her eyes darting to the princess.

Anise raised her voice and declared, "No, you can't! What if they have an angyr, too? Talya could have been lying! She may be stronger than you, too, like Tobias was for father!"

Merelith interjected, "There isn't another angyr, Anise. There has been no sight of it for months now and it's safe to say that if it *was* Galrend's, it would have made its move already. It has likely headed on towards the wildlands."

Or was the angyrian witch all along? I can't say that aloud. I can't even begin to explain THAT mess in the middle of THIS mess!

"Y-you can't! It is too risky, Mama!"

"Propose an alternative, Anise. Genuinely, we will listen."

That's not fair! I…damn. We can't endure a siege. We can't lose Torhal.

It all felt futile. Annelle nodded slowly then restated her plan, each word boring an icy hole into Anise's stomach.

"Orren and I, along with the crown guard, will entreat Tobias to parley. It will be the closest I can get to him outside of battle. Anise will prepare a storm to render Torhal a difficult, if not impenetrable target, should the siege go ahead and likely succeed in creating a breach. Merelith will lead the royal guard in defending the castle, Lord Regis will lead whatever defenders remain for the rest of the kingdom."

The queen paused, sighed, then said the worst part of all.

"None of which will be needed if my part succeeds: we will surrender to Tobias, I will get as close as I am able, and encase the three of us in as much ice as I can manage. The resulting loss of leadership should cause ample chaos."

This is my fault. She got the idea from me and that stupid rune.

"Mama…" Anise began, but the queen held a hand up to cut her off.

"It will provide Talya several choices: attempt to kill me, save her husband, lead the army without Tobias, or flee. Torhal is an ordered people capable of defending themselves without Orren and me. I sincerely doubt Galrend is the same. Especially if the bloodletters are as awful as our survivors described."

Orren nodded and whispered, "They are, my love. They may set upon *us* rather than fight."

Anise shuddered at the thought, as did Merelith, yet the guardian then nodded and asked a hesitant question.

"If this fails…if, if Talya somehow stops you and you are both forfeit? What then?"

"You preserve the future, Merelith. At any cost. *We* are loyal to Torhal, Guardian. *You* are loyal to its lineage" Annelle looked to Anise and added, "*You*, Anise, must survive whatever comes."

Whatever comes. No more pretending. Shit.

"Yes, Your Majesty" replied the princess.

Annelle forced a grim smile then motioned toward the window.

"Come, let us walk the wood again. I know a few spots perfect for tomorrow's work. Orren?"

The king hesitantly replied, "Yes, my love?"

"Have the seamstress deliver my favorite fur coat to our best smith. I want Talya to have a glimpse of what a *real* sorceress queen looks like."

Merelith snorted with muted amusement. Orren only gave a serious nod. The queen made for the door then waited for Anise to follow. The princess cast a wary glance to both her father and sister and found them both looking back with grim acceptance.

"For Torhal," the queen said behind her.

For Torhal. For me, its future. I don't want to be its future.

Anise took one last look at Merelith, forced a smile, and followed her mother. Tomorrow, she decided. Tomorrow, she would set it all in motion somehow. Torhal needed a better future than her and she knew *exactly* who that future should be. Anise hoped Merelith would agree.

32 – Everything Considered

Anise

Anise wandered the queen's wood, alone. Every half hour or so she felt her mother's magic nip at her, the queen ensuring her youngest was still where she'd last been. It would have felt comforting, maybe even endearing, if not for the events of the last month. Now, her mother's presence felt oppressive and looming. Much like the thin circlet upon Anise's brow.

She wore the crown constantly, now, a symbol of her status and a reminder to her people of their future. A future Galrend was bent on destroying. To be fair, Anise realized she wanted to destroy that future, too. Or, perhaps more accurately, wanted to replace it with something better. *Someone* better.

Yesterday's meeting had left Anise still trembling. Her mother's plan was nothing short of a spectacular risk. Noble and selfless, maybe, but a risk all the same. What bothered Anise, though, was that they didn't fear their deaths nearly as much as she and her sister. Merelith's fury had flooded the room, but Anise had been surprised to find it comforting, unlike her mother, who had gazed at the guardian like a misbehaving hound rather than a rightfully worried daughter.

All this time, we've wanted the same thing…we just went about it differently. Would mother listen to Merelith if she were crown princess?

Equally distressing, though, was Merelith's open proposal to *be* given away. If only to have a chance at killing Tobias Galrend. That bloodlust bothered Anise, and it took a great deal of rationalizing to understand it. She *could* rationalize it, though. Merelith loved their father deepest of all and Anise didn't blame her. She wondered if he would love *Anise* the same, were she the angyrian guardian.

The people would not fear me as much as Merelith, I don't think. I certainly wouldn't struggle to stay at Merelith's side. I have seen why her life matters. Seen how it matters beyond the throne. Bah, enough. I need to focus.

Anise endeavored to push the myriad worries from her mind. She paused in a small clearing and let a shiver roll down her spine at the bitter breeze. The queen's wood echoed with the rattle of empty branches, a cacophony of pops and crackles. The crown princess listened to that breeze, felt it on her lips, and inhaled it. She tasted the wild magic in it. A tang of minerals, from the mountains it had swept over. A velocity that raced to keep up with a movement as wide as the continent. Wider still.

She exhaled the breeze and tasted that vast movement compressed, interrupted from its natural progression then released into a new, natural progression. From a breeze that had wandered from beyond the Wardens surrounding Torhal to a breeze that had emerged from warm, wet lungs into the freezing, harsh dryness of winter.

A storm is nothing more and nothing less than a breeze curled in on itself. Snow is but a frozen drizzle. Lightning is simply the energy of air compressed to a finger's width. We marvel at the fury of nature, Anise, but find ourselves boring. Yet we are alike and the same. Courage is just curiosity unbound. Discipline the culmination of many small steps. To make a storm, my daughter, you only need a breeze. To make a breeze, you only need breathe. To breathe, you only need the wild magic in you, of you, be itself.

Anise inhaled the breeze again and the wood grew still. Birdsong ceased, as did the crackling of the trees and the tinkling of icicles. The world around her was still, as if robbed of its own breath to feed her. When she exhaled, a gust broke forth before her and shattered the nearest tree into splinters of wood and frost.

Then she inhaled again, and the gust ripped back, shards of bark flying past and embedding themselves in the trees behind her. Then she exhaled a third time, and the trees behind were uprooted in a hurricane gale. Like five battering rams, the trunks hurtled forward and crashed through the wood ahead. When she next inhaled, she turned her head slightly, and the storm birthed then swirled around her.

A whirlwind fit to shred flesh echoed around the young sorceress, the five trees circling in a roar of noise as they tore along with the debris caught up in the gale. The ground cleared around her as the snow was lifted into the vortex, thinning then sharpening into spines of ice. She exhaled and the whirlwind expanded in diameter. Five trees became thirty, and Anise found herself in a clearing fit for a small festival. She felt the dim nip of her mother's attention but ignored it. Ignored that the nip had been coated in approval and praise.

Anise looked down at the ground and inhaled sharply, as if seeking to suck the earth right into her mouth. The storm surged skyward, a temporary tornado of wooden detritus, ice, and stone. Then she looked outward and exhaled every bit of air in her lungs. The storm widened to cover most of the queen's wood. Spread so thin, the trees and most of the stones fell from the sky back to the forest below, leaving only those snow flurries that had not been sharpened into ice.

To make rain, you only need water. To make water, you only need to cry. To cry, you only need the wild magic in you, of you, be itself.

Crying was easy for Anise. Had been since her first nightmare when the bed had come alive, not to eat her but scrabble down the hallway and eat her father. Just as she had thought Merelith might. Now, she cried for taking too long to see the curse infecting them both. The tears flowed off her cheeks and into the swirling vortex above, crystalizing into salted snow. From the stream of her heart poured an ocean of grief, from that ocean fell a rain of bitterness.

Snow is but a frozen drizzle. To freeze something is to rob it of the ability to change. To destroy or remove its wild magic. It is worse than death, to freeze something. Madness awaits those who cannot change.

The lesson pierced Anise's heart, the truth of her mother's words finding new meaning even as she stripped back the wild magic from the rain until it softened into snow. And so, the storm was complete: a rippling hurricane of her breath, an ocean of her tears, a barrier of her inability to change beneath it, yielding a blizzard that began to consume a generous portion of the queen's wood. To cover it with the essence of the crown princess.

Anise gazed up at her storm and struggled to describe it for herself. It was both beautiful and depressing, incredible yet horrifying. It did not feel right, to be able to so easily see herself in the sky. Yet everything else felt wrong beyond that storm.

"It is too easy for you."

She smirked at the words, not out of pride but agreement. It *was* too easy, to feel this way. She looked down from the storm to see a familiar, black angyr lacking its wings. The witch tilted her head in appraisal. Anise returned her steady stare.

"Such big emotions for so small a head."

Anise removed her circlet, glanced at it, and replied, "I confess that this does not seem an adequate lid for it."

"You have considered, then. And your sister?"

Anise furrowed her brow. She knew, without a doubt, she wanted this change. Her heart seemed undecided on Merelith, though. She and Eric were madly in love, and while the guardian did struggle with her new body, it was evident she did not *hate* it. Not like the angyrian witch's sister had, anyway.

"I don't know what my sister thinks," Anise answered slowly.

"You have not asked?"

"I have not."

Anise studied the circlet and envisioned it upon Merelith's brow, her red hair flowing under it. It was a difficult image to conjure. Already, in such fleeting time, Anise saw the muzzle of her sister rather than her winning smile. Considered her silver-rimmed eyes, rather than the beautiful hazel they had been before. A tiny voice whispered into her ear it was not too late to change. Another whispered in her heart that there was no greater sacrilege than to force the change.

"I cannot decide for my sister," Anise finally said, looking at the witch, "But I *can* give her that chance. Will you meet with her?"

"What you seek is not possible if she rejects it," the witch warned.

"If she rejects it…if she can live with what she is, then so can I."

The angyrian witch nodded then huffed with amusement.

"You are different, Anise, when you choose to not pretend."

The crown princess accepted the praise with a warm smile. Then she opened her hand towards the witch and repeated her question.

"Will you meet with her?"

"She's *your* guardian. The question isn't *if.*"

"I swear no harm will come to you," Anise replied.

The witch cackled at that, and Anise felt the barest twinge of anger. It was almost certainly the case that Merelith posed no threat to this ancient creature. Yet, a small part of Anise completely trusted her sister to protect her if such violence was needed. The witch steadied herself then turned away. She pointed with her nose toward the Silver Alpha and bared her teeth in a grin.

"When do you wish to meet?"

Anise faltered, not certain of how to answer. *Right now*, she wanted to say but knew better than to do so. A viable excuse would be needed to whisk her sister away from the castle. An enemy army would soon camp beyond the walls, afterall.

Perhaps it is best to wait until the war is concluded? Let Galrend falter and…No. No, if mother's plan fails…Merelith would be a prisoner, but she'd live. And I would likely die if I couldn't escape. Torhal needs her more, though. As an angyr or a princess, it doesn't really matter.

"Tomorrow night," Anise said, forcing her voice to sound confident.

That left another night until the parley. If Merelith agreed, they would change places. Or at the very least agree to change places *after* the war. The burden on Anise's shoulder already felt a hair lighter at this thought. If Merelith rejected the opportunity, Anise could go into these next days at peace. Her sister, too, she hoped.

Perhaps even my parents. Mama would understand, I think, after the fact. What if Merelith DOES accept? The cost is everything, afterall. That cost is still less than the hurt we've both felt. If she accepts, she's in as much pain as me. The cost is worth it.

"Tomorrow night, then," the angyrian witch said with an air of solemnity, "I suggest bringing a warm change of clothes."

Anise ill-hid her hope as she asked, "You think she will accept?"

"No, but I think you'd prefer she didn't nearly freeze. Again."

The crown princess took the jab in stride and nodded her head with a smirk. The angyrian witch nodded back then wordlessly set off across the vast clearing made by the storm. Anise looked skyward and considered what she would say to Merelith. Or Eric, for that matter, if this worked. A plan formed in the back of her mind as she breathed into the storm and grew it ever wider over Torhal.

Whatever happened, Galrend's troops would no doubt have taken notice of the arcane blizzard on the distant horizon. It was both a warning and a promise, but also a distraction. Somewhere in Castle Torhal, the queen was preparing her own spell. Anise pushed down the quiet fear that said trick might end up being for her, instead. Her mother's wrath would be more proof of the witch's truth: pretending could only hurt others.

Anise stuck out her tongue as she walked back to the castle, tasting the salt in the snow as she went. It was perhaps the most *Merelith-Thing* she had ever done. She twirled the circlet in her hand as she continued back to the castle, barely containing the urge to just toss it into the storm and never see it again.

Soon. For both of us. Whatever she chooses. Freedom. Soon.

33 – Sisters of Choice

Merelith

"Guardian? The crown princess has requested your presence. She has sensed a disturbance in the queen's wood and wishes to investigate."

A disturbance? Interesting. What are you up to now, Anise?

"Certainly. Inform Lord Regis, please. He'll need to know our plan in the event we return after the king and queen."

"Yes, Guardian."

The royal guard bowed then trotted out into the training yard. Merelith had decided to spend the last days before battle observing the royal guard and establishing rapport. Though she hoped her mother's plan worked, the guardian recognized it was her duty to be prepared for the worst. Lord Regis' raised eyebrow warned the crown princess might not get her way.

"It is not advisable to go out, Guardian" the lord said by way of greeting.

"Let's see what she has to say, Lord" Merelith answered.

Tal smirked at the lord's annoyed huff. Kara worried that his opinion of the guardian had lessened. Merelith shrugged them both off and led the way back into the castle. Behind her followed the lord commander of the royal guard along with nearly thirty of his men. Merelith hoped the sensation of hairs raising on her neck didn't mean her hackles were up, too. The sound of their boots, leather armor, and swords put both instincts into a state of unease.

The queen's wood is a strange place to want to go at all. Nobody in their right mind would be out there in the middle of that enormous blizzard Anise made. A surprise attack wouldn't come from the one place Mama would be strongest. So, what IS Anise sensing?

What was equally odd was that Anise was asking for *her*. She could have just as easily taken the royal guards posted around her. So, why ask for the guardian? The *monster*? All Merelith could figure was the destination: the one place the royal guard *wouldn't* go was the queen's wood without express permission from its namesake: Annelle Torhal. Were it anywhere else in the kingdom, the royal guard would have demanded to accompany the crown princess and her guardian. The queen's wood, though, was the one place they did not impose such strictures. It was an unspoken law that *nobody* entered the wood without express permission of the Torhalian family, security in war be damned.

Merelith and the guard arrived at the throne room to find Anise nervously pacing before the throne dais. Kara immediately began to fret while Tal had the guardian surveying every single guard posted nearby with lethal curiosity. Both instincts flared in worry at Anise's greeting.

"Sister! Thank goodness you're here."

What. The. Fuck.

Anise hastily said, "I have sensed something…strange…in the queen's wood. It could be a problem with my spell. We should investigate immediately!"

"Mama and Papa are still away, sister," the guardian replied cautiously, tilting her head slightly to acknowledge the scowl Lord Regis wore.

The angyr plopped down before Anise then rose to sit upright, bringing her head closer to her sister's height. The guardian's wings were rigid with concern as she motioned with a paw to state the obvious.

"A disturbance could be related to Lady Talya of Galrend, too."

Anise gave a tiny nod and replied, "Yes, which is why we are investigating it," she then glanced at Lord Regis and said with as much authority as she could muster, "Alone."

The lord replied, "Your Highness, I appreciate your faith in the guardian, but…"

"Prepare her horse, Commander" Merelith cut in, "and find Knight Smith."

Anise cocked an eyebrow at her sister's command. Merelith merely tilted her ear in benign curiosity back. Her sister was up to *something*, but it likely was not dangerous. Perhaps the princess merely wanted away from the castle – and ears attached to gossiping mouths – to discuss the next few days. That said, Lord Regis would need placating. Merelith was only just fit to fight, and certainly not in any protracted battle. Having Eric along would, hopefully, assuage his fears. The guard began to question Merelith's suggestion, but the crown princess interrupted.

"That should be sufficient protection. Knight Smith will be ample escort. His knowledge of the wood in these conditions also marks him the best for the task. I will ride with him" she paused, smirked at the guardian, and asked playfully, "If the Guardian agrees."

Touch him the wrong way and I'll ensure you never do it again!

*Tal. Seriously. Shut up. She's my sister! She doesn't even like Eric.
She can offer him all those things we can't…a home, children, a life…*

Merelith didn't have a reply for Kara, the instinct's thoughts too raw to muster a comeback. The guardian eyed her sister with mirth, but she hoped Anise felt the pull of Tal's threat. The warning to keep her hands off Eric reverberated in the magic surrounding them. The guardian looked to the commander and snorted with amusement.

"We'll meet Eric at the gate. Inform the king and queen if they return before us."

Lord Regis warned, "Guardian, are you certain…?"

"That is an *order*, Lord!" the angyr snarled.

The sudden onset of aggression had the man stepping back with a raised hand before bowing lower than normal. Then he and the others set off to find the knight, leaving Anise and Merelith alone. The angyr studied her sister in silence as they waited. Anise seemed to simultaneously stare at Merelith and avoid her gaze. Then the scent hit her, and she knew.

"You mean to visit the mysterious angyr. *Again*."

Anise struggled to hide her surprise. Absolutely failed to hide her terror at being found out. Merelith was still honing the skill of sensing other's emotions but reading Anise had become unusually easy in the last week.

Anise replied quietly, "What do you mean, sister?"

"Can he be trusted? I have smelled him on Eric each time he hunts the beast."

"Eric has returned every time, hasn't he?" Anise replied slowly.

"Two hunters did not."

"I do not know if she did that."

She? The mysterious angyr is a male. Golden eyes.

"She? You've met a *different* one?" Merelith whispered.

"No…she…it's hard to explain. Here."

"Is she aligned with Galrend?"

"No."

"Is she Aunt Reeta?"

"No! No, definitely not. I…Merelith, please."

Anise said it with as much confidence as she could muster. Which meant the thought *had* occurred this could be some sort of trap. Yet the princess obviously wanted to take the risk anyway, which was very much *not* like Anise. Tal considered the various potential threats and ran headlong into Kara asking the most important question: Anise was trusting Merelith with this. Why wasn't Merelith trusting her?

Merelith only nodded then asked, "What does she want?"

"I…" Anise stumbled for words and then said, "I can't say, here. I want you to meet her."

"Me?"

That threw both instincts and Merelith found herself alone in her mind. Another angyr wanted to meet *her*? A litany of questions arose but the crown princess held up a petite hand before Merelith could give voice to one of them.

"You will see. As will Eric. I'm glad you asked for him. Come on, the quicker we go the quicker we return. I'd rather be here when our mother returns, if only so we can explain ourselves instead of the guard."

Merelith considered her a final time then nodded.

"Hmph. Fair. Lead on, sister."

. . .

Every time Eric's arm slipped around Anise's waist to brace her against a gust, Merelith felt Tal's fury rise sharply before crashing against Kara's calm reproach. Her sister had no feelings towards the man, and she was confident Eric held no warmth towards the crown princess. He was loyal to the crown, true, but in love with *her*. Kara exuded delicious warmth at the thought and even Tal seemed to recede, albeit in a huff of righteous pride. In the swirling snow of the storm, neither human could see the angyr bare her teeth in a brief grin of satisfaction.

Human.

The grin subsided as Merelith pondered their journey deep into the queen's wood. Her ears gyrated about at every small sound beneath the roar of the blizzard. Anise hadn't even tried to deny they went to meet the mysterious angyr, though they'd both agreed to not tell Eric. It seemed strange that the knight hadn't put up any concerns. He'd merely shrugged, flashed a grin at Merelith, and declared he'd happily escort the two deadliest women in Torhal. Neither sister had bothered to remind him that Queen Annelle would easily outmatch them both, together.

"How are you faring down there, Beta?" called the knight, stopping Sneak so that Merelith could draw up beside them.

She easily ploughed through the snow, her legs and arms essentially complete and only lacking in the muscle that would come with practice and exercise over time. Just yesterday she'd snapped a branch as thick as a man's arm between her paws, surprising and no doubt frightening several of the soldiers that had taken bets on her strength. She shook her wings free of accumulated snow and gazed up at the handsome man clad in furred armor.

"Better than you, I bet," she replied with a smirk, "Your dick would have fallen off an hour ago."

"Merelith!" Anise retorted, her cheeks flushing with embarrassment.

"You always were frigid down there. Probably feel right at home, *Guardian!*" Eric goaded.

"KNIGHT SMITH!?" the crown princess bellowed in abject shock.

Merelith crowed laughter along with her man, both reveling in Anise's shame.

"Oh, come now. Can't be any colder than yours, Princess" Eric teased the crown princess.

Anise had no time to reply nor Eric to even laugh. That Sneak didn't so much as move a muscle was a testament to the horse. One moment, Knight Eric Smith was in the saddle holding the crown princess steady, the next he was buried under three feet of snow and with a thoroughly *furious* angyr atop him. He didn't even get a chance to sputter out a demand before a heavy paw with thick claws pressed right against his throat, razor sharp teeth filled his vision, and a voice that did not belong to his beloved whispered a lethal command.

"Apologize. *Now.*"

Anise was too stunned by the speed of it all to speak. Eric, too, judging by his wide, unblinking eyes staring up at the angyr. The Kara instinct kept Merelith from drawing blood to force the apology, but the Tal instinct gave her permission to roar the demand again.

"APOLOGIZE NOW, ERIC SMITH!" she bellowed.

"I-I-I'M S-SORRY!"

Somewhere, under the circling instincts, Merelith felt her heart bleeding with regret. She loved this man. She had no right to treat him so brutally. Yet the instincts had come on so quick, unbidden, she'd not had a chance to stop them. Her heart bled for Eric's shock, but it hummed angrily for Anise's pride. Any hurt, *any* slight to her sister gave rise to a fury she'd not felt since the last time she'd wandered these woods. She blew hot air into Eric's face before lifting her paw from his throat.

"She is *my* sister, Eric," murmured the guardian, stepping off him so he could rise.

"M-Merelith?" asked the crown princess.

"I'll not suffer any harm to you, Anise," Merelith replied, "Not even from him."

She felt the words settle in her heart and the bleeding staunched. She sighed as Eric slowly stood and brushed himself off. He glanced at the angyr and, to her quiet delight, nodded then flashed a small smile.

"Would that I had your gift, Merelith, I could love as fiercely as you."

"Save it for when we return, Eric," retorted the guardian.

Eric looked to Anise and bowed low as he said, "Forgive me, Crown Princess. I meant no real offense to you."

The young sorceress snorted and said, "Considering I *can* freeze yours off, I'd suggest choosing your insults carefully. In case Merelith isn't there to save you."

The knight grinned as Merelith threw back her head and guffawed. Then they were on their way again, Anise still not saying where they were going even as she bid Sneak onwards with Eric's aid. Merelith couldn't help but wonder at the strange quartet they were. A fifteen-year-old sorceress, an almost twenty-year-old knight, an eighteen-year-old angyr, and…

"How old is Sneak?" Merelith suddenly asked, realizing she did not know.

Eric replied, "Twenty-four! Old bastard is going to make it to thirty if only because he's so quiet nobody remembers he's on the battlefield. Why?"

"I can't say I expected him to just…*not care* an angyr had struck his rider from him."

"Oh, he cares when it isn't *you*. I suspect ol' Sneak knew I deserved it."

The angyr plodded along beside the horse and met his calm gaze. She'd spent many an afternoon lovingly petting that long face, waiting for her scout to leave the barracks with his latest orders. The gelding regarded her with what felt reassuring warmth. Why the horse didn't fear her, when every other in the kingdom did, forever puzzled Merelith. A pang of regret hit her as she realized she could no longer ride the gentle beast.

"Guess you and I will be seeing each other down here a lot more?" she murmured.

"What was that?" Eric called.

"Nothing. Just telling Sneak how handsome he is," Merelith called.

"We're almost there. See?" Anise suddenly said.

They'd reached the edge of the wood, where the slope suddenly rose up into the surrounding Wardens. In the poor afternoon light of the storm, it took a moment for Merelith to realize where they were: almost exactly where she had found Anise weeks prior. The crown princess pointed upwards and, through the snowy haze, the angyr barely made out the twinkle of a lone campfire amongst the treetops.

Tal tensed at the sound of steel being drawn. Kara curled her wings tighter as she went ahead of Sneak. An unspoken plan formed between her and Eric as they shared a glance. Merelith would scout it out, Eric would keep the crown princess safe as they approached. The climb was long but eventually Merelith came to a cave illuminated with flame. Within, she beheld a woman of extraordinary beauty, staring out into the storm. She tilted her head, then gave a wolfish grin.

Right at Merelith.

34 – No More Pretending

Anise

The angyrian witch remained seated by the fire as the trio drew up to the edge of the small cave. Anise forced a smile back to her, then noticed the runes and held out a hand to stop Merelith.

"What will happen if she enters?" Anise asked, her eyes darting between the cave walls and witch.

The witch shrugged and replied with disinterest, "Nothing. She does not wear a collar as I do."

"Wait here," Anise said to her sister.

Merelith's growl was low but quiet, yet the guardian nodded. Anise glanced at Eric, then his blade. She gently spoke her command as she motioned towards his sword.

"She is not an enemy, Knight Smith."

"Not yet, she isn't."

Anise furrowed her brow even as the witch chuckled in that sing-song voice. Merelith's hackles rose to an impressive height. The angyrian witch smirked as she stood from the fire and held open her arms towards the knight.

The witch asked, "Oh, Eric. When will you learn to trust?"

"When you give me what I want. What I've always wanted," he replied coldly.

Before she could blink, Anise found the knight's blade across her throat. Before she could scream, Merelith was already launching at Eric, teeth bared in fury but eyes wide in terror. Before the crown princess comprehended her fatal mistake, the guardian was pinned by roots and gagged by vines. Through it all, the angyrian witch only smirked at the knight, who continued to glare back.

"Well done, my hound. Here!"

The witch pulled the collar from her neck and tossed it at Eric. The knight caught it and in one smooth motion slapped it around Anise's neck just above his blade. Instantly, Anise felt *very* cold, her magic that had warmed her on the journey vanishing. Terror clawed at her throat as the witch's smirk grew to a menacing grin.

"It only took one touch for it to be bound to you, Anise. So much in that little head, so little of it common sense. Release her, Eric."

"No."

The witch's smile fell, and she tilted her head to the side, her look of amusement ill concealing the anger beneath.

"No? We need her. *Alive*. We have her."

"No. *I* have her," he said through grit teeth, "I have her blood. You *know* what I want."

Anise gasped as the blade bit into her neck. So tight was the steel against her she couldn't even stammer out a question or plea. The angyrian witch threw a hand up, first in a commanding gesture, then palm up in supplication.

"Eric, *mate*, let us reason through this. Tobias will kill us both if either dies prematurely."

Mate!? TOBIAS!?

"Tobias owes me his life. I could have helped Orren. I didn't. The bastard can wait his turn."

"I'd hardly call jumping in front of a bolt *saving* an immortal," quipped the witch.

"A single bolt, a single distraction, was all the King of Torhal needed."

"A single drop of her blood is all I need to end *you*, Eric. Don't make me choose between you and Tobias. Not right now. Not when we are so close."

Anise felt the knight shudder with fear, but he still managed to retort with calm wit.

"Choose? I chose *you*, Talya. I chose to find Lorath, *for you*. I chose to stalk this land, *for you*. I have chosen you over and over, and I'll gladly do it again IF you finally choose me, just once. *You know what I want!* And I now know you can do it."

The witch eyed Anise with wariness then sighed and nodded. Nearby, Merelith growled and roared through her bindings, to little avail. Anise could just make out the angyr's eyes darting about. Though the collar suppressed her magic, the crown princess felt as much as saw Merelith's swirling emotions with each look: rage, terror, and despair.

"More blood than is here is required, Eric. We'd need to return to the camp…"

Eric whistled, interrupting the witch. Sneak nickered then plodded his way up the slope, onto the ledge, and dutifully stopped beside the traitor knight. Anise's eyes widened in horror as the witch chuckled.

"Did you think I didn't read about the ritual myself? This should be plenty."

"Ever resourceful, Alpha," replied the witch.

Talya raised a slender, skeletal root from beneath the horse. It weaved along the belly of the beast before pausing at the base of its chest. Then it pierced the loyal steed.

. . .

Merelith

Sneak was in death as he had been in life: quiet, obedient, and unbothered. Merelith watched in horror as the witch's summoned tendril stung directly for the horse's heart. When the tendril retreated, blood gushed from Sneak as he collapsed to the ground. Talya then drew the blood up into the air, into her cave, and began to paint the ground around the fire with it.

MONSTER! BITCH! WHORE!

Anise, I have to get to Anise!

ERIC, WHY!? WHAT ARE YOU DOING!?

Mama! Papa! Someone has to help us!

I'LL DESTROY YOU! I'LL DESTROY ALL OF YOU!

The angyr struggled mightily against Galrend's sorceress but nothing came of it. Young angyrian strength couldn't trump roots that felt as stiff as the earth beneath her. She tried to scream for Eric's help, but the knight ignored her, as if she weren't even there. Merelith roared for Anise to fight back, but the younger sister could only watch in horror as Talya weaved her ritual from Sneak's blood. Only when Merelith deigned to whimper, to cry, to plead through her wooden gag, did the knight look at her.

"Relax, Merelith. It's going to be ok," he said with a smile full of love.

It's going to be ok. Is, is this all a trick? Is he playing Talya, too? Seems that way. Maybe…maybe everything is alright?

Merelith stopped fighting and did as she was told, relaxing and observing. He nodded at her with sincere appreciation then turned his attention back towards Talya. She loved this man. She trusted him. Clearly, he'd been lying to her but…she'd lied plenty herself, hadn't she?

Not to Eric, I haven't.

She smelled the blood of the horse and felt her instincts drive her to act, but she forced them back. She was trapped, anyway. So, she observed, smelled, tasted, listened. Her senses sharpened and she beheld truths she didn't want to.

Eric had said it was twins in Anna, but Talya smells the same as them. The scent of the mysterious angyr is all over both. Eric always knew where to look next. That day Anise found us, he sent them away. He said he saved Tobias' life: Papa thought Eric was trying to protect him, but he was only distracting the crown guard. Tobias could have killed Eric but didn't. Talya obviously trusts Eric, but Eric is forcing her to do this ritual.

He said he chose her. Over and over.

Merelith felt her heart seize with pain as she considered her thoughts.

You know what I want. Would that I had your gift, I could love as fiercely as you.

"You understand, *Guardian*, don't you?" teased the witch.

Merelith turned her baleful gaze upon the Consort of Galrend and found her smiling apologetically back. She motioned to the completed ritual site, shapes and eldritch writing formed from blood. At its edges were two circles, one beneath the angyr and the other beneath the knight.

"This is what *everyone* wants," she said with seriousness, adding, "Everyone. Even her."

She pointed at the crown princess before dropping her arms to her side and commanding Eric to let the princess speak. Eric eased his blade enough for Anise to cough and clear her throat.

"P-please, release her! She, she isn't part of this! She isn't…" stammered Anise.

"Stop your whining and tell her the truth, Anise!" Eric snapped in her ear.

"N-no! No no no!"

Eric yelled, "TELL HER!"

Trust your instincts, Guardian. They will never fail you.

The way he cuffed her sister's ear. How hard he gripped the sword against her neck, just enough to breathe and speak. His teeth bared in hate, his eyes full of angry desire. Merelith's heart broke and broke and the instincts within seemed to scatter into the depths of her soul, as if fleeing from the impending flood of grief and rage and shame. She loved this man and could not understand how.

"TELL HER YOU WANTED TO TRADE!" hollered Eric, and the crown princess screamed back.

"ALRIGHT! IT'S TRUE!"

The world stopped for a flicker of a moment. Time itself stood still, Anise's mouth wide with sorrow as her words echoed in Merelith's twitching ears. Eric stood taller, as if strengthened by the admission. Talya's eyes twinkled with victorious mirth at her servant. None of them saw Merelith. Or rather, only Merelith saw them. A tiny shock seemed to ripple across her wings then strike deep into her chest. For that briefest of moments, Merelith sensed her heart was not beating. Then, it lurched into motion and the worst day of her life continued.

"It's true!" Anise sobbed, "I wanted to trade! I, I wanted to be angyr!"

Why?

Merelith couldn't even muster the strength to ask. Her heart throbbed painfully, and her body suddenly felt too heavy. She collapsed beneath the binding roots, which saw fit to constrict her even further. She didn't fight them. Eric saw, his eyes wide with excitement. Anise's eyes welled with tears as the witch explained for her.

"The crown was too heavy, Merelith, and *your* burden too light. Anise came to me seeking a way to *change it.*"

"I didn't know it was her! I-I thought..."

"NO, YOU DID NOT!" crowed the witch, cackling, "You didn't think at all! Poor little *crown princess*, woe is me! Woe is my castle and my power and my kingdom and BOO-HOO-HOO. Merelith gets *freedom*, Merelith can do whatever she wants, Merelith has it all!"

Anise shut her eyes against the witch's tirade and flinched as if being struck physically by the words. Merelith could only watch her sister, her strength all but gone as she listened. Her heart thundered with grief. She wished her instincts would help her fight, but they were nowhere to be felt. Perhaps, she realized, they had been slain as she had.

"Enough, Talya!" barked Eric, "Do it. Transfer her power to me."

What? Transfer my...power? To Eric?

"You'll need to release her, mate."

Eric tightened his grip on Anise as the witch held her hands out with a tender smile.

"I choose you, Eric. Trust me. You are right. I owe this to you. I need protection from both those men, Eric, and only you can do that. Just as you've always protected me."

The knight grunted in satisfaction then shoved Anise away, towards the witch. Roots and arcane symbols swirled about the crown princess, binding her beside Talya. Merelith and Eric were left as the sole occupants of the bloody ritual, until Talya stepped into it. The blood seemed to shimmer, as if in recognition, as the witch went to the traitor knight.

"Take off your armor. Your clothes. They'll only get in the way of your new, glorious body."

Eric grinned with vicious lust, tossing his sword aside and doing as he was told. Talya watched with her own hunger. When Eric stood naked before her, she wasted little time taking hold of his erection while sealing her lips to his and very visibly plunging her tongue into his mouth. Anise watched in horror and disgust. Merelith, though, sighed in defeat. Then time stopped again.

I hate this. Why is this happening? Where did I go wrong? What did I do to deserve this? I love this man. Why? Why do I still love him?

This time, she knew her heart had stopped. The pain returned, sharp and awful, and she felt her entire body tingling at the sudden loss of blood flow. She was dying, literally.

Is this what a broken heart feels like? Is this what they mean?

All along, this had been his goal. She had loved Eric for nearly five years, now. Ever since that first romp in the woods, she'd known this man loved her. Hadn't he? The moment before her stood frozen in time, proof that she had only known half the truth. He was a skilled hunter and scout, but not for her father. He loved as wildly as she did, but he didn't love her, just her body. Moreso as it changed. It had all been for this moment.

Would that I had your gift, I could love as fiercely as you.

All he wanted was to be…me. Not to have me. To have what I am. Why do I love you?

Spasms wracked her body, the lack of blood flow starting a catastrophic chain reaction of organ failure. None of it seemed to register, her mind too focused on every line of his face. Every inch of his naked body, pressed to someone else. Every ounce of his desire, lust, and love focused on what came next. Not Talya, Merelith realized, her eyes widening in understanding.

He doesn't love her. He doesn't love me. He does not love. If he does not love, and he wants to be me…Do I not love?

She cried out in pain, and curled in tighter on herself as spasms wracked her body. Sound returned, as did the wind of the storm beyond the cave. She heard the wet, sloppy kissing of the traitor knight and evil queen. She saw the terror in Anise's eyes as Talya stepped back and began pouring power into the ritual. The blood's red ichor turned bright and before Merelith could react, a line between Eric's circle and hers lifted into the air then plunged right into each of their hearts.

"I give this gift to you, Eric, but you'll have to fight her for it," Talya said over his scream, "I do hope your wild nature can overcome hers."

Eric fell to his hands and knees, gasping and sobbing in pain. Merelith cried out in her own agony. Then heard him cry along with her. He flexed his hands into fists, and she felt her paws do the same. Eric shot a look of pure lust and longing at her and the angyr found herself staring right back. Merelith realized she could feel *everything* he felt. *Hear* his very thoughts, too, as if they were her own.

"Give it to me, Merelith. It's too much for you to carry," he said between grit teeth.

It felt as if her skin was being peeled off her back, so great was the agony. Perhaps it was, for she saw fur begin to bristle along Eric's naked back. He roared with pain but smiled with triumph.

"MORE! GIVE ME MORE!"

Her wings felt as if they might be breaking and bending at the wrong angle. Her tail was on fire. Her belly scraped and ripped with foul magic. Merelith felt his hunger in her own gut, the consuming *need* to become something else.

ANGYR! I…I CAN BE ANGYR IF YOU ALLOW THIS!

Human. I…I can be human if you allow this.

She howled as he howled, and soon Eric was more angyr than man and Merelith…she managed to see her fingers and felt bile rise in her throat. *Fingers.* Hair fell down along her face. *Hair.* She looked across to Eric and found his form swelling in size, covered in fur and strange shapes forcing their way under the skin of his back. Wings soon to emerge.

"YES! MAKE ME ANGYR! MAKE ME WILD! MAKE ME PERFECT!" screamed the traitor knight with wicked glee.

Perfect. He thinks I am perfect.

I WILL BE PERFECT!

My sister hated her life so much as to allow this.

MY LIFE WILL BE FOREVER!
My father trusted me to protect her.
EVERYTHING CAN BE MINE!
My mother…
SHUT UP! SHUT UP! SHUT UP! FUCK YOUR MOTHER! GIVE IT ALL TO ME!

She was almost human now. Eric was almost angyr. He shouted into her heart as much as aloud. Yet the flow between them stagnated. He roared in fury and somehow doubled down on drawing it out of her. Nothing flowed. His rage felt impotent and meaningless.

DO NOT STOP! YOU ARE NEARLY THERE! THIS IS WHAT YOU WANT!
No. It isn't.
YES, IT IS!
No. I do not want this.
YOU DID NOT WANT HER TO BE QUEEN! YOU DO NOT WANT TO BE GUARDIAN!
I want…
YOU WANT TO BE HUMAN!
I want…
YOU WANT YOUR PAPA? YOU WILL NEVER HURT HIM AGAIN! YOU WANT THAT!
I want…
YOUR MOTHER!? SHE ABANDONED YOU! SHE WILL DIE! YOU WANT THAT! GIVE IN!

He could feel her thoughts just as well as she could feel his. Yet he did not understand. She focused on her mother, on the queen that had left her in the snow, on the woman who had chosen this life, this fate, for her firstborn. Merelith knew she had never had a choice to be anything other than angyr. Presented now with the chance, Eric's determined pull was still not enough to convince her.

SHE DID THIS TO YOU! LET ME UNDO IT!
My mother wanted this. Wanted me.
BUT YOU DO NOT! YOU DO NOT WANT THIS! GIVE IN, MERELITH!
I want this.
NO! NO! NO!

Talya's eyes widened, just slightly, as the flow betwixt angyr and woman began anew…backwards. It was slow, but inexorable. Eric roared aloud in defiance. Somewhere deep within their entwined hearts, something snarled back from Merelith.

I want this. I have always wanted this!

STOP! NO!

With Tal I protected my sister all those years ago! Who are you to take her from me? Who are you to bring harm to my sister? How dare you threaten her life!

ENOUGH! SHE HATES YOU! SHE HATES EVERYTHING YOU ARE!

Yet Kara loves her! I love her! I do not care if she hates her life, I do not care if she hates me, I only care that I love her! I am her guardian! I am her sister!

STOP! STOP! STOP! NO! STOP IT! YOU CAN'T!

I can and I will, Eric Smith.

NO! I AM ANGYR! I AM NOT ERIC! I AM FREE! I AM WILD!

You do not know what it means to be wild.

YES, I DO! I SHOWED YOU! I TAUGHT YOU!

No. They taught me. Dig deeper, Eric. Find my wildness and I'll let you have it.

To his credit, Eric didn't waste time plunging his desire straight into Merelith's shattered heart. There, in the darkest corners of her grief he found the essence of wildness. The nugget of what made Merelith an angyr. In this arena of the mind and heart, Eric made himself the penultimate predator: an angyr himself who bit down with fearsome jaws upon this last piece of wildness in his unwilling prey.

In the arena of reality, his eyes opened in horror as the essence bit back. As they *both* bit back. Merelith pulled back from the root in her mouth just enough to utter the last words the knight would hear in this life.

"Let Tal and Kara teach you, too."

Merelith watched with cold fascination as the ritual gathered pace in its reversal. Talya had spoken true: it was his wildness against hers. Within her heart, she beheld a bloodbath: Eric's angyr little more than a ragdoll thrashed and tossed between the voracious instincts. Tal and Kara tore his throat out, rent his back with claws, and roared in twin voices of authority and protection over the broken pieces of her heart. Utterly destroyed, true, but still theirs to lay claim to. Wings spread in a show of dominance and her core radiated with purified calm.

Within the ritual, Eric's fate was even more bloody. As Tal and Kara thrashed him within, Sneak's blood and the tether between her and Eric seemed to lash at the traitor knight. Merelith grunted, screamed, and roared as her body was returned to its true self. As she swelled in size once more, hair fell out, fur sprung forth, and wings ripped through fresh skin. None of the pain compared to what she could feel in Eric as his body wilted into that of a man once more.

Worse than a man.

NO! STOP! Stop! Please, don't do this! I-I-I…

Less than a man.

It hurts! It hurts, Merelith! P-p-pleaaaAAAAAAHHHH!

The scream was guttural and deafening in her heart and ears, once more sensitive beyond comprehension. She wanted to revel in it but could not. Even now, she loved this man. Her instincts, though, did not. The wildness within her did not know love. Not anymore. Her body returned to her and the tether between Eric and Merelith looked ready to thin and snap. Just when the guardian thought the ritual was broken, the man defeated and still human, twin pulses of luminous white rushed down the tether towards Eric. His mouth opened into an 'O' of terror, but it was too late.

I still love you, Eric. I don't know why, but I do.

The man shuddered as the twin lights of energy struck him.

Forgive me. I can't stop them, for they love me just as fiercely. They are wild.

His hair turned grey. His eyes sunk in. Once strong bones grew sharp against aging skin. Eric tried to howl but his voice came out a wheezing gasp.

We can't help it. Maybe that's why you did it. You couldn't help it, neither.

Tears streamed down his ancient face, mingling with blood as his body weathered further and further beyond a natural lifespan.

It's not that I'm wilder than you. I'm not. Everyone is wild. Mama told me so.

Merelith cried, too, as the twin streaks rushed back along the tether and settled into her. The warmth of aggressive pride, the cool of satisfied calm. Twining within each other around her agonized heart. Eric collapsed upon the blood of his faithful steed, his eyes going dim as the last of his life faded.

You didn't want to be wild. You wanted to be free. Now, you are. I would have loved you for eternity. I did.

Skin shriveled then peeled into flakes that blew away in the wind. Eyes and tongue withered into dust, swept up and past Merelith. Even the bones bleached into nothingness, mixing into the blood on the earth before dissipating. Anise gaped in horror, Talya in surprise, and Merelith in plaintive understanding. The twin instincts had gone into him in search of something given freely before this awful night: an eternity of love. Merelith was content to leave it with him, but Tal and Kara were not. They had stolen it back, leaving Eric the hollow shell he had always been.

"Eric, my mate, why?" whispered the sorceress, "Why was I not enough for you?"

Nothing else was said as the sorceress queen bound her prisoners tighter. Talya threw her cloak about her shoulders, transforming into her fake angyrian form, then drug the daughters through the snow. Deeper into the mountains and away from their home. Anise cried bitterly and fought against the collar and wards binding her. She shouted at her sister to resist, too, but Merelith was oblivious to her cries.

The guardian watched the cave fade away into the growing dark of evening. The instincts roared at her to fight yet more, but their cries only echoed into the void in her chest. She had killed the man she loved. He was free, now. Free of his ambitions, free of his hatred and lust, free of his empty, mortal suffering.

What kept Merelith quiet, though, was knowing that Eric Smith was free of her, too. The instincts had taken back an eternity of love, perhaps in the hope of helping her fight on. Now, an eternity of rejection pooled in her broken heart, his words never to be heard again. The instincts circled and cried, but they went unnoticed in the endless silence within the guardian. A void, empty and dark, yet comfortable, shielded the guardian from everything.

Even herself.

35 – Mother of Nothing

Talya

The angyr was as still as death, her breath so shallow as to be undiscernible to the consort. Talya reminded herself, over and over, that Merelith was *not* dead. Nor was her own angyrian child, wherever that bastard Lorath had taken her. At least she'd finally held the babe before the advisor had left. It had been a supremely *stupid* risk to take, but the man had relented.

She has your eyes, My Lady. Have you come up with a name?

No. I…I do not know how to name something so precious. So beautiful and wild.

Well, succeed in Torhal and I will arrange for a…strategic separation of you and your husband.

It was a piss-poor promise Talya had no choice but to accept. For better or worse, she had to oversee the toppling of Torhal because Tobias was too busy fantasizing about how he'd torture Queen Annelle or where he'd hang Merelith's pelt when it was all over. Even the commanders of his army had taken to avoiding him, the walls of Torhal better company than the swelling ego of their king.

She glanced at the second cage, where the crown princess sat like a quivering ball of grief and shame, and almost felt pity. Almost. Anise had bought the lie and not thought twice about trading the security of her throne for a chance to be…what? *Free?* Talya shook her head and wondered if her ploy had been too good. Perhaps the Torhalian line really *was* cursed with heartless queens and insane angyr.

Not heartless. I heard that cry. I know it.

The sorceress shivered, as if to shake off the lingering effects of Annelle's otherworldly wail from earlier in the night. It had come just as they'd arrived back at her king's camped forces. Eric had preemptively delivered a letter informing the Torhalian monarchs their children had been taken. Annelle's reply had been a wail so loud and powerful, the very storm over Torhal had taken on an angry hue of red and the air now tasted of salt, not just the snowflakes.

It had carried such profound grief and rage, laced with accusation fit for a goddess of judgement. Not even the legends of Antila spoke of such power. Which begged the question: if Eric, in all his reckless *wildness* couldn't overcome an idiot eighteen-year-old…what chance did Talya stand against Annelle?

The ritual can only be forced through sheer will, My Lady. Claiming the princess' power will be of no trouble. The trick to claiming Annelle's will lie in breaking her beforehand. Complete the tasks set to you and your hound, and you will hold the keys to her power.

It had sounded so simple until that wail had sent Talya to the ground, crying in the tongue of a creature she had fabricated, unable to move a muscle as grief and shame and fury ate at her. As if Annelle had damned all of creation and had the authority to do so. Or, Talya wondered, perhaps creation itself had damned itself for her. The consort's heart prickled at considering the fear her own daughter might have felt as she was carried in the arms of a man with too old eyes, somewhere on the long, cold road to Tarn.

"Why are you crying?"

Talya looked up from the ground, where she had been staring in deep contemplation, toward the crown princess. Anise Torhal sat upright, her hands folded in her lap. Or, rather, she tried to. The collar made it difficult for her to keep her head upright. Talya lacked the means to control the pentarchy relic, and its prisoner, but the collar's basic function remained: total suppression of any magic, supposedly even void magic. It was an ugly, heavy thing forged from a metal that seemed to pulse with shadow rather than reflect torchlight. A large ruby was set into it, along with a number of various, smaller specks of gems and crystal.

"That looks terribly uncomfortable," Talya retorted, skirting the question.

They had attempted to put another collar on Merelith. The angyr had ripped the man's hand clean off, Talya's bindings not as tight as she had thought. Even when properly restrained, the collar had reacted unexpectedly, as if compelled by unseen forces *away* from the angyr. Ultimately, the consort had given up and settled for heavy chains and a thorough lashing to cow the guardian into submission. Anise had screamed for them to stop, but a punch to the mouth had laid her out in just one blow.

Now, Anise's jaw bloomed purple as it quivered with hopelessness. Merelith's back had already healed from the lashing, though the blood, fur, and skin that had been carved away still lay about her cage. 'A reminder' Tobias had said, when asked if it should be cleared away. That had been around midnight. A heavy blanket had been wrapped around the chained princess to ensure she didn't freeze to death, but otherwise she had endured the gathering winds of her storm slowly stretching beyond the Torhalian border. Merelith had been given nothing.

"Ah! She is awake! I trust you slept well, Crown Princess?"

Talya watched Anise shiver with fear before it suddenly ceased under a mask of barely contained fury. The consort almost smiled at that. Then she heard the rustling of chains and turned to see Merelith twitching and, presumably, waking. Galrend's king strode right up to the caged angyr and snorted.

"Ah, and the angyr who is meant to be hunting me. First time, I take it?"

The consort was of a mind to tell her prisoners to not reply, that nothing good could come of it. Merelith raised her head a fraction of an inch, then twisted her neck just enough to cast an eye upon the immortal king. Talya saw in the corner of her own eye that Tobias seemed to tense. Then he flinched as the angyr whispered her reply with unnatural calm.

"For me, it is."

Tobias huffed a chuckle, pretending as if neither daughter of Torhal had seen the fear flash across his wicked grin. The sorceress consort, though, furrowed her brow in confusion.

"There is no one else, *pup*," he crowed.

"You would not know, *boy*," replied Merelith.

Then the angyr did something that enraged the immortal. She closed her eye, turned away, and lay back down. As if he was little more than an unwelcome distraction from a much-wanted nap. Anise cried out when Tobias drew his sword and clanged it against the bars of Merelith's cage. The angyr didn't so much as flinch. Not until Tobias drove the blade straight into her left haunch. Chained tightly, Merelith could do nothing but howl in agony.

Tobias bellowed, "LOOK HERE, YOU FURRY BITCH! LOOK AT THIS BLOOD UPON *MY* BLADE! YOU ARE ALREADY DEAD! YOU ARE ALREADY LOST! SOON YOUR

FATHER AND MOTHER WILL BLEED ON MY STEEL AS WELL!"

Anise sobbed and screamed as Tobias withdrew his sword and threatened to stab again.

"STOP! Stop! M-Merelith! Merelith, talk to me! A-are you alright!? STOP HURTING HER! STOP IT!"

Tobias whirled on the crown princess and looked ready to drive his sword tip into her leg, too. At the sound of Merelith's furious roar, he stumbled back, his fear not at all concealed. Even so tightly chained, Galrend's King took no chances. He began to advance again, no doubt to punish Merelith for scaring him, when Talya's voice rang forth.

"Tobias, Sweety! Stop harassing the children. Annelle's surrender depends on the promise of her daughters remaining unharmed."

The consort gently rested a hand upon his heaving back. He tensed at that touch, then a false calm settled over the king. His wicked grin returned but Talya saw the fear still lingered there. The consort turned her husband to face her and ran a finger down his jaw. His grin turned lascivious, and the crown princess cringed as she watched the queen indulge the roaming hands and tongue of her king.

What have men ever created without a woman…Oh, Eric. Why were you such a fool?

The angyr looked away and Talya felt a tightening in her throat. She pulled from Tobias' wandering hands and forced a smile. Lorath had been right about Eric, too. The consort could only trust he was right about Galrend's impending victory. Tobias cast about casually then did what he did best: ask the worst questions.

"Tell me, my wife, where has that dog of yours gotten off to? I wish to reward him for his work in securing *our* victory. You may be getting a crown out of it all, but Eric deserves a treat, don't you think?" Tobias murmured.

Talya felt her heart stop at the sound of Eric's name. Or perhaps because Merelith seemed to twitch at the same time. Or maybe because she saw in Anise's face the unmistakable shadow of grief before she replied.

Merelith loved him, too. Truly. She would have given in if not for Anise. Powers unknown…

"Eric is dead, My King."

The king cocked an eyebrow but didn't seem to show any sign of surprise.

"How?" he asked plainly.

"The angyr killed him."

Talya's choice of words wasn't a mistake. Tobias went rigid, briefly, then let out a forced guffaw. He cast a hand towards the caged guardian but didn't look as he taunted her.

"*She* killed him? After all the fucking they were doing?! Do you mean to tell me that Merelith Torhal *killed* Eric Smith? I don't know what is more surprising, that she had it in her or that he was foolish enough to allow it! How?! *How*, Talya, did this come to pass? Do tell."

The queen clenched a hand to her side, though embers of hate seethed between her fingers. She visibly gulped before answering, not in a sign of fear but self-control. If Tobias Galrend knew that he was stepping on his wife's heart, he didn't show it. That awful, amused smile merely danced on his lips as he waited for her answer.

Talya whispered, "Eric attempted the ritual of transfer with Merelith."

The glee in Tobias' eyes ran away and was replaced with something else, an emotion the sorceress couldn't place.

"What?" he whispered.

Talya nodded and said, "His wild nature against hers. He nearly succeeded."

"Was he a child of ritual, too?" asked the king.

"No, but I also do not think angyrism is related to lineage."

"You mean to tell me…he could have succeeded?"

"Possibly. If she were to allow it."

Talya motioned towards Merelith, who remained as still as ever, though her ears were clearly tilted towards the monarch and consort in rapt attention. Talya knew little of angyrism, if it were a curse or a gift or a spell or some other magic. All she knew was that the boy she had raised to be her lover and spy had chosen this creature over *her*. His mate. Or so she'd thought.

"So, you chose your life over his, then?" Tobias drawled towards the chained angyr.

To Talya's surprise, Merelith looked back at the king and *smiled*. The sight of her teeth had the intended effect: Tobias visibly swallowed. The consort barely hid her own fear at the guardian's words.

"Maybe I chose *you*, Tobias. Just like she chose Eric."

Tobias didn't miss the stiffening of his queen at his side. Eyes full of condemnation swung onto Talya, who only stared straight at

Merelith with thinly veiled hatred. The angyr turned away again. As she settled her head upon a thick iron link, she whispered before either monarch could retort.

"My mother kept me. You should have kept yours."

Tobias shot back, "It is kept in an unmarked grave, mutt, that such evil as you can't be used!"

It. He won't even acknowledge she was his. How dare she dredge up something she doesn't understand! She has no inkling of what I have done to SPARE my daughter!

"I am glad to not endure her temperament. Yours is taxing enough!" Talya spat.

Merelith retorted, "Why am I not surprised to learn you killed a baby *girl*, Tobias?"

Talya didn't stop Tobias from raising his blade once more to drive it into Merelith. The angyr kept still, no doubt waiting for the punishment. Yet it didn't come. Talya cocked an eyebrow as Tobias faltered then turned his gaze upon her. He stared at his consort as he asked a new, terrible question.

"*Her.* How do you know the babe was a *girl?*"

Oh no. No no no!

"I am a wild sorceress, Sweety. I knew what she was in the womb."

Tobias' stare was almost too long to bear, then he huffed and turned away. Whether the king had bought the lie, Talya was not sure. Tobias looked upon the angyr's back and returned to crowing over her.

"I look forward to my consort stealing your mother's power. All thanks to your sister."

"*What?*"

Both Talya and Tobias looked to Anise as the crown princess realized she had spoken aloud. Tobias glanced at his consort then smiled with victorious malice. Happy for a change in topic, Talya laid bare their plan for the queen of Torhal. Anything to distance Tobias' mind from the child who was meant to be in an unmarked grave.

"The ritual of transfer is an ancient rite for passing on accumulated power. I'm surprised you don't know of it, but then again, your grandmother died before she could complete the rite with Annelle. A shame, really. Centuries of Torhalian magic lost to an unknown assassin."

Tobias continued, "My lovely wife will be taking your mother's power and, someday, yours as well. However, it requires a specific ingredient!"

A malevolent hand was cast toward the chained angyr. Merelith didn't look but the consort was sure the angyr knew all the same. Afterall, she'd just survived that very ritual.

"The blood and a feather of angyrian kin. Hence why Torhal has *always* kept its angyrian children. Oh, did you think she was meant to be your *protector?*"

It was evident that Anise was struggling to believe her ears. Yet Talya beheld realization creep across the girl's brow. Eric had nearly become angyr, proving the ritual functioned. Whether it could work on an angyr didn't matter anymore. Torhalian might had a dark secret under it, one the crown princess obviously had not figured out until now.

"She protects the future, Anise. Isn't that what dear Mama and Papa told you both?" taunted the sorceress, "Forgot to tell you whose future, though, didn't she?"

"But you are not kin to us?" Anise said, trying to muster a tone of defiance.

"Oh, my sweet child, we need only be kin by a single thread. The mad pentarch has mothered countless bastards in her unholy research. You think the Torhalian line is the only one to survive the War for Freedom?"

The horror of Talya's truth settled onto Anise's face. The plan had been Lorath's and, despite Eric's claim, Talya was confident Lorath had found *them*, not the other way around. How long had Eric stalked Torhal, undetected because the magic surrounding him was kin to Anise and her forebears? How easily had Talya slipped in, both as Maybury and the Angyrian Witch, never once detected except in physical tracks and minor slips? The questions danced plain as day in the princess' widened stare.

"We are all children of Anisterosa, here," Tobias said with satisfaction, "Her husband was Galrend, the sixth immortal slain to form the Pentarchy. Their son, Tamar, is my ancestor. Even you and I are related, albeit through over a millennium of bloodlines. Isn't that something?"

He chuckled then shrugged.

"I suppose, after today, maybe you can start calling me Uncle Toby. Or Papa, if you're so inclined, seeing as Orren won't live to see the next sunset."

Anise had no words and, apparently, neither did Merelith. The angyr merely tensed at mention of her father. Tobias didn't notice, though. He took Talya's hand and left their prisoners to freeze in the dawn's light. In a few hours, Tobias promised over his shoulder, they would see their parents for the last time.

"Then," he trumpeted ahead to his soldiers, "The Empire of Galrend will begin anew!"

The cheers of his men didn't drown out Anise's sobbing. Nor the faint growl of her angyrian sister. Worst of all, it didn't calm Talya's nerves as she realized Tobias was squeezing her hand too hard.

36 – Colliding Crowns

Merelith

Beyond the wall of towers, Torhal's border was loosely defined by three major landmarks: the warden mountains that stretched to either side of the wall, the town of Silverton that rested in the shadow of the southernmost tower, and the point at which the Torhal River turned directly east, eventually flowing into a small marsh known as 'the split'. Directly over the bend in the river was an ornate, wood and stone bridge that marked the official entry to Torhal's lands. The forests beyond it were all regarded as belonging to the people of Anar Tota.

The bridge had been commissioned centuries ago and, over time, expanded in width and grandeur. By the time Tobias Galrend and his horde arrived, it could fit eight mounted horses abreast, though their riders likely had trouble doing so on account of the bridge's stony keepers: the first ten guardians of Torhal, five to each side atop pillars that supported the bridge. Carved with lifelike detail, merchants from the world over had learned to cover the eyes of their beasts of burden when crossing the infamous Guardian Bridge.

On the western side of the bridge sat a lone watch tower of meager height, originally built as a toll house but gradually transformed into a signal tower to notify the wall of approaching dignitaries or, in more recent days, an enemy host. Like the bridge, its architecture left no doubt to which kingdom had built it. The brass knocker on the door was fashioned into the likeness of a roaring wolf framed with iron feathers, and four miniature angyrian statues lined the simple crenulations of the tower, each leaning forward and down, as if ready to plunge off the tower and take flight.

As the sun peeked over the forests of Anar Tota and bathed the top of the tower in dawn's light, Merelith studied the four small statues, marking every detail that made them unique from each other. Her and her sister's cages had been placed before the watch tower, in the heart of Galrend's most equipped soldiers. To either side of the bridge stretched a host of nearly six thousand. Almost two thousand had fled in the night after her mother's otherworldly cry. Not enough to make any real difference, considering Torhal had less than fifteen hundred men to defend the four towers and wall.

Anise had spent much of the morning attempting to loosen or damage her various restraints, interspersed with random bouts of crying. Each time Merelith had looked at her, the crown princess could only stare back for a moment before casting her eyes away in shame and biting back sobs.

This is her fault. Whatever comes next, Anise did this.
That isn't true, Tal. Stop.
She was just trying to help, though it was a poor way of doing so.
Maybe, Kara, but I might have done the same.

It was odd, again conversing with her instincts as if they were separate people. Perhaps it was because there wasn't much else to do. Tal had plotted and craved the death of every soldier twice over, Kara had studied every tear on Anise's face. Merelith had laid in her cage and let the instincts have free reign. She was bound in iron; it wasn't as if they could do anything. Yet.

Mama and Papa have a plan. It will still work. She called for help in that wail of hers.
They will not trust me to help. Anise's security is first, they will be afraid I'm broken.
They should not trust me to help. I need to taste Tobias' blood. Talya's, too.
I am the guardian. They will trust me to control the two of you.
The wild cannot be controlled.

Merelith shuddered at the answer of the instincts, enough so that her chains clinked and drew Anise's attention. It was unlike Tal and Kara to outright disagree with her, but then Paol and Polo had warned such a thing could happen. The instincts weren't wrong: her parents had every reason to not trust her, given the circumstances. Merelith reminded Tal that it was crushing that ember of hope in her. She felt the bloodlust relax in tacit agreement, albeit with a huff of annoyance that brought a small smirk to her lips. She reminded Kara that it didn't matter if her parents trusted her, she trusted them. Kara hummed uncertainty but resumed its patrol around Tal in obedience.

She could almost hear the crunch of her heart-shards under its paws when she realized what she heard was the approach of many boots on the gravel of the road to the bridge. She looked up and over to find Anise watching, too. From their vantage by the river, they could see all the way to the Elder Tower in the distance. What remained of Torhal's army stretched beneath the wall, seemingly insignificant compared to the horde of Galrend, which the enemy troops were quick to point out with jeers and cheering. Tobias Galrend and his queen sat atop warhorses just beyond their prisoners. The King of Galrend raised a hand for silence as a unit of calvary broke from the center of Torhal's lines to approach.

King Orren. He is not fit for combat. I can see his wounds troubling him as he rides.

Queen Annelle. She is armored, too. Do they mean to fight right here on top of us?

They can't use the original plan. There is no way to protect all of us.

The crown guard flanked the pair of monarchs as they rode ahead of their small army. A white flag was hoisted by a familiar face: Knight Polo. As they drew to about fifty yards away, Merelith's ears focused on the men that had sworn their lives to defend her parent's throne. What she heard gave pause: not words, but the distinctive clank of hidden chains and the rattle of many crossbow bolts.

They've come prepared to kill me.

Merelith felt her nostrils flare with Tal's anger.

Or they are prepared to steal Anise away in the confusion?

The guardian quivered with Kara's worry and fear, her eyes darting to Anise. The crown princess now stood, her bloodshot eyes gazing towards her parents. Merelith tried to sense what emotions her sister felt but could not. Perhaps it was the collar upon her, but the angyr wondered if it might be because Anise felt nothing at all. Both instincts stilled at the thought.

"TOBIAS GALREND! I HAVE COME TO PARLEY!"

Orren's voice did not waver as he shouted his greeting before kicking his horse forward until he was half the remaining distance to Galrend's frontline. His queen followed alongside him, one hand upon the reigns of her charger while the other rested in her lap in the form of a relaxed fist. Tobias' chuckle was loud enough for all to hear. He did not move forward as he spoke.

"Dismount and come stand before me, both of you, or I'll turn your pet into a pin cushion."

Merelith kept her eyes steady on her father, even as Orren blanched at the sound of ten crossbows being raised and aimed directly at the guardian. One of the men grunted a snort of amusement, but then she heard him mutter a curse when her tail flicked in his direction.

Don't do it, Papa. Make him come to you.

"Very well, Tobias."

Weak.

He only makes himself more vulnerable!

SHUT. UP.

The instincts were cowed by Merelith's inner command. In truth, she agreed with them both but didn't need that reminder on top of her own racing thoughts. The king and queen of Torhal quietly dismounted their steeds in a fluid motion that looked choreographed. Both pet the necks of their mounts, both stepped in time with each other, both looked ahead to the conquering king with determination. In all the years of watching her parents, Merelith had always saw them as passionate lovers and wise rulers. Now, she saw them in a new light: unbreakable monarchs.

Orren stopped ten feet short of Tobias, far enough he couldn't be immediately harmed, but close enough he had to look up at the immortal of Galrend. Which, no doubt, was exactly what Tobias wanted judging by the sneer on his lips.

Tobias declared, "I will only accept your capitulation and execution. Kneel and accept your defeat, and I will spare Torhal's people. Your daughters will be pressed into service of Galrend's throne. In time, they may earn their place at my side or the side of Galrend's allies. Those are my terms. Accept them or accept their deaths in place of yours, and the death of all your people, who have marked you as their voice."

Tobias held his head high as Orren considered him. Then the King of Torhal looked to Lady Talya and, strangely, cocked an eyebrow as if in surprise to see her there.

"Talya Bodisnia. You are far more beautiful than I expected."

"And here I thought the King of Torhal had manners," Talya replied, "You may address me as *Queen* or not address me at all."

"You wear neither crown nor ring to mark you as such," Orren said back, a smile curling the edge of his lips.

Even at this distance, Merelith saw Talya go rigid at the jibe. She almost grinned when her mother spoke next.

"That should not be surprising, love. Do you not remember? Tobias bought me a *chair*. Angyrian fur, was it not?" Annelle glanced at Tobias and her smile dripped venom as she added, "It was a *lovely* piece, Tobias, truly, but I am glad you took it back. It simply did not match the décor I already had. White fur is so hard to clean."

The angyr felt it before she saw it: the rush of wild magic between the two queens. It was apparent that one had a far more powerful draw than the other: Annelle Torhal cast her gaze onto Lady Talya and

Galrend's Sorceress twitched. In fear or rage, Merelith could not tell. She was inclined toward rage as Talya shot a glare at Tobias. The King of Galrend, though, seemed to find it all quite hilarious.

"You should have kept it, Annelle. Unlike you, my queen will be lounging on it long after your corpse has rotted to nothing. What did Orren give you? Perfume? As fleeting as your reign, I suppose. Now then, enough theatrics. *Kneel.*"

Tobias snapped his fingers and the crossbowmen surrounding Merelith, as one, lifted their weapons and took careful aim at her. The angyr felt Tal surge with fury at the sight of fear flashing across Orren's face. She forced herself to a standing position, the chains held up by the resolve of Kara to exude calm in the face of death.

Whatever happens next, I am ready. I will do what I can. Even if all I do is die. Let them see that I trust, even if they don't. Let my sister see I have always been ready to take her place. Not on a throne, but in a grave. I am the guardian. I was born for…huh? What is that sound?

Near the edge of her peripheral, Merelith heard the distinct sound of a landslide. Yet the land was flat here? Her ears filled with the tumbling and cracking of stones, as if careening down the side of a mountain. A deep reverb echoed beneath it, as thunder in the far distance, that she could feel in her head. Yet nobody else heard it. Merelith looked toward the sound and barely caught sight of a flash of white at the edge of the woods behind them. She looked back towards her parents to see Queen Annelle had also seen it, her eyes wide.

Is this part of some plan?

"KNEEL!" Tobias shouted.

Orren grimaced but then looked on with shock as Annelle immediately dropped to her knees and went as far as to throw her arms forward in shameless submission.

"STOP! D-don't kill her!" she pleaded, casting her war-crown from her head and prostrating herself before the King of Galrend, "Please! Please, Tobias, spare her."

"Annelle?!" Orren said, but the queen shouted angrily back at him.

"Kneel Orren! Do as he says!"

The king glanced between his queen, Tobias, and finally to Merelith. All the guardian saw was confusion and worry. This was *not* part of the plan. Merelith considered her mother in equal confusion, the reverb in her head suddenly ceasing. She had read about that sound, before.

Nobody else heard it, but mother saw something, too. It sounded like thunder, but Anise's storm has no lightning in it. A flash of light can only mean one thing: quickening. Oh, no. OH NO!

Merelith's eyes widened in horror as she began to scream her warning. Yet she was too late. From thin air she beheld the appearance of a monster only seen on the pages of ancient books and in a mirror. It was larger than her, more mature, and far stronger. It leapt from the peak of the lone tower directly towards the kneeling queen and her bewildered husband, not yet realizing death itself was descending upon them.

"*MOVE!*" screamed the guardian of Torhal, but it was drowned out by the roar of the other angyr.

It was a blur of red fur and feathers, crashing down into the queen. It took hold of Annelle by the shoulder with its outstretched forearms, and the pair went tumbling away from the other three monarchs. Orren unsheathed his blade, only to be shot through with spines of ice by Lady Talya. Tobias drew his own sword but, rather than deliver a death blow to Orren, he whirled on his queen.

"TRAITOROUS BITCH!" he seethed, swinging at her with murderous intent, "YOU SUMMONED IT HERE, DIDN'T YOU?!"

Talya narrowly avoided the attack, and Merelith saw her face was full of fear and confusion. Orren struggled to free himself. Anise screamed in horror and banged her bindings against her collar. The crossbowmen had abandoned their post around the guardian and scattered at the sight of the new angyr. The instincts in her roared to get loose, but the chains were too heavy for her to do more than see what others could not.

See that the angyr had thrown Annelle from the vicinity of Galrend's forces and now stood over the queen's limp body. It did not harass or kill her. It did not even *look* at her. Rather, Merelith saw silver-rimmed eyes focus upon Tobias Galrend with an emotion she knew too well. Primal fury. Lethal calm. Then there was a flash of light and the angyr had vanished again for all but Merelith Torhal, who watched with rapt awe.

The sound of its quickening was terrible and beautiful, the reverb of it washing over her smaller pair of ears as the sight filled her eyes with white light. Time split for Merelith, reality slowing to a crawl while the quickened angyr, wreathed in lightning, ran toward her. *This.* This was the power of her birthright. Merelith could only gape as the angyr ran to her cage then, in an instant, time realigned and the lightning was gone with a second boom.

It reappeared right beside Merelith and, with a mighty tug, ripped the iron door clean off her cage. It bit into the very chains and crushed them into bloodied shards, stinging Merelith with the force of it all. Death incarnate breathed on her, its face showing signs of intense pain despite having no wounds. Quickening, twice, for such long distances in so short of time was taking a toll. Merelith unsteadily rose from her bindings. She looked at the face of her rescuer and was overcome with the uncanny feeling of gazing into a mirror. Silver eyes, a face of red fur, and the stare of a guardian, not a monster.

The wail. Mama was calling for you. And you answered.

"Reeta," whispered Merelith.

"Save sister," replied the older guardian.

Then Reeta was gone, hurtling into the nearest soldiers as chaos broke loose in Galrend's lines. The Battle at the Guardian Bridge began in earnest.

37 – Guardians

Anise

Anise thought her throat might somehow shatter and split open, so loud and painful was her scream as the strange angyr plowed into her mother. But then the monster just *disappeared* in a flash of lightning, leaving her mother's still form just beyond the reach of the Torhalian Crown Guard. A second burst of light saw the princess stumbling back and tripping over her own chains, falling in the cage as she took in the creature flaying her sister's cage open and *biting* the chains off as if they were little more than twine or sinew.

"Reeta."

Even over the shouts and screams as the two armies converged, as the crossbowmen rushed to defend their king, oblivious the threat had already moved into their midst, as Tobias and Talya spewed curses at each other while her father tried in vain to escape…even above the cacophony of battle breaking out, she had heard Merelith speak. And Reeta, too.

"Save sister."

It was the voice of a *thing*, not a woman, rough and graveled as if broken from disuse. Anise looked on with rapturous terror as Reeta leapt onto the nearest crossbowman and rent his head, left shoulder, and arm from his body. Blood arced in the morning light and before it hit the ground the angyr had already slain three more. Anise was so entranced by the unnatural destruction she didn't see Merelith at the edge of her cage until the angyr roared her name.

"ANISE!"

"Wha…!? Merelith! A-are you…?"

"Stay down, don't move, I'll find a way to get the collar off!"

The crown princess nodded dumbly and did as she was told, the commanding tone of her sister both foreign yet comforting. Merelith was already barreling toward another crossbowman in the direction of the squabbling monarchs before Anise could beg her to go to their mother instead. She hunkered down, flinching as a crossbow bolt whizzed into her cage and shattered against the iron bars, showering her in splinters.

From this vantage, Anise could see little, but she heard much: the clash of steel as the armies collided. The whinny of the crown guard's horses as they charged into the fray to aid their king. The singing of arrows and bolts fired back and forth, sometimes accompanied with the dread thud of flesh pierced. Above and below these sounds of war, though, she also heard the most awful sound of all: the voracious aggression of a sister wronged.

Two of them.

. . .

Merelith

"TOBIAS, YOU FOOL! WHAT ARE YOU DOING!?" screeched Talya.

Tobias sneered, "I KNEW IT! I KNEW YOU KEPT THAT FOUL THING! WAS IT LORATH!? WHO DID YOU BED TO SNEAK IT OUT? DID YOUR DAMN DOG BRING IT HERE!?"

Even as Merelith ripped through the nearby guards and soldiers, desperately searching for keys to her sister's freedom, she listened to the arguing conqueror and consort. It was a small wonder Talya didn't just freeze Tobias, too, like she had the king of Torhal. The guardian glanced towards her father and tried to ignore the rising fear of Kara. His death was mere moments away, a single sword-stroke, but Tobias was too busy throwing a tantrum over an angyr he thought might be his firstborn.

She's just like mother described. Just like me! Reeta. She came back.

"You ungrateful buffoon! THAT ISN'T OUR CHILD, YOU MORON! IT BELONGS TO THEM!"

"YOU SAID THERE WAS NONE LEFT BUT MERELITH! YOU LIED TO ME!"

An entire army was swarming away from them and into Torhal's lines, ignoring or oblivious to Tobias' futile attempts to attack his own sorceress. Orren cast a glance towards his queen behind him and yelled. Merelith saw Talya look, too, but heard a promising jingle as the consort yanked her horse back from Tobias' charger. The guardian prayed the keyhole on her sister's collar was the obvious solution it seemed.

"ANNELLE! *ANNELLE!*"

Yet the queen did not stir from the earth, even as the crown guard broke into three groups: some went to surround the queen and defend her from Galrend's troops, Paol and Polo charged right at King Tobias, and the rest barreled into the fray around them. Merelith heard the distinct twang of two bolts being loosed and saw Tobias knocked from his horse as they found their mark.

Talya. Get the keys!

"MY KING! HOLD FAST!" cried Knight Polo.

The knight drew one of his hunting blades and swung it down at Orren's icy prison, hacking away at the watery spears and breaking him loose. Paol continued towards Tobias, an iron lance with a chain attached to his saddle in hand. The immortal of Galrend recovered to his feet just in time for Paol to run him through the shoulder. Merelith took some satisfaction in seeing Tobias' eyes widen in fear before the chain drew taught and Paol was dragging the immortal behind him in a wide circle back towards Orren.

"T-T-TALYA! H-H-H-HELP!" hollered the king of Galrend as he bounced away.

"YOU DAMN FOOL!" screamed the queen back, hurling magic at her king.

Whether Talya was trying to help or hinder her husband, Merelith didn't care. The guardian bolted straight for the sorceress and leapt at her, only to be surprised by a blast of wind blowing her sideways. The consort smirked, even as Merelith managed to land on her paws and whirl about for a second attempt. Then she pointed.

"I didn't keep mine because it would have failed me, just like you failed them."

Merelith took the bait and stole a look.

"STAND READY, MY KING!" Polo commanded, breaking the last of the ice shards.

Orren nodded grimly and prepared his own blade as Paol drug the immortal of Galrend right back to his former prisoner. One strike was all it would take. One quickened strike to end the bastard that had threatened his people, stolen his daughters, and deprived his wife of peace and safety. Orren hefted his blade high as Paol darted by only to realize Tobias had seen the ploy and had his own blade ready to spear the exposed king. Merelith reacted immediately.

"PAPA!"

Orren's chest caved in a little as Merelith leapt into him, forcing her father back before Tobias could run his blade through the

Torhalian king. Instead, his sword point ran through then out of Merelith's hindleg and she roared in pain.

"MERELITH!" Orren hollered, tumbling loose of his daughter.

The Torhalian king had little time to check how severe the wound was: Tobias was already charging at him, the chain to his embedded lance broken by supporting magic from Talya. It made for a grisly sight: the King of Galrend rushing forth even as the iron spear protruded through his shoulder. Orren barely parried the first blow, stumbling backwards and nearly tripping over Merelith before quickly rounding off another blow from Tobias.

"PAPA!" Merelith hollered, rising to join the fray until Orren shouted her down.

The embattled king ordered, "SAVE ANISE! I HAVE THIS!"

She didn't feel his words to be true: Tobias had an encumbrance but was otherwise healthy. Orren fought deftly with his left arm, but it didn't change his right lacked the power to effectively block with two hands. Let alone his left leg quivering at every swift maneuver against a superior swordsman. Paol and Polo circled, hurrying to load their crossbows to give aid. Merelith scrambled out of the way, not sure how to help as she willed her leg to heal itself.

Survive, Papa, dammit! Just survive!

Where did Talya go!?

Just when she thought the knights might aid him, their horses reared in terror at the sound of Reeta's too-near roar. Their bolts missed at the absolutely worst moment, allowing Tobias to disarm the Torhalian immortal. Tobias sneered and prepared to drive his blade home for the kill. Merelith saw her father's impending death and turned about to prevent it. The guardian surged forth, just like the blade of King Tobias. She wouldn't make it in time to stop the evil king.

Orren raised an arm up in pitiful defense, only to see that blade run right into the thick, red fur of an angyr. From across the field of battle, all heard a familiar scream of sorrow. Tobias was pulled down by the weight of the creature upon his blade. In a fluid motion, she flipped the immortal king onto the ground beneath her, leaving Tobias staring up into the shocked gaze of Orren Torhal.

. . .

Tobias

Lightning now cracked from the red blizzard as Tobias glared up at the angry, unnatural storm. A bolt struck into the flank of Galrend's forces, instantly cooking some fifty men in their own hide. Annelle's magic surged into the storm and Tobias knew his army would be beaten without Talya's help. Salt stung his eyes, from the magic snow or his own tears, Tobias could not tell. He felt the angyr upon him still breathing, though he was pinned such that he'd lost any grip on his blade sticking through the monster.

He looked up to see the surprised face of his opponent. Orren Torhal raised his sword high, and Tobias began to think of a curse to spew.

"DO IT! DO IT YOU FUCKING COWARD!"

Then the king faltered, his eyes not on Tobias nor the angyr, but in the distance. Tobias twisted his head to see the queen of Torhal rushing towards them, face streaked with tears, waving her arms. Surely the queen wasn't trying to *save* him?

No. Not me. This…thing.

Orren nodded slowly in understanding. The king lowered his blade, and a cold fear gripped the king of Galrend. He was trapped. His army was without leadership. His consort was void-knew-where.

All of it for nothing. NOTHING! DAMN IT! IT ISN'T FAIR! NONE OF THIS IS FAIR! I DID ALL OF IT RIGHT! I DID EXACTLY WHAT I WAS MEANT TO DO!

"Bastard! DO IT! Coward! You are not fit for your crown! You are not fit for HER! GET THIS FUCKING MONSTER OFF ME AND FIGHT ME LIKE THE IMMORTAL YOU ARE! COWARD! DO IT! *DO IT!* TALYA! TALYA, YOU BITCH! HELP! HELP YOUR KING!"

Annelle fell to beside the angyr, as if ignorant to the very much alive immortal underneath it. Orren looked on with equal parts sorrow and annoyance, Tobias still yammering away. The king of Galrend felt his heart fracture with hatred so hot he hoped it would burn them all alive.

"YOU'RE A FUCKING COWARD! AND YOU, ANNELLE! A WHORE TO A WORTHLESS MAN WITH A WORTHLESS MONSTER FOR A PET AND A WORTHLESS…"

"R-Reeta? Sister?!" Annelle stammered.

Tobias stopped ranting at that. *Reeta.* Talya had been telling the truth! He decided to start thrashing, hoping to get the angyr off him or perhaps cause her enough pain to move on her own. Orren's blade hovered dangerously close, yet the king of Torhal seemed unworried.

No. Not her! NO!

"Sister?" growled the angyr.

"Y-yes! Yes, it's me, Annelle! Reeta, I'm here! I-I-I…"

"Smell…like…Mama…"

"Yes, I'm your sister, I…"

"…killer."

Annelle stilled at those words, as did Tobias. Orren's eyebrows shot up and the grip on his blade noticeably tightened. Tobias felt the color drain from his face.

"What?" whispered the queen.

Reeta answered, "Mama…killer…"

Annelle stammered, "No, I…I didn't kill her! I, Reeta, it's ok, you're j-j-just…"

"NO!" growled the angyr, "NOT SISTER! Man…*this man.*"

Orren muttered, "Tobias. *Of course.*"

Tobias began screeching, "WHAT!? NO! I HAD NOTHING TO DO WITH THAT BITCH MOTHER OF YOURS! SHE DESERVED TO DIE BUT I WAS N-N-NOT *MMPH! MMMPH!*"

Tobias struggled to say much more as Orren's sword pressed into his mouth, its edge pinning the immortal's tongue at the back of his throat. He soon gagged on the steady trickle of blood pooling around the sword's tip. Tears welled in his eyes as the hatred splashed down into a deep, dark well of fear.

"H-H-Him?" Annelle asked her sister.

"No," Reeta replied, "Smell him. Not…him."

Orren asked slowly, "Whoever killed Queen Anise was near to this man?"

The angyr nodded slowly, though blood dribbled from her mouth as she did. Annelle gasped and sent her magic through the angyr, probably to see the extent of her wounds. Tobias' worry deepened, knowing his blade had likely nicked her heart. Suddenly, death by angyr seemed far less awful than torture by Annelle Torhal shortly after her long lost sister died.

"Can you save her?" Orren whispered.

No. Not then. Not now. Hmph. Fitting, really, that it all ended this way.

"Save sister, yes?" Reeta asked.

"Oh, R-Reeta, I…I can't…I…"

The angyr snorted, coughed blood, and asked again, "*You.* I…save *you.* Yes?"

Annelle's sobs broke as she nodded vigorously, throwing her arms around the great head of her guardian while crying pitifully. Words pent up for two decades spilled forth. The king of Galrend listened, surprised at what he heard.

"Yes! Y-y-yes! You saved me! You saved me, Reeta."

"S-sorry not…not save…Mama."

"Do not be," Annelle chided between sobs, "It wasn't your f-fault! It was n-n-never your fault."

"Papa?" croaked the angyr, "Papa…home?"

Annelle shook her head and whispered, "No. He went looking for the killer. For…for you, too."

Tobias wasn't sure if her words were true. Or rather if the intent of Doran's search would make sense to the dying sister. Did Reeta know her own father was hunting her? Or did she think King Doran was searching for his lost daughter to bring her home? Reeta's answer said enough.

"Try…help…Papa. Try give…smell. *This* smell. Papa…attack. Take it."

Reeta shook violently as she lifted a limb forward. Tobias saw that the angyr had wrapped around its foreleg a tangle of faded cloth, the color long since lost to dirt and grime. Reeta's eyes seemed to widen with clarity as Annelle gingerly touched it.

"Take," the angyr commanded, "Take! Give to new guardian. Find Mama killer."

Annelle nodded and did as she was told, even as Tobias squirmed again beneath the mounting pressure of a dying angyr. And Orren steadily leaning down on his blade. The queen removed the tattered cloth and carefully held it before her so that Reeta saw. The fragment had once been white, and an ornate pattern marked it as being part of a beautiful cloak or shirt.

"For Papa," Reeta whispered, "For Mama."

"For you and for me," Annelle whispered back, stroking Reeta's head as it grew heavy in her hand.

"Sister?" mumbled the angyr.

"Yes?"

"Love…guardian?"

Annelle murmured, "Yes. I love you. I have *always* loved you."

"No."

"No?" Annelle asked, her lips trembling.

Reeta's eyes shuttered, briefly, then seemed to fight to stay open as she asked again.

"Love…*new*…guardian? Yours."

Annelle laughed. How, Tobias did not know, but she did. It was a joyful sound, or enough so that Reeta's lips curled upwards in a smile. Thousands of questions flooded Tobias' mind.

How? How is there love between this creature and you? Do you not see a monster lays here!?

"Yes!" replied the queen with haste, "I love Merelith so, so much! She is so much like you. I love her very, very much. As does her Papa, Orren."

Reeta cast a tired eye on the King of Torhal. Orren stilled beneath that gaze, as if awaiting judgement. The angyr's nostrils flared, taking in his scent, then she settled back into Annelle's quivering hand.

"Good."

Reeta nuzzled her bloody maw into Annelle's fingers, took a shuddering breath, then breathed out her last words. Tobias felt the full weight of the angyr bear down on him, enough so that the sword in his mouth let off his tongue a little.

"Not…save Mama…bad. Save sister…good. Reeta…good?"

Annelle nodded her forehead against Reeta's.

The queen replied, "Good. Always."

"Always," sighed the angyr.

"You have always been good," Annelle repeated.

But her guardian did not reply. Annelle cried silently into the face of her dead sister. Tobias tried to shriek against the blade of Orren, to tell him he could help them if they would spare his life, but the immortal king of Torhal continued to gag Tobias on the blood of his own tongue. The trapped king thrashed, half hoping to kill himself on the sword, then stilled at his opponent's words.

Orren said with lethal calm, "I have one question, Tobias Galrend. A name for a swift, painless death, though you do not deserve it. Do you know the pattern upon this cloth?"

The defeated king shook his head vigorously, but Orren did not release his blade, instead glancing at his queen. Annelle looked back, her eyes shot red with grief as she absentmindedly stroked the head of her sister. Tobias felt his skin crawl as she spoke.

"It is the cloak of a Saltsword, Orren" she managed with a raw voice.

"A Saltsword?" Orren asked.

"An ancient order of assassins. Tamar founded them, after the War for Freedom. Ask *him*" answered the queen.

Orren looked to Tobias and saw the man had grown very still. Too still. Annelle looked around her sister's prone form, past the beautiful fur she had once pet as a child, over the glorious feathers she had collected in the aftermath of that awful week, to an immortal she had considered wedding with eyes wide. Not in terror, but recognition. Tobias beheld beauty in her grief. He also witnessed cold judgement that seemed all too familiar.

Lorath. Of course. You wise old ass. You started this. All of it. A glorious future for Galrend, starting with the fall of Torhal. Except you didn't count on this monster coming back. Bastard.

"Who, Tobias?" she asked.

Orren lifted his blade, and Tobias didn't immediately speak. When he did, he closed his eyes, knowing his death was imminent. Ever full of vengeance, Tobias spoke the truth and hoped his advisor met an even worse fate, though he doubted this lot would ever find him.

"Lorath Saltsword. My advisor. He goes to Tarn," the king stated.

"Thank you," Annelle said, as if content with that answer.

Tobias' lips curled in a cruel smile as he said, "You won't fin…"

Tobias Galrend didn't finish the last curse as Orren Torhal rammed his blade straight through the back of the fallen king's throat. Tobias felt the tingle of quickening fail to heal the wound, give way to the blood rushing out the back of his neck, the strange sensation of not feeling any of his body below his head.

I am dying. I…I have been killed?

Orren let go of the sword, looked to his wife, and mustered the strength to ask a final question. One that may have left her colder than the death sweeping over Tobias' face.

"This battle isn't done. Where is Talya?"

Annelle dove into her magic, then shivered in recognition of what it showed.

"The woods. She has Anise. Merelith is following."

The Torhalian king's face drained of color. Without a word, Orren wrenched his blade from Tobias' yawning mouth, which the defeated immortal did not feel, and secured a mount from a nearby knight. In a fluid roundabout, he charged by his queen and hoisted her as they made their way towards the woods. It was rather romantic, Tobias thought, as he saw Annelle fade from his peripheral, still staring back at her fallen sister.

I want that.

Perhaps staring at the fallen king of Galrend, too, whose last vision was of snow, fur, and feathers. It was lovely, really. Except, even as his life faded away, it still tasted of salt.

38 – The Dead do not Lie

Merelith

Merelith had felt more than saw her mother scream. She had watched Reeta quicken a third time but come up short, unable to assault Tobias. So, the angyr had done the unthinkable and saved *Orren*. A man she didn't know. The guardian had looked on as Reeta was impaled, sparing her sister's husband, and trapping Tobias Galrend beneath her sheer weight. Before Merelith could go any further, a second scream had issued from behind Merelith, and the instincts ripped her attention away from her parents and aunt.

Anise!

She had looked back to see her sister dragged from her cage. Talya had bound the princess with roots to the back of a horse and promptly fled east into the forest.

"*ANISE!*" roared the guardian.

Everything had fallen away in that moment. Merelith ignored her mother's cry, paid no mind to the quiet voice wondering about Reeta. Not even her father's fate was of concern. The angyr ducked and weaved, dodged and bounded through the rear lines of Galrend, her eyes ever on Anise's screaming face.

Sister.

Into the woods disappeared the consort of Galrend, a crown princess bound at her back and a young angyr in hot pursuit. Tal pushed Merelith's muscles to their breaking point, Kara willed the deep wound in her leg to knit close. Speed the likes of which the guardian had never known became hers as she dug paws into the salt and snow and raced after her sister. She gave herself fully to the instincts: to possess and protect. Just two words echoed in her mind, words only a guardian could feel as much as think.

Save sister.

· · ·

Talya

Talya Bodisnia, first and last of her line, rightful ruler of Galrend, sorceress *queen*, and descendant of the mad pentarch, fled as fast as her horse would carry her. Every ounce of her magic poured into sustaining the beast's stamina, strengthening living bindings holding Torhal's crown princess still, and ripping through low tree branches and brush before her. She was no stranger to being hunted but every sense in her body, mind, and soul told her death itself followed.

She had known. Said it right to our faces, and we laughed. Merelith knew another was coming.

At least the mature angyr was impaled on her husband's blade. By now, Tobias was surely dead, a loss she didn't mind in the least. With luck, Annelle Torhal was still dazed and Orren Torhal too busy leading his meager army against an unruly horde promised riches and blood. Yet Merelith, the whelp, was gaining on her. It was not how Talya had planned, but all things considered it was going rather well.

Even in death, you're still useful to me, Eric. Lorath will rue the day he thought to twist you and me. To take my child and use her as a bargaining chip. I will deal with this pup, then I will find that ancient bastard and take back what is mine. What has always been mine!

Talya knew little of angyrism beyond the books she had read in Galrend's diminished library. Those books, fortunately, had been focused on how to kill or trap angyr, not their biology or psychology. The sorceress had long ago learned the value of backup plans, and backup plans for the backup.

Eric had been an unfortunate but not all-too-surprising stumble. If not for the intervention of the other angyr, Talya would still be faced with figuring out how to eliminate her immortal husband. She tried to balance her satisfaction of Tobias' imminent demise against the grief of losing her favorite playmate. Eric had been such a wild lover. Too wild, it seemed.

Still, a dead lover had his uses. Talya pressed her steed forward, steeling a glance back to see the angyr was closer than she'd expected. Her heart pounded with terror, but she was sure her eyes lit with excitement. Soon, very soon, she'd get what she wanted *anyway*.

A woman like her always did.

. . .

Anise

Anise could do nothing but watch her sister hurtling behind them. The gag of wood felt like it might break her jaw; it was so tight she tasted her own blood leaking from cuts in her lips. Her arms and legs were pinned against the horse beneath her, but the pain of being bounced along at breakneck speed didn't register. All she could feel, all she could see, was Merelith watching her.

She is so beautiful.

Tears streamed down her face, the thought ripping through her heart. Merelith didn't stand a chance against Talya. Anise already knew that her captor was simply luring the angyr away, again. Perhaps Merelith knew, too, but it was apparent in those silver-rimmed eyes she did not care. Reeta had come back for their mother. Merelith had already come back for Anise before. Now, she did it again. Would keep doing it again if they somehow survived this.

She will always come for me. She will always be bound to me. Talya was right. She isn't free. Not at all. She is a slave to me. To my future.

Canine legs were a blur of power and speed, enslaved to a singular hunt. Wings were tucked tightly, sometimes flaring to aid in swift maneuvers around brush, rocks, and stumps. Only the tips of her elongated fangs flashed in the sunlight dappling the earth beneath the barren canopy, her mouth cinched in a grim scowl. Long, red tufted ears were tucked back, sometimes standing to attention whenever Talya spurred her horse down a new trail. And the eyes…

How many times did I dream of a hero coming for me? A man, wild and fierce for me with eyes so intense. No man is coming, though. Only her. Always her.

Merelith's pupils were dilated so wide as to render her eyes like obsidian pools contained in a dish of purest silver. Anise knew that, if she could access her magic, she would feel the instincts of dominion and docility reaching out from those pools, stretching to take hold of their prey. Not Talya – no, Merelith didn't care if Talya lived or died – but her sister.

I am the prey. It is me she hunts. Has always hunted. So many years, I hated that feeling. I hated that she always found me. What a miserable life, to be slave to someone like me! This is all my fault! I did this, not mother, nor father. Not even her. I did this. I led us into this mess. Again. Again and again! And she followed me. Again and again. Always, she follows.

And so, Anise watched her sister follow, grief and shame eating the crown princess alive. If humans had their own instincts, hers were at war: dominion desperately wanting Merelith to not give up, to take possession once more, to *always* be her guardian.

Docility wished the angyr would give up. To stop following. To be free.

. . .

Merelith

Save sister.

When the trap was sprung, Merelith barreled headlong into it. So absorbed with following her sister, the angyr didn't register the magic binding her until she tumbled and smacked her jaw on a jutting rock, the distinctive crack of a hairline fracture lost to the grunt of pain, in turn swallowed by a roar of impotent fury. Talya had led the angyr to a clearing that had been prepared for this exact occasion. Yet, before Merelith could fight the magical bindings steadily constricting her she went still at the sight of who walked from behind a tree.

Eric!

Tal and Kara both vanished into the void of her heart, drowned out by her mind racing with questions, hopes, and fears. Talya pushed Anise off the back of her horse without a second glance, then dismounted. A familiar red glow emanated from the ground of the clearing and Merelith saw she was once more within a ritual circle.

Talya cooed, "I'll make this simple, *Guardian*. You allow your sister's power to flow to me, I allow Eric to pass on. Anise lives, Eric is free, *you* live, I am free. Everyone wins. I disappear into the unknown, never to trouble Torhal or even Galrend, ever again."

Talya didn't wait for an answer, pumping magic directly into the ritual and drawing up a three-way tether between her, the crown princess, and the angyr. Merelith felt her sister's magic pull back in terror and Talya's surge forward in hunger. Of the guardian's own, there seemed no sign. Much like the ritual with Eric, Merelith apparently controlled the flow once again.

"Choose, Merelith. Give me what I want, or I kill both of you."

"It's ok, Merelith," whispered Eric, "We…we can figure this out. After."

It was him, of that she had no doubt. If this was an illusion of the sorceress, Merelith couldn't tell. He watched her from the shadow of a dead tree and then seemed to force a grim smile. Her heart-shards rattled, the smile too familiar and too real.

"You died," replied the angyr, "I saw you die."

Talya scoffed, "Dead and gone aren't the same, girl."

The tether wrenched on Anise and her sister shut her eyes tightly with pain, her gag too strong to allow the scream of agony to escape. That seemed to call the instincts to the forefront once more. Merelith roared but the magic held her in place. Talya didn't deign to stop the guardian from spewing hate-filled threats.

"I WILL DESTROY YOU! LET HER GO! I WILL RIP YOUR THROAT AND TEAR YOUR LIMBS AND PLUCK EVERY HAIR FROM YOUR DEAD HIDE! RELEASE MY SISTER! RELEASE MY ERIC!"

"*Your* Eric? Your sister?" replied the traitor knight.

He stepped from beneath the shadow of the tree and seemed to shimmer slightly. His smile fell into a disapproving frown as he surveyed the angyr. Merelith looked back in equal parts shock and dismay. A ghost. Talya had bound his spirit. As if reading her thoughts, Eric nodded and then motioned to the crown princess, then Merelith.

"Dead. Because of her," he said, pointing at Anise, "Trapped. Because of *you*."

"M-me?" the angyr stammered.

Eric's specter paced towards the crown princess then kneeled over her terrified form, shaking his head with serious disappointment.

"I just wanted what you wanted. To be free. I could have had it, in time. Merelith would have traded and you, you could have given her the crown then. You didn't want to be an angyr! You just wanted to be free! I could have given that to you. But no, you only think for yourself."

Anise grew still, her eyes welling with tears. Talya waved a graceful hand, and the gag was released. The crown princess darted her eyes at Merelith, gulped, then spoke.

"The dead do not lie, Merelith," she whispered.

Talya nodded and replied, "No, they cannot. Ask whatever you want of him, Guardian. He can choose to not answer, mind you, but he cannot lie. Precisely why I summoned him."

The dead cannot lie. What is she playing at? Does it even matter? Either I let Anise's power pass on…or we die. Why bring him into this?

"Did you love me?" Merelith asked, trying to stall by playing the game.

Eric smirked then said quietly, "As you mean it? No. I did not love *you*, I loved what you *are*."

The guardian replied, "Did you love *her*?"

Merelith motioned her snout towards Talya and saw the sorceress tense. Maybe she was pretending, but angyrian instincts said otherwise as Eric shook his head.

"No, but I was closer to her than you. Talya almost gave me what I wanted. The shapeshifting clothes, the power to hunt men with ease, the raw urges of true wildness. Yet, when I met *you*…I was ruined for her. How did she say it? Ah, yes, I was tired of *pretending*."

He looked at Talya then shrugged. The sorceress regarded him with cool indifference, but Merelith felt the pain surging beneath that icy exterior. The sorceress had loved Eric, even if she'd gambled his life and lost it to Merelith.

Eric went on, "Much like your sister was tired of pretending. She started all of this, after all. Because of that power she has. All of this…" he cast a hand around the clearing, "…because of her *cursed* gift. A curse you can now pass on to someone else if you choose."

Merelith asked, "What do *you* get out of it?"

Eric considered her for a moment then seemed to soften his smirk into a genuine smile.

"I am trapped, Merelith, because of you. Ask your sister."

Merelith glanced at Anise and said, "What does he mean?"

Talya, though, answered instead.

"Eric, our handsome man, cannot be at peace because of how he died. The rules of death are fickle and loose, but wherever it is that life threads return to requires certain *truths* to be acknowledged. Often by the living. Think of it as unfinished business."

Merelith listened but kept her eyes on Anise. The crown princess considered her words before whispering her own answer. It didn't make any more sense to the guardian.

"Your love keeps him here. He is unworthy of it."

"What does this have to do with you? Us?" asked the guardian.

Talya's answer was soft but full of malicious confidence.

"That same love keeps you from saving your sister's life."

I love her too much to allow this.

Just as I love Eric too much to allow him to move on.

Merelith sighed and felt the tether go taut once more. Anise whimpered as Talya tugged on her power, but it held firm. The angyr heard the evil sorceress growl in warning. Eric chuckled and shrugged.

"I told you, my mate."

"SHUT UP!" barked the sorceress.

Eric ignored her, opting to move to beside Merelith then kneel, where his face loomed before hers. She wasn't sure how, but her heart seemed to reassemble and shatter, over and over, as her eyes studied his lovely face. The lips she had tugged and bit, the strong jaw that had rested in her neck, the severe nose that had breathed the scent of her hair, then her fur.

"I cannot lie, Merelith. I want what you want, in this moment. *Quicken.*"

Merelith whispered back, "I can't! I, I don't know how!"

"Sure you can. You already have. Twice."

Merelith's eyes widened. Talya and Anise both shared a glance of shock and dismay. Eric continued, an eagerness tinting his voice.

"I saw it with my own eyes. Just like the books said! You've already done it before. Do it again."

"I...I can't. I don't think..."

"Eric, what are you talking about?" demanded the queen.

But the ghost ignored her, though a small smirk crept onto his lips.

"I know you can, Merelith, but I do not know how or why. The first was when I had my sword on your sister's throat. I felt it, a slight tingle. Then it happened again right before you...ha. Before you showed me how wild you really are. It was terrifying yet also exhilarating."

"NOW, MERELITH! GIVE ME HER POWER NOW OR I'LL GUT YOU BOTH AND THEN YOU CAN WANDER WITH THIS TRAITOR!" demanded Talya.

Spines of ice shot to within an inch of Anise's throat. A similar pair had stopped right before Merelith's keen nose. The crown princess had flinched. The guardian hadn't even noticed them. Her eyes were taking in the odd sight of the spikes piercing her former lover's translucent face. He really was dead. Eric seemed unbothered.

"Quicken, Merelith. Break the magic, kill Talya, save your sister."

"Shut up, you undead idiot! We had a deal! Don't ruin this, too, you, you *dog*!"

Merelith saw Eric's face spasm at the insult. Then he was calm again. Her instincts became acutely aware of his expression as he stood: disappointment that masked deep sorrow.

"Fine. You're right, Talya. She isn't going to do it for me."

What is he doing? Why is he going towards Anise?

No. No no no NO NO NO!

Merelith struggled feebly against her bindings as Eric bent over Anise and, from nothingness, seemed to draw a blade of ethereal light. Anise's eyes widened in horror.

"The dead cannot lie, Merelith. Talya is too desperate to kill your sister before getting what she wants. Me? I care not. I only want what you want."

"I don't want her to die!" bellowed the angyr, "STOP! STOP!"

"Release the magic, *Beta*" commanded the ghost.

Merelith hesitated, even as the tether tightened once more. Talya's will roaring against Anise's, the guardian's own power acting as an impenetrable barrier. Talya couldn't force this, Merelith knew, but the alternative…Eric nodded at her then drew the blade along Anise's throat. To the guardian's horror, blood trickled out of her sister's neck.

"NO! OK! I'LL DO IT! STOP!" screamed the angyr.

Just like that, the barrier came crashing down. Anise screamed in pain, Talya screamed in victory, and Merelith screamed in grief. Eric shook his head, looked at Anise, and sighed. Over the hollering of the three, only Anise and Merelith heard his whispered words as he tilted the blade up into her neck, its bite forcing the princess to raise her head to meet him eye to eye.

"You know she's going to kill you anyway, right?"

Merelith could only shudder with shame as she watched Talya steal Anise's power. Tal and Kara both pined in worry. What difference did it make, dying now or dying in a few minutes? The guardian held out hope someone would intervene. That the ghost would attack Talya instead, or that her parents would arrive, or some other fluke of fate.

I love her too much to allow this. I love her too much to stop it.

I loved him too much to see the warnings.

I loved and it cost everything.

39 – The Cost of Everything

Anise

Is this what it felt like? What he did to her?

SHUT UP GIRL AND GIVE IN!

Anise had never regarded her magic as being *part* of her. It had always felt more akin to a reservoir or formless satchel from which she drew her power. A thing that could be spilled, or set aside, or unleashed if the aperture to it was wide enough. Right now, that opening felt like a hole ripped right into her chest. Painful, searing, and rapidly emptying its contents.

She's going to kill us anyway.

BE SILENT AND GIVE IT TO ME!

The ghost of Eric Smith regarded her with a stare that was somewhere between sympathy and anger. He didn't say anything else, though the blade was steadily tightening against her throat. She'd studied the dead many times throughout her mother's tutelage. Spirits of warriors were among the most lethal, for they often possessed the means to still harm the living. Yet even as the traitor knight held her life against his spectral blade, she wondered.

You are already dead. Why aren't you killing me? You could spite Talya. Deprive her.

POWERS UNKNOWN, YOU REALLY DO THINK TOO MUCH! PERHAPS KILLING YOU WILL BE A RELIEF?

"What was the deal?" Anise ground out, focusing all her efforts into not screaming at the pain of her magic rushing away. Or at Talya's thoughts comingling with her own.

Eric's eyebrows flickered in amusement.

"It is already complete: I was allowed to be here, to see Merelith one more time. In exchange, I tell her the truth. A poor deal, admittedly, but it seems to be working as Talya planned."

Seems to be working.

IS WORKING. IF YOU'D FOCUS ON GIVING UP, THIS WOULD BE FAR LESS PAINFUL FOR US BOTH!

Eric tilted his head, and a smirk joined his bemused face.

"I had hoped Merelith would quicken and kill her. It seems I was wrong."

Seems he was wrong.

THAT FOOL BOY GAVE ME UP, AND FOR WHAT? TO BE A MONSTER RATHER THAN HAVE THE GIFT OF APPEARING AS ONE!? I HAD OFFERED HIM EVERYTHING! EVERYTHING A MAN COULD WANT!

Anise whispered, "Why? Why are you doing this?"

Eric's features smoothed into contemplation, even as Anise bit down another scream as Talya dug yet deeper into her magic. Merelith wept, powerless and defeated. The crown princess was so *tired* of seeing that brokenness. So *angry* she kept being the cause of it. When the ghost spoke, his whispered words carried a hint of pride and sorrow.

"I didn't love her, Anise, nor you, nor your family nor any of Torhal. I loved what Merelith is, though. Call me selfish, for it is true, but I wanted to see it. *Just once!* I wanted to see her become what I dreamed of. What could save her now. Seems she can't let go of control, though. She loves you too much. She always follows you. Never choosing her freedom over yours."

Seems she can't let go of control. SHE HAS NO CONTROL, THAT'S WHY YOU DID THIS!

She loves me too much. SHE IS A MONSTER! MONSTERS DO NOT LOVE.

Always following. ALWAYS HUNTING YOU. YES, I SEE HOW THAT TROUBLED YOU!

Never free. NOPE. NOBODY IS FREE. LEAST OF ALL YOU! HAHAHAHA!

Anise looked to Talya and saw the sorceress glowing with wild magic far greater than she'd ever had. The crown princess looked to Merelith and found the angyr shaking her head in apology, even as her eyes darted around, hopeful for some intervention. An intervention Anise knew would not come. Even with the collar stopping her magic, Anise knew, deep down, nobody was coming. She looked at Eric a final time and forced her quivering lips into a firm smile.

The ghost mumbled, "Her love has finally reached its limit."

"Love does not have limits, Eric," Anise ground out.

"Your sister does," he replied matter of fact.

"No! Not anymore."

The crown princess couldn't stop the flow of magic. She could barely raise her head off the blade of the ghost. Her strength was faltering, fast.

She locked her eyes to Merelith, forced as big a smile as she could, and shouted.

"MERELITH! *SISTER!*"

The angyr seemed to still, even as Anise felt the last of her magic draining away. Talya had begun to laugh with triumph, the ritual nearing completion.

"I love you! Be free for me!"

"Anise?" questioned the angyr, before shouting in terror, "ANISE! NO! *ANISE!*"

The crown princess looked at Talya, whose victorious grin warped as the crown princess winked at her and said parting words.

"No more pretending, Talya."

Then Anise Torhal slashed her own throat upon the spectral blade. The last sound she heard was that of Merelith bellowing her name. The crown princess began dying, no longer fearing that beautiful roar.

. . .

Merelith

The blood of her sister's neck was still on the blade when it happened. Anise's eyes remained open. She still had a warm smile with a slight smirk tugging at the right edge. Time stuttered, then Anise was falling to the ground, an arc of red around her neck.

I'm quickening.

But the guardian wasn't quickening the right direction. Merelith didn't know *how* to move around time. It was still moving forward, in a jerky motion that made her sister's suicide so much worse.

It's not fair.

She tried to will herself backwards in time, but all it did was stutter Anise forward, like a twitching rag doll, towards the earth, her smile faltering to match the curve of blood gushing from her neck.

No.

NO.

NO!

Merelith's heart stuttered, too, and the pain was unbearable, but she held onto the feeling in her chest. The profound loss. The inevitability of it all. There was nothing she could do but watch her sister's last moments be drawn out.

She smelled the blood. Saw the blade in her lover's hand, and the strange acceptance in his eyes as they slowly looked towards the angyr. She felt the tether with Talya snap, the ritual completed or ended prematurely with Anise's death. She heard the tinkling of ice crystals growing, Talya willing the ice spikes before Merelith to finish the angyr.

And in her own mouth, she tasted salt. Tears that flowed faster than time, or slower? She didn't care. She cried into this void of between, her body warning her she would soon die from quickening instead. Merelith didn't care. If Anise was dead, what was the point?

I love you.

Kara spread its wings. Anise loved her. Truly. She always had, but in this moment, her sister had loved her too much. No, no that wasn't right. Love had no limits. Not anymore. She'd heard her say that to the ghost. Merelith felt her own wings press out against her bindings.

Be free.

Tal pushed itself off the ground of her heart. All her sister had ever wanted was freedom. Freedom from a crown, yes, but freedom from being something *other* than a sister. They had understood each other in this way. Everything Merelith had done had been for her sister, not a crown. She had been free to choose differently, hadn't she?

For me.

It was a command, not from crown princess to guardian, but sister to sister. Merelith's heart seemed to steady, the pain in her body evaporating. Tal breathed in wild magic, and the quickening stopped all movement. Anise's eyes were still open, but Merelith saw they were full of love and hope. The guardian took a step forward and Talya's bindings around her fractured and collapsed beneath the touch of timelessness.

She tore her gaze from Anise and settled on the ghost, who was looking at her now. Eric's face betrayed a softness she had known many times. Kara breathed out wild magic, and the angyr began to plod forward, one paw at a time, making time for herself. Yet she did not go towards the specter that held the suicide weapon. There was no point. She didn't know how to go backwards.

Merelith turned her silver-rimmed eyes onto Talya Bodisnia. The angyr was slow in her approach. She studied every inch of the woman's face as she drew near. Both instincts became focused in their purpose. The quickening couldn't be sustained much longer, but it didn't need to be. The angyr let all her mind fall away until only a few words echoed in it, as empty as her shattered heart.

I love you. Be free for me.

Then she let the wildness take hold. As one, Tal and Kara hunted.

. . .

Talya

That damn dog!

Talya wasted no time commanding the ice spikes before Merelith to plunge right into the angyr. Yet by the time she looked, the whelp was nowhere to be seen. Just a receding flicker of lightning. She tried to curse aloud, but found she had no voice because she also had no throat.

The shock of the pain felt delayed, perhaps because her mind was trying to work out when, exactly, half of her neck had been torn out. She tried to raise a hand to the grisly wound, but it was gone, too. Its bloody wrist was leaking on the ground beneath her. She collapsed to the earth, the agony of her wounds taking an eternity to catch up to her thoughts.

That damn dog. He made her do it. She killed me. I'm dead.

The creature stood over Talya's twitching body as she bled out, its maw dripping with blood. Hers. Silver-rimmed eyes bore into Talya's very soul. The sorceress wanted to beg, to scream, to curse, but she could not. Then she wanted Merelith to speak, to yell, to gloat. As her life thread unwound, Talya became vaguely aware that, perhaps, Merelith could also not speak. What stared at her was not a person. Not anymore.

The nothingness in the angyr's gaze wasn't beautiful. It was perfect. Just like Lorath had once said. Talya Bodisnia died wondering if her daughter would be the same way.

. . .

Merelith

The bad woman was dead. Merelith turned toward her sister and the ghost that stood beside her. Pain rippled through her heart, both real and imagined. The quickening had hurt, but not as much as seeing sister dead. She went over to the body, passing through the man that wasn't really there.

He'd never really been there.

She nuzzled the back of sister's head and whimpered. Her ears perked at the dull clank of a collar opening and falling to the ground. No words were spoken, no questions. A peculiar warmth radiated off the not-man behind her.

"I have to go, Merelith."

She ignored him, her whimpering becoming more frequent. She pawed at sister, was she dead? She wasn't earlier. The collar stank of death, though. The warmth in the not-man increased and she recognized it. Remorse.

"She is gone."

Merelith either didn't hear him or did not care to hear him. The warmth became a sorrowful heat as the angyr pressed her head into the bloodied neck of her sister. She pulled the body into a furry embrace, curling her wings as if to protect it. Much the way she had the not-man, not so many nights ago.

The not-man's warmth began to fade, and so did he. She didn't care. He'd never really been there. She didn't like that sister was so cold, though. No matter how tight she held on, sister was getting colder. And so still. So very still. It was not good.

"Find love again, Merelith."

The not-man vanished without a trace. She did not care. She considered the woods and wondered if there was a better place to take sister.

Protect. Keep.

Warm. Relax.

Survive. Save.

She did not know these woods, nor its sounds. She did not recognize the taste of the blood in her mouth, nor the feel of the cold body in her embrace. Only the scent of it. It smelled safe, kind, and gentle. It smelled of memories she didn't know and of feelings she couldn't recall. Above all, it smelled like *hers*. Whatever it was, or had been, it was hers. Had always been hers. Yet a different sense called her away from that smell. A calm but focused tug on her spirit.

Come.

No. This is mine.
Come.
I will stay!
Come.

The angyr growled at nobody. The call was strong but her will to remain was stronger still. She drew in the thing closer to her, burying her snout into its long hair. She whiffed that smell and felt the tingle of recognition. She whiffed again and the strength of that smell blew away the distant calling. She couldn't place it, didn't know why it held her so.

It was a scent that was more. Not just more, it smelled like *everything*. So, she stayed.

40 – Wild and Heartless

Merelith

The sun was high above, but it was not warm to the angyr. Like the snow around her, everything felt cold. Not too cold to be dangerous, but cold enough she slept. The thing in her grasp was as cold as the ground, now, but it still smelled pleasant. Exhaustion from killing the bad thing, from enduring the not-thing, from keeping the good thing warm…it was all so much. So, she slept.

In her sleep she heard voices but didn't understand them. One was low, warm but fearful. The other was soft, broken but kind.

"N-no!" whispered the soft voice.

"Love, she may hurt us," warned the low voice.

"Let her!"

"Annelle…"

"Better us than our people, Orren! Better here, where she can go home without harming anyone else in Torhal."

"The Wildlands? No! Her home is with us."

The angyr became aware something, several somethings, were nearby. They didn't smell bad or dangerous, so she ignored them. She was tired.

"There has to be a way," the low voice whispered.

"There is," the soft voice mumbled, "Her way."

The things came closer and the angyr reacted. She leapt to her paws, whirled about, and spread her wings wide in a show of dominant aggression. She had her fangs bared, silver-rimmed eyes wide with terror, and body positioned in a defensive posture. The things looked like hers, but not cold. They saw her thing and stopped.

The one with the soft voice fell down and let out a strangled cry, its eyes on the neck of the angyr's thing. She growled in warning.

MINE! STAY BACK!

The soft voiced thing reached forward and the angyr snapped her jaws at it. No! This thing was hers and she would not give it up.

"Annelle! Stop! She isn't herself!" warned the low voice.

It stepped forward and took hold of a silver thing at its side. The angyr's eyes swiveled onto it and, for the barest moment, she felt a flicker of curiosity. She'd seen that silver thing before. Just like this. She had protected her thing from it before. Then the fierce beast was back, snarling loud so that her four ears rang with the noise.

"Merelith! It's me! Papa!"

Merelith? Papa?

These sounds were familiar. Was it a trick? The angyr bent low, as if to leap at the low voice, but then spread her wings even farther over her thing. The low voice gripped his silver thing – a sword, that's what it was! The angyr bared her teeth.

"Anise," it whispered, "She's protecting Anise, Annelle."

The soft voice's sobs momentarily halted as it finally looked away from the dead eyes below to the eyes of the angyr. The angyr did not like that stare, and her own seemed to dart between Orren and Annelle. The angyr sensed the fear in the low voice give way to a different feeling: recognition. The angyr felt less threatened and eased its snarling jaw closed.

"Merelith?" whispered the soft voice, "Love? I-i-it's me. M-Mama. Annelle."

The low voice added, touching a hand to his armored breast, "Orren. I'm Papa. You are Merelith. We are family."

Mama. Papa. Hmm. Not bad. Good? Merelith. Merelith? Me. Family? What is family?

Merelith's eyes darted to Orren, and she bared her fangs again in a low growl. Annelle curled a hand into his and he dared a glance at her. Tears streamed down her cheeks, but her gaze was hard and her words even harder.

"She can sense your heart, Orren. Calm it, or she won't know you."

"How does one *calm* their heart," he asked, wincing at the terseness in his voice.

Annelle's lip quivered as she said, "Remember she's still here."

Still here. Mama said? No, Papa said! Hmm. I am still here? Where have heard before? King. King said I am still here. What king? Papa king. Mama queen. Who?

Orren almost flinched as Annelle spoke again. Interestingly, the angyr flinched, too.

"I'm s-so proud of you, love," whispered the queen, "So very proud. You did your best and protected h-her."

Orren followed his wife's lead and said, "W-well done, Guardian. You, you've done well."

Merelith's wings seemed to relax a fraction, but the growl and gnashing of teeth remained. Annelle started to inch forward on her knees, and the angyr stomped a paw with a threatening roar. Annelle flinched and the angyr nearly took off the tips of her fingers with a powerful bite.

STAY BACK! Mine! Mine. Thing…this thing mine?

"Tal and Kara," Orren whispered, "The instincts. I can see them, love."

The words struck a chord in the angyr and, for the first time, her ears flashed forward in apparent curiosity. Annelle gasped. The king swallowed his hope and kept speaking.

"Guardian."

Merelith tilted her head. Fangs were still bared, but now she breathed through her bloodied maw rather than growled and grumbled. Orren kept his eyes on hers, trying to hide a desperate smile as he saw the pupils slowly dilate smaller. He seemed to fumble for another word, then found it.

"D-daughter!" he whispered in earnest.

Her ears now swiveled about, as if taking in the surroundings for other threats. She even dared a look towards Talya's destroyed corpse before snapping her gaze back to her parents.

Guardian. I am guardian. Daughter? I am that, too. So is my thing. It is mine! No, it is ours. Mama and Papa and Merelith. Thing is ours. What is thing? Why cold? No, no, no…

Merelith heard her mother gulp several times before she mumbled her word. It broke through. Of course it did, for only Annelle Torhal could guess the name Merelith would always remember. The only name a Torhalian guardian would never forget.

"Sister."

Sister. Thing is sister. My sister. Mine! Sister is cold. Sister is so cold!

The wings crumpled to the earth. Her legs began to violently shake. Her mouth opened and closed, the whimpers piteous and mournful. Yet it was her eyes that struck her parents. Gone was that wild fear, replaced with the all-too-familiar gaze of a broken child. Tears welled and began to trickle onto her snout before free-falling onto her sister's matted hair. Annelle sobbed again when the angyr ground out just two words in reply.

"Sister died."

Overcome with grief and motherly need, it was apparent Annelle could no longer stop herself. Before Orren could react, the queen had her arms around the neck of her eldest daughter. Merelith, though, still looked at him, her whole body now trembling with grief.

Sister is dead. Anise. My Anise. My sister! She…

Merelith choked out her answer again, "Anise *died*, Papa."

Orren forced his throat closed and took his time stepping towards the guardian, kneeling, and gently resting a gauntlet against Merelith's furry cheek.

"I couldn't…I tried…I-I'm sorry…" stammered the creature.

The king brought his nose to hers and Merelith's eyes went wide again in stark terror. The shaking stopped, the jaw tensed, and the wings straightened. Tal warned of imminent danger, Kara pleaded to flee from it.

Anise died. Papa will be angry! Mama is hurt! Anise…oh, Anise!

"Wherever we go, you go. It's ok, Merelith. It's ok, love."

Annelle began to wail, though no power accompanied it this time. She wrapped her fingers around the limp hand of Anise beneath Merelith, but she kept her face buried into the angyr's neck. Merelith's brows danced as the king's words seeped in, the shaking returning once again.

Orren intoned, "Wherever we go, Merelith, you will go, too. This changes nothing. You will *always* be our daughter. You will *always* be Anise's sister. It's ok, love. It's going to be ok."

Even Annelle's sobbing stopped, if only for a moment, at the sound of Merelith's howl. A cry so low that it felt as if all the world's sorrow had been condensed into a single, warbling note of profound grief. Then the queen wailed alongside her daughter, giving herself entirely to that wild song of sadness. Orren cast his arms around his wife and child and allowed a shrill cry to escape his own lips. The trio huddled over their dead kin, consumed with grief and shame.

Beneath them, Anise still smiled.

41 – Burying the Future

Merelith

Much of Torhal had known when the crown princess had died. One moment, the blood-tinted blizzard that tasted of salt had been roaring over the kingdom and the remnants of the battle just beyond its walls. The next, the storm had evaporated and been blown into wisps of nothing by a winter breeze. For a time, a great terror had seized much of the army: Tobias was slain, but the king and queen of Torhal had ridden off into the woods of Anar Tota, alone, and many feared the storm's sudden disappearance heralded their queen's demise.

The crown guard had taken charge in their absence. At Talya's dramatic departure, the bloodletters had turned tail and fled into the wilderness. Tobias' death had heralded a near-immediate surrender of over half his remaining army. A picket line stood watch at the bridge well into dusk, waiting for the return of their monarchs and, hopefully, the children of the throne. When the Torhalian family emerged, a hush fell over every man and woman, soldier and prisoner of war alike. The silence was crushing to Merelith's ears.

Orren Torhal sat upon his borrowed horse, blade drawn but rested across his lap, guiding the steed towards the bridge in a slow walk. His queen and sorceress wife walked beside him, though some distance apart, underdressed in little more than a teal shirt and matching pants. All eyes fell upon who walked between the pair of monarchs: a creature of legend and nightmare somehow made human. Her sense of emotions now fully strengthened, Merelith knew none feared the sight of her. How could they? Upon the back of an eternal predator had been laid the body of her sister, wrapped in Annelle's armored dress.

Not one soldier spoke a word to their king or queen, opting instead to make way, then form the beginning of a column that would stretch to the steps of Castle Torhal. In hindsight, many would wonder aloud in the coming days why not a single person cried aloud at what they saw. Perhaps Annelle's wild scream of fury had removed any ability to do so again, or maybe the people were too stunned to comprehend the terrible price that Galrend had extracted in its failed battle. In the moment, Merelith believed the people were silent because they had never beheld a ruined future before.

At the castle, many had expected Orren Torhal to speak, considering the man looked to have his wits about him more than his wife. When he cast his eyes down from the gathered, they looked to Annelle Torhal, but found her eyes also cast down in defeat. Only then did the people of Torhal look to the guardian, who looked back at them with eyes full of sorrow.

Merelith felt the weight of their gaze and found it to be nothing compared to what was draped across her back. The twin instincts twined around her grief but also encouraged her to speak. The king had yielded the words to her, Tal growled, and so they were hers to say. The queen was too broken to speak, Kara sighed, and the people needed to hear what Annelle could not say herself. The guardian rose her head as high as she could, took a deep breath, then shuddered under the weight of a ragged sob.

Easy. They need to hear something. Anything.

So do I! I need to hear HER, again, just…just once more.

I love you, be free for me.

Oh, Anise…what would you say? It is you they need to hear, not me!

Merelith steadied her breathing then tried a second time, only to feel her jaw seize up in a bid to keep another sob escaping. If she lost herself here, now, it would only hurt them all the more. Yet she was an *angyr*, not a woman, the *guardian*, not the princess. The present, tasked with explaining the future had been killed.

What do I say, Anise?

Everything I ever said…it wasn't enough. I was wrong.

I didn't want you to be…

The angyr blinked and, before she knew it, Merelith was speaking.

"I didn't want her to be my queen."

The ripple of shock was unmistakable, but all held their tongue as the angyr let them stew in her words. Merelith herself was surprised, but then felt Tal nudge her onward while Kara reminded her *why* she had said that the first time.

"I just wanted her to be my sister."

Many cast their heads down in sorrow, shame, and regret. A few nodded understanding, her father among them. Others clamped hands over their mouths to stifle sobs, like her mother. The guardian wondered how many of the host gathered had felt the same of their own families.

She sighed, swallowed the tremble building in her throat, and felt it settle into her shattered heart instead.

"In the end, Anise Torhal wanted the same – and she died saving *my* life. My future."

Merelith blinked back tears and willed her throat to remain wet just a little longer.

"I'm s-sorry," she finished, "I am so sorry she d-died."

The guardian turned into the castle gates, unable to meet even the teary-eyed gaze of her parents. Only then did the mourning begin. It started as the few, frail cries of women and mothers looking upon their broken queen. Then was joined by fathers given permission by the gentle sobs escaping Orren's stoic face. Finally, the children cried, too. Not because their parents did, but because the sight of the sorrowful angyr plodding away broke their too-small hearts with too-big emotions.

.   .   .

The funeral was held three days later, heralded by every tree in the kingdom of Torhal sprouting leaves of ebony in the dead of winter. Merchants who had dared to return to the kingdom, hoping to make easy coin while the nation mourned, found themselves barred at the gate beneath the Elder Tower. When they demanded entry, as the greedy oft will in the face of tragedy, the soldiers of Torhal drew their blades and uttered but two words: *She died.* That was enough to silence even the blackest of hearts.

The formal grieving began in the throne room of Castle Torhal, the king and queen presiding over the open casket that contained their youngest child. Anise was bedecked in a gown of flowing emerald satin with elegant sleeves of silver and gold lace. In life, the crown princess had never worn a scarf, but in death her neck had been wrapped in a high collar of red fur with a trailing scarf of auburn feathers, each plucked from her sister's own wings. A circlet ringed her head, with an icon at its fore depicting Torhal's tree in silver filigree.

Her hands were clasped in quiet composure, though between them rested a sword. The blade drew attention, for it seemed unusually *simple* compared to everything else in the casket. It was a short, scouting sword. Only those with keen eyes recognized it as the guardian's former blade, gifted by the late Knight Smith. That man had been honored yesterday, though the guardian had been conspicuously absent from her lover's wake. Today, though, Merelith held pride of place as the honor guard.

She could tell that, for many, it was an uncomfortable visit to the casket to pay respects. Merelith Torhal sat at the head of her sister, erect and motionless, though her wild eyes tracked every single person that approached her fallen kin. Normally, the honor guard would fall to a number of trusted knights of the crown guard. Afterall, even as an angyr, Merelith was technically now crown princess herself, and was meant to be sat beside her mother and father on the thrones overlooking the casket. She had almost laughed when her mother had shown her the unusual throne built for an angyr to sit on. Almost.

Yet Merelith refused, unable or unwilling to relinquish the title she prized above all others: guardian. So, she instead stood watch over her dead sister. When the mourners weren't gazing upon Anise's peculiar sword, they lingered on Merelith. Or, more precisely, on the pale circlet fitted to rest between the guardian's four swiveling ears. Many whispered that there had never been an angyrian princess before. None of them knew Merelith heard every word.

Visitation ended at high noon, when all were asked to leave the castle as the royal family prepared for the final procession. King Orren and Queen Annelle emerged an hour later upon their most beautiful steeds. Again, the king rested his unsheathed blade across his lap; it was a ceremonial tradition indicating him as the first line of defense for the dead. Queen Annelle, beside him, held aloft the banner of her kingdom in one hand and a chalice of glass; the banner was to declare the heritage of the dead and the goblet symbolized the collection of the kingdom's tears earlier that morning. In truth it only held three droplets, each one salted but kin to the dead.

Behind them proceeded the casket, now closed and topped with a bouquet of lilies whose petals were a shining obsidian. At their center was a lone, white rose tied with an emerald string. Ten knights, dressed in ceremonial tabards with a single armored shoulder to bear the weight of the casket, marched in step behind their monarchs. As they did so, they grunted and sighed in unison. Not out of stress or exhaustion, but as an ancient soldier's hymn: a sharp inhale to meet grief, a hard grunt to face loss, a deep inhale to remember life, and a soft sigh to accept death.

Next followed the guardian and, once again, Merelith drew more attention than her sister. The angyr strove to be nearly silent as she walked, a testament to her increasing grace given the amount of armor she wore. It shone brilliantly, encasing her breast and back in polished silver but shaped to have the appearance of the fur beneath it. Small plates and chainmail tinkled along her legs and the top of her paws. Her wings were gilded in three pendants each that draped delicate chains in great sweeps along her trailing feathers. She'd spent most of her life dreaming of wearing that armor. If not for her mother's pleading eyes, Merelith wouldn't have worn it at all.

Nobody had donned the armor since Merel; Reeta had never felt worthy of it and Queen Anise had never said she was. That guardian had been buried yesterday, too, right on the spot where she had died. Torhal had many traditions when it came to death, and for its protectors there was no higher honor than to be buried where they'd fallen in battle, roads or houses or walls be damned. Across the kingdom were such shrines. Reeta's would be the first to an angyr, for no Torhalian angyr had ever died defending the soil of its own home.

The remainder of the crown guard marched behind Merelith, and behind them followed the royal guard. After the royal guard came the castle staff, then the many denizens that surrounded Castle Torhal, and a plethora of people from across the kingdom. It was a somber if somewhat noisy affair right up until the edge of the queen's wood. Then only the royal family and the ten bearers continued on. All the others waited beside Antila's stream, where Torhal ended, and the domain of its sorceress queens began.

The burial site itself was nothing of note: a hole dug out beneath a tree chosen by the queen the day before. The monarchs dismounted beside the tree then, after a silent nod from each, watched the bearers carefully lower the casket onto roots that stretched across the hole. The king raised his blade to point at each of his men, who in turned bowed their heads and backed away one step. Once all ten had done so, as one they marched back out of the wood, leaving the royal family alone with their dead.

Orren sheathed his sword and, for the first time that day, sighed. It ended with a small shudder that threatened to topple him when his queen held out the chalice to him. He cupped the glass in his left hand and studied the tiny pool of tears in it. The king couldn't tear his gaze away as yet more fell in. He heard Annelle rest the banner against the tree but was startled by the sensation of her forehead pressing into his. His tears came more freely as a second dribble joined his. Merelith looked on, certain that her armor was dragging her into the earth where she belonged.

Annelle gripped her husband's arms then tugged him down. Their heads together, they kneeled at the head of the casket. The goblet shook enough that the growing pool within it sloshed a little. So, his queen moved a hand atop his to steady it. Orren had earlier said he thought the thing a terrible tradition. It was obvious he now hated it all the more. He attempted a joke to lighten their moods.

"Well, I can see why it is so large. It'll be full in the hour at this rate."

Annelle tried to chuckle but only another sob came. Followed by his. Merelith drug herself to beside them and pressed her head into theirs, her breathing hollow. Orren's eyes widened as they took in hers. *Why* the goblet was so large suddenly made sense, for Merelith cried into it as freely as her parents. When a pause was finally had, Orren tried to lead them onto what was next: the spreading of the tears, the lowering of the casket, the speaking of words he had spent three nights preparing, as much for his family's sake as his own.

Yet the immortal seemed unable to move. Or, rather, he was unable to stop *feeling* the same things, over and over. Like a battering ram against her own, shattered heart, Merelith's instincts sensed his grief and shame. Unbidden, Kara gave words to those emotions.

She died. My child died.

My beautiful, delicate Anise died.

The queen instead moved, taking up the goblet and forging ahead. Annelle Torhal's hand shook so violently that half the tears in the goblet showered past the casket and into the hole or onto the surrounding snow. Merelith knew her mother did not care. Nor did she care when the goblet slipped from her fingers and shattered upon the casket's lid. A dark, twisted emotion hoped the noise would wake her daughter from that dreamless slumber. The queen desired her king would scold her, or that her eldest daughter would fix the goblet somehow, but both only looked at her with awful, sad smiles.

Her father was meant to be saying something special, now, as her mother commanded the roots to lower the casket. The king's silence made it clear he'd either forgotten his speech or, more likely, no longer cared to speak it. A quiet, selfish fury laced the queen, as if begging to lash out at him. Their daughter deserved those words! Yet Merelith also felt a motherly instinct wash over the fire in her mother's heart, as if to point out Anise was no longer there to listen. Unbidden, Tal spoke for Merelith's mother.

No!
No parades to lead, no festivals to plan, no suitors to wonder about.
No more lessons. No more words! No more anything.
My child is no more.
My Anise.
No.

"Annelle."

The queen flinched at her whispered name then gasped in horror at what she'd done. The casket was partially crushed, the roots having lowered only halfway before encircling it. A mother's last embrace, too tight and unyielding to even death. The queen blanched and began to stammer an apology, but the king held up a hand to silence her. The queen's heart throbbed with desperate hope. Perhaps for Orren to say his words. Or for Merelith to speak instead, as she had at the castle three days ago. Merelith could only stare at the fracturing casket with empty eyes.

Orren said, "It was so long ago, that first time you hugged her with arms of wood."

Annelle sobbed and nodded. Merelith did, too. *It was.* It was so, so long ago now.

Merelith added, "She was laughing and screaming. I was sure she would be scared the first time, but she wasn't. Anise knew, even without seeing, that it was *you*, Mama."

The king nodded and began to cry again. The angyr looked up from the grave, right at her mother, and the queen's sobs stilled under that patient, wild gaze. Tal commanded the queen and Kara told her why.

"She'd know it was you now, too. It's ok. Wrap her up, one more time."

Any other time, the sound would have been sickening to Merelith. Dirt and stone collapsing in, roots twisting and crushing, the sound of the ornate casket splintering and shattering before it was swallowed up by the earth. The tree itself creeped over the grave, its ebony leaves shaking loose as the sorceress queen set a new guardian for her daughter. Annelle cried through it all and, when the deed was done, she fell to her knees with a long, familiar wail. Merelith heard, and felt, the wild magic in that wail cascade out across Torhal.

As one, every tree shed their ebony leaves, leaving only barren branches once again.

The burial site of Crown Princess Anise II was nowhere to be seen, an empty tree atop it no different from the tens of thousands of empty trees that made up the queen's wood in winter. Somewhere, throughout that forest, were other trees harboring secret graves, too. Other places where families, just like Merelith's, had grieved the dead.

I'm not the guardian anymore, am I?

Merelith watched her father go to his wife. He cried as loudly as she did and the angyr felt the instincts stir at the sight. Strangely, it was Tal who was loudest. It was a different kind of possession that tingled in her heart, a bit of pride wrapped up in a new emotion: compassion. She beheld her suffering family, and it was *Tal* who sought to comfort them. She felt Kara step back and sit, as if in quiet acceptance. Was there such a thing as dominant empathy? It seemed so.

The angyr plopped down beside her parents and wrapped them in her wings and furry arms. Her chest heated with grief, but Kara *fought* that sorrow. Intense calm held back the tide of shame and guilt, the instinct ferociously guarding Merelith's broken heart while Tal obstinately projected peace to her parents. It made little sense to her, this pair of instincts, but she let them lead.

As the afternoon wore into evening, Merelith felt in her parents – and maybe in herself – a sensation beyond her five senses. The wild instincts acknowledged this as if it were a friend. Only when the king and queen let go of each other and embraced their surviving daughter did she realize what it was: forgiveness. Forgiveness for the king that had failed at Anar Tota. Forgiveness for the queen that had abandoned her daughters. Forgiveness for the guardian that had lost a life.

Merelith gazed up into the darkening sky as her parents held her and wondered when, if ever, she would forgive herself for losing Anise. Perhaps never, she reasoned. It felt strange, being able to so easily forgive Eric but not herself. To accept her mother's unfair wrath and fear, or her father's overconfidence in himself and others. She didn't understand why she could forgive everyone else but not herself. All the while, a persistent voice whispered in the back of her heart, made louder by her own uncertainty.

Come.

42 – Returning the Past

Merelith

Queen Annelle Torhal lifted her chin in regal consideration before nodding, once. The sculptor before her grinned and then bowed his head with gratitude.

"It will be a masterpiece, Your Majesty! I swear it."

"It need only show the truth of her, Master Stone," replied the queen.

He wasted little time nodding again before rising and departing the throne room, the last petition for the day. The queen glanced at her daughter and found the angyr watching her with too-familiar intensity. Merelith knew, for she sensed her mother's heart swell with pride, grief, and love. The queen often stared at the guardian now, sometimes making others uncomfortable, but not Merelith. The guardian knew her mother saw her daughter as much as her sister.

A long, unbroken silence filled the space between queen and princess. The king was away in Anna, overseeing the reorganization and replenishment of the army after the battle at the guardian bridge two weeks ago. It was a miserable day but, despite the queen's pleas to wait out the current *natural* blizzard, King Orren had been determined to leave. No doubt to give his 'she-wolves' time to sort out what came next. Given there was now only two of them.

Soon to be only one.

"How fares the calling?" the queen finally asked.

Merelith replied, "It isn't so bad, today. The storm helps. I think."

"Oh? Why is that?"

The guardian finally broke her mother's gaze, instead looking into the great hall beyond the throne room. Towards a particular tapestry. Her mother's heart twisted but the pain was less every day. She still had nightmares. Orren had finally convinced her to sleep in Anise's room, both to help her grieve but also to protect the new furniture in the monarch's own room. Merelith had taken to sleeping at the foot of Anise's bed on random nights.

Or seemingly random. The nights Merelith slipped into her sister's room were often the same nights Annelle was certain she would have another nightmare. They did not come in the presence of the angyr that reminded her so much of her own sister. In a way, it helped Merelith to sleep, too. She had avoided the room for so long, it felt both wrong and right to spend as many nights there as she could before she left.

Merelith replied, "The calling is *strong,* but it isn't *demanding.* It's as if the instincts recognize that today is a poor day to travel. Or a poor time. I'm not sure. I can't ignore it but neither does it trouble me. It's a bit like looking at a cracked door to a room you've never seen. I'm curious, but not enough to feel unable to resist."

Annelle nodded, fear comingling with curiosity. The angyr sat beside the queen tilted her head, her ears flicking forward at a sound Annelle could not hear. Then they gyrated back to the queen before her head followed. Once again, that intense gaze fell on the queen.

"Where will you place her?" Merelith asked.

Annelle considered the question before answering. Merelith asked of the sculptor's proposed, now approved, project: a life-sized statue commemorating Reeta Torhal. A scribe had already been commissioned to draw up a brief history of the queen's guardian. Annelle had been strict in her instructions: *every* truth of Reeta, even her infamous rampage, was to be included.

She wants the world to know the weight her sister carried. She wants her descendants to know the sins of her father and mother. Her own sins. She wants our people to know Reeta came back, even when she had every reason not to.

"I am of a mind to set her beneath the tree, just beyond the gate."

"You said her favorite place was by High Lake? I was sure you'd want her there."

Annelle smiled and shook her head. It was true, Reeta had loved to wander off to the lake. Away from her cruel father and distant mother, away from the little sister who didn't know or trust her.

"I want her where she should have been all along."

Her predecessors had long waited under the tree, though, a visible guardian to the people and royal family. Merel had loved greeting the people coming and going from the castle: the children excited to see the guardian up close, the foreigners terrified of the beast of legend that laughed and smiled, the soldiers of Torhal who saluted with deep respect.

Merelith could not read her mother's thoughts, but the angyr could literally smell Annelle's emotions. Whether the now-princess understood, Merelith didn't say, but she did nod her head in acceptance. Merelith then sighed. Her silver-rimmed eyes turned sad and troubled, her brow pinching as she looked back toward the great hall.

"Speak, love. What is it?" asked the queen.

"He's still out there."

Lorath Saltsword.

The arm of the throne chittered beneath Annelle's grasping fingernails. The angyr looked back at her, eyes dancing with surprise and a hint of shared fury beneath. Merelith became very still as her mother sighed and nodded. *This* was the conversation Orren Torhal had left for. The king had made it clear that wherever the monarchs traveled, Merelith would be welcome *first* as their daughter. What Orren had never really considered was the possibility that Merelith might travel somewhere her parents could not.

"He is," the queen managed, before sighing heavily and adding, "and that cannot remain so."

"No," Merelith replied, "It cannot."

The silence returned, this time charged with tension and worry. Merelith knew her mother would not want to have this talk. Would not want its outcome. She saw the queen's mind running and decided to beat her there.

"What if he targets another family? We cannot allow that. Anar Tota is in ruins, Galrend in upheaval, and our kingdom weathered. If he did the same to Tarn…the whole of the freelands could be at war before next winter."

The queen nodded agreement then released a rush of air. For too long, Torhal had ignored the affairs of other kingdoms. It had been safe, if somewhat isolated, but it had been *safe*. No longer was that the case. Whatever this assassin was after, Merelith was confident he would strike again. Though it was not Torhal's responsibility to preclude such a threat, a blood debt was owed. Two of them, as far as the guardian was concerned.

"Torhal is too weak to send anyone else, Merelith," Anelle began, before raising a hand to silence her daughter's impatient growl.

The queen stared down her angyrian daughter. Finally, Merelith relented with a heavy sigh and inclined her head in a show of patient listening. Despite the demands of her instincts, Merelith *needed* her mother's approval. She needed to know her family was behind her for this.

"My father will have left Tarn by now. It could be months before I have the means to send him another message. Even then, I trust absolutely *no one* with the knowledge our family now has. Not even him. The fewer who know, the fewer that can warn."

The angyr nodded and asked, "What do we do? What *can* we do?"

Annelle forced a smile. Tal was chomping at the bit. Merelith wasn't asking what could be done. She was asking for permission to go and *do* it. The guardian knew her parents had already discussed the possibility of sending Merelith. It had been a tough conversation, but in the end Orren had admitted nobody else could possibly track their daughter's killer down *except* an angyr.

"You will be alone, Merelith," Annelle said quietly, "and in a kingdom that has a long history of murdering their own angyrian children."

Merelith countered, "King Aaron helped pay for Tobias' army. We need to know why. We need to know if there is more coming!"

The queen visibly tensed in anger. In the aftermath of Galrend's defeat, news from Anar Tota's surviving council members had revealed a terrible secret: many of Tobias' mercenaries slain at Anar Tota had been carrying coin from *Tarn*, not Galrend. The implication was obvious: King Aaron Tarn had helped finance Galrend's war effort. Annelle nodded slowly but continued her warning.

"If you are discovered, you will be slaughtered without a second thought. Your only advantage is that nobody knows you are coming. Once discovered, once even *rumored*, your survival will be perilously difficult."

Merelith began to reply, to say she understood and to not worry but paused at Annelle's upheld hand. The queen's words were hard, even as her lips trembled when speaking them.

"I have already lost Anise. I do not wish to lose you, too, Merelith."

Merelith ground her fangs but then stopped. The anger at invoking Anise's death was fleeting, quickly doused by the reality of that death. The former guardian nodded slowly, sighed, then sat up on her hindlegs and crossed her forearms as best she could, as if to try and be regal. It would make for a comical sight if not for the deadly serious tone of the surviving child. Annelle's eyes hung on the silver cuff that now adorned Merelith's left foreleg.

"Reeta never gave up. Nor will I."

Only you could possibly understand, Mama. I cannot let this go.

"Compromise with me, daughter: I will send you *if* you are prepared to hunt. The hunger for vengeance isn't enough. Show me you can survive the *wilderness* of a hostile city, and I will commission you to carry on Reeta's final task."

Merelith's eyes sparkled as she replied, "The wild do not compromise."

Annelle pursed her lips but the humor in Merelith's eyes made her think twice. Then she smiled back, this time with ease. It was strange, playing the part of witty princess. Perhaps Anise had been right: Merelith would have made a fine crown princess, had she been born second. Yet the guardian was glad, in this moment, she had not been. Though she would give anything for Anise to be alive, Merelith was glad her sister did not face this quest nor its burden.

"You will train to prowl a city undetected, to survive the wilderness, and to begin mastering your quickening. When you have shown competence in these three, I will send you. *No compromise.*"

Merelith bared her fangs as she answered, "It will be done, Your Majesty."

. . .

The king of Torhal wandered the queen's wood, aimless and alone. This was the third time he had tried, and Merelith wasn't sure if she should feel shame for letting him try so many times in the first place. Yet, he had not asked for her help, and she had not been ready. Not until today. Buoyed by her mother's acceptance, the guardian had followed the king.

She waited until he stopped and fell to his knees, crying. It was a terrible tradition, Merelith agreed, but one full of lessons. Still, the guardian reckoned it would break Anise's heart to know her father couldn't find her. So, the angyr plodded out from the shadows of the dormant woods to beside her father.

"She's this way, Papa."

To his credit, the king neither startled nor asked how long Merelith had followed him. He merely wiped his nose, stood up, and nodded in the way only a king could. They walked in silence the entire way. When Merelith stopped, he didn't ask if they had arrived. All the trees looked the same, but the angyr could smell the corpse just beneath the snow and dirt. The king sat down in the snow. He started to pat a spot beside him, paused, then simply held out an arm. Merelith didn't hesitate to press into his side.

They sat there until it was almost dark. Orren could feel the cold, but it did not harm him. Merelith, too, but her fur and wings provided ample protection against the harsh bite of deep winter. It was strange, to be in the presence of two people whose hearts no longer beat, yet one was alive, and the other was not. Stranger still that Annelle had chosen the very tree Anise had sought safety in, ten years ago, when a wild wolf tried to eat her. Merelith had wondered if her mother had marked it, all those years ago, or if the guardian was alone in recognizing it.

"Why did she never understand, Papa?" Merelith whispered.

Orren answered, "I think she did, love. She just pretended not to."

"But why?"

The king thought for a time before shrugging and hugging his daughter closer.

"I don't really know, Merelith. She was so afraid of what you might be, rather than aware of what you are. She had once said she'd rather have been first, so that if it came to the worst…it would be her, instead of you. I think, in the end, Anise just wanted to be more like you."

"So did Eric."

The king shook his head.

"No. Eric wanted to be angyr. Anise wanted to be a sister."

"Or a monster," Merelith sighed.

Orren sighed alongside his daughter and Merelith cringed. Kara warned she shouldn't have said that. Tal remained stalwart in its belief that the truth needed to be said. Merelith *was* a monster. She had nearly hurt her father, again, and her mother. Nearly.

"I'm sorry," Merelith said, "I…I shouldn't say that."

"Do you know what a monster *is*, Merelith?" Orren replied.

The angyr perked up her four ears, the question eliciting a vast array of emotions. When Merelith couldn't decide on an answer, she shrugged. Tal wanted her to say *Anise was*. Kara wanted to say *I am*. Neither felt right nor wrong. The king nodded at her silence.

"A monster isn't a person, Merelith. It has no heart. It does not care. Monsters aren't always dangerous, nor are they incapable of kind acts. Monsters can do anything you and I can do. The difference, the *only* difference, Merelith, is that a monster does not care about *anything*. Not even itself."

Heartless. That is what Talya said to Anise. She called her a monster in a different way. Was she? No, Anise gave herself up for me. But she also did all those things, said all those things.

"I told her that, on the day she found out what you are. What I am. I was so sure she'd think *me* the monster: a man that couldn't be killed except by age or other immortals. I showed her how my wounds could close themselves instantly, but she only marveled. To her, learning her Papa could not die was the greatest gift. The mind of a five-year-old is astonishing. Of course, *you* were thrilled to learn you'd become *this!* What interesting little girls to raise."

The guardian managed to snort as Orren chuckled. Then the mood turned serious.

Merelith said, "She was afraid of me from then on. Afraid I would hurt you. Or kill you, when I became *this*."

"Yes," was all the monarch whispered.

"She doesn't have to be afraid anymore," Merelith whispered back.

"No."

"Are you afraid?"

The question must have stunned Orren, for he sat straight up and looked right at Merelith. The king considered the angyr. Merelith considered the still heart of her father. There *was* fear there, but it did not feel like Anise's fear. Tal recognized it as fear of loss. Kara knew it as fear of harm done to another.

"I am," he finally answered.

"Why?" asked the angyr.

"I am a father, Merelith. I will always be afraid," replied the king.

She is my sister. She was always afraid. For me. For us.

Merelith cried as the weight of her sister's fear lightened just a little.

43 – Hunting the Present

Merelith

No ceremony was held for the guardian's departure. Nor was there an announcement that Torhal's princess would soon be disappearing for an unknown amount of time. The royal family had agreed that Merelith's best chance at catching Lorath hinged on him not knowing she was coming. Or, at the very least, not knowing when she had left Torhal. Considering winter would last another two months still, she would hopefully have most of spring before anyone beyond Torhal knew that an angyrian princess was missing.

Officially, the royal family was making a quick trip to the town of Taris. The logging village had been ransacked by Galrend and was struggling to survive the winter, much like all Anar Tota. King Orren and Queen Annelle, escorted by a chosen royal guard, were to meet the three surviving councilors of Anar Tota's former ruling body to deliver aid in the form of food and blankets. Unofficially, King Orren would be asking Anar Tota to bend the knee to Torhal or face the civil strife boiling over in Galrend alone.

Unbeknownst to any outside a select few, Merelith Torhal would be splitting off from them before they ever reached Taris. As the convoy of aid proceeded past the monarchs and guardian, a pair of knights paused to greet their king and queen. Then say farewell to their princess. Knight Polo looked fit to cry, something that Merelith couldn't help but chuckle at. Knight Paol, though, had the stoic carry of a man saying farewell to a fellow soldier. Seeing as Polo was sniffling, the elder twin spoke first.

"They can't kill what they can't see, Guardian," he began.

Merelith dutifully replied, "They can't hunt what they can't track, Sir Knight."

Paol's face softened into a sad smile. The angyr groaned.

"You can't *both* cry, Paol."

Polo's sorry laugh was joined by his brother. Paol nodded, more to himself than the angyr, then he knelt onto a knee. From a pouch he withdrew a leather cord with a thin metal whistle attached to it. He held it out to the angyr and beckoned her closer with his other hand. Merelith obediently drew herself to before him and sat, her large ears betraying genuine curiosity at the proffered gift.

"A whistle?" she asked.

Paol nodded and said, "A *dog* whistle."

Ears pinned back and Paol chuckled. Yet the angyr patiently waited for him to explain.

"None can hear it but you and animals sensitive like yourself. It will frighten most wolves, but in a city like Tarn? It'll set the whole place to howling. An old trick from our mercenary days…when we sometimes drank before we could pay. A final lesson: they can't hear what is silent. Sometimes, the best silence is too much noise. May I?"

Paol pointed to her right paw, and she smirked, flashing fangs. She then raised a leg up to him and he tied the cord just above her paw. With only four dexterous fingers, it'd be a pain to remove or tie elsewhere, but Merelith would manage. She lifted the whistle to her snout and, with a long tongue, drew it into her lips. She blew and winced, the piercing tone setting her ears back in discomfort. Paol chuckled. The king laughed as a stray following the convoy further up the road took to barking at nothing.

"Hunt well, Princess Merelith!" said the knight.

He knuckled his forehead then stood and backed away, casting a sad smile onto his twin. Polo gulped, sighed, then started tearing up again. The guardian rolled her eyes, sat up on her hind legs, and beckoned the knight to hug her. The queen tittered as an armored knight hugged a giant, winged hound like it were his favorite puppy. Merelith let the man compose himself before speaking.

"I'll be ok, Polo. I swear it. You and Paol have taught me well."

Polo stammered, "H-huggin' a damn angyr. I'm hugging an *angyr*. You're something else, Merelith."

The guardian answered, "No. I'm just *me*, Polo. You, on the other hand, are something else: a mercenary and brother turned knight and soon-to-be husband."

The angyr snorted then licked the knight's ear, prompting him to chuckle. She forced the man back, her forelegs bracing him as she stared into his wavering eyes.

"Tell you what," said the angyr, "I'll make you a deal, Knight Polo. For every child you have, I'll be the honor guard at *their* wedding. I'm still sore to be missing yours."

"Natalie isn't…" laughed the knight, "…but I'll take you up on that deal, *Guardian*."

Merelith beamed at the knight and, though his lips quivered, he grinned right back. Then his grin ran away, and he became serious as he clapped a pair of gauntlets onto her furry shoulders. Eyes that had hunted angyr searched hers as he spoke.

"Nail that bastard, Merelith."

The angyr growled back, "I will. I swear it."

Polo nodded then stepped back. The twins looked at each other, then the guardian, and saluted her. Together, they said their goodbye.

"For Torhal!"

Saluting was an awkward motion for the angyr, so she opted instead for a different acknowledgement. She had found a portrait of Merel Torhal saluting his king and father in a history tome and tried to mimic it. She half-spread her wings, relaxed her forelegs at her sides, and raised her head with regal confidence. The angyr puffed out her chest and, with a bit of concentration, *quickened*. It was but a split second of extra time for her, her heart barely registering the pause, but enough for the knights to see lightning dance across her feathers and fur in normal time when she stopped

"For Torhal" she replied, her fangs bared as their eyes widened in astonishment.

The knights regained their composure, silently saluted their monarchs, then hurried after the convoy. Merelith remained on her hindlegs as she watched them go, before turning her eyes on her mother and father. The king and queen watched her with vastly differing emotions on their faces.

King Orren shared the shock of his knights, his eyes wide with awe. He stepped towards the guardian and then kneeled before her. On *both* knees, Merelith noticed. The immortal opened his arms wide, and the guardian wasted little time embracing her Papa. Orren's voice was steady as he whispered into the tufted ears of his daughter.

"You were *made* for this, Merelith. All your life, you have been angyr. A protector. A hunter. I say to you again: *do not be afraid,* guardian. Trust your instincts and they will guide you."

"I am what I am because of you, Papa," she replied, "I trust you. I will endeavor to trust myself."

"See that you do. I *love* you, little Alpha."

It was that pet name that saw her begin to whimper. Orren chuckled into her mane then leaned back, taking her furry jowls into his hands as he smiled. The king studied the dampening, silver-rimmed eyes of his daughter. Merelith tried to take in every detail of her father. She knew it would likely be a long time before she saw him again.

"I'm sorry I'm leaving," she offered.

"I was, but now I am not," the king replied, "You were *made* for this. I love you, and though it hurts, I have loved seeing you become what you are. I am proud, I am awed, and I am humbled. Remember well the lessons you've been taught. *Survive*, Merelith, and return home. Never forget, despite all that happened, Reeta knew her home was *here*."

Orren motioned between himself and the queen.

"It is here, Merelith. This family. You and any you lay claim to will *always* have a home in Torhal. Go forth, Guardian, and protect your home. As you *always* have."

Merelith nodded as the king hugged her again then stood back. The angyr turned towards her mother and found Annelle still watching her with a wry smile. Where the knights and king had been shocked at the display of her quickening, Annelle had seemed amused. Tickled, even. Like her husband, she kneeled into the snow before the angyr and pulled her eldest daughter into a magically warmed hug.

No words passed between them, but Merelith felt her mother's magic count every hair, trace every feather, and take in every inch of her life thread. Tal greedily pulled at the queen's magic with each deep breath of the angyr. Kara threw it back, like a child happily tossing stones into a calm lake, marveling at the ripples left behind. Beneath the five senses, Merelith felt her mother's magic respond with loving reflection.

Then the instincts were, again, confused. Tal had been roaring to be on their way, to hunt the assassin that had orchestrated so much pain. Now, the dominant instinct pined to remain, nearly refusing to let go of its mother. Kara had been dragging its paws, reluctant to leave the family that still lived. Now, the docile instinct turned its intense calm to the south, towards Tarn and a quest it was made for.

"Such wildness, my child," whispered the queen, "Such a wild, wild heart you have."

Merelith felt her instincts shift again, both turning inwards towards her heart. A terrible void was still there, filled with fragments and shards she was not sure would ever resemble a heart again. The twin instincts focused on that shattered mess, on *her*, and the angyr found her mother's words to be untrue.

My heart is not wild. I am wild…and heartless.

"What is it, love?" asked the queen, leaning back and showing concern.

The guardian eyed her mother for a long time before speaking. In no small part because she wasn't sure *how* to explain what was wrong. She tried to think of a gentler way to say it, to phrase it so that her mother would not worry. Yet the instincts pressed against that void and, finally, forced out words that were hers by instinct, not choice.

"I don't have a heart anymore, Mama."

Annelle's smile was full of sorrow, but she didn't correct her daughter nor admonish her. Instead, the wild sorceress laid a hand over Merelith's furry breast and tapped in time with the physical heart she *did* have. The queen then tilted her head, as if seeing the void therein with her own eyes. She nodded in quiet agreement.

"Then you shall have to hunt for one, love."

I hope you find love again.

Eric said that, there at the end of it all.

"I don't know how," Merelith whispered, the void aching in her chest.

Tal and Kara curled into each other in that void, watching the endless dark. Not with fear or anger, nor sorrow. The instincts felt expectant. As if they waited for something or someone. Another instinct, perhaps, Merelith wondered to herself. The queen seemed to sense this shift, too, for Annelle said as much aloud.

"It isn't a question of *how* we love, Merelith. Only that we do. Be wild, my daughter, and you will find your heart again. Or, maybe, you will have a *new* one? One big enough to hold the love of your mother and the courage of your father. So large that even the grief of your sister will fit."

Mention of Anise brought tears to Merelith's eyes again and she couldn't help but whimper. The angyr hung her head, the shame eating her alive even as the queen pulled the creature into a warm embrace. Annelle tapped fingers upon Anise's cuff, her nails tinkling against the silver, all the while whispering words of encouragement and soothing.

"Stay, Merelith. Stay if it would bring you peace. Vengeance will not return her to us. Stay if it would hurt less, my love. Stay if you would sleep more soundly. Our love for you is *endless*, daughter. Wherever we go, you will always be welcome."

She heard the gentle plea in her mother's words but *felt* the undercurrent of a command below them. The queen was begging her to remain. Her mother was commanding her to go. The angyr made her choice and she felt the woman nod with acceptance into her forehead. A final, tight hug was shared, one in which the angyr surrounded her mother in wings of auburn and white. Then it was over, and Annelle Torhal stood before her guardian, princess, and daughter.

Annelle held herself stiff, though a smile played at her lips, as she commanded the angyr.

"Merelith Torhal, first of your name, first of my line, guardian of our home, Princess of our kingdom, I charge you with carrying on the work of your predecessor, Guardian Reeta Torhal, and avenging the murder of my mother and your sister, of the same name: Anise Torhal. Go forth from Torhal as our sword and shield, a weapon of eternal fury and a bastion of ageless love. Remember your *home*, remember your *family*, but above all my angyrian daughter, remember *yourself*. Do you accept this charge?"

Merelith saluted her mother and Annelle's eyes flickered with the lightning dancing across the angyr's body.

"I accept this charge," the guardian answered, surprised at how confident she sounded.

"For Torhal," the queen replied.

"For Torhal," the king added.

Merelith began to reply, then paused and shook her head. The king and queen looked on with raised eyebrows, no doubt wondering if their daughter's resolve had finally crumbled. The angyr glanced down at her cuff and considered the silver guardian etched upon it. Considered that Anise had seen who Merelith had wanted to be all along. Both monarchs beamed at her words.

"She told me to be free. No more pretending," the guardian paused, nodded, and finished, "For me. I do this for myself."

A final hug and farewell were shared. Then, with nothing more than a birthday cuff and a dog whistle, the guardian turned her nose south. Towards Tarn and the man who smelled of salt and blood. Merelith Torhal settled into her instincts as the hunt began.

Epilogue

Lorath

The road to Tarn was long, cold, and silent. Talya's babe cried only once, on a random day nearly a month into the journey. Whether the sorceress consort had met her end, or an angyr had perhaps drawn too close to Lorath, the Saltsword didn't know. Nor did he care. By the time he arrived at the outskirts of the great city, rumors already said Galrend and Torhal were at war, that Anar Tota was under siege, and Tobias Galrend might soon rule the north.

Lorath's arrival in Tarn did not go unnoticed. He had not made it twenty minutes into the city before a guardsman approached him, saluted, and asked him to follow. Five minutes later, Lorath was lounging in an ornate carriage, the babe was fast asleep on a pillow stuffed with goose down, and the King of Tarn was studying him with silent expectation.

Neither said a word all the way to the castle's perimeter.

Tarn's central keep was a behemoth of architectural genius, perhaps matched only by the famous Port of Glass on the faraway shore of the Silver Sea. Rising over the bustling city, Tarn's keep was an incredible *twelve* stories tall, complete with lavish ball rooms, four libraries, multiple kitchens, and no less than six internal barracks housing the immense force of guards that patrolled the keep day and night. Yet none of this was what made the structure stand out.

Lorath broke King Aaron's gaze as they drew near to the keep's base. Peering out the carriage window, he looked up, up, up to the twin spires hanging off skybridges from the central keep: the queen's tower and the royal observatory. Both structures were horribly impractical but striking all the same. Of course, the queen's tower had been vacant for nearly two decades now. An unfortunate waste of a rather beautiful suite.

The king stated, "Arius' magic remains useless."

Lorath turned his gaze back on Aaron Tarn and simply nodded.

Of course. As expected.

"I want you to observe him. Find what his tutor is doing wrong."

"Yes, Your Majesty," Lorath answered.

"I then want you to sit with Lord Alton. He has many questions regarding defense against angyrian threats. You will answer them."

"Yes, Your Majesty."

King Aaron nodded then turned his gaze on the sleeping babe. Stoic, unmoving, the immortal looked upon the child as if it were an interesting rock and little more. Yet Lorath knew the king was perplexed at her presence. As times before, King Aaron often asked questions without speaking. Yet Lorath knew to not answer them aloud. A king should only be spoken to when told to do so.

"They remind me of her. I cannot place why."

Oh? Hmm. That is somewhat surprising. I'd expect you to forget her.

"What is their name?" the king asked.

"She does not yet have one, Your Majesty. Her mother died in birth."

"How unfortunate. The father?"

"Unknown, Your Majesty."

"How came you to possess her?"

"By chance. I required shelter during a blizzard just south of Anar Tota. I found a farmer's hovel, knocked, only to be greeted by a wet nurse frantic with fear."

"You aided them. Why did the nurse not deliver it to others?"

"The nurse feared the death of the mother would be blamed on her. She fled into the blizzard."

"Foolish."

"Yes, Your Majesty."

"Why keep her?"

Ah. Still practical as ever. Splendid.

"The Blooders were already too close for my liking," Lorath paused, shrugged, "It is not the first time I've raised an abandoned child. Tarn will make a fine home for her."

King Aaron allowed a rare smirk and nodded. Just in time for the carriage to stutter to a halt on the cobbled bricks of the keep's inner courtyard. A door was opened, and the king departed without another word. Lorath lifted the babe, shushing it with fatherly calm as it began to startle awake, and followed the monarch.

The welcome party was sparse: a dozen guards and just two servants. The first, a spindly man, bowed deeply to the king and indicated a meal was prepared and waiting. The second, an equally thin woman, curtsied and informed Lorath she would take the babe to his quarters to be cared for. The Saltsword didn't hesitate to hand over the nameless child. Yet he still felt the distinct sensation of an empty shoulder and arm that had been occupied for nearly two months of travel. He endeavored to hide the surprise he felt.

I miss this. Strange! Perhaps you will fare better than the others? If only because I may care this time.

"We will convene in three days to discuss what you have learned, Sir Saltsword" the king said by way of farewell.

Lorath replied with a deep bow, "Yes, Your Majesty."

. . .

The six barracks were staged around the perimeter of the castle, each forming the foundation for turrets. Five of them were of equal size, but the sixth – situated in the rear of the castle relative to its main entry – was petite. Here was kept the king's personal armory, a private training ground, and the housing of his most loyal and appreciated guards.

King Aaron's skill with blade and bludgeon was well-known, but hardly legendary. Certainly, Aaron did not possess the athletic skill of Lorath's previous host. Yet Aaron's tactical intellect made Tobias seem like a simpering child. There was someone who, supposedly, possessed even greater tactical skill: his son, Arius Tarn.

Most kings would be thrilled that their heir could outwit them in games on the board or the field, but it was not so for Aaron. The trouble, as Lorath was seeing firsthand, was that Arius was a *genius* trapped in the body of an ordinary man.

"That is exactly correct. Well done, Your Highness."

"It will not work."

Lorath stood in the shadow of a pillar upon an interior balcony overlooking the king's personal training yard. In the yard were just two men: Prince Arius Tarn, the sole heir to King Aaron, and his tutor, a famous sorcerer hailing from Gwentia named Failon the Infallible. An unfortunate title, considering Lorath knew *exactly* what was about to transpire.

"Now, now, I am confident this is precisely correct! Have some faith, My Prince!" declared the sorcerer tutor.

The prince drawled, "For you. It will not work for me."

"Nonsense, I am certain…"

Etched into the dirt of the yard was a simple, foundational rune for summoning fire. Elementalists inclined towards flame often started with such a rune, both for learning and practicality. The irony of magic was that 'runes' weren't so much constructs of magic but rather written instructions to follow. A rune wasn't remotely necessary to conjuring a given element, rather, it aided in the focusing of the mind. Lorath had long preferred the analogy of runes to recipes. The pages of a recipe book had nothing to do with the cooking, but for an apprentice they may as well be a required ingredient.

By that logic, Failon should have had no trouble utilizing the rune. Lorath could see Arius had indeed perfectly etched it, meaning it was an excellent focal both visually and mentally. Yet when Failon went to summon a gout of flame, only a few sparks fizzled before sputtering into nothingness. Lorath couldn't help but smile as he watched Failon stare at the rune with bewilderment.

"It is as if *your* magic is suppressing mine" the sorcerer mumbled.

What a tragically inaccurate assessment. Hmm. I like it.

Arius snorted and said, "That is unlikely. My magic is too poor to influence yours."

"Yet I am unable to use your rune?" countered the tutor.

Failon tried again and, once more, little came of it. Lorath's smile widened to a grin as he saw fear flash across Failon's face. In the Saltsword's experience, most sorcerers of any skill – and Failon was indeed such a person – only feared two things. The first was the loss of their power, which was understandable since so many built their identity upon it. The second was encountering power they could not comprehend. Failon was experiencing *both* fears.

The prince rolled his eyes, sighed loudly, and said, "The rune itself is flawless, which means the fault lies in *your* magic, not mine. Elemental manipulation is driven by mental and emotional grasping of the elements of reality. If you are failing to use a rune – *any* rune – it is because your own ability to grasp the element is compromised. Observe."

Arius pointed a finger at the rune and a small flame erupted from the rune. Too small, but there all the same. Failon's eyes bulged with surprise and confusion. The prince extinguished the flame with a snap of his fingers, then proceeded to snap his fingers over and over, dancing the flame in and out of existence all around the training yard. Yet it never grew in size. Lorath saw the prince's frustration begin to surface.

"I *can* feel this element. I can feel *all* of them, Failon. I can grasp them. I *cannot*, though, expand them. Grasp more. Use more. THAT is why you are here. Not to teach me runes I memorized fifteen years ago. Not to give me a pep talk. Not to coddle me like a *fucking child*."

Failon held up his hands in supplication, but the prince did not relent. Instead, he began to stalk towards his tutor. The sorcerer obviously felt threatened as he took a step back for every two steps Arius made toward him. Lorath found it all comical. The prince was shorter than Failon, obviously weak in his magic, and his reddening face made him look exactly *like* a child, rather than the angry heir to the most powerful monarch in the freelands.

"You are here to *unravel* this problem, Failon. To understand WHY this does not work. Your role is to *prove* your title, or do you wish to report failure to my father?"

"M-m-my Prince! I understand your frustration, I-I…"

"CAN YOU OR CAN YOU NOT SOLVE THIS!?"

"I-I-I don't know!"

Arius screwed up his face, balled his fists, then stopped. In an instant, his face fell to one of pure apathy. Lorath felt his heart squirm with delight. The prince whispered his command.

"Out."

"Your Highness, I…"

"*Out*. Now. Find a solution or don't come back."

"O-of course! Right away."

Failon the Infallible scurried from the yard, not even bothering to grab his ostentatious cloak left on a training dummy. Which meant, Lorath presumed, the sorcerer was *not* going to find a solution but rather flee Tarn as fast as possible. Rumors abounded that the prince's previous tutor had been quietly executed. Aaron had paid for a tutor to 'fix' Arius. Arius was not fixed. Ergo, the tutor had committed *fraud* against the *king*.

I imagine one does not get the title of 'Infallible' being a cocksure fool.

"Worthless" muttered the prince.

Lorath looked on with interest as Arius paced the rune, shaking his head and repeating the word over and over. He spoke with quiet certainty, rather than anger or shame.

"Worthless. Worthless. Worthless. Worthless."

You are not referring to your tutor, are you?

Arius Tarn's troubles were well-known, as well as a constant source of annoyance and shame for his father. The king was meant to have a powerful, sorcerer son that could influence wild magic itself. Instead, he had Arius: a young man that could conjure enough flame to light a brazier or fill a goblet with water, but little else. That was only the start of Arius' crippling problems.

His mind was rumored to be as sharp as Aaron's tongue, but the prince had the face of his mother – soft and weak – and a body to match. Court gossip had him pinned as preferring men over women, that the prince wet himself anytime he had to spar, and his only true skill was the ability to empty a bottle of wine in one gulp.

Weak, Frightened, and Alcoholic. Poor, poor Arius. Precisely as expected.

Lorath had long feared Aaron would tire of the boy and allow an 'accident' to befall his only heir. Instead, this particular portion of Lorath's plan had manifested precisely as desired. King Aaron *needed* his royal sorcerer. He needed a suitable heir to woo a suitable princess. Aaron's ambitions were as large as Tobias', but unlike the mad king from Galrend, Tarn's king knew how to execute his vision. Tarn had long produced kings and queens that understood generational power. Aaron's own status was the result of centuries of carefully planned marriages, excellent economic policy, and strategically deployed armies.

The king knew all of this and had every intention of perpetuating that perfect model forward with Arius. If only the son was just as willing. To be fair, Arius' upbringing was full of tragedy and expectation. Yet the hollow of a man standing below Lorath, predictable as he was, still managed to surprise the Saltsword. Moreso when Arius sighed, shook his head, then left the yard. No additional outburst, no monologue, not even a dirty look at the cloak left behind.

Nothing.

Wildness in a cage of nothing.

Perfect.

Lorath withdrew from the balcony above and began making his way toward the entry of the keep. There, Lord Damian Alton no doubt waited with bated breath. A great many things were transpiring along the outskirts of Tarn. More news of the war to the north would begin to trickle in soon. Perhaps word of Torhal's angyr surviving or dying. Lorath knew where his bet was.

News that King Aaron had helped fund Tobias' war would begin to circulate, too. Lorath had made certain of that at Anar Tota. It would all go one of two ways: the world would know Tarn and Galrend were allies, or that Tarn and Torhal were now open enemies. Both outcomes led to the same place, precisely as orchestrated: the broken prince who stood between them.

Lorath kept his grin all the way across the castle.

. . .

TO BE CONTINUED IN...

APEX

Book Two of *The Wildlands*

PLEASE LEAVE A REVIEW!

Your feedback and criticism are essential to improving my writing and success. Please take time to leave a review. I read *all* of them and, just as importantly, your review helps more people find *The Wildlands.*

I sincerely hope you enjoyed *Guardian* and are excited for *Apex*!
-Tyler

. . .

SUBSCRIBE FOR MORE!

Want to keep up with progress on *The Wildlands*?
Do you enjoy chapter previews?
Short stories in the same universe?
Want a chance to beta read *Apex*!?

Visit www.TylerTillerson.com and subscribe to my newsletter, *THE DIRT*! What does it cost? *Nothing!*

THE DIRT IS FREE!

Subscribers receive a monthly newsletter with book series reviews, lore dives, and updates on Tyler's current book project. They also gain access to short stories, chapter previews, and more on the website. Join today!

Acknowledgements

Guardian wouldn't have been possible without a very specific person: my wife and soul mate, Rachael. *Years* have gone into arriving at this moment, where an acknowledgements page is actually needed! You were the first to say I could *and should* do this.

I often said I am writing for me. Thank you for giving me permission to do so. I love you and am forever grateful I get to do life with you.

In addition to my lovely partner, I want to thank my beta readers: Haley Meredith and Angela Patti. Your feedback for *Guardian* was invaluable and I cannot wait to put the next book in front of you! (I just have to, y'know, *write it*.)

Lastly, I want to acknowledge my patrons – paid and free – for supporting Story Tiller over on Patreon. Your encouragement, or even your silent presence, is a daily reminder that what I'm working on matters to somebody other than me. It is empowering, slightly anxiety-inducing, and extremely gratifying to know there are people waiting to read what happens next.

Miela er Fen
-Tyler

Resources: Lore

Name Pronunciations

Merelith Torhal: Mehr-ah-lithe Tor-hall
Anise: Ah-neese
Annelle: Ah-nell
Orren: Or-in
Reeta: Ree-tah
Merel: Mehr-el

Eric Smith: Ehr-ick Smith
Regis Hardy: Ree-jus Har-dee
Thadeus Starling: Thad-ee-us Star-ling
Paol: Pahl
Polo: Po-lo

Talya Bodisnia: Tal-yah Bo-dis-nee-ah
Tobias Galrend: Toe-by-us Gal-rend
Lorath Saltsword: Lor-ath Sahlt-sord
Maybury: May-berry

Anisterosa: An-eh-stir-oh-sah
Antila: An-til-ah
Woden: Woah-den
Tamar: Tah-mar
Kalligan: Kal-eh-gan
Tal'Ar: Tal-ar

Places and Words of Importance Pronunciations

Angyr: Ahn-gear
Angyrian: Ahn-gear-ee-an
Pentarch / Pentarchy: Pen-tark / Pen-tark-ee
Autarch / Autarchy: Ah-tark / Ah-tark-ee

Tal / Kara: Tal / Kah-rah
Damaria: Dah-mar-ee-ah

Naming Conventions and Torhalian Family Tree

The first name of each entry is the angyrian child. The second name of each entry is generally the crowned ruler, however, Torhal is a matriarchy: the crown always passed to the first *daughter* born after the angyrian child.

For example: Anne Torhal, the third queen, had a secondborn son – Woden II – but the crown went to her third child, Antila II. Knowledge of *how* to conduct the wild binding is passed exclusively from queen to heir. Sons of Torhalian royalty never attained quickened immortality, as demanded by Antila when she first set down the traditions of her rule with Woden. Rebellion against this has been rare in no small part to the guardians ensuring the crown heir is *never* threatened by her siblings.

After Antila assumed control of her mother's territory in the aftermath of the War for Freedom, she married Woden Torhal. Together, they continued the ritual of wild binding. Their firstborn, Meretah, was the first angyrian guardian of Torhal and – just as important – the first angyrian 'soldier' to not be collared and controlled.

Interesting Note: Unlike their human siblings, Torhalian angyrian children are *never* named exactly as their predecessors. For example, there is no Meretah II. Instead, Torhalian royalty has always chosen unique names for their guardians based off the first three guardians: Meretah, Reetari, and Atina. This tradition was started by Anisterosa as a means to 'set apart' Darasti as being distinctly different from the angyrian soldiers the autarchy had commanded. It is one of the few family traditions Antila kept for herself after rebelling in the aftermath of her father's absence.

Many Damarian names, especially amongst commoners, keep the first two to three letters of a first name to denote lineage. This is the result of an ancient accounting system used by the Autarchy for millenia to manage their slave populations and track the most effective bloodlines in their many experiments and projects. The exception to this is, of course, those descended from the autarchs themselves. Unique names were one of the many ways the Autarchs separated and elevated themselves to the god-like status their subjects regarded them with.

Prior to the War for Freedom, Autarch Anisterosa and Autarch Galrend had three children: Darasti, Antila, and Tamar. Darasti was the only named angyrian soldier at the time, a point of pride for

Anisterosa. When Galrend was ritualistically sacrificed, Darasti initially sided with his mother until wildness overtook him. Antila defeated her mother and drove Anisterosa from the Northern Keep, now known as Castle Torhal. Tamar assisted his elder sister in this endeavor, then continued to lead the rebellion across the eastern continent that would become The Freelands.

As the war progressed, Tamar focused on reclaiming his father's vast territory while Antila focused on securing her mother's. After marrying and mating with Woden Torhal, she renamed the kingdom in his honor as yet another way to prove the methods of the Autarchy were gone for good. Together, they had two children: Meretah and Anistia, the first guardian and crowned princess of Torhal, respectively.

Names are in order of birth, left to right.
First name is always an angyrian child.
Bolded names are the crowned heirs.
"Name + Name" signifies the crowned heir and their husband.

Meretah, **Anistia** + Reginald

Reetari, **Anne** + Darten

Atina, Woden II, **Antila II** + Jakob

--- Centuries Later ---

Arten, **Antira** + Uhltan

Artani, **Anne VI** + Richard, One Other Sibling

Artensa, **Annabelle** + Harold, No Siblings

Merel, **Anise** + Doran, Four Other Siblings

Reeta, **Annelle** + Orren, No Siblings

Merelith, **Anise II**, No Siblings

On Siblings: Most Torhalian queens opted to only have additional children until a suitable heir. As a result, small families like Annelle's are quite common: just the guardian and their little sister. Some scholars suppose the reason may have been to avoid internal conflict: no additional sisters to vie for the crown, as few sons as possible to harbor resentment for being passed over. Whatever the case, Torhal's simple, condensed royal lineage is a peculiarity in the freelands. Though not nearly as peculiar as their tradition of the angyrian guardians.

Queen Annabelle and her husband, Harold Cotton, is a solitary exception with a total of *six* children, including Merel. The reasons for such a large family are varied, but most historians point to a failed assassination attempt against the royal family, the first in many centuries. Annabelle's sister and guardian, Artensa, died during the attack. Merel narrowly saved his father and little sister, Anise, from an attacking angyr. It is thought the assassination attempt spurred Annabelle and Harold to have more children as a form of insurance against future attacks, should they succeed.

Princess Anise I watched her aunt die and brother kill at the age of six. She was perhaps the youngest person in Torhal, ever, to witness the savagery of an angyr firsthand since the War for Freedom. Once again, a guardian stood between their crowned sibling and certain death.

Yet Princess Anise never forgot the day her aunt died. She would later lament to her daughter, Annelle, that in many ways her brother also died that day. Annelle wrote in her own diaries that her mother's coldness towards Reeta may have been born out of trauma rather than malice: the strict queen could not bear the thought of losing kin again, so she never treated Reeta as such in the first place.

Queen Anise's four siblings all left Torhal shortly after she married Doran, on account of *none* of them approving of the marriage. Where they went and what became of them is not found in Torhal's records.

· · ·

If you would like to know more about the previous guardians, history of Torhal, and other lore, visit my website and subscribe to my newsletter, *THE DIRT.* You can find short stories, lore dives, and much more!

www.TylerTillerson.com

Resources: Reader Wellbeing

One of the dangers of reading, regardless of genre, is encountering authentic scenes that can be triggering. This is both normal and, believe it or not, fortuitous.

Triggers do not have to be directly related to the trauma – the sound of a garage door or a distinct ringtone can just as easily trigger a traumatic memory as reading about domestic abuse or intense loneliness.

What is important to know is that while triggers can't always be removed or eliminated, they *can* be managed in a healthy manner!

If, dear reader, you were triggered at any point during this story and have *not* sought counseling, I highly encourage you to do so!

Having a safe space is critical to wellbeing and counseling services are a great place to learn healthy coping skills, process trauma safely, and develop response strategies for triggering events.

Put simply: counseling is a great place to begin *living well*.

You deserve to live well, to feel well, and to *be* well. A nobody author expounding on mental health might not be the greatest pitch, but take it from me: it really is worth it. Below are some web links to help you get started.

A final note: whether it is for counseling, a 12-step group, or some other function…sitting in the parking lot and *not* going inside is ok. What matters is effort, no matter how small, towards taking care of yourself. Lots of people are rooting for you – me included – but the most important encourager is inside of you.

They *are* in there.

They will *never* give up.

Psychology Today

www.psychologytoday.com

Hands down the *most* beneficial resource on the web is Psychology Today. It has excellent articles on mental health, trauma, and trending news in the field. It is also a great site to explore and learn about wellbeing. Most important of all: Psychology Today is where counselors frequently register their services so they are easy to find and contact.

Alcoholics Anonymous

www.aa.org

Alcoholics Anonymous is a 12-step program that is excellent for addressing addictions. The website allows you to locate a meeting near you.

Narcotics Anonymous and

Sex Addicts Anonymous

www.usa-na.com
www.saa-recovery.org

If seeking assistance with an addiction *other* than alcohol, AA can still help but there are specific organizations – all born out of the extremely successful program of AA – that directly address those needs.

NA (Narcotics Anonymous) frequently partners with AA groups to service individuals struggling with drug addiction or legal woes arising from that addiction. SAA (Sex Addicts Anonymous) is similar, focusing on individuals addicted to sex or sexual media.

There are specialized groups for many other addictions, most of which can be found with a simple search or through Psychology Today. In *all* cases, I would still encourage a counselor to assist in guiding recovery.

Jesus Christ, Son of the Living God

Yes, yes, I know…you just read a book with *monster sex* and it ends with a Christian testimony? What can I say, I'm a weird person. Yet, I am also a *content* person. I know where my eternal future is and that gives me hope in a world darker than that of Damaria.

Secular help is good, and there is *nothing* wrong with seeking it. I put those resources *before* this part on purpose! Get a counselor if life is overwhelming. Yet, there *is* a point at which secular services can't help. Mental and emotional health both stem from *spiritual* health – and when the soul is neck-deep in a shitty world, it's hard to bother with things like hygiene, self-worth, and optimism.

Look, I'm not going to wax poetic. If you think people chucking bibles at you in the streets is annoying, imagine how it feels for someone who already believes! Fact is, there are a *lot* of Christians who seemed to have missed the fundamental message: love God, love your neighbor.

So, who is this Jesus guy?

He is this incredible, *real* person that loves you and wants a relationship with you. Not to control you, certainly not to abuse you. I'm not going to recommend going to a specific church – the Lord knows half of them would put me to the stake if they read this book – but I *am* going to recommend you read *the* book: the bible.

Grab a bible, any edition, (I like the older stuff like King James version, but it's hard to read if you're not into stuffy language) and sit down with it. If you want an easier read, try the New Living Translation (NLT) or the Contemporary English Version (CEV).

This is the easy part: read the Gospels. The bible is split into two major sections: The Old Testament (Pre-Jesus) and the New Testament (Jesus and the ministry of his disciples). It'll read like a history book because that is what it is: a historical (and accurate) explanation of who this God guy is, who Jesus is, and why they matter.

And why *you* matter. That's the really important part.

Start with the New Testament (I know, I know, that's skipping ahead! Trust me.) and read the first four chapters, known as the Gospels: Matthew, Mark, Luke, and John. These are *the* chapters containing Jesus' life, his words, and his story.

Before you do anything else – throw the bible in a fire, attend a church, or ask a stripper for spiritual advice – read the Gospels. The message will either make sense…or it won't, *and that is ok*. What I'm asking you to do is *judge the book* before you judge the people. (You'll find out you're not supposed to judge people, a lesson Christians are *great* at. Yeah, I know.)

But why? Why should *I* bother with this, Tyler?
<u>Because you matter.</u> **And if you think you *don't*, the Gospels are a great place to start understanding why.**

Look, life isn't supposed to *suck*. You're not meant to go through it feeling lost, or like time is slipping, or that when you finally croak…it all amounted to *nothing*. That's why we call it the 'Good News' – Christ died for you. You! Someone who never met him in person, someone who may not have even heard of him until the backend of a *fantasy* book. If it sounds crazy, well, welcome to the club. Trust me, weirder stuff is in the bible on *both* ends of Jesus' ministry.

Yet it's true, and I'm hoping you will know and feel its truth. What you do with that truth, well…that's up to you! I'm here to tell you there *is* hope. There is a better way to live your life. It *does* work. You *will* be different, in a better, more contented way. But *you* have to choose to look for it. That is the catch, the only catch, to this faith. You have to choose to seek Jesus. Don't sweat it: it doesn't mean believing what he says from the first page.

Be curious. See for yourself. Like everyone else the first time. Find out for yourself. Read it and be the judge of it, *for yourself*. It might sound flippant, but…you have *nothing* to lose except a little time, and an eternity of peace and joy to gain.

Good luck and may God bless you on your journey, wherever it leads. For what it is worth, He is *wild*. In the best way imaginable.

About the Author

Tyler Tillerson

Tyler was born and raised (all over) the great state of Texas. When he is not working on *The Wildlands*, Tyler writes fantasy short stories for his website. He enjoys all things fantasy and sci-fi but avoids writing the latter because, "Explaining mermaids in space is quite hard."

(The working title was *Space Merines*. It's buried in a drawer until he figures out how to effectively mash fantasy and sci-fi. *Guardian* became his first book instead. *Phew!*)

When not writing, Tyler wrestles eighty-pound German Shepherds, explores the world from a kayak, or plays videogames. He has a great love for experiencing the outdoors and game media with strong storytelling elements.

Above all, he adores his wife and son that, somehow, always end up being a better story than any he can dream up.

Tyler has very real concerns that his wife might be a sorceress. The boy is *definitely* showing signs of wildness.

Learn more at www.TylerTillerson.com

www.ingramcontent.com/pod-product-compliance
Lightning Source LLC
Chambersburg PA
CBHW032115310726
48972CB00001B/234